The
Violet Hour

ALSO BY VICTORIA BENTON FRANK

My Magnolia Summer

The
Violet Hour

A LOWCOUNTRY TALE

VICTORIA
BENTON FRANK

GALLERY BOOKS
New York   Amsterdam/Antwerp   London
Toronto   Sydney/Melbourne   New Delhi

To Carmine

The
Violet Hour

PROLOGUE

~~~~

Violet

I was born with salt air in my lungs and pluff mud between my toes. As a girl I wore seaweed in my hair and seashells around my neck. I was raised knowing the tide tables along with my ABCs. I knew not to swim in August or April, because I didn't want to keep company with the jellyfish, and I understood that oysters were best in the fall. I took my afternoon naps alongside the dunes and learned to walk lightly on the hard-packed sand. My backyard was the ocean, and I would always call it home. Although I am named after a spring flower, I am an island girl.

There is something different about women who were born by the sea, baptized in salt water, and raised by the tides. We were mermaids, adapting to the temperamental whims of storms that brewed beyond the shores. I lived at a different pace than the people on the mainland. We called it "island time." We moved a little slower and smiled to ourselves at the city people. The thick humid air bound us to a secret only we knew: life was a little sweeter at the beach.

Being born on an island meant you were also in tune with nature. All women are daughters of the moon, but our relationship is strengthened by the ocean. Along with the water, we belong to her phases. I grew up with an appreciation for the cycle of life because I saw it play out so clearly in front of me. I respected the ocean because it deserved and demanded it. I knew there were places that would swallow you whole if you weren't careful. Riptides took out a few clueless tourists each summer. Us island folk knew better. Oceans are not always joyful; in fact, very quickly the water can turn dark, roll in and roll out to cover and uncover deep secrets. The ocean, if it wanted, could make you lost forever. Reaching up and pulling you into its mouth, never to be seen again. People have gone missing at sea for as long as we have ventured out on her. The ocean is beautiful, but also wild and mercurial. The beach at noon is not the same beach at dusk.

We appreciated the gifts of the ocean and understood how it could also take away.

Anyone born next to the rolling tides of Sullivan's Island knew a lot about the natural world, especially its weather. Island people know about hurricanes. They will tell you crazy things happen during hurricanes. Tragedies, too. Heart attacks and early births. I had lived through many storms, but as all island women knew, we were always ready for the next one.

Somewhere along the way, though, I had become timid about life's storms. I had learned to keep my mermaid nature wrapped and hidden. If I had an inner siren, she'd become muzzled in the process of growing up. I'd grown scared, I guess, that if I let my hair out of its tight bun, if I acted on my wild and tempestuous impulses, I would lose control and then be truly lost at sea.

This is the story of how I found myself, out there in the storm, and learned my own true nature.

CHAPTER ONE

~~~~~

Violet

It was a balmy almost afternoon on Sullivan's Island, and I decided to escape from my desk for once, take my work outside and enjoy the beautiful afternoon. There was a gentle clinking of wind chimes, danced around by a breeze that promised a hotter tomorrow. The bright Lowcountry sun was spilling out through the palmetto fronds, warming my shoulders and bathing me in golden light as I spread out a handmade quilt on the soft grass that surrounded Gran's garden. It was all lovely, but my mind was on work, on the wedding I had to photograph tomorrow, obsessively going over the checklists that helped me keep track of all the shots I needed to capture between the ceremony and the cocktail hour, memorizing the wedding party names. It was all that planning, those little touches, that had put me in high demand among the brides of Charleston.

Summer was right around the corner, and the wedding season would be coming right along with it. That meant good money for a girl in my line of work, but it also meant a lot of old dreams were about to be right up in my face. For a moment I got distracted by the wind chimes and the heat of the sunshine, allowing myself to slip into the cushions of my imagination and fantasies of another life.

It was comfortable living at my gran's. I had originally moved in to help her recover from a surgery she'd needed after an accident a little over a year ago, but then my business had started to take off, and it just made sense to stay. She was finally starting to get back to her normal self. I helped with the cleaning, but she'd make us dinner most nights or order takeout. I had some wounds that were slow to heal, too, and things were simple there. It was great to have company, and I could dedicate a lot of time to my photography.

The home I used to live in, back when I thought I was going to live that picket fence life, was currently being rented out. I got good rates for it on Airbnb (Charleston was a hot destination these days), and I was glad to have an excuse not to live in that house all alone.

My phone buzzed in my pocket, taking me out of my head and back into reality. I picked it up, expecting a frantic message from one of the brides who'd contracted me to shoot their upcoming weddings. But it wasn't that. My chest got tight, then filled with sweet air at the sight of a message from Chris, my boyfriend—or ex-boyfriend, I guessed. Our status was, well, complicated. The family life we'd planned together had been snatched away, but we still owned that house in Byrnes Downs together. For almost a year now, he's lived in Japan on a job that was meant to last only a few months. We were in touch, though. Part of me thought I should move on to new things, but I liked that easy familiarity and the sense that there was someone out there who cared about me, that we could start up again at any moment and it wouldn't be starting over from scratch with someone I didn't know at all.

I tapped open the message.

> Hey, I got an alert for funds available in our shared account . . . do you know what that's about?

Oh shit. My stomach dropped. I *did* know what that was about, though I hadn't planned to tell him about it yet. Or maybe ever?

Though maybe he deserved to know I'd been renting out the house. Squirreling away money for who knew what. My fantasies changed all the time. A Vera Wang gown for a harbor wedding, or a Caribbean elopement?

That's weird, I typed.

Had I sent the last renters the wrong account number? This wasn't the kind of mistake I usually made. Had I somehow done it subconsciously—like, accidentally on purpose? I *had* been really busy. And I'd tried to simplify some of my admin when I was putting in a few security measures—a camera, a lockbox—and maybe I'd mixed a few things up?

I'll look into it.

For what seemed like a long time he didn't reply, and then for what seemed like an even longer time those three dots rippled in the gray speech bubble.

Then his response came, and my stomach dropped again.

Violet, I miss home.

My heart started to race. This was not a normal message to get from Chris. Our exchanges these days were almost entirely practicalities about the house—making sure the flood insurance was up to date, that kind of thing. Sometimes he would text to tell me about a strange or cool discovery he'd made. Mostly pictures of food. It hadn't been romantic in a while.

Everything okay?

We have a lot to talk about. I think I need to come home.

Well, you are overdue for a visit.
I'm sure you miss your Bessinger's Barbeque.

My words were easy breezy, but my fingers trembled as they hammered at my phone.

That's not all of it, Vi, although I do miss their pulled pork.
That's not what I meant by home, though.
I think I miss us.

I stared at the screen on my phone.

I guess on some level I had been longing for a message like this, a direct plea that we go back in time, or forward in time—that we form a real, official couple again and sign up for all the official couple things. But now, clutching my phone, I felt nervous. Maybe I was projecting anyway. Did he mean he missed seeing us regularly so we could all hang out? Or did he mean *us*, like us sharing a home again, and maybe a bed?

I felt a little foolish. One *I miss you* and I was imagining the whole domestic world that had almost been ours but had been flung back into orbit. I chewed on a fingernail.

Speaking of nails, I hadn't gotten a manicure in a hot minute.

My mind whirred with insecurities, little fears—what would he think of me now? I had a lot of lady maintenance to do if he really was coming home.

Somewhere along the line, after my world was turned upside down, I didn't recognize myself; I didn't know anymore what I used to know. New corners of my heart had been ripped open, and what had mattered before seemed to hold less space now. I had buried my grief in work. I had become sharp and laser focused on becoming the most successful photographer in Charleston. If my chance of having a more domestic life was taken from me, I figured I'd better commit hard to something else. I shifted, placing myself in the center of my own attention. If my work got good enough, was noticed by someone at *New York* magazine, say, then maybe I could transition and do some editorial work, or even travel a little. I was a new version of myself, and I was still figuring her out.

How much of the old me was still in there? The one who was a perfectly toned size four? The one who knew exactly where the salad fork went, and how to write the perfect thank-you note? That was the version Chris and I both knew. But I had changed since he'd been gone. My time now was spent in the gym or working on my photography. My weekends weren't open to days spent on his boat; they were spent at weddings, or in the darkroom, or at my computer editing. When Chris said he missed me, I wondered if he meant the old me.

He didn't know the Violet I was trying to become, and maybe I didn't, either.

The door of Gran's truck slammed and out popped my sister, a blaze of copper red hair floating behind her as she ran toward me.

"Hey, girl, whatcha doin'?" she called out, crossing the yard.

We were so different, my sister and I, though we'd always been close. I was small, and Maggie was on the taller side. I had dark, straight-as-an-arrow hair; hers was wild, curly, and red. Her eyes were green; mine were brown. She was loud and impulsive; I was quieter, more calculating. I liked tradition, and she broke the mold. So dating Chris, who happened to be my sister's ex-boyfriend, would always make me feel a little naughty, whereas Maggie got a kick out of seeing us together. On some level the fact that Chris and I got together probably let her off the hook. It had been my opinion, and still was, that she was a fool for letting him go, but the pull of New York City made her heart sing louder than he did.

She plopped right down next to me and sent up the perfume of garlic. Maggie—my sister the chef—brought her work with her wherever she went. She stretched out, rolling her pant legs up and leaning back to accept the sun's kiss. She shook out her hair so that it caught the sunlight, lit her aflame.

"How goes the kitchen?" I asked.

"Oh, you know, another day, another review for the Lantern," she replied with just a hint of bravado. "Lots of pressure, but I'm whipping out some classics."

"Like what?" I was still feeling a little unnerved by the Chris thing—my mistake, and his comment—and wanted to be told something good.

"Like a mussels dish in a saffron cream sauce with garlic toast."

That explained the garlic smell. My mouth watered a little. "Yum. I'm sure that will be a hit."

"When in doubt, go French to impress," Maggie replied with a wink.

"You've come a long way from the Fire Department Cook-Off."

She grinned at me. "I had those boys beat when I was in high school."

"Oh, I know," I replied, grinning right back. "The article from the newspaper is still framed on Gran's mantel."

"As it should be." Maybe Maggie noticed my grin slipping, because she tilted her head and asked, "What's up?"

For some reason, I didn't want to tell her about the text from Chris. I didn't want to admit to myself, much less to her, the hopes it had kicked up inside me. Instead, I asked, "Do you miss New York City restaurant life any?"

"Sometimes." My sister shrugged, released a sigh. "But I learned I don't need to chase destiny up the coast. I have everything I need to achieve my dreams right in my own backyard."

Maggie ran our family's restaurant, the Magic Lantern. It was an institution on Sullivan's Island, right up the road from our childhood home. Our great-grandmother Daisy started the place and handed it down to her daughter, my grandmother Rose, who handed it down to my sister, Magnolia, or Maggie as we all called her.

"You look dark, Violet." She squinted in my direction, sizing me up, coming to one of those snap big-sister judgments. "You need some playtime."

"Maggie, my fellow workaholic. You of all people should understand. I have zero free time, except for the next thirty minutes, and I'm actually working. See my pretty planner?" I held up my perfectly color-coded planner, complete with a violet cover and containing a very full to-do list.

"That's exactly why you need to rekindle some old friendship flames and maybe catch a date? Stop working for a moment."

I couldn't help laughing a little at the irony. "You should talk!"

"I know, I know. But Sam is all I need."

Must be nice, I almost said, but I managed to hold my tongue.

Sam was Maggie's doctor boyfriend of a few years. He was a catch—I knew, because I used to date him. Yes, if you are keeping score, then that's correct—we kind of swapped boyfriends. Sounds scandalous, I know, but in truth there was no juice in that fruit. He was the kind of catch that didn't really do anything for me. We were better as friends, and he was just right for Maggie somehow. He was a good southern man from an old Charleston family who had been farmers for about a hundred years on Johns Island, a barrier island off Charleston.

"I have Aly," I said. Aly was a new friend, but we had become close fast.

"That's not the same. Speaking of needs," Maggie said, a twinkle in her eye. "You could use your coat shined."

"'Coat shined,' good lord, Maggie." I giggled at our family phrase for, well, *you know what*. I hadn't had sex in . . .

But Maggie, not noticing my embarrassment, forged right on ahead. "Time to dust off one of your Lilly Pulitzer shifts! Maybe wear less black? Jimmy just moved back, you know—he needs a companion. A single girl—I won't do, shacked up as I am. So maybe y'all will go out?"

Jimmy was our childhood best friend. He was the best dancer, the best dressed, and he had the sweetest heart I'd ever known. He was loyal to a fault and had looked out for my sister and me since our sandbox days. But he had gotten closer to Maggie when they were both living in New York, and I hadn't seen him in a minute. "I thought Mr. Hollywood was too busy for us. Where is he living?"

"He's technically a soap opera actor; is that considered Hollywood?"

"How should I know?"

"He's here for the summer, staying with his aunt on the island. His show doesn't film in the summer."

"It'll be good to have him around again." I bit my lip, resisting my sister's suggestions. "I wouldn't even know where to take Jimmy. Except for wedding venues, that is. I'm so out of it."

"Vi, your sister is a very important chef in Charleston. Maybe try a new restaurant? You know I love Vern's. Their chicken is totally Last Supper status." She made a playful face and said, "Maybe loosen that tight ballerina bun?"

These days, I never had a single hair out of place; it was always the same style. I slicked it back with my wax stick, parted it down the center, and wound the rest of it into a bun so my hair was off my neck. It had become my signature look.

"Yeah, we could do that. I'd like him to get to know Aly, too," I said noncommittally. "I haven't been to a restaurant other than the Magic Lantern or a banquet hall in a long time. Maybe the three of us could go out? Or the four of us?"

"Violet, what's wrong?"

"Well . . ." It hurt when I swallowed just then, but I figured I should come clean, tell Maggie what was on my mind. My weird little secret, and the emotions coursing through me. "Chris sent me a text today." For a moment, Maggie didn't say anything, so I added, "Just house stuff at first, but then he sent an 'I miss you' text."

"Not the 'I miss you' text; come on, Violet! Don't fall for it!" Maggie groaned.

"I'm not falling for anything, Maggie." My words were tumbling out of my mouth fast and defensive. "But he might be coming home."

"Yeah, okay. Who cares? Why would he send you that? I thought the romance department was closed with that guy."

"That guy." I must have repeated her words a little too sharply, because she flinched at the sound.

"Violet, I love you. I'm not saying this to start a fight; I just think you need to be careful with him. Why would he send you an emotional text out of the blue . . . It seems fishy."

"Does it? I mean, we own a house together; it can't be totally out of the blue . . ."

"Don't you dare say you told him you miss him too." Maggie's eyebrows were about at her hairline.

"Maggie, I'm not going to pretend like the fire is totally out. I wonder sometimes how things could've been if—"

"Stop, I'm not entertaining that, and you shouldn't either. Have you told Chris about the Airbnb thing yet?" she asked.

My irritation with my sister faded as my guilt welled up. "No, not yet . . ."

I mean, I should feel guilty. I was lying by omission. I had initially done it just to get a little extra cash for house maintenance and didn't think Chris needed to know about it, but it proved lucrative, even more so once I moved into Gran's and could rent out the whole house. Not that I had shared the money with him.

"He's on the deed!" Maggie said.

"I know I need to tell him. I'm just waiting for the right moment . . ." I looked at my toes, which, as it happened, could really use a fresh coat of paint.

"You are always waiting for the right moment for everything . . . but you know when the right moment comes? Never."

I didn't have an argument for that.

"So, speaking of the wrong moment, Mom's coming home soon."

"Yeah, back from another European adventure."

"At least we'll have Jimmy to roll our eyes with. Hopefully this time won't be so dramatic."

"It's Mom we're talking about here," I said. "There's always drama."

Maggie nodded. Just like that, we were on the same team again.

Our mother was a true handful, to put it midly. After years spent as an aspiring ballerina, she had a warped relationship with food and a tendency toward the operatic. Years ago, when we were small, our father died in a motorcycle accident after a dance with some narcotics. That woman was no stranger to drama.

"Is Gran inside?" Maggie asked me.

"Yeah, she was knitting something in her chair and dozed off. She's been sleeping for a while now, so we might want to head in."

"Huh, she okay?" Maggie jumped up and disappeared into the house.

I followed her but stopped at the gallery wall of pictures by the stairs and straightened out the framed image of Grandmother Daisy that was always falling to the left. I tiptoed in to find Gran staring out of the glass door that overlooked the marsh, a wistful look on her face.

"Gran?" I whispered.

"What? Oh!" She collected herself and gave me a glancing smile. "I was just remembering."

"Something sweet, I hope?"

As she turned to face me, she gave me the once-over. "What's on your mind, Violet?"

"Nothing."

"You look like you're hiding something."

"I'm not hiding anything . . ." It was hard to lie when Gran was staring right at me. With a sigh, I admitted, "Chris wants to come home."

"Oh, lord. How do you feel about it?"

"I mean, I don't know. It's complicated."

"And right when Lily is coming home, too." Gran reached out and cupped the side of my face. "It all happens at once, doesn't it? You might want to go see Malory over at Stella Nova Salon. I know I always feel better when my hair's looking good. If Chris is coming home, he needs to see what he's missing."

"How do you know I want him to miss me?" I smiled and put a hand on my hip.

"Violet, I've known you since before you knew yourself. You've been moping around this house, not going on any dates. You two almost made a family together. It makes sense. You have unfinished business. We all know you miss him, even if you are busy with work. Maybe he's made some mistakes in the past . . . but so have you, right?" She gave me a warm smile. "Everyone likes second chances!"

It took a special bond to be able to speak like that to each other. I was grateful when she did that, cut right to the chase. She always saw through me anyway, and her saying it out loud gave me permission to feel what I was feeling. The little tug at my heart made me realize I was actually excited to see him, too.

"Thank you," I said with a smile.

"There you are," Maggie said, emerging from the next room. "I was looking for you in the other room—Violet said you were in your chair. Keeping secrets, are you?"

"What? No . . ." Gran glanced from Maggie back to me. "I was just going out, actually. Want me to pick you up something to eat?"

"No, thanks," I said. "I'm meeting up with Aly at the Co-op."

"Then have a shower, Vi," Maggie said.

"Okay, y'all, I get it. I'm going to see Malory tomorrow; everyone relax."

"Thank goodness," Maggie teased. "Did you tell her to caffeinate?"

"I'm sure she knows she has her work cut out for her. It's been a minute," I replied, catching my reflection in the mirror. How long had it been, exactly? They had a point. I had stopped caring about my hair; I just tucked it away and went to work. But I had stopped making time for things like hair appointments. I had just been so busy making everyone else look good. All my brides needed to capture perfection, yet a woman's hair in the South was a very serious matter of pride and, according to my mother, fifty percent of a woman's looks.

"Gross, Violet!" Gran said, swatting my hand away from my mouth before I had a chance to bite my nails.

"Y'all, I'm going to run over to the Nail Place on Main Street."

"Yeah, you don't want Chris seeing you like that," Gran said.

"You're gonna need a fresh sharp set, in case you need to scratch his eyes out," Maggie said. She was smiling again, but I still couldn't tell if she was joking.

CHAPTER TWO

~~~

Aly

There will never be a colder Christmas than the Christmas after my mother died. I'm a midwestern girl, but I've lived in Charleston long enough that my internal thermostat isn't set to normal. A little chill in the air was felt much more dramatically here in the South. Yet nothing has ever felt chillier and more vacant than that December. I was a shell of a woman, and I know that now. I was drifting in and out of my days like a ghost through walls. I didn't know how to show up to my own life. I had forgotten how.

They say you are never truly an adult until you lose your mother, and the morning after I lost mine, I had to remember how to breathe. I remember waking up in hot, damp, nightmare-riddled sheets thinking that it had all been a dream. Opening my eyes to a raw new world in which she wasn't, so foreign and strange. I remember telling myself not to attempt anything bigger than micromovements. *Pull back the covers, go to the bathroom, turn on the shower, and then get in it.* Every choice was hard, because I no longer had a mother to care about what I did. She had saturated my entire identity, and that was wonderful. Living without her was like drinking sweet tea without the simple syrup. It quenched my thirst, but it wasn't as fun anymore.

I was still trying hard to thaw out and warm to my life.

My mother was a small-town star. Everyone in Charleston knew her, her stories, and the town lore that she contributed to. She'd expanded her brand in recent years with a line of home goods at Crate and Barn that had gained a cult following in the Carolinas. People still say she was born under a hydrangea bush, one so blue it rivaled the sky. The same color as my mother's eyes and the ribbon she always tied around her ponytail. She was lovely. She moved through rooms like music, like jazz. You could tap your feet to her beat, even if you didn't know the tune. My mother was a true beauty, glamorous and thoughtful. Nothing she did was by accident; every decision was exquisite and deliberate.

She had left our tight-knit family—me, my two siblings, and my father, her soul mate in every sense of the word—a little unraveled. Maybe that's the youngest child's view, but I don't think so. My brother still lived in Michigan, where we were originally from, and my sister was in Los Angeles now. I lived in Charleston, with my dad, in what was once our family vacation home, now turned full-time home, on Sullivan's Island.

I moved in after my mother passed, when neither of us could bear being alone. We'd both grown used to the arrangement.

Grief isn't one-size-fits-all; it looks different on everyone. My dad and I were, for whatever reason, hit the hardest by her loss. Probably because my sister was so busy with her job, and my brother was married with kids. So my dad and I bonded over our shared trauma of losing Callie—Momma to me—and joked that the only good that came from losing her was our newfound closeness.

And here was another layer of complicated heartbreak: I had been working for her.

Callie Knox. She went to New York to begin her career but then moved back to Michigan to start a family. She designed homes all over the Midwest and Texas. She began to put her designs on Instagram and TikTok, and in less than a year she was a full-blown star. People were drawn to her warmth and the beauty of her lifestyle. She always looked as if she had everything together, and, in truth, she always did. She was glamorous and down-to-earth at the same time. Her genuine personality resonated with women across the country. She went viral with her *Car-Line Confessionals*, where she would talk about the constant struggle for work-family balance. She was relatable and aspirational. In one video she would be setting a table with expensive china, and in the next she would be unloading her dishwasher. I loved her content, despite being her daughter, and so did a whole universe of fans.

When she was younger, she vacationed on Sullivan's Island, and with all her success she had decided that it was time to move here full-time. She and my dad bought a giant house on the beach, and it quickly became our refuge. A sanctuary. When she relocated to Charleston, she opened up a small boutique, where she sold some of her homewares and did a YouTube decorating show, and her brand became more closely associated with the city of her childhood. She had designed a line of linens that seemed to be on everyone's table. A few years ago, everyone had a "Callie mug"—they were *the thing*. I was lucky to be a part of her empire, professionally and personally.

I wanted to be brought in front of the camera eventually, or at least that was the long-term goal. To evolve a single-woman show into a mother-daughter act. But I didn't feel like I had honed my own style enough yet to be worthy of sharing her stage. So I was learning how to be her. She had been grooming me to take over for her one day in the far-off future. She had been on top of her game, so stepping back wasn't on the horizon.

My mother was a force larger than life, but the past summer, out of nowhere, cancer took a bite and didn't let go. We lost her in eight weeks. It was a devastating shock. Dad was absent in his own body without his person. I witnessed him crying for the first time in my life. I figured I needed to keep an eye on him. I left my rented place downtown and moved into the apartment over his garage.

The boutique my mother owned closed the moment we found out she was sick, but I had been keeping her social media accounts going, maintaining her virtual community. I wanted to keep them true to her—I was afraid to post anything personal, anything of my own. I did post about Charleston, and that seemed to generate more attention. I was trying to find my own style and perspective, but so far all I really posted was old content of hers and pictures of our home, throwback projects, projects she never got around to. I went on trying to still engage her old audience. As it was, her lines at Crate and Barn and a few local stores were still selling, and her cookbooks were in print and stocked at our favorite bookstores.

After attending the College of Charleston, I had fallen into the world of influencing on Instagram. I started by taking pictures of my friends, the things we did for friends, and I threw in a few clever hashtags. I didn't have to do too much work to get people to like the pictures and blogs I was writing. After all, my subject was one of the most beautiful cities in the world, and I hopped on that bus at just the right moment. Charleston had been a hidden gem for too long and was ready to be shared. Not yet the number one tourist destination for the last twelve years in a row, like it is now. As the city got hot, I got more attention. But I was still small-time, as far as my own influence went.

I wasn't putting out viral videos like my mom had, and I wasn't making a ton of money—not yet, anyway. Really all I wanted to do was share what I found beautiful, or delicious, or fun. But on the other hand, once I realized I had an opportunity to make a career from what I was already doing, it seemed foolish not to at least try. My father, who was in finance, had another point of view. He hated the influencer thing. He liked to roast me about that expensive college degree in biology, how it was just gathering dust.

When I started my blog in college, it was right at the beginning of the social media craze. Facebook was phasing out, and Instagram had hatched. It was just my little corner of the internet, where I could share my love affair with Charleston. But now the competition was getting fierce. It seemed like every time I opened my Instagram these days there was another girl, against another house on Rainbow Row, with a little paragraph about the Lowcountry lifestyle. I felt the pressure to hone my voice into something sharper. I needed my perspective to be unique. I vowed to myself that this summer would be the summer when I found my own style.

Enter Violet.

I met my best friend, Violet Adams, by accident. I was a bridesmaid in a wedding, and she was the photographer. I felt an instant connection with her, and she was so funny, making us pose in creative ways. We became fast friends—she was the native, while I was a newbie to the greater Charleston area. When the pictures from the wedding came back, I was astonished that not only had she made me look beautiful but she had also captured my personality. She had just made me so relaxed in front of the camera. I had never gotten myself to look that way; it was almost as if she had bent the light to make my tired face look angelic.

On this particular morning on Sullivan's Island, it seemed like all the birds were singing. A perfect day for the new beginning I had promised myself. The air was warm and scented with the jasmine that crawled all over the lattice on my dad's porch. My mom had planted it the spring we bought the house, and it had since gone absolutely crazy. The porch looked like it was wearing a cardigan.

As I walked down the driveway to pick up the newspaper, a salty breeze lifted my hair, and I looked up at the robin's-egg blue sky, so bright that I slid my sunglasses down to look at the clouds. Giant puffs reminded me of the cotton pads my mother had always used to remove her eye makeup. It was going to be a good day, a good week, and a great summer. It had to be! The winter had been long and bruising.

But first I needed some coffee.

I found my dad in the kitchen filling the French press. He stood there measuring out his water, dressed in tailored khaki trousers and a lime green button-down. Not one single wrinkle on it, and not one single strand of his hair out of place. He looked up at me through tortoiseshell glasses and gave me a warm smile, then shuffled over to the cabinet and pulled out a Herend Chinese Bouquet mug. It was my parents' wedding china. I loved that rust color.

"Morning, Minnow." It was the nickname he had bestowed upon me because of my love of swimming.

"Hey, Dad. How'd you sleep?" I gave his cheek a kiss and slid the *New York Times* over to him.

"Not great. But you know I don't sleep very well these days. It's a big bed."

"I think it's time you got a dog, Dad."

"Aly, I do not want a dog." My dad made a face of disgust. "All that hair?"

"They make dogs that don't shed, you know."

"Yeah, but those are froufrou dogs. Real men have Labs, and Labs shed," he grumbled. "And *chew*. Also, there is no way in hell I'd let a dog in my bed."

I sipped my grainy French-press coffee. "What about a cat?"

"Aly, can we be serious for a minute?"

I sat up a little straighter, hearing his tone. "Yes?"

"I am doing a little work on settling Mom's estate."

"Okay."

"The lines you all were working on—Crate and Barn wants to let the collaboration deal lapse, now that Mom is gone."

"No!" It felt like a lance through my heart. That would be like losing her all over again. It was such a big revenue stream for Callie Knox—the whole thing might fall apart without it. "They can't do that."

"Well, actually, they can. *She* was the product in many ways. Her sensibility. Without her as pitchwoman . . ."

"But I mean, someone could take over," I said fast, before I could think what it might mean.

"Someone could." He leveled his deep-blue eyes at me. "What about you?"

"Me?"

"I think you should consider officially taking them over. Otherwise . . ."

I frowned. What he was suggesting was a dream in some ways, but it gave me a sad, scared feeling in the pit of my stomach. "I'm not ready for something like that. I only have, like, five thousand followers. Of my own, I mean."

"How many does Mom have?" he asked.

"Still over two hundred and fifty thousand."

"And you've been part of maintaining that audience, right? Seems to me like the best, most natural move for you is to officially take over her account and start the crossover."

"Dad, I've never designed anything in my life on my own except, like, a few rooms and that one towel set . . ."

"It's time, Minnow. You have to start stepping into your own. You can do it."

Maybe this was the push I needed? But how to go about it? Would I start with interiors as she had done, or should I go directly to the homewares? Or could I do all of it at the same time? My brain was firing before I even admitted to myself that I wanted this.

"You know," Dad said, putting a hand on my shoulder, "it wasn't *entirely* my idea."

"It wasn't?"

"Your mother used to say you had the star power. And the taste. I stay in touch with Rosemary, your mother's business manager, and I mentioned this as a possibility. Who else can create like her? Who better than her own daughter? You know the operation. You've already done most of the training." He smiled at me, and I felt that sweet, sad arrow going through his heart like it was piercing mine, too. "You had the best teacher."

"Maybe." I knew he was right—I would be good at it, and honestly there was nothing I'd rather do. But something kept my enthusiasm tamped down. "Let me think about it."

"Good. Think on it, but don't think too long. This could be a good move for you. And if we can't find an heir for Callie, first that deal will expire, and then people will stop buying her books, and we'll have to sundown the operation."

"I thought you wanted to try to sell the brand."

"I did, but your brother and sister don't want to sell. After we talked, I agreed they were right. We can't lose her *and* her life's work."

"You've already asked my siblings?"

"Yes, Aly. They each own a share in the company. But the vote has to be unanimous. If you don't think you can handle it . . ."

"I can handle it." I spun my mug on the table. That beautiful table we had gathered around as a family, that rust-colored mug she'd chosen when her family life was just beginning. "I just worry that I won't be as great as she was."

"Minnow, you'll be different. I wouldn't suggest it if I didn't think you could do great."

The way he was looking at me set off a sunburst of pride in my chest. He believed in me. Mom had believed in me. Maybe I could really do this.

"We did have that idea for the magnolia-scented candle with the glasswork from that artisan on King Street . . . Maybe I could pick that up again?"

My dad nodded. "Give Rosemary a call."

"Okay. I will. I'm excited, Dad . . . This could be . . ."

"Wonderful."

"Yeah." I was beaming now and flushed with adrenaline. "Thanks, Dad."

My dad turned to the paper as though that was settled.

When he flipped to the business section, I noticed that he'd removed his wedding ring.

And just like that, I fell from cloud nine. "Dad, where's your ring?" I asked.

"Well, I—" He gestured with his hand. "I have a date tonight."

I was not proud of my tone of voice when I said, "*A date, Dad?*"
My heart was feeling very tight. I mean, I didn't want him to be lonely,
but I also didn't know how I felt about his moving on so soon.

"Time to get back on the horse."

"Not a superfan of you calling a woman a horse, but . . ." I swallowed, tried to make myself sound neutral-ish and curious. "Who's the
date with?"

"A woman who—don't you worry—is age-appropriate and financially comfortable."

"Oh, so not a gold digger or a bimbo," I quipped, wishing I didn't
sound quite so bitterly sarcastic. "That's good, Dad, that's really good."

"Your old man doesn't need that noise."

"Okay, well." I filled my cheeks with air, trying to think what a
supportive daughter would ask next. "Well, where are y'all going?"

"Chez Nous, downtown."

"Wow, that's romantic."

"Yes." He cleared his throat. "That's the point. Maybe you should
try getting out there. You never know who you might meet."

"I don't know. My life feels pretty full right now."

"Okay, Aly, you know best. Except . . . you might need some new
shorts. Those look a little worn-out. Can't be a Callie Knox CEO in
shorts like that."

"They are cutoffs; they are meant to look like this." I gave his hand
a pat, trying to appear breezy and untroubled, then hurried back to my
garage apartment. I opened the door to the floor-length gold mirror and
took a look at myself. My outfit that day was beach chic—a long-wrinkled
button-down and my favorite faded cutoff jean shorts—something
Dad would never understand, though my mother would have given him
a slap on the back of his hand, winked at me, and said, "Men don't get it."

I could feel my eyes start to well up with tears.

It was another sad milestone—how many would there be? The first
Christmas without her, my birthday, whenever I had a hard day and

couldn't call her to kvetch. But the past twenty minutes were a special kind of mindfuck. The suggestion that I take over my mother's entire company at the same time my dad was declaring himself ready to start dating.

Grief was a mean little bitch.

Most of my grieving I did in private, not wanting to upset my dad. Whenever I could, I would text Violet.

> Dad's got a date.

Oh, shit. You okay?

> Nope!

Well, that's normal. Who's it with?

> Some woman. He said she's quote age appropriate.

Let's all pray that means over fifty.

> I have a long list of prayer requests.

Girl, me too. Maybe you should go for a swim?

> I need one, I think. Go clear my head a bit.

Yeah, do that, then maybe meet up for nails and then lunch?

> Okay. I need to run some things by you, too.

My little apartment over my dad's garage was lovely, but I still hadn't fully moved in. The apartment was a blank space, all white everything. I missed being downtown sometimes, but the serenity of the beach couldn't be beat, and the ocean was excellent for healing a wounded spirit. The window in my bedroom had a view of the water. I could watch the harbor all day long in any weather. Being close to the ocean anchored me.

Today the water seemed to be dancing as it sparkled with sunshine.

I tripped on one of the moving boxes that I had never gotten around to unpacking.

I struggled to find anything in that mess. I walked across to the other side of my apartment, by the kitchenette, and looked out on my mother's garden. Neither Dad nor I had stepped foot in there since she passed. It was her favorite place. The weeds had claimed her herb patch, but the thought of going in there and messing it up hurt. Everything hurt then, and when grief wanted me, it was best to give in and let it pass.

This apartment might be a great place to start. Maybe actually decorating it and making it my own wouldn't just be a great distraction from my broken heart; it could be content for my Instagram account, and my mother's. If I was going to decorate, might as well share it, and maybe this would look like an organic transition onto her account. She had a ton of followers still, and a lot of them still engaged with the account, knowing I was the one curating her feed now. It would be wasteful to just flush that captive audience.

But then another memory of her popped into my mind, a memory of us laughing over a color swatch, and then another of us giggling uncontrollably over some joke when we did a photo shoot together. I loved style and décor because it was something I got to do with *her*. I wondered if I could love it, enjoy it, or even do it without her.

What would she tell me to do?

I sat down at my kitchen table. My throat was painfully constricted. I was missing her. If she were here, she would say, *Go for it, girl*. The same way she told me to go for team captain of the swim team in high school, or encouraged me when I auditioned for the class musical *Annie*. She made me believe I could do anything. I felt her blessing.

My eyes filled up with tears. I could hear her laughing at me and then scolding me for being emotional.

"Momma, I miss you so much. What if I fail?" I said out loud to the empty apartment.

Then I heard her voice again, deep in my heart.

But what if you don't?

CHAPTER THREE

~~~~

Violet

I took a fast shower and then threw on a black maxi dress. I slicked my hair back into a bun and added some thick gold hoops. When I turned my car on, the radio began playing my favorite song, "Gypsy" by Fleetwood Mac—a good omen.

May was the time of year when either the air-conditioning would be super cranked or the door would be open. South Carolina summers were sneaky. It would be springtime in the morning and the height of summer by the afternoon.

Sullivan's Island had, almost overnight, become like the Hamptons. I was grateful to already live here, I guessed. Now you couldn't get a house on this island for under a million dollars, even one of those ratty run-down beach shacks. But it was strange to see my hometown transformed into a playground for wealthy outsiders. People were moving here from all over, snatching the properties, tearing down the houses, and throwing up giant mansions. It was true that with the gentrification came fun shops, restaurants, and some new blood, and let's face it, the island was more beautiful than it ever was before . . . but sometimes I missed the island of my childhood, unpretentious and unfussed.

Also, a time when you could get a Caesar salad for under thirty dollars.

I rolled down Middle Street, watching groups of people empty out of their Land Rovers and spill into the new chic restaurants or pull their fabric wagons filled with kids in designer clothing—smocked, to resemble peasant wear—while their parents wore linen caftans, espadrilles, fedoras. A part of me wanted to be one of those fashionable mamas, and I wondered if Chris coming home meant I would be before too long. But I also wondered who had the time to iron all that linen and considered their dry-cleaning bill.

That's when I spotted him. The dial of time was turned down. My attention was stolen. My eyes caught sight of a tall, toned, tan man jumping out of his vintage burnt orange Ford Bronco. His white, unbuttoned, crinkled linen shirt flared out with the breeze, revealing an impressive six-pack. His dog popped out, following him. The man and the white Lab. His dark hair shone in the sun, and even at a distance I could see his eyes were bright blue. This was one of the perks of living on an island—everyone was always in some state of undress . . . Actually, that could be a negative thing sometimes, too.

He saw me looking at him, gave me a little nod. I waved back, cracked a smile, and then got startled by the beep of the car behind me.

Oh, lord, help me, I was staring at this strange man and stopping traffic.

What was the matter with me? I hit the gas.

Maybe I needed to eat sooner than planned. I quickly texted Aly, offering to pick up something before, instead of after, the salon. Then the bright bubblegum pink awning of the Co-Op caught my eye, and I knew I had to have their turkey sandwich and an iced latte. Inside, I saw Olivia, who lived a few doors down from us. She was in high school but already working the cash register.

"Hey there, Olivia! I didn't know you worked here!"

"Oh, hey, Violet! Yeah, my first big-girl job. What can I get you?"

"The turkey sandwich and an iced latte."

"Oh, man, I love the turkey, but have you tried our chicken salad? It has grapes in it."

"Gimme both, and might as well add another latte."

As I stood there waiting for my order, looking around at the fun T-shirts, the signs, and the frozen-drink machines, I saw the man with the blue eyes and his dog pass the window, and I panicked and ducked.

"Violet, are you okay?" Olivia shouted, a little louder than I would have liked. I lifted my head to shoot her a look but then realized the man with the abs and the dog had come into the Co-Op. Shit.

I then, stupidly, decided to act like I had dropped my keys.

For a few moments, I did my best improv, pretending to search for keys on the dark concrete floor.

A smooth voice poured into the air: "Can I help you, miss? Did you lose a contact lens or something?" I detected a slight British accent.

It was the man. Bronco, abs, dog, accent.

Double shit.

"I actually seem to have dropped my keys," I said quickly, before realizing I had them on a key chain bracelet around my wrist. "Oh, I'm wearing them. How silly of me." I was sounding slightly British myself. What was happening?

I looked up at him then and was lost in the sharpness of his jaw-line, so pleasantly sprinkled with stubble. Just the right amount. His eyes, beautifully fringed in thick lashes, crinkled when he smiled back at me, flashing the whitest teeth I'd ever seen.

It was probably a pity smile. Jesus. How dumb could I look?

"It's all right. I'd lose my head if it wasn't attached to my neck." The man was probably relieved to turn away from me, inch toward the cash register. "Hey there, Olivia! May I please have the Masters sandwich and a Coke?"

Meanwhile I was still on the floor. Slowly I rose to my feet and smoothed out my dress.

"Sure thing! Violet, your sandwiches are ready! Here ya go!" Olivia said, handing me my bagged lunch. I slipped the sandwiches into my bag and grabbed the lattes in a carrying tray.

"Violet? What a beautiful name. Same as my grandmother." The Brit gave me another pure white smile. I wondered why full eyelashes were wasted on men.

"Oh, thanks. All the women in my family are named after flowers," I blurted.

"Oh, that's lovely. I'm Henry." He held out his hand for me to take, which I did, and I immediately felt a jolt of fire in my . . .

God, I needed to get it together. Was it possible to be made immediately stupid by a sudden burst of attraction for someone?

"Uh, Henry! Nice to meet you! Like, King Henry the Eighth?" What was happening to my mouth? I was sweating from my armpits and my palms.

"Yes, but I don't tend to cut off my lovers' heads," he said with a sly smile.

"Good news!" I replied, nervously giggling.

"See you around, Violet?"

"Yes, sure. Yes, sir. Your Majesty." Then I did a little curtsy.

Oh. My. God. I. Was. So. Lame.

"Here's your order!" Olivia said.

"Thanks," Henry replied. Then he arched an eyebrow, gave me what must've been a polite chuckle, and went out.

Me, I was going to need this coffee to be a little more Irish.

"Wow, that was something," Olivia said.

"Yeah, let's all pretend that didn't happen."

"You know who that was, right? Henry Tucker. He's some big shot from London, I guess. My mom got the gossip from Emily down at High Thyme on Saturday. She said he was a big deal . . . Fancy family, I think, or some kind of investor or something."

"Great, great." Time to focus on my nails and erase that unfortunate display of my most awkward self. I waved goodbye and got back into the car.

I found parking easily right on Middle Street, went inside the large nail salon, and was greeted by Eridani, the owner. She was one of the most beautiful people. Long, thick, raven black hair and a smile as bright as the sun. You would think that she could not be as nice as she was, but you'd be wrong. She was even more beautiful on the inside.

"Hey, Violet! Nice to see you! Been a while."

"Hey! Y'all got your work cut out for you on these nails."

"Please." She shot me a wink. "They can't be that bad. Let me see."

I held out my hand and she bit her lip.

"You must stop biting those fingers! Pedicure, too? We'll fix you right up. Can I get you something to drink? Diet Coke, right?"

The Le family owned two nail salons in Charleston. One on Sullivan's Island and another downtown. They were both beautiful, and after a while television casting companies had picked up on them and filmed often in their spaces. With the money they earned from the shoots, the family had franchised their salons and now had four.

Eridani led me to a black leather chair with a foot bath that swirled lavender and vanilla perfume into the air. I removed my flip-flops, got into the chair, and immediately found the remote for the massager. I slipped my feet into the hot water and let myself relax. I felt the massager roll into my shoulder blades and release a good two weeks' worth of solid stress.

A nice woman introduced herself as Emma and sat down at the pedicure station while another girl offered to start on my hands.

"Here, love, you can put your wedding rings in here." The girl offered me a ring dish. I blushed. Didn't she see I didn't have any rings?

"Oh, I don't have any jewelry."

"No, like, your engagement ring," she said. "The rings you probably never take off?"

"I'm, um, not married," I said, wondering why she was so persistent. "Or engaged."

"Oh, sorry!" she said, and went to get her nail tools.

I sat there, my stomach turning. I hated how everyone assumed I was married, and I hated it even more that I was self-conscious about it. Chris and I had bought a house together; we had planned a life. I had agreed to those things. I truly did want to marry him. Or I had, at the time. I knew life never went exactly as planned, but still I felt cheated. I had seen enough local weddings to know that not everything always went as we hoped, and marriage was complicated. I'd seen brides get cold feet the day of the ceremony. I'd seen entire weddings called off and couples who separated right after the big day.

Nope, things hadn't gone according to plan with Chris. I mean, it was obvious that his mother, Karen, pictured her son with a pearl-necklace-wearing debutante from Charleston. Not an island girl with sand in her hair. Okay, I didn't have literal sand in my hair, but try as I might with my Lilly Pulitzer dresses, even if I could look the part, I was never officially one of the cotillion crowd. Even though Sullivan's had become chic, the older crowd still viewed us as island brats. The worst thing about her not liking me was that she was everything I used to admire about a woman. She was smart and successful, came from a great family, and was the Emily Post of southern etiquette.

His mother often referred to me as "his almost baby momma," never as her son's past girlfriend, or just Violet. It was like her to name me by my big failure, my big loss. Karen had disapproved of Maggie, too, and had probably been thrilled by her son's transfer to Japan. It probably represented a convenient break for her.

Just then Aly came in to save me from my ruminations. She had her hair pulled back, and I noticed the angle of her jawline, so sharp, a great contrast to her soft mouth and large brown eyes.

I couldn't help noticing things like that. Occupational hazard.

"Hey!" she sang as she plopped in the chair next to me.

"Hey! Feeling better? Did you find out who your dad is going on a date with?"

"No, but I feel like my hands will feel better soon, and my feet," she said as she pulled out a book. I knew she would tell me more later. Even though Aly had a blog and put a lot of her life on the internet, she was actually pretty private.

"Oh, what are you reading?" I asked.

"The latest Kristin Hannah. It's so good."

"Book nerd."

"Hot girls read, Violet. Catch up."

Emma was doing the lord's work on my feet, and I almost forgot all about Chris and my former life. The plush pink chair pillows snuggled me and gently massaged my back. Once the foot massage started, I closed my eyes and felt sleep creeping over me.

I woke up when I heard myself snore.

"Oh my gosh, I'm so sorry!" I mumbled as I wiped my mouth with the back of my hand. Not only was I snoring, I was also drooling. I was mortified.

"Don't worry, Ms. Violet. You need rest! By the way, I saw that wedding you photographed in *Charleston Bride*. It was incredible!" Emma said as she drained the tub.

I realized then there were a few women looking at me.

"Sorry, y'all!" I said, feeling my cheeks deeply blush.

"Aly! Why didn't you wake me?" I hissed at my friend.

"And interrupt that colossal slumber? No way. I even took pictures!"

"Ugh." I rolled my eyes. I looked down to find ten perfect nails on beautifully moisturized, happy feet, which I was pleased to recognize as mine. Gone were my hobbit toes, and here were the feet of a queen.

A nice woman with beautiful silver hair sitting next to me leaned over and said, "You never stood a chance. Once Emma touches my feet? I'm out! No shame in it."

As embarrassed as I was, I felt refreshed. I just prayed I didn't wind up on someone's phone headed for a TikTok. I did not need to go viral.

"Miss Lucy, you fall asleep because you are out all night dancing!" Emma said.

"All night dancing!" I said, raising my eyebrows to my neighbor, who looked old enough to collect Social Security.

"She's right! One of my boyfriends likes to salsa, so I do my best to keep up!" Lucy said, pretending to fluff her hair.

"Salsa? That's what we're calling it now?" her friend teased her.

"More like 'Mambo No. 5'!" Lucy cackled.

I couldn't believe what I was hearing. "Good for you!" I laughed. "Aly, did you catch this?"

"I did. Y'all are scandalous." Aly closed her book and cleared her throat. "Do you gals know a George Knox?"

"Nope, no Knox yet. Why, is he single?"

Aly shrugged. "Seems like it," she said cryptically, and went over to get her hands done. The talk about dating seemed to make her nervous.

"Well," I said, to cover for Aly, "I admire your stamina. I'm not even forty, and I can barely find the energy for romance. I'm Violet Adams, by the way."

"I'm Lucy Lane, and since I moved back to Charleston, I'm having the time of my life. Keeps me young to be busy!"

"Yeah, *getting* busy," said a grumpy voice from the other side of her.

I scooted forward to identify the owner of the snarky comment and saw another silver-haired beauty, this one with a sharp scowl.

"Hush, Susan, you're just jealous because you keep getting ghosted by the bee," Lucy said.

"Lucy, it's called Bumble, not the Bee, for heaven's sake!" Susan replied.

"Whatever. The boys are buzzing in my direction! Maybe you just need some sweeter honey." Lucy's eyes closed as she did a little wiggle in her seat.

I smiled at their bickering, and also at their energy and zest for life.

"Oh, don't you know about Twilight Connection?" Lucy said to me.

"Oh, um, no, ma'am . . . You mean the book?" I said.

"No, silly girl, the dating site! Changed my life! Although ole Susan over here can't seem to hook a fish!" Lucy made a face at her friend. "I've got a new beau every few days! I was so conservative when I was younger. But now that Martin has gone to glory, my dance card is full!"

"You just get on every horse that comes to the barn, Lucy. I have higher expectations." Susan pouted and added under her breath, "At the very least they need to have all their teeth and hair."

"Oh, you're too picky. Bald men save money on shampoo!"

I laughed for real at that. "I hope when I grow up I can be just like you," I said.

"Well, honey, all I have now is time on my hands. My husband died, I sold our big house, and I wanted to have fun again. I love to dance, and so I put myself out there. It wasn't hard to figure out."

"Are you really dating that many men?"

"You bet! I have a few who are foodies, a few that are dancers, I even have one who likes to bowl! I have a tennis partner and a golf partner. I have a partner for almost every activity now! It's wonderful. One day maybe I'll settle down again, but for now I just want to have fun, travel, and spend my retirement money," Lucy said.

"I have to show this to my gran. She needs some new company, I think."

"Who's your gran? Do y'all live around here?" Lucy asked.

"Rose Adams, and yes, ma'am. We live right here on the island."

"Rose Adams! Lord in heaven, I haven't seen her in ages! I went to high school with her at Bishop England! Oh my god, how is she?" Susan asked, brightening up. "I lost touch when I was living in Atlanta, then Dallas, San Francisco. Does she still tickle those tiles?"

"I'm sorry, what tiles?" I was confused.

"Mah-jongg tiles! She was our class champion all four years! God, she was something! Does she still play?"

"I'm not sure I even know what you just said. I'll have to ask her and google mah . . ."

"Mah-jongg, babe. It's all the rage now. But in our world, it always has been! We have a small club, if you ever want to come learn. Bring Rose! We'd love to see her." Lucy gave me her card and a couple of cards for an organization called Holy Mahj, and I promised to be in touch. Then I went to get my fingernails done, caught up with Eridani, and paid. Aly and I went across the street to the park to eat our sandwiches.

"Mah-jongg," I said. "Have you heard of it?"

"Oh yeah," she said through a mouthful of sandwich. "It's super popular right now. Your younger baby boomers are into it, but so is Gen Z. Maybe that would be a good crossover topic for my Insta?"

"Here, take one of these," I said, handing over one of those Holy Mahj cards Lucy had given me. Then I blurted out what I'd been holding in. "Chris is coming home. For good, I think."

"Wow. Okay, how do you feel about that?" she asked, and I felt a rush of gratitude. Why couldn't my sister be like this?

"Not ready. But kind of . . . excited?" As soon as I said it, my cheeks flushed hot.

"Oh, so you're still in love with him," she said, giggling at my obvious embarrassment.

"Whoa, Aly, I wouldn't say that!"

"You don't have to; your chest is getting blotchy! I mean, you said he's super handsome, right?"

"He's a tall drink of water."

"Oh, girl, you definitely still have a yen for him . . ."

"Maybe. I don't know. I might just be nervous. I'm not the same girl he left when he went to Japan," I said, feeling hot. "Or maybe I just don't want to be like Lucy and Susan, still fighting over the few decent male specimens five decades from now." When I saw Aly's face, I felt bad for saying anything. "I'm sorry, I mean it's great they're dating. And it's good your dad is dating, too."

"Or maybe it's horrendous?" Aly said, balling up her sandwich wrapper. "Sorry, I know I sound crazy."

"No, you don't." We sat there for a while, watching the fashion show of tourists pass by. I reached out and squeezed her hand. It wasn't until later—after we'd said goodbye and I was driving home—that I remembered she'd said she had something she wanted to run by me. At least, she'd texted something to that effect. I'd been so distracted by Chris, and then that handsome Brit, I hadn't remembered to ask. I hated making mistakes like that, being less than a perfect friend.

We'd have to get together soon, and next time I wouldn't forget.

CHAPTER FOUR

≈≈≈

Violet

Gravel crunched, and I walked up the pink-and-white azalea-lined driveway. *What was it Aly had wanted to talk about?* I wondered as I passed Gran's garden. A bright orange monarch butterfly landed on a flower. The southern sunshine illuminated his wings, making him look like a moving patch of light. I climbed the stairs, old wooden porch floor creaking underfoot, and pulled the door open to find Gran at the kitchen sink, washing dishes. Over the rush of water from the faucet, I heard her sigh.

"Hey, Gran," I said, loud, so as not to scare her. She turned, and for a moment I saw the fearful surprise in her eyes. Then she recognized me, and her shoulders went down from her ears. "I'll clean up; please don't do that."

"I'm not too old to clean up, Violet," Gran snapped back in a harsh whisper.

"Gran, I'm sorry . . ."

"No, I'm sorry, I shouldn't have . . ." She paused and gazed out the window. "I was just thinking about something."

"Gran, it's okay, but are *you* okay?"

"Yes, I . . ." She pursed her lips, then brightened up. "What's going on with you?"

"Oh, just trying to get myself beautified before Chris comes home. Comes *back*, I mean. To Charleston. Hey, do you know about the game mah-jongg? I met these funny ladies at the nail salon, and—"

"What?" Gran's eyes had grown large. "What were their names?"

"The one I mostly talked to was Lucy . . . She said y'all used to play this game together in high school."

"Play?" Gran gave a small chuckle. "Baby girl, we *slayed*."

I gave her a look. "Slayed? Gran, really?"

"I'm hip, too, you know, and back in the day I won the championship. I was a tile queen."

"I've never even heard of that game."

"Just goes to show you how cool I am, kid. I know things." Gran shook her head, a faraway smile playing on her lips. "Man, that Lucy was something else. How'd she look?"

"She looked good, Gran. She just moved back, she said."

Just then my phone buzzed; it was a text from Maggie.

Food emergency. Please bring me rosemary from Gran's garden. That's what I came over for this morning, and then you distracted me with your Chris news. My supplier didn't drop it off with today's order, and I can't exactly do my roasted chicken with rosemary fingerling potatoes without it, and I already posted about it on Instagram! Help!

I pursed my lips, put my phone away. I wasn't sure what Chris had to do with Maggie forgetting to grab rosemary, but I could help my sister out anyway. It was my restaurant too. But I couldn't help the swirl of memories it provoked in me. I had been there enough times since *it* happened—I should be fine to go there tonight, do my sister this favor.

"I need to swing by the restaurant," I told Gran. "Maggie asked me to snag some rosemary from your garden for roasted chicken with potatoes. Doesn't that sound perfect? Do you need anything while I'm out?"

"No, but if Maggie is serving that carrot ginger soup of hers, I wouldn't mind if it found its way to my dinner table. When you return . . . I think we should talk."

"Everything okay?"

"Yes. Just time for a chat."

I wondered if she was tired of having me around. Was it time for me to get my own place? I smiled brightly, not wanting her to see how unsettled I felt, and gave her cheek a kiss.

That's odd, I thought to myself as I made my way down the walk. It wasn't like her to schedule time to talk. Normally, she just said whatever was on her mind.

CHAPTER FIVE

~~~~

Violet

One Year Earlier

The air in the dining room was buzzing with voices of well-fed customers, thick with anticipation over the incoming storm. The prongs of forks and the blades of knives hit the plates, and glasses clinked as the diners discussed their storm prep and debated over whether they should have evacuated or not. The weatherman had called this a hurricane, but the restaurant was full. It made me question if everyone really believed there was a storm on its way. Heck, if it was as bad as the television was saying, it could knock the power out for a few days . . . or worse. However, this was South Carolina, a rebel state, and we islanders had never truly been afraid of a big ole act of nature.

"All right, folks, this just in. The storm has been upgraded to a cat two hurricane, with a possible drop at landfall to a cat one."

I put my hand on my lower back, adjusted the weight I was carrying, craned my neck to see the television, and raised my eyebrows at Frankie, manager and sometime bartender.

"Aww, Violet, we aren't afraid of a little rain, now, are we? A little wind?" Frankie shouted over at me.

"Well, you know what I always say: 'Cat two we see it through, cat three we flee,'" I said as I delivered a glass of Chardonnay to table six.

"That's right, Ms. Violet. The true islanders don't get our feathers ruffled over a rainstorm," Bubba, a regular, said to me.

"We haven't been really scared since Hugo! Remember that?" his dinner companion asked. "Blew my momma's roof clean off. Had frogs in the living room for days!"

"Well, y'all are welcome to ride out the storm here; we do love a good old-fashioned hurricane party. The wine is flowing, and the bathrooms are clean!" Frankie said.

Bubba gave my belly a significant look. "How much longer, *Miss Violet?*"

"I'm in the homestretch; last few weeks? I feel it in my back, that's for sure," I said, rubbing my giant tummy.

"Well, take care of yourself, sweetheart," he said.

"Don't you worry. I have the truck out back, and she's full of gas if we need to make a quick escape."

The customers were all in agreement that the weather station had become far too dramatic and apocalyptic these days.

I was working at our family's restaurant to help out while Maggie, my sister, got settled in as chef. I should have listened to everyone, including the island knowledge I grew up hearing, but I was too determined to be helpful. I was very pregnant and so tired, but also aggravated that my physical abilities were limited.

I had refused to sit this service out and rest at home like my sister wanted. Hurricanes were not good for the elderly or the pregnant. The drop in pressure caused early labor and heart attacks. I, however, put up quite the protest, and my sister, not wanting to fight, allowed me to work. I wasn't going to sit at home alone and stress myself out. Even though I was waddling all around the dining room, and my feet ached, I did what any good southern girl would do: I threw on my pearls, and a black wrap dress, and swiped on some lip gloss. I had it together, even if I looked like I had swallowed a watermelon.

Around six thirty, the wind started to pick up, and customers went from normal to concerned. Everyone's phone went off at the same time receiving a warning about the incoming storm. Frankie turned up the volume on the TV over the bar. The news anchor was talking about the radar, and it was not looking good. Some customers at the bar started grumbling about their cars and how downtown Charleston would be a mess. We were below sea level, so flooding was a normal event. I was glad I had taken my bright pink rain boots to work.

There were a few cheers from some older guys at table eight as their beers disappeared and the wind began to pick up to a howl. I bet if the rain really started to go nuts, they would declare it a hurricane party for sure and stay put till the storm blew over. I cherished the memories of past hurricane parties, where we locked up the restaurant and kept the bar open throughout the storm, collecting everyone's keys for safety. I recalled my younger years in low-rise jeans and tube tops, throwing back beers and yelling at the weather station, egging on the storm as it raged.

Somewhere between college and Chris, my recent ex–almost fiancé, I ditched my glitter belts and jean miniskirts for monograms and pearls. I wanted a husband, and my mother made sure I knew that the kind of man who would give me the life I wanted wasn't found at a sports bar or a keg stand. Momma always said, "You can marry more money in five minutes than you can make in a lifetime." Back then I was an aspiring wedding photographer, and while I waited for business to pick up, I waited tables, but I wasn't getting anywhere near to what I wanted with that. It seemed that I was never going to get the life I had put on my inner Pinterest board.

We had friends from college who now owned million-dollar homes. They had all married doctors or lawyers or were from wealthy families. I think the pressure of achieving got to Chris. He came from a nice family, but not from one with a gated community, Herend dinnerware, and a country-club lifestyle. I grew up on Sullivan's Island before it turned into the Beverly Hills of the South. Sure, we could probably sell our family home for a ton, but it wasn't mortgaged, and it was our identity. We were a beach family . . . even if we drove a beat-up truck and not a Land Rover. Things mattered to Chris and me, too. We wanted a beautiful life. So we had to work, and that meant taking opportunities wherever they came up, even in Japan.

But after Chris took the job in Japan and hadn't coughed up a diamond despite our growing life inside of me, I cut him loose. I had decided to do this on my own. I was terrified, but with the support of my family, I could make do, and maybe if Chris decided to come home, we could figure it out . . .

Outside, it was getting darker by the second. I always got a little excited by storms, all that electricity in the air. I was helping a four-top to their table when I felt a stabbing cramp come out of nowhere in my lower abdomen. I knew it was exactly what I had been dreading. But I remembered that it could also be a Braxton-Hicks contraction. Could be nothing. I winced a little and closed my eyes.

"Violet!" Maggie called across the dining room. When she caught my eye, she gave me a thumbs-up in question. I rolled my eyes at her and returned the gesture. Probably just back pain, and besides, even if it was labor, most babies didn't just shoot out in five minutes! I decided to pop my head outside and take a look at the weather. Nothing beat a hurricane sky right before it went crazy. I found my grandmother outside, locking up the shutters over the big window.

"Wind is getting pretty crazy out here," Gran said.

"Maybe we should ask some of the kitchen crew to help you?" I suggested.

"I'm not too old to do this yet!" Gran said.

"I know, I know," I said, smiling.

The wind blew a giant gust and shook the palm tree in the front yard of the restaurant so hard it almost bent over.

"Yeah, maybe go ask the boys to get the windows in the back," she said, and finished up locking down the shutter. "God's gonna show his strength tonight."

By seven fifteen, the dining room had thinned out to about half capacity. The rain started all at once, dumping gallons, then stopping completely before starting up again. The rain got heavier, and the wind got stronger; the weatherman on the TV went from television nervous to real-life nervous. The station changed to live coverage by the College of Charleston downtown, where the water was up to the anchor's knees. He was blown around a bit, and I saw a few people at the bar looking nervous. *Must be out-of-towners*, I thought. This could be over in ten minutes. I'd seen rainstorms look this bad and then roll right out to sea. I grabbed Frankie's elbow to get her attention.

"Hey, what about making a batch of dark and stormies for the bar? It might change the vibe a bit, get the mood up," I said.

"Better idea, why don't I do what you said and then post on Instagram that we're selling pitchers of them? Like, we could invite people to wait out the storm with us?"

"Actually, that's not a bad idea, but just post that we don't want anyone driving here . . ." I had to think about liability. No one else in my family did.

"Got it!"

I took a look outside again, and truth be told the wind was way worse than the rain. It would just be a big rainstorm. I turned up the music in the dining room. It was time for a little Fleetwood Mac. The evening settled into a good pace, the Instagram post actually pulled in some people for the pitchers, and as the rain fell and the wind howled, we had a full-blown hurricane party on our hands. I thought it was a good appeal to the true island people, too. Our bar was full, and there was a level of electricity in the room.

I made my way back to the kitchen and bumped into Maggie.

"Maggie, can we turn up the air-conditioning? It's so humid in here, I'm sweating like a pig!"

"Violet, you're *sweating*. Are you okay?"

"Yeah, but my back hurts," I said, deciding to say something just in case.

"Please take a break. That's all we need, right? Labor during a hurricane!"

The kitchen was busy, keeping everyone at the bar happy with appetizers. It was really nice to see the crew enjoying what they did, too. Even though we were working hard, there were finally smiles on faces and jokes being made.

Maggie had turned our restaurant around, making it a new hot spot on the island. She never doubted for a moment that people would embrace the original Magic Lantern's menu, even though it had a few new twists. She had added our grandmother's and our great-grandmother's recipes and kept the hush puppies on the menu as well. We didn't have to have a gimmick to make money and keep our lights on; we just needed to consistently present good food.

I realized then, standing in the middle of the kitchen, that she had reached her goal. I was proud of my sister then; she had done what she had always wanted to do. She was feeding people food with a story. Every item that came through our kitchen was linked to history in one way or another. A good restaurant was a melting pot of skill and ingredients. She had brought the Lantern back to its former glory. I looked over at Maggie; she was beaming. She must have felt what I was feeling, too.

Just as I was thinking everything was looking up, there was a huge clap of lightning. The restaurant shook. The lights flickered, and I said a silent prayer. The lights buzzed back on, and there was a cheer from the dining room. The tin roof of the restaurant hummed with the pounding of raindrops. The hurricane had arrived.

My cellphone buzzed, and I saw a text from my mom.

Hey, just checking in. How's the restaurant? I'm watching the storm on the television at home.

Yeah, we're open. All good over here.
Old islanders holding down the fort at the bar.
I think we may wait it out.

And how's my Violet?

My back hurts. But I'm okay.

Sore back? Keep a good watch on that. My labor always started in my back.

Great. Didn't know that. Something else to worry about. Time to alert Gran. If something was going to happen, she needed to know. I went into the office, thinking she might be there. Suddenly there was another flash of lightning, and as if in sync with the storm a huge wave of pain shot around my middle. I bent over and put my hands on the desk, swaying my hips back and forth, thinking I could move the pain.

"Uh, Vi?" Maggie had followed me into the office. "Violet, let's go to the hospital. We need to get there before they close the bridge and we get stuck," she pleaded.

"This is probably nothing, Maggie. It's early yet, and first babies usually come late."

"Are you having contractions?" she asked.

"Yeah, I've been having them for a few days," I admitted.

"What? What do you mean *days*?" She was almost shouting.

"Maggie! They are called Braxton-Hicks, and it isn't really labor," I said.

"Violet, I am sure you are very in tune with your body, but do you want to deliver on the floor of this restaurant? For the love of god, let's get you to a hospital so a medical professional can rule it out. For me?"

"Maggie, stop being so dramatic," I snapped as I held down a little contraction. "I'm going to get a Coke."

We went back into the dining room. I looked up at the television and heard what I had been dreading.

"The Ben Sawyer Bridge is now closed, as the wind strength is too dangerous. This is going to be a whopper, folks. Stay inside and be safe."

I caught Maggie's eye.

"Y'all need to just simmer down. I can't take all these looks. I am just fine, okay?" I stood and winced, and then my water broke all over my legs, the floor, and my beloved Tory Burch flats. "Oh god," I said, and doubled over.

The hours that followed were not filled with happiness, joy, and the overwhelming love that I had expected to feel.

Instead, I held my stillborn baby.

CHAPTER SIX

~~~~~

Violet

It was a perfect sunny day in May. I went out to Gran's garden, looking for the rosemary Maggie needed for that chicken dish. The garden took over our entire front yard, which was no easy feat, since we were blocks from the beach and the soil was fussy. But Gran could make anything grow. Neatly raised beds lined our yard, all full of plump tomatoes, shiny eggplants, beautiful bright flowers, and wild quantities of herbs. Martha Stewart would've seethed with envy.

The herbs we had planted when we were little girls, and the giant rosemary bush was now almost as tall as I was. I took the gardening shears and clipped a big bouquet. There was plenty left—I could trim that thing like a poodle and it would grow back overnight. I loved the smell and rubbed it in my palms. They say planting rosemary is lucky. I wrapped it in a damp paper towel, threw it into my large brown leather bag, and hopped on my bike.

The Magic Lantern sat on the corner of Main Street and Ben Sawyer Boulevard, next to the gas station. Its giant brass lantern was turned on, signaling that the restaurant was open. So much chicer than a neon sign. I walked up the front porch stairs and pushed open the giant heavy door.

It was late afternoon, but the bar was already packed. This was typical; it was a local hangout for the old salts of the island, who usually cleared out around dinnertime to make room for the new, hip crowd. For the bar, Maggie had a small menu available, mostly items that were staples on any southern table. Hush puppies, fried green tomatoes, boiled peanuts, and pimento cheese—unfussy plates for customers to snack on. The dining room menu was more elevated. She'd still have the fried green tomatoes, but they would be served with a local farmer's goat cheese, and the tomatoes were heirloom from Johns Island. It was a delicate balance of clientele: the old salts of the island liked the way things were, and usually kept to the bar area, but the new city folks came for my sister's genius. She did a great job of keeping everyone happy.

"Hey, girl! Good to see you!" Frankie greeted me.

"Hey, Frankie! What's new?" I said, returning her bright smile.

"Oh, you know, same old stuff. Your sister is bringing her A-game tonight, let me tell you what. She's doing this fancy French rat-a-tat thing. Delicious!"

"Frankie, do you mean ratatouille? You better pronounce that right; otherwise Maggie will fire you!"

"Oh god, I know. I'm calling it the Pixar special. She didn't like that."

"Jesus. Well, I'm here to drop off some rosemary for her chicken dish—she in the back?"

"Yep." Frankie waved and went back to helping the bartender handle the regulars.

I walked through the dining room and pushed the doors of the kitchen open, only to be immediately hit with the dense, heady aroma of lemon and thyme and garlic.

Man, it was heaven back here.

"Hey, girl, you got my goods?" Maggie called over the banging of pots, slicing of knives, and whirling of people. Everyone was busy but focused and moving. It was a hidden world back there.

"Yeah, I clipped a ton." I handed over the towel-wrapped bouquet.

She grabbed it and inhaled. "Gran's herbs are the best. They are probably better than my supplier's. Thanks, Vi. Are you staying to eat?"

"I wasn't going to, but of course now that I'm smelling this kitchen I'm starving."

"Then I still got it." She shot me a wink.

"Never lost it." I stayed a few extra minutes saying hello to some of the cooks, blew my sister a kiss, and went back into the dining room. It had already moved into full dinner mode—the bar was emptier, and the tables were filling up. Fleetwood Mac played over the speaker system. It felt good in there.

I found a stool at the bar and hung my bag on the hook underneath. I looked over at the chalkboard and spied a flounder special with that lemon thyme garlic sauce. Yep, that was what I would be having. Frankie brought me a glass of white wine, and for a little while I just relaxed and soaked up the atmosphere.

I was waiting on my fish when a tall man sat down next to me. Older, salt-and-pepper hair, and a leather jacket. Smelled like cinnamon. I gave him the kind of smile that conveyed you were enjoying your solitude.

Frankie appeared again with my fish dish. I felt my stomach do a happy dance.

"Here you go, Violet," she said, setting a beautiful plate in front of me.

"Good lord, it smells divine!" A deep-yellow sauce dotted with green encircled a plump piece of white fish; gently seared golden skin nestled in a smaller circle of plump cherry tomatoes. There was a small handful of lemon-pepper-drizzled arugula salad with shaved slices of Parmesan cheese. I slid my fork into the side of the fish, popped the opaque flesh into my mouth, and tasted thyme, the ocean, and actual sunshine. I didn't know how she did it. My sister was cut from a different cloth. Sure, I had my photography, but she was heaven-sent.

"Goodness, I guess that tastes as good as it looks," said the older man.

"It really does. My sister is the chef here, and she's very talented."

"I can see that, and I know. I had her Barolo braised short ribs the other night. How does she get her grits so creamy? They could have been polenta!"

"Salt, heavy cream, butter, butter, and more butter," I said.

"Oh no!" He put his hands over his chest, a mock heart attack.

"I know, I know. Turns out all the good stuff is bad for you," I said.

"Not everything. Some wholesome things are good for you, too."

The man had a nice way about him, and I found what he had just said oddly reassuring. I took a sip of wine, trying to think how I should reply. But then my phone buzzed against the bar, and I saw that it was Chris texting. It was early morning in Japan, so I picked it up immediately, not even bothering to make an excuse to the bar customer.

Hey, we need to talk.

Chris, no good conversation ever began with "We need to talk." What's up?

My whole body had tensed up. I glanced toward the older man to apologize, but he must've already been on his way out, because he was gone.

Meanwhile, another text had come in from Chris.

I just got a receipt emailed for the installation of a security camera.

I thought we should have one. Just in case.

In case of what?

I don't know, in case someone steals my Amazon deliveries?

Well, it's my house. I think those things look tacky.

Yes, I'm sorry, you're right. But I'm there by myself,
you know. Sometimes it's scary at night . . .

You're right. I'm sorry.

It's okay.

I'm coming home, Vi. You shouldn't be alone.

I stared at the last message, wondering how my little lie had spi-raled and resulted in Chris becoming suddenly protective of me and the home we'd shared.

"Hey, girl! How's the fish?"

Maggie had appeared out of nowhere.

I almost jumped, I was so surprised to be brought back into the real world. I turned my phone over in a hurry. "Gold Dust Woman" was play-ing. The man who'd been sitting next to me had left a big tip on the bar.

"Hi! Fantastic, Maggie, really, it's so good."

"Good. Well, here," she said, putting a bread basket in front of me. "I just pulled some fresh sourdough out of the oven. Wouldn't want you to waste that sauce."

I flipped back the napkin, tore into the warm crusty loaf, and almost started to drool as I saw a tiny little pot of yellow butter sprin-kled with coarse sea salt. "Let me at this!"

"Nothing like warm bread," she said.

"Truth. Hey, do you have any of your carrot ginger soup?"

"Gran?"

"Yes. She asked me to get some if you did."

"We might. I'll go look."

"Does she seem off to you, by the way?"

"Huh. Not that I've noticed." Maggie shrugged, and then she left me to go back into the kitchen. I finished my delicious fish. Feeling fortified, I texted Chris.

Sorry about the camera, Chris. I should've
asked you about that.

No, don't worry. I'm sorry. I am for sure
moving back.

Okay.

For real this time, Vi.

The bread felt stuck in my throat, a big sourdough lump. I didn't
know what to say . . .

We need to see each other face-to-face.
We've lost a lot, but I haven't been there for you . . .
I'll see how soon I can get back. Most of my cases have
wrapped.

Okay. Send me your flight information.

I glanced up at the bar. I felt like my phone had sucked me into
some other world. All around me people were drinking happily,
carrying on loud conversations, and I was half in this conversation with Chris. He was financially holding half of my house—our
house—and here I was making money off his half, not telling him
about it.

Why couldn't I just tell him why I wanted a security camera,
what I'd been doing on Airbnb? For some reason being honest
about it felt hard. For some reason I didn't want to give him the
money.

We could always just sell the place. Charleston's real estate market
was hot.

I felt the prick of tears in my eyes. A wave of self-pity over my
situation was looming, and I hated feeling sorry for myself. Then I
remembered that Maggie would be back any minute with the soup,
and I didn't think I could face her—I wouldn't be able to hold any

of this in if she came back. I waved Frankie over and quibbled with her about settling the bill, but as usual she won and wouldn't take my money.

So I left her a big tip and made my way home to Gran's empty-handed.

CHAPTER SEVEN

~~~~

Aly

I had spent much of the day trying to brainstorm a reason that Crate and Barn should keep up the relationship with Callie Knox now that I was the face of the brand, and I'd been coming up blank. Crate and Barn had recently done several successful lines with influencers, and my mother had secured a lucrative partnership a few years back. It represented a substantial portion of her company's budget. We were against the clock now, because my mother had just begun planning a holiday collection with their team when she got her diagnosis. It was to be the biggest collaboration yet, but she hadn't been able to see it through.

In desperation, I turned to my old journals, pages from when I was just starting my blog.

Charleston is a love song. A great melody that instantly becomes your favorite the first time you hear it. That tune you wind up humming while washing your dishes, or lather, rinse, repeating in the shower. Charleston is the timeless beauty from high school, too cool from a distance, but once you get to know her, she makes you feel like you've known her forever. It is soaked in history and decorated with culture. It smells good. Walking down the streets of downtown, it isn't uncommon to hear horses trot along cobblestone streets, pulling carriages behind them. The past is present here. I wasn't born here, but my soul must've been. Charleston is my muse. There is something about the palm-lined streets, brightly colored buildings, and wrought-iron gates leading into secret gardens that made me want to reshape myself in its image. It wasn't just the buildings, or the beaches, or the sprawling homes that made me fall in love with the place. Or even the history. It was the people, the fashion and style, how they conducted their day-to-day lives. All that made me feel called to share their way. I was charmed by the sweet tea in cut-crystal glasses paired with linen napkins on polished silver trays. Where I grew up, I never used a fabric napkin in my life! I loved that those silver trays were monogrammed, but the monograms were their great-grandmothers'. Charlestonians are proud of legacy and traditions, and they (we!) are not afraid to be fancy.

Was that it? Was that my brand? Or had I just written what any Midwest girl visiting Charleston on a bachelorette party might?

I decided I had been working on the problem too hard and set my journal aside.

I thought about what my dad had said—that he was dating, and maybe I should, too—and glanced over the apps I kept on my phone but mostly neglected. All the single, straight males aged twenty-eight to forty-two who lived within a thirty-mile radius and maintained a dating profile seemed unlikely to be actually single, unsafe to be alone with, or just straight-up unreal. So I sat down on my bed and pulled out my phone to check the recent engagement on a post I'd shared earlier that day. It was a picture of my bike up against a beach marker. Station 25. My audience loved to see me on the beach. It had garnered above-average likes and a lot of sweet comments, but I didn't find that as satisfying as I usually would. How was I going to transition to my mom's account? She was able to bring in women of all ages, not just Gen Z. She made things beautiful, but it was through a heart connection with her followers, not just glossy images.

I tapped my screen, pressed my lips together, puffed up my cheeks, and blew out my frustration.

I needed to just talk to Rosemary, like my dad had suggested.

Was it too late to send an email? I didn't really know. I'd never had a real-deal office job. I'd been a waitress, a bartender, an influencer, but I didn't know how the people with MBAs and kitten heels did it. And if being my mother's daughter was the reason I'd gotten the opportunity, well, it was also the reason I was going to be scrutinized ten times as hard.

Oof. I needed to stop second-guessing myself. CEOs didn't second-guess themselves. Did they? Whatever. I began to type:

> To: RosemaryHarper@callieknox.com
> Hey, Rosie!
> I know it's been a minute since we last spoke, but my father shared with me that there has been a discussion about me potentially stepping into my mother's shoes. I think this could be wonderful, and I'd obviously love to talk it through with you. Can we get together for coffee this week? I can make myself available almost any time.
> Looking forward to speaking with you!
> Hope you are well!
> Aly

I read the message over, pursing my lips. Did I sound too eager? Not eager enough? Too young? Or was I supposed to sound young? Ugh, what a punishment, experiencing this world through the cruel prism of a human brain.

My dad knew Rosemary. This had all been his idea! Hadn't it? Maybe he could reassure me that I was overthinking this, that I could be informal, that I could be myself and no one expected me to walk in tomorrow with fully developed girlboss swagger. But when I went to my window to see if he was still awake, I was a little surprised to see that not even one light was on in his house.

So. He was still on that date.

The light from the full moon spilled through the palmetto fronds and splashed on my hardwood floor. I went around turning all my lights off. When he got home, I didn't want him to know I was awake, peering through the blinds, wondering where he'd been. I suddenly felt like a mother waiting for her teenager to come home after curfew. This was late for Dad. His date must be going well, I thought, otherwise he'd be home with a glass of wine in front of the tube, watching a movie with his feet up. He was usually asleep by ten. It was almost midnight.

"Where are you?" I said out loud to my empty apartment.

I held off on texting him, because I always worried he'd try to text me back while he was on the road. He was getting older and didn't have the greatest set of eyes. Night driving had always made him jittery.

The sane part of me picked up my phone and reread my email to Rosemary. I tapped my fresh French manicure on the screen, wondering if I should brainstorm more before I reached out. What if she responded right away, asking for ten new ideas, and I had none?

I refreshed my email and saw that I had a new message from Rosemary.

Had I accidentally sent my probably totally inadequate checkin? Panic zipped up and down my spine. But then I realized I hadn't emailed her—this wasn't a response to my timid little outreach. Instead, she had forwarded a message from Crate and Barn about the holiday line, laying out their concerns about moving forward without a Callie Knox to move the product. The PB rep said she knew that I had taken over Callie's feed but expressed that my reach was too narrow and too niche and "not sophisticated enough." My heart sank at that.

Rosemary had forwarded the email with a one-line comment to me:

Think you can get to 100k sophisticated followers by August? xo RH

What was wrong with me? Why had I thought I could do this? I wanted to cry, and to yell at my dad for making me dream of something I couldn't possibly succeed at.

Then I heard the wheels of Dad's car crunch the gravel in the driveway and my mind buzzed that away. It was really late—what had he been doing?

I went to the window and peered through the blinds. Just to make sure Dad was in one piece, of course. I couldn't see him, though. What I heard made my stomach turn. Giggles.

Wait, what?

Dad got out of his car and strode around to open the passenger-side door. This tall woman with long legs and a short skirt poured out onto the drive, *giggling*. She allowed him to take her hand and pull her along like some kind of Hollywood vixen.

"What's one little ole nightcap?" Dad asked, sounding very debonair.

"Aren't you too old for this?" I laughed to myself. At least he was having fun.

"Oh, it's a little late, isn't it?" the woman said, not protesting nearly enough, IMHO.

Which was when my dad began singing, "But, baby, it's cold outside . . ." even though it was currently the opposite of cold. Shortly thereafter, they disappeared into the big house.

"Oh, gross," I said into my partial reflection in the window glass, but then I erupted in my own fit of giggles. I guessed it didn't matter how old you were, you could still misbehave . . . or engage in a little late-night action.

Good for him.

I looked over at my laptop and remembered the email from Rosemary. I couldn't believe that I'd dared to dream. Who did I think I was, trying to fill my mother's shoes? I was giving myself impostor syndrome, and the best thing I could think to do was go to sleep. I found my headphones, opened up my white noise app, and took a melatonin gummy.

Until I was college age, my family lived in Michigan, where we only had lakes, not salt water, so to wake up to the sound of ocean waves changed everything for me. I had only ever seen my parents work like crazy, always stressed, always rushing around to get to their next work-related event. But soon after moving into the Sullivan's house, we all realized our pace of life was changing. Mom would say that the house taught her to "stop and smell the camellias." We started entertaining at home, she joined a book club, and my dad got into golf. Our quality of life improved so much that we never went back to Michigan, except once in a while to visit my brother, Mike, and his family.

And as a bonus, that quality of life became a beautiful and celebrated brand.

Our house was located on the water facing the harbor. My mother planted rosemary and bright pink camellias in the front yard, and two enormous Blanchard magnolia trees curtained the home. We had a wraparound porch sprinkled with rocking chairs and a porch swing. Through the years, that porch hosted countless parties (including my brother's wedding), nursed many heartbreaks, and was the place my mom and I would spill secrets.

But that wasn't the vibe the next morning.

I woke up hungry and agitated. All the real food was in the big house, where I made most of our meals. Just in case Dad's little rendezvous had gone into the morning, I lay in my bed for thirty minutes, waiting. I wanted his date to have some time to slither out the door. When I heard the front door close, I just about broke my neck rushing to the window to watch this slender redhead walk out, wearing *no pants* and one of Dad's button-downs! She cast a sultry look back at my father and blew him a kiss as she climbed into the waiting Uber. The expression on Dad's face was really something. He looked like a kid on Christmas morning.

In consideration of his feelings, I gave him ten minutes before throwing on my robe and venturing into the house for some coffee and breakfast. The whole situation felt weird to me, but also kind of funny. They must both have lived several lives already, and here they were, acting like teenagers. Everyone deserved a little thrill now and then, I guessed.

"Morning, Minnow!" Dad called as I entered the kitchen. "Can I make you a coffee?"

"Sure, Dad." Then I joked, "Should I light you a cigarette?"

He blushed but took it in stride. "I know, your old man is wild!" He chuckled to himself. "Some things stay the same, though. Cradle to the grave, women are crazy. All of you want to get married!"

"In your seventies?" I tried not to look horrified by the idea of my dad getting married again. Also, I wasn't sure if he was right about that, but it wasn't what was foremost in my mind. "What's the point?"

"Exactly! I've had my children. I have my house. You know? I don't want to change anything. I just want company. Someone to catch a movie with, or a flight."

"But not feelings?" I said tentatively.

"What?"

"Catch feelings, Dad. It means—"

"Oh! Got it. Yeah, no feelings. I mean I would *like* to feel *some-*

thing . . . but I'm not looking for a soul mate." He poured us two coffees from the pot. "I have one of those already, and she's saving a seat for me in heaven."

"Kind of a strange sentiment when I just saw a woman exit in your Brooks Brothers oxford."

"You're seeing things, Aly. That was Gap."

"Right."

"Aly, I'm just having fun. Nothing to stress about." He patted my hand and turned away to the buzz of his phone.

"Who's calling you this early?" It wasn't even eight.

"Sharon."

"Who's Sharon?"

Dad just couldn't help grinning a little when he said, "A friend."

"A friend?"

He pumped his eyebrows. "A *blond* friend."

"Okay, I'm gonna go fill my pockets with stones and walk into the sea."

"Ha ha."

"Well, be safe, Dad," I joked. "Make good choices." But as I made my way to the door, I wasn't feeling so easy breezy as I had tried to sound just then. "Wait, was Sharon from this morning?"

"No. That was another friend."

"Popular guy."

"These women have great taste."

"Gross." I rolled my eyes at him and headed back to the apartment, not even realizing until I got upstairs that I hadn't asked him anything about Rosemary or how I should proceed. I picked up my phone and tapped out a quick reply:

100k by August? No problem. xx!

CHAPTER EIGHT

~~~~~

Violet

"What happened to you last night?" Maggie asked when I finally answered one of her many calls.

I was driving out to Mount Pleasant and glad to have the distraction of a big job ahead of me, what with questions of Chris bubbling in my head and Gran acting so off.

"Had to get my beauty rest for the big wedding!" I replied, trying to sound careless and sassy, but not totally succeeding. I knew that if I told Maggie the truth—that the text from Chris and the memories of losing the baby on the floor of the Lantern had gotten the better of me—I'd be in for a lot of sisterly concern and judgment I wasn't really in the market for right now.

"Smart," my sister said. "Well, see you there, then!"

"Oh—at the Martin-Hayworth wedding?"

"Yeah, girl!"

Of course Maggie was going to be there, too. She was a hot chef in town; she was invited to everything. After we hung up, I drove in silence, popping my gum to distract me from picking at my fingers. I was really trying to curb that habit.

I tried focusing on the landscape I was driving through, a glimpse of the Cooper River in the distance, a splash of hot pink azaleas up ahead on the side of the road. The way the southern landscape was splashed with wild, unexpected colors always seduced me and imprinted on my soul like a footprint in the snow. Condé Nast had named Charleston the best city in the world to visit, and that had opened the floodgates for thousands of tourists.

I turned left at the brick columns; the two large black iron gates were open. Gran's old truck rolled down the gravel road, which was covered with a canopy of old live oak trees dripping with Spanish moss. Morning sunlight sparkled through the treetops. The entrance to Boone Hall Plantation was stunning and right out of a romance novel, and yet the history was complicated. Many people felt that couples shouldn't get married at former plantations. At the moment this was just my job.

After I parked, I spotted Malory's car and walked over to where she was unloading her equipment. She had braided some very glamorous long extensions into her hair and had them woven and twisted on top of her head, giving the look of a turban. She waved me over to her, gave me a hug, and passed me a tiny ice-cold bottle of Coca-Cola. She knew I loved them, and the small hit of sugar gave us the oomph we needed to get through the morning. There was just something about those tiny bottles that made the Coke taste better.

"The dream team is back at it again!" Mal gave me a squeeze. This was our fifth wedding together this year.

"Your hair looks so great!" I said.

"Oh, thank you! It took forever to do, but it's getting hot, and I needed my braids off my damn neck!" She smiled.

"Well, my hair could never," I said.

I looked up from the printed layout of the Cotton Dock. "I have to shoot the bride and bridesmaids as they get ready, so I'll head to the Camellia Room. Could you help me with my tripod, umbrellas, and hard cases over to the covered deck where the ceremony will take place?" I asked Mal. "I can help you carry all those cases. While you set up, I can snag some exterior and scenery shots," I said.

"Yeah, I got you!" Malory said, slinging a tote over her arm.

The Cotton Dock was rustic on the outside, but pure elegance inside. The bride and her four bridesmaids were wearing robes, ready to have their hair and makeup done. The bride was your classic Charleston girl, with all three *t*'s—tall, tiny, and tan. It looked as if she hadn't consumed a carbohydrate in a year. As much as that might seem crazy to notice, all southern women knew that brides took their appearance very seriously. The year leading up to a girl's wedding was intense. It was drilled into you that you were your most beautiful on your wedding day, and therefore you had to be perfect. For a moment, I was thankful for having dodged that stress. The old me would've gone nuts. I wondered if I'd ever have my own big day. The thought no longer terrified me.

The bride's nails were polished in that popular shade of milky pink. It showed off her enormous halo cushion-cut diamond. Her hair, displaying a rainbow of blond from hay to platinum, was swept up in a clean French twist. She was gorgeous. The kind of girl you didn't have to ask if she'd been a debutante or a sorority sister. You knew she'd been a cheerleader and prom queen, and she confirmed it when she looked at you with all the sunshine of a southern sky in her Carolina blue eyes. I wanted to hate her, but when she saw Malory, she squealed and gave her a big hug, then introduced her to everyone, and I was charmed by the bride's genuinely friendly disposition.

"Violet, I'm Anna Grace. My mother is *obsessed* with you, and I've heard all about you through Maggie, of course," the bride said. "Please make me look beautiful!"

"Wow, thank you! I won't need to work hard, Anna Grace; you already are beautiful." I smiled at her as she blushed. She couldn't possibly think she was anything less than perfect, right? This was just modesty.

"Oh, girl! Please call me AG. Everyone else does!" She gave me a hug. I let out a little laugh. "I've heard so much about you from your amazing sister! I'm so glad she's home now. The moment Grant and I get back from our honeymoon, I am coming directly to the Magic Lantern. I love sitting at the bar there; honestly, I was so flattered when she accepted our invite. She's so fun, I want her to be my best friend!"

"I'm honored to help out on your special day," I said.

"I'm so lucky to have you and Malory Starr. Can you *believe* Momma snagged her?" AG went on good-naturedly, "Malory, you've been booked for, what, a year out?"

"I'm popular because I love what I do, just like Violet here, and you are lucky enough to get her because Maggie is your friend. Today will be perfect, I just know it . . . and if it isn't, we'll make it *look* perfect!" Mal smiled a megawatt smile, her brown eyes sparkling underneath gold eye shadow. She could pull anything off.

"AG, it's your day. Now, tell me, where do you want me to start?" I asked. "Should I start taking pictures of the details?"

"The details?"

"Yes. Like y'all's wedding invitations, the rings, the flowers, the cake, and even your dress—the little buttons, lace close-ups, you know." All the things I still fantasy-planned for my own big day in my idle moments. With my most professional, caretaking smile, I explained, "It's nice to get that stuff out of the way before the actual wedding."

"You're so smart! Yes! Everything is set up already: we only have a few hours before go-time. Do you think you could do my pictures and the bridesmaids' before anyone gets drunk? My maid of honor, Mary Katherine, is already half in the bag, God help me."

I looked over at the bridesmaids, smiling. I saw some things on these shoots. One of the bridesmaids was refilling everyone's glasses and swaying a little. That had to be Mary Katherine. Malory glanced at her, too, then raised her eyebrows at me and lowered her chin. I knew what that meant. Okay, I'd keep an eye on the maid of honor so she didn't ruin my group shots.

We moved over that way.

Mary Katherine was fanning herself theatrically and saying, "All right, ladies, drink up! Gosh, I am so nervous about my speech. I'm sweating like a hog over here!"

"Oh, honey, it'll be fine! You've done pageants before; this isn't any harder! I love you no matter what you say over a microphone in front of everyone I know." AG had on a forceful megawatt smile. "Kidding, no pressure!"

Just then the mother of the bride came in.

"Anna Grace Sophia soon-to-be-Hayworth, you need to get into your dress before Daddy comes in!"

"Oh gosh, you're right, Momma!" AG said, and all the girls squealed.

"Big day, big day!" said her mother as she took the wedding gown off the rack and held it out to her daughter. I realized that for her this was a special, unplanned moment and quickly started to snap a few shots. Like that, my impulse to feel jaded about drunken bridesmaids drained away, and I refocused on the task at hand. I had my camera around my neck, ready for the sweetest moments, the moments that were thought to be unnoticed.

Malory's two assistants showed up and started on the bridesmaids, and I followed at an unobtrusive distance, capturing the happy little tears sparkling at the corners of AG's eyes as her mother helped her into a tiered lace confection.

I took out my checklists of which pictures had to be taken and when. "Okay, y'all, here's the plan." I read the schedule to the women, who clapped their hands and whooped in excitement. I carefully adjusted the lighting and the positions of the bridesmaids to make all of them look beautiful, complimenting them and making easy chatter to put them at ease. Malory had AG done in record time—though to be fair she was working with an easy client. All that girl needed was ChapStick and she would be angelic. Somehow Malory had made her look even more beautiful.

"Hey, AG, come over here a moment, and you, too, Mrs. Martin." I directed them to stand in front of the window. Just then the florist showed up, and everyone got their bouquets. AG's mom pinned her daughter's veil in her hair, beaming and tearing up at the same time. My camera caught every poignant moment. The sunlight shone through AG's veil as her momma fanned it out. I let out a deep sigh; it was a gorgeous shot, and I loved that I'd gotten it—I felt myself setting into the rhythm of my work, calmed by doing these tasks well.

I didn't usually cry or get emotional at weddings, but when her daddy came in and saw his daughter in her wedding gown, I felt it. I caught the moment when he took from his breast pocket a patch with AG's new monogram on it. He pinned it to her bouquet and kissed her forehead. Just like that, my chest was tight again over everything I might not have for myself—the white dress, the handsome groom, and, either way, there wouldn't be a daddy to walk me down the aisle. Weddings could dig up deep and ugly feelings from the back chambers of your heart.

A half hour later, after we had moved out to the lawn, where I took shots of the bridesmaids and the groomsmen, everyone assembled on the Cotton Dock's covered deck, which overlooked the tidal marshes. Guests sat in the ten rows of chairs that had been arranged on each side of the aisle, with more guests standing in back.

The ceremony was beautiful. I watched from the back as AG and Grant pledged themselves to each other. It was so hopeful and pure. Every time I watched vows, I hoped it was forever.

Sam and Maggie came up to say hello.

"They look so happy," Maggie said. She was in a slinky gold dress and looked stunning.

"They sure do," Sam said, looking right at Maggie. She giggled, and he kissed her cheek.

"Sam!" Maggie playfully shrugged him off.

"Couldn't help it," he said.

They were so enamored of each other, they didn't even notice me slipping away to take candid shots of the party. I spent the rest of the cocktail hour feeling awkward and embarrassed, but I did find some solace focusing on the happy couple, capturing shot after shot of AG and her groom.

When the bride and groom led the guests into the elegant dining room, where a band was playing, I made my way through the crowd. By the time I saw Maggie and Sam again, I was back to feeling like myself, busy and useful. "Okay, y'all, help me round up the wedding party for some more photos before the serious partying gets underway. In the meantime, I'll start shooting the guests."

I was surprised to see that Sam had followed me. "Hey," he said, "can I talk to you?"

Why did everyone have some secret agenda they needed to discuss with me lately? "Sure, but I am working here; just help me out for a moment . . ."

As we started the roundup, I spotted Mary Katherine taking shots with the bartender. She was knocking them back like a sorority girl on a game night mission. I elbowed Sam in the ribs and jerked my head in her direction. "I think we may have a little problem over there, Sam."

"She wouldn't be the first bridesmaid to overindulge at a wedding."

"I know, but—"

"No, I see what you mean. I'm on it." He made his way in that direction.

I watched Sam charm a drink out of her hand and heard her ask him if she could practice her speech on him. I almost felt sorry for her. Poor thing, she *was* nervous. But I didn't want her ruining my client's day, or my shots.

"You know, Vi," Maggie said, coming up beside me, "I feel kind of awkward because I had a weird interaction with Sam's momma."

"Oh, Maggie, I wouldn't worry about it. I don't know why you have an edge about Bunny; she's *so* sweet."

"Uh, are we talking about the same Bunny?" she asked, eyebrows sailing upward. "Bunny Smart?"

"Yeah! She was probably just joking. Look, I'm sure she'll spot me and come over to talk, or I'll spot her, and you'll see she isn't so bad," I said.

"No, thanks. I don't need any more time in the rabbit hole."

"Maggie, why don't you take a break and get some food? I'm going to get some quick shots before everyone else devours it."

It was a classic southern spread. Shrimp and grits, red rice, biscuits, mac and cheese, pulled pork, and a ton of other sides. It smelled delicious. I made myself a little pulled pork sandwich with Carolina BBQ sauce on a Hawaiian roll. It was even better than it smelled. I made a note of the caterer. Hamby. Of course. Hamby Catering was *the* caterer; they did all the best events in Charleston. We both wolfed down the delicious chicken salad sandwiches, huge helpings of mac and cheese, and two biscuits that were lighter than clouds—not as good as Maggie's, but pretty good.

I guessed I was starving! Which made sense, as I'd been on the go since sunrise . . .

"I love women who can eat," Sam said, looking at Maggie's and my empty plates.

"It's my profession, Sam," she said.

"A moment on the lips and a lifetime on the hips," said a cool voice. *Bunny.*

"Hey, Ms. Smart, it's so nice to see you! I just couldn't help myself, it's so yummy! Can I fix you a plate?" Maggie quickly said, trying to sound happy and helpful and not seething as I knew she was.

"No, thank you. I am perfectly capable of helping myself, and I don't really like this kind of food." She waved her dainty hand over the heavenly spread. "I prefer lighter fare."

"Momma, come on, now. There's no pulled pork in the world as good as yours! You love southern food, and you're the best at making it!" Sam grabbed his mother around the waist. "Don't be so mean!" He gave her a kiss, and she looked like she might swoon.

"Oh, you like to cook! I didn't know! That's wonderful," Maggie said, apparently deciding to take the high road.

"Yes, but for others, not myself. That's how I got the name Bunny. My daddy always said I ate like a rabbit," she said, giving her son a wink.

"Mmm, wow, this is a great song!" Maggie said, changing the subject.

"Well, we can agree on that," Bunny said. "I do love the Rolling Stones. Sam, why don't you take your momma for a spin around the dance floor? I want to work off that biscuit that jumped into my mouth." And off they went.

"Ugh, how exhausting to be so caught up in one's body image," AG said, coming out of nowhere, shaking her head. "It's generational, I guess. Like being thin your whole life is an accomplishment!"

"AG, you are so right, but I don't think Bunny can help herself. Although, Maggie, she was never as sharp around the edges with me . . . You must bring it out in her," I said.

"She probably gets territorial around you because she can smell the threat," AG added.

"Thanks for speaking truth! But, um, shouldn't you be enjoying being the star of the show right now?"

"Oh my god, I am, but you know what? This being-the-bride thing? It is a *j-o-b*, and I need a lunch break. Ugh, these old southerners and their heirlooms and traditions. It's nice, but I would have preferred my own gown!" she said, slathering honey butter on a biscuit.

"What's with that? It's your wedding day!"

"No it isn't—it's hers." AG closed her eyes, savoring her bite of that biscuit. "She and Daddy are paying for it. Whatever. I got to choose the menu. Hence the mac-and-cheese bar!" She polished off her biscuit and took another from the basket.

"Well, it's a beautiful wedding, and that dress is amazing, old or not!" Maggie said.

"Aww, shoot, Maggie, don't make me blush. Anyway, spill the tea. What's with Bunny?"

"I have committed a mortal sin by dating her son," Maggie said, rolling her eyes.

"Maybe she thinks Maggie will lure Sam to New York. Where's *her* husband?"

"Out fishing, she said," I told them.

"Yeah, he's been out fishing for the last fifteen years. Well, whatever. Sam has never looked so happy. I've known that family for so long. Oh, damn, they are coming this way!" AG said, and mocked dropping dead. I let out a laugh.

"Anna Grace, darling, you make such a beautiful bride! You're *radiant*. Your parents must be thrilled," Bunny said. She double air-kissed AG, and without Bunny or Sam noticing, AG made a face.

"You know, I need a drink," Bunny said, and off she went to the bar. But before she left us, she paused and gave Maggie the once-over.

"Maggie, you look good out of those chef whites. You should wear more clothes in that color: brings out those eyes my son gets so lost in." She gave her a smile. Maggie's mouth hung open. "Close your mouth, darlin', you'll catch flies! Now, where's that drink?" she said, and left.

"Was that a compliment?" Maggie asked the empty space.

"Sam, why don't you take Maggie out on the dance floor? You are the best dancer in Carolina! I remember our cotillion classes; you were my partner and the sole reason I passed," AG said.

"You flatter me!" Sam said. "And, yes, I do believe Momma has softened, Maggie. She asked me when I was going to ask for her ring."

"Really? I'd love a spin," Maggie said. "Should I get a manicure, Sam?"

"But can you curtsy? I must marry a lady!" Sam asked.

"Absolutely not!" Maggie said, laughing out loud.

"Well, may I have this dance?" Sam bowed. It was such a silly gesture, but Maggie responded with her best curtsy, and Sam pulled her out onto the parquet, where he held her close. I watched my sister gaze lovingly into his eyes. And yet I couldn't help that low thrum of wistfulness. Maggie had found her person, and Sam had found his.

The music slowed, and I decided that the moment was so beautiful, the light was perfect, that I just had to get over it and take some pictures of them dancing. Maggie's red hair shone copper from the fairy lights, and Sam had a smile on him that lit up the room. AG and Grant danced nearby, looking like they belonged in Hollywood. As much as I had wished it were me, I felt a rush of happiness for my sister, for AG and her new husband, and for Sam.

I felt a tap on my shoulder, and I turned my head to see Henry, the Brit I'd mortified myself in front of at the Co-Op. I was surprised to see him—seemed like everyone knew AG. Standing there smirking at me and looking nothing short of delicious. His cool eyes and his tan skin against a small sweep of stubble on his sharp jawline. I caught a whiff of his cologne and felt my stomach tighten. God, he was handsome.

"Well, hello there, Ms. Violet," he said.

"You sure do clean up nice." I decided to flirt a little—why not? Maybe it was the mood of the evening.

Henry smiled at me. "You look nice as well."

"Oh, I'm just in my work blacks."

"But all black is very chic . . ." His eyes did a scan. My body immediately shivered. I wondered if Chris and I were already back together enough that this would count as crossing some line.

"Are you cold? Would you like my jacket?" he offered.

"No, but I should get back to work. Nice to see you, Henry!" He caught my hand before I could scurry away. I looked over and saw that AG was coming toward me. She saw me standing with Henry, made a gesture like she was fanning herself. I giggled.

"Something funny?" Henry asked.

"No, I just . . . I didn't expect to see you here."

"Violet! Gimme this camera—I want you to enjoy yourself, too!" AG insisted. "Why don't you let Henry take you for a spin on the dance floor?"

"Anna Grace! I am a professional, and how do y'all know each other?" I asked, swatting her away.

"Him and Daddy worked together on some big deal in fancy New York City," Anna Grace said in her southern drawl.

"Really," I said. My face was feeling hot. "It wouldn't be professional if I let you take the pictures."

"Okay," Anna Grace said. "But it's my day, right? Just one?" And she lifted the camera to take a shot of Henry and me.

The barn door was wide-open to the dock, and a warm breeze off the water wrapped around us. I inhaled the salt air and stepped closer to Henry, felt him moving closer to me.

What was going on with me? I barely knew this guy and yet I felt like I wanted to kiss his handsome face off, but I was at work and I was supposed to fade into the scenery. Also, I had a boyfriend? It must be that old wedding razzle-dazzle, making every single girl a little mad for whoever would dance with her. The tempo of the music picked up again, and all around us people moved toward the dance floor. I took the camera from Anna Grace and stepped back, smiling at Henry to show him it had been fun but had maybe gone too far.

The clinking of a wineglass signaled the beginning of the toasts.

"Well, that's my cue," I said, moving away. "I have to get some shots of the toasts and then the cutting of the cake."

It was getting late in the evening, and the toasts seemed to go on forever. The first two, from the fathers of the bride and the groom, were lovely. The second two, from the groom's brother and the best man, were pretty standard—a blend of funny anecdotes, testaments to the bride's and groom's sterling characters, and forecasts of their future happiness. Then it was time for the maid of honor.

Mary Katherine approached the small platform where the microphone was set up with the slow, liquid gait of someone who'd started drinking at breakfast. Taking tiny steps, she made it up there and squinted into the light. She lost her balance but steadied herself and grabbed the microphone, holding it as a rapper would, wrist at her mouth, elbow in the air.

"This is such a big day, y'all!" Mary Katherine said in her cheerleader's voice.

"God, Anna Grace, you just look so . . . freaking beautiful. Like an angel in that white dress, which is ironic, huh? Because, well . . . you know . . . Anyway, I love you so much, girl!" She had started to kind of rock back and forth. "I've known AG my whole life. We went to school together, college together, were Girl Scouts and sorority sisters. Go, Kappa!" She swung a fist in a circular motion. "We've gone from diapers, to braces, to SATs, to homecoming court!" Her voice was getting louder. "Guess who was queen? Of course, it was Anna freaking Grace!"

Uh-oh. Good ole MK was really on a tear.

"That girl is just the *best*. Isn't she? Just super-duper. Super blond, super tan, and super smart! So smart she nailed down Grant, she took him *down*! And what a catch! I fell in love with him first because . . . Wait, oh shit, I meant *she* fell in love with him at first sight. Ha ha, joke!"

Mary Katherine's parents were there. I knew this because I had seen some photographs the wedding party had submitted. A list of people who were important to take pictures of.

"Oh, Momma, stop it! I am not making a fool out of myself. It's trendy to roast the bride these days. I'm being *funny!*"

Mary Katherine's mother was waving at her to get off the stage, but Mary Katherine was not moving.

"Oh, AG, I love you so. Listen, y'all, AG is a cat. She knows exactly how to get what she wants. Don't you, little kitty cat?" Mary Katherine started to lose her center of gravity and was wobbling now. "Meoooooow!" Sadly, on the "ooow" she pulled away from her mother, lost her balance, and fell off the stage in the other direction, right into Sam's arms.

I saw AG's father signal the band to start playing, and Sam twirled MK around to the opening measures of "Twist and Shout" and then danced-carried her away from the party. MK's mother ran after them. Grant pulled AG onto the dance floor, and the guests cheered and followed them, everyone twisting enthusiastically to the rowdy Beatles tune.

A few minutes later, Sam returned. "Her momma dragged her into the ladies' room."

"Sam, I name you and Jerry, the bandleader, MVGs—most valuable guests. That was brilliant! I got the best photos of you turning a near disaster into a sweet, funny moment. And the shots of AG and Grant twisting are fab!" I gave him a big hug.

"Violet, about that thing—"

"Sam, not right now: this is when I get the best shots!"

I stepped away from him into the fray, feeling a little bad. Sam was such a good guy, and moments like these reminded me of the hard fact that when we'd been together, we'd never had any chemistry. Chris and I had. Did. I mean, Henry the Brit and I had it, too, or at least I had it for him—but I couldn't go chasing everyone with a dash of stubble and a capacity to make me light-headed. Maggie and Sam were going to end up married sooner rather than later, I could feel it coming, and if I wasn't careful, I might end up playing the fool like MK at their wedding—jealous and drunk and mortifying to myself. But right now I had to get it together, and I could keep it together, I thought, as I moved through the crowd, lifting my camera, ready for any moments that presented themselves. By the time the wedding was over I could not find Sam.

As I packed up, I decided that I had to stop chasing fireflies and give it a try with the one I was with—or the one I already owned a house with, anyway.

And in the meantime, I'd keep my head down. There was work to do.

CHAPTER NINE

~~~~

Violet

Although I was getting sort of excited for Chris's return, the secret I had been keeping from him still lingered in the air like a heavy mist after a temperature change. That last wedding job had worn me to a pebble, and I had slept deeply, but my dreams had been tinged with loneliness, full of happy memories smashed to pieces.

I had to talk with someone about Chris coming home, but Gran was off lately. She seemed preoccupied with some old wound of her own. Yet I could not get her to talk, and Maggie seemed pretty hostile to discussing Chris at all. Part of me thought, *Oh, just get on with it. He'll come home and then I'll know what I know.* Southern women were bred to fix our lipstick and hide our messes under the rug.

I knew how to do that, but not Maggie. Maggie lived her life out loud. If something was wrong with her, everyone knew it, and if she thought something was wrong with *you*, she'd tell you, like it or not.

I really didn't want to hold this one in, though.

There was my mom, too. She had just passed her year mark of full sobriety, so ostensibly she should be a sturdy font of wisdom, and she was set to return any minute. But somehow, I didn't trust that yet . . .

Then I knew who I could talk to. Aly. I took a hot shower, put on some comfortable clothes, and texted her.

> Drama, need a problem solved. You busy?

What kind of drama? Man, work, family?

> Man, mostly . . . but family, always . . .

Well, you've come to the right person for
family drama . . .

> I need to consult an expert. Beach walk?
> Meet me at St.25?

The beach on Sullivan's seemed to always solve everything. I grabbed my sunglasses and headed out.

When I met Aly in the driveway, she handed me an iced coffee.

"Where did you get this? It's delicious."

"The Co-Op; you know that. They have the best."

The giant gray sand beach stretched out like arms welcoming us into a hug. The sun was warm, and the gulls were calling to one another. It was low tide, and the beach went on forever. It felt gigantic, and made me feel tiny and insignificant but right somehow, too.

"So, what's going on?" Aly asked.

"Ugh, where do I begin . . . ?" Suddenly just being with a friend felt better than circling the drain on an impossible situation. I inhaled the salty air, and we took a right toward the lighthouse. "Honestly, I'd just love to hear what's going on with you. You were going to tell me about some news at the nail salon yesterday, and we just got off track somehow. What was it?"

"Oh, well . . ." Aly took a breath, and her eyes got bright. She looked excited, but maybe also a little afraid. "I had this conversation with my dad earlier, about me stepping in to continue Callie Knox in some way. My mom had such a large following and brand; it would be great to keep her creation alive. It would, you know, keep *her* alive in a way. And I could even eventually do my own stuff."

"That's huge!"

"Yeah, but I don't have the . . . full vision of where I want it to go. My mom's business manager, Rosemary, is supportive, but she's worried I'm too niche, that I won't be able to keep my mom's audience, so now I'm nervous about that, too. I need to build an audience, a bigger, broader one. I said I'd get to a hundred thousand followers by August!"

"Whoa. Okay. But I mean . . . why not?"

"Honestly, I'm worried I need a professional team behind me. My mom had me helping her out, but she also had a host of assistants. I can't afford that at the moment. Plus, they all got other jobs."

"What am I, chopped Spam?"

"I hate to rely on the kindness of friends, but, my god, would you help me?" she blurted out. "Would you be open to taking some pictures of me? Maybe shooting some videos? Help me create some content for my social accounts? I'll find a way to pay you!"

"Oh, like you need help elevating your brand, Miss Thing, and you know I would never take money from you . . ." I teased. "Not until you start earning the big bucks, anyway. How about you tag me for exposure?"

"I need to up my game, and I feel like a total ass when I take my own pictures!" Aly looked happier and more at ease already. "I think I need to be putting out something more polished."

"Absolutely agree. People really respond to your selfies and outfits of the day. Aspirational, though, and not so relatable?" I whipped out my phone, pulling up her Instagram account. "Look at the likes on this picture of you in your bikini on the beach. Maybe more of your achievements, not just thirst pictures."

"Yeah, but I feel so cringe."

"Why?" I asked. "You're Callie Knox's daughter! The daughter of a style queen!" She was really beaming now and elbowed my ribs. "Embrace it!" I said, proud of my friend, wanting her to feel proud of herself, too.

"I know, but I want it to be more lifestyle versus, like, me in outfits. I want more substance, something more meaningful. My mom had a following based on her genuine gift for helping to elevate other women's lives. Gardening, cooking, decorating, beauty tips. She sprinkled magic on everything. She knew how to make genuine connections. Mine is just like . . . *me*."

"Okay. What if that's not a problem, though—what if you just need to do that more? More you? I don't know. Let me think about it. Let's do a brand strategy meeting this week."

"Are you sure? I feel like I'm really asking a lot of you . . ."

"Well, actually, I need a little help with something that might be very on-brand for you, or very on the brand you're building, anyway . . ."

"Okay. I'm game. What is it?"

"You know that house I own with Chris that I may or may not have been Airbnbing for extra cash and that he may or may not know about and that he may or may not be coming back mad about . . . ?"

〜〜〜

A short while later, I pulled up to the little brick house and let myself in. The Airbnbers had cleared out already, and the cleaning company had come. I normally would've looked around and liked what I saw—I had grown up without a steady sense of home and had taken a lot of pride in creating this one—but now the house made me a bit sad. It was cute and cozy, but something in me felt like I had outgrown it, like it was my old life. I didn't fit in this space anymore. It didn't feel like home, and I knew it never would.

The front screen door slammed, and in walked Aly, holding two more giant iced coffees and wearing a massive smile. The clouds of my thoughts about Chris, the house, my family, lifted with her sunshine.

"Hey, girl! Long time no see," Aly joked at me, showing a million white teeth at once.

"Hey, Al! Or should I say, my new life architect?"

"Life architect. I like that. Here's some liquid '*Get 'er done!*'" She giggled and handed me my iced coffee. Then she looked at my face, and she must have seen the traces of my sadness. Aly gave me the once-over. "What's going on with you? I mean besides the obvious. There's something else."

"Nothing, just Chris," I said, hoping to change the subject. "Did you decide on the next post, your outfit and location, all of that?"

"When is he coming home? Tell me what is really going on—then we can talk about content." She ushered me to the couch.

"Aly, I'm a mess. Chris is coming home, and I just . . . I think I'm still in love with him . . . but feel like it's been so long that my feelings might be misplaced? Or imaginary? Or so deep at this point that I'll never get rid of them? I don't know . . ." I trailed off and swallowed hard. "I hate to admit any of that, because I was supposed to be over him. The baby would have connected us, at least superficially, but that lie is gone. I don't want him to think he can just waltz in and pick it back up with me anytime he wants, you know?"

"Sure, but of course you miss him."

I took a beat. Was I allowed to miss him? Was it obvious to everyone that I was still hung up on him? "I haven't told Chris about the Airbnb thing."

Aly shrugged, God love her, like who cared that I had been carrying on this lie for six months? "I mean, is there a reason you don't want to tell him?"

I thought about that for a minute. It was funny, but I liked having this little cushion of money, and if I told him, I'd feel obligated to share it. That felt hard to explain, though. And it wasn't the only reason. "I guess it was our home, where we were going to bring our baby home to, you know? And I guess turning it into a hotel makes it seem like it won't ever be a home again . . . And maybe it shouldn't be?"

"Well, you could always sell it. That would solve all of those problems!"

"The location is amazing, right? So close to downtown! I just . . ." I frowned. It made a lot of sense. Why was there this big block inside of me, resisting that simple solution?

"Probably could get a great price for it," Aly mused. "All these people moving to Charleston, buying those little saltbox houses and fixing them up." But then my friend read my face, cocked her head, and changed her tone. "But that would be you letting him go for good, right?"

"Yep. That's exactly it," I said, relieved to hear her say out loud what I had been feeling but had been unable to put into words. "I feel nervous about *anything* being 'for good.'"

"Well, that's reasonable given that your situation with Chris isn't exactly black-and-white."

"Yup, lots of gray. Maybe we'd get a good price, but what would be my next move?" I shook my head, feeling a tidal pull of loss all over again. "If we wanted to make a home together, we'd never be able to afford a place like we have now!"

"What do you think Chris wants?" Aly asked with an arched eyebrow.

"It's pretty hard to communicate that kind of thing across such a big distance. I'm sure it's frustrating for him not being here."

"You know what would fix that? Coming home," Aly said, a fresh sharpness in her voice.

"Aly, he's coming." I hadn't meant to sound quite as defensive as I did . . .

"Heard that before. Look, maybe there is just a reserve tank of rocket fuel you both need to burn off. You need to figure this out, and maybe it's a little gray between y'all right now . . . but you need to define your relationship, and you can't do that while he's not here."

"I know that, and so does he. I appreciate that, but it isn't so easy for him . . . for us." I hated the way I was sounding. Aly looked at me, and I could tell she wasn't buying it, either.

"You know what you need? Some sweet tea!"

"You know I always leave some here just in case," I said, heading to the kitchen. "I'm addicted to the stuff."

"I think when we are dealing with matters of the heart, we should be drinking something sweet, not this jet fuel," Aly said, taking our iced coffees and following me into the kitchen.

"A little sugar wouldn't hurt," I said, and went to the fridge and pulled out a bottle of sweet tea. I always left some as a little welcome touch for renters. I poured it over some ice cubes in two tall glasses. It was the perfect afternoon pick-me-up, delightful, refreshing, and with a little boost.

"All right, Miss Lady," Aly said as we headed back into the living room. She sat, patting the cushion on the couch next to her.

"Aly, I'm tired. The wedding jobs are high stress. This might be too much. I have more on the horizon. I have a bridal portrait session; I have a ton of editing I need to do. The house isn't ready . . . for whatever needs to happen with it. Look, it's like a sanitized hotel in here! I feel like I'm spiraling."

"You are, a little bit, but it's normal. There are a lot of decisions you need to make. A lot of new information. Life-changing information."

"I know," I said, and drank that goodness down. I did know, but I didn't want to face it. What if this relationship with Chris wasn't really a relationship at all, just two people a world away from each other? He hadn't made any real promises to me, or commitments, not even before he left . . . but I was putting all my mental energy into it as if he had. I started to panic a little. "Aly, I'm afraid he might not come back forever like he said."

"Might not." She shrugged.

"Aly!" I said.

"What? That's entirely possible. You need to think about that. Seems a lot easier for him over there. If it was so bad, he would have come home by now."

"This is not making me feel any better, Aly."

"Well, you need to face that possibility instead of putting everything else on hold waiting for him to come around and finally be the man you want him to be. Maybe you need to be with someone who is already the person you need."

"Ouch."

"Well, truth hurts. But so do constant heartache and disappointment. Your call. I love you, whatever you decide."

"It's not that simple!"

"It's not that complicated, Violet. You can make things simple by looking truth right in the eye, or you can complicate them by covering the truth in excuses. Whatever you choose, just choose it. Stop sitting around, feeling sorry for yourself, crying over a man who is doing exactly what he's always done. At least *he's* making *his* choice."

"This is not my favorite conversation," I said, and started to get up.

"Well, what's the most pressing problem?"

"The house," I said. "If this house didn't look so much like an Airbnb to me right now, if it looked like something special, I could face the other problems. Okay?"

"Okay?" She raised that eyebrow again.

"Yes, okay. I want it to look like something Chris wants to come home to . . ."

"Fuck Chris!" Aly said.

"Aly!"

"Listen, you need to do what's right for you. Not what's right for him." Aly sighed. "He's in Japan. If he wants ownership of this life, then he needs to take ownership of this life, starting with his being present."

"He will be, or at least that's what he said," I replied.

"Let's marinate on your next step. A fresh start for you, and maybe someday the both of you. You don't become a woman overnight," Aly said. "It's not an all-of-a-sudden change. We have to choose to be an adult, a woman, a mother, choose that path over and over. That's what Callie Knox would say if she were here. The right thing is hard; that's why the wrong thing feels so good. It's easy."

"Oh, man, Aly," I said. "You are really sounding like your mother's daughter. Full of magic and wisdom!"

"Well, when I woke up this morning, I was peeking through my blinds like a madwoman, trying to get an eyeful of the creature my dad's replacing my mom with, so maybe don't speak too soon . . ."

"Oh, boy."

"But listen, I have a great dad, he lives right next door to me, and you never even got to know yours. I got my momma for over thirty years and then I lost her, and now I can't imagine trusting anyone with my heart. You are pretty amazing, trusting people with your heart as you do. So maybe I should shut my mouth, count my blessings, and listen to *you* a little . . ."

"Thank you, Aly. Really can't say it enough times: I'm so grateful for your friendship, my wise one," I said, and gave her a hug.

"Anytime, lady. I'm here for you."

"Likewise."

"Okay, now take some great pictures of me making your house look great!"

We fluffed pillows, vacuumed, and removed personal touches. Aly removed a few decorations so the ones that remained popped. She brought some props out of her car. She really did have a great eye.

We posted a few images of Aly at work—"Change your décor, change your life," that kind of thing—a little more personal than her usual thing. It was still her looking great but doing something for a friend, something with real purpose, and I could see that the response was immediate and positive. Then we cleaned our glasses and left. I gave her a few assignments to think about for her own brand-building and sped back to the island for dinner.

~~~

When I arrived at Gran's house, I went upstairs to change and took a look around my childhood bedroom, its faded purple walls, my bed covered in an ancient family quilt, posters that I'd made as a teenager. Collages of actresses in golden age Hollywood movie stills. Shots from a *National Geographic* I had found in Gran's basement when I was thirteen and been obsessed with. It had a story about Iceland, with the Northern Lights, and remote lighthouses, and these fisherwomen who looked like ancient Norse mermaids. Outfits I liked from *Seventeen*. Precursors of the vision boards I made for weddings now. Looking at those images, I knew Aly was right as usual—I needed to *choose* my life. I walked over to my bedside table and picked up my camera. I felt the weight of it settle into my hands.

I went to the mirror over my dresser and snapped a picture of myself, a self-portrait in this open-ended, unwritten moment of my life.

I threw on a black tank dress and let my hair hang loose. Sprayed on some perfume for a change and liked what I saw in the mirror. I took another picture—me, trying to choose life!—and went to join my family.

As soon as I closed the bedroom door behind me, the smell of garlic and olive oil sailed through the air and tickled my nose. Nothing in the world got me hungry faster than garlic. Oh, man, if I wasn't mistaken, I was smelling the start of my favorite meal in the universe.

Spaghetti and meatballs. Now, that might seem simple coming from a sister and granddaughter of chefs, but it was a classic for a reason, and the perfect Sunday meal. I knew that there would also be more than a few garlic bread loaves and a giant green salad with a lemon vinaigrette, probably topped with goat cheese.

In the kitchen, I found Maggie rolling out little meatballs alongside Gran.

Gran was the same height as Maggie, and looking at them was always heartwarming. They moved in the same way and shared so many mannerisms. Gran's hair was up in her usual bun, fastened by a gold claw clip. She wore her pearls, which peeked out of a dark blue starched denim shirt, and her classic khaki trousers, which were cropped short. She was barefoot, but I noted her toes had gotten a fresh swipe of her signature OPI Big Apple Red to match her fingernails.

Maggie must have cheered her up. I saw a smile that had been on vacation the past few days return to Gran's face as she threw her head back in a laugh, shaking her dangle earrings, which caught the light. For a moment, everything seemed beautiful and homey and serene.

Then the door swung open, and in came my mother, Lily.

CHAPTER TEN

~~~~~

Violet

"*Ciao, la mia famiglia!*" My mother's voice rang through the house with a badly overpronounced Italian accent.

She turned a corner and stood there, arms thrown wide, in a white fedora, a bright pink blouse, white slim pants cut off at the ankles, blue loafer mules, and a white trench coat rakishly flung over her shoulders. Her hair was platinum blonde, hanging straight and slicked back behind her ears, and her eyes were obscured by the largest mirrored sunglasses I had ever seen. She had gone hard with the self-tanner. The result was an unnatural shade of apricot. It had been two weeks since she'd been gone. Left as a Charleston lady, came back as . . .

"*Mi sei mancato, bella!*" She kissed both of my cheeks, gave me a mildly disapproving head-to-toe look, and strutted on toward the kitchen.

As I followed down the hall—lagging a little, if I'm being honest—I noticed my great-grandmother's photograph, the one from when she had just started the restaurant. I used to pretend that she was watching over us as we continued to uphold her legacy with the restaurant. It was known to always be off-center, and I was used to finding it crooked, but now it was perfectly centered.

Like, unusually perfectly centered.

Was that a sign? Were things on the right track?

I touched the framed photo as though it might rub off some bit of good luck, keep things moving in the right direction. Then a postcard fell from behind the frame. It must have been wedged there. By Gran, I guessed. Who else?

The picture on the postcard was of a New England–style bay, gray-green and dotted with picturesque sailboats. A ripple went through me at the words written in blue ballpoint: *Loving and missing my girls. —Dad.*

At the bottom, a little doodle drawing of a magnolia and a violet. Maggie and Violet.

I was having a hard time breathing.

A postcard from our dad? When had he sent this, and why had Gran hidden it?

The stamp had been ripped off, but the postcard itself was well preserved for its being decades old, or however many years ago he must have sent it. The time stamp was unreadable. He had died before my third birthday.

And the funny doodle. So, he was artistic? Maybe Maggie and I got our creativity from him?

I wondered if it was true what Aly had said, if it was a miracle that I could trust any man given that I never really had a dad to hang on to. Or maybe all this time I was hanging on to a shadow, and that meant my love life was all shadows, too . . .

My ruminations were cut short by the sound of my mom going on and on in that over-the-top Italian accent in the kitchen, and I felt sick at the thought of what the rest of my family would say.

Mom, who was always switching careers, always about to strike it rich with some new, wild plan, had recently become a travel agent, which meant she now finally lived her dream of being a world traveler. None of us had ever seen her shine so bright. When Momma was happy, the waters were calm, and life could feel normal. I hoped it would last.

I tucked the postcard in my back pocket. As I came into the kitchen, I rolled my eyes at Maggie, who was staring at our mother like she was a monster—mouth hanging open, the hand that had been stirring the sauce frozen in place.

"Mama, *come stai?*" my mother said.

"Hey there, Lily, *come stai* yourself," Gran replied, breaking the silence. "You speak Italian now?"

"Well, that's all I've got. But the cabdriver on the way to the airport said my accent was perfect! Oh, Violet, you would die to take pictures in Roma! Wow, your hair looks—"

"Thanks, Mom," I replied mildly, cutting her off. If I were going on a photography trip, it would be to some wild, rugged coast. Iceland, maybe—one of those lighthouses on a sea-battered rock, something remote and mystical. "I'm sure I would."

"Oh, lord," Mom went on, picking up a strand of my hair, "seriously, you need to go see Malory right away!"

I smiled thinly, took the least wrong option, and changed the subject. "How was your flight?"

"Perfect! They upgraded me to business class once I told them I had such a large following on Instagram. Almost as many followers as you have now. I gently suggested that it would be free PR and made a little video of it. Didn't you watch my stories?" She whipped out her phone and showed everyone the video.

"Wow, Mom! It looks great!" I said. "Seems like you're having fun."

"Well, I think I earned it after the past few years! I finally get to see the world like I've always wanted! Finally, my life is my own!" She giggled and did a little twirl. "Okay, I need to use the WC." And off she went to the bathroom.

"The WC?" Gran said, raising a dagger of an eyebrow.

"It's Euro for *bath*—" I began.

"Oh, hush, I know what it means! I was born at night, but not *last* night. I just hope she doesn't stain my white toilet seat pumpkin!" she joked.

"Well," I said, and everyone nodded and got back to setting the table and working on dinner. Meanwhile I felt a host of secrets haunting me. The ex who was maybe coming home. The postcard in my pocket, which had almost stopped my heart. The nearly ten thousand dollars I'd stashed away, for what purpose I did not know. To bring up anything would change the vibe. I went into the cabinets beside the sink, expecting to pull out our old red-and-white dinner plates, but found a stack of low-slung bowls instead.

"Gran, are these pasta bowls?" I said, impressed that she had bought anything new.

"Blates," she responded over her shoulder as she dropped a handful of spaghetti into her stainless steel pasta pot. "I got tired of everything being chipped."

"Excuse me, what?"

"Blates. All the rage in the food world now, Vi. Bowl and plate together! You can use them for anything!" She did a little wiggle, proud of herself for being on trend. "Maggie told me about them. They are actually from Callie, Aly's momma's line at Crate and Barn!"

Well, well, well, Gran!" I said, pulling them out for closer inspection. They were very pretty dark navy blue low bowls, a little wider than your usual pasta bowl, heavily glazed and shiny. I was excited to use them. I set the table for five, but Gran saw me and told me there would be seven.

"Who else is coming?" I asked.

"Well, Jim is coming, and he is bringing a surprise guest," she said.

"Oh, yay! I was wondering when we were going to see Jim."

"It'll be a proper welcome home for Jim," she chuckled. "I can't wait to hear all the juicy gossip about the show."

Jim was an actor on a soap opera that was filmed in New York City. He'd had a supporting role for several years, but it never went front and center as he'd hoped. However, from time to time he'd call Gran to update her with some gossip about the actors. She was a fan.

I pulled out Gran's bright yellow gingham print place mats and her mismatched silver. I loved that it was eclectic, homey. I set out the blates and placed the silverware in its correct positions. Snagged some wineglasses and matching napkins. Gran grabbed them out of my hand and shoved them back in the drawer. I looked at her, confused.

"Oh, I'm sorry, Princess Violet, our butler, Jeeves, is out. Are you going to iron these? Bounty napkins are just fine. Spaghetti sauce all over my nice napkins. Come on, now!"

"Oh, okay," I said, and replaced the linen napkins with paper towels.

The doorbell rang, and Lily answered. I heard her singsong her Italian greeting for Jimmy and cringed. Then I reminded myself how hard she'd always had it and bit my cheek.

"Oh, wow, Sophia Loren! I didn't know you were coming to Sullivan's Island!" Jimmy said as he entered the house. "Hey there, beautiful, I brought Momma some of her own juice."

"My famous friend! How nice we are having dinner with a celebrity! Welcome home!" I said, and got in the spirit, giving Jim two dramatic air kisses.

"It's good to be back. *You* look good!"

"Thank you! It's all my sister's cooking!"

"Body by Maggie? A new biz venture?"

"Ha! Carbs for curves!" I said, wiggling my butt.

God, I'd forgotten that about Jimmy, how easy it was to be with him. He knew exactly what to say and do. The wine he'd brought wasn't expensive, but it was good tasting and would wash the family crazy down nicely.

"Hey, Violet, I have someone I want you to meet. This is Henry Tucker." Jimmy gestured behind him, and there he was: the man I'd made a fool of myself in front of at the Co-Op and who'd then appeared during my wedding job to distract me with his handsome dimples and swaggery charm. He was grinning and holding the leash attached to his beautiful dog. I made direct eye contact with those deep-ocean-blue eyes.

I knew the normal-person thing to do here would be to say something, but my mouth had gone inoperable. Then I remembered to breathe and managed to stick my hand out.

"Violet, right?" Henry shook my hand, and it was like shaking a warm baseball glove. His hands were large and strong but soft, like . . .

"Hey there! Nice to see you again. Welcome to our home." Was I sounding normal, or like a robot? I made eye contact with Jimmy, who appeared to be trying very hard not to laugh at me. I guessed he was getting that this guy was unnerving me. I bent down and gave Henry's dog a pat, and the dog gave me a giant lick in return.

"Nice to see you, too," I said to the dog.

"Ah, *bello*, let me have those! I can open them up straightaway!" My mother took the bottles from Jimmy with a little too much exuberance. But when she noticed Henry she straightened her posture, stuck out her chest a little, and said, "My, my, my, aren't you just gorgeous! I'm Lily, Violet's mother!"

"No, that can't be true. You have to be Maggie! Her sister, right? Jim told me there were sisters living here." Henry kissed her hand.

Then my mother did an odd thing and blushed. "You can put that handsome boy on the porch!" she said, gesturing to the dog.

"I'd like to eat at the table if that's okay," Jimmy joked. "Oh, wait. You mean the dog?"

"Oh, stop it! But flattery will get you everywhere with me, darlin'." My mother switched from the Italian Riviera to the back porch of the Deep South real quick. She grabbed the leash on Henry's dog, leading him to our screened-in porch. Then she swished off to the kitchen, leaving me alone in the room with Jim and Henry . . . and Henry's nicely built frame, ever so slightly hidden by his crisp blue linen shirt.

"Thank you for the wine," I said. "I'll make sure that sweet boy gets some water!"

"I'll drink wine, thanks. Oh, sorry, you mean the dog again!" Jimmy joked. "Don't worry, I have backup in my car. So, she speaks Italian now? Wow, quite the educational trip."

"Yeah, that accent is amazing."

"Mine or hers?" Henry said.

"Hers, Henry. Yours is not even fair. Hers, however, reminds me of something between *Borat* and, like . . ."

"*Borat*. Oh my god," I said, remembering that over-the-top movie. That dang accent had been imitated so many times I hated it. "Mario!" I said, and giggled.

"It's-a-me-Lilllly," Jimmy said, and giggled right back.

"I'm afraid I can't keep up with you two," Henry said.

"Well, it is hard to soar with the eagles of comedy. Thank God you're British; otherwise you'd never have a chance with the ladies next to me," Jimmy teased.

"Lately I've been fortunate enough to be welcomed into this southern society with the best host," Henry said.

"Nonstop women!" Jim did a little dance, and I burst into laughter; so did Henry. There was some noise behind the front door—Sam, holding another bottle of wine.

"Hello, I'm Henry Tucker." Henry shook Sam's hand.

"Nice to meet you! I'm Maggie, Vi's sister. Sam, let's go help Gran," Maggie said behind me, greeting Sam at the door.

"How was service at the restaurant?" Sam asked.

"Fine, but crazy busy. Lots of orders for the goat cheese quiche, thanks to your zucchini!" Maggie said with a wink.

"Zucchini? Isn't it early for those?" I asked.

"Yes, but it's been such a warm spring," Sam said with a shrug. "Momma wanted me to unload some of it. Maggie was happy to add it to her order."

Sam's mother and father still ran a gorgeous family farm. Maggie had arranged for a few plots of land to grow crops just for the Magic Lantern. They were so good, I often photographed them. Maggie had hung some of my prints in the restaurant: giant dark green bouquets of kale, huge violet and beige turnips, bloodred beets. All delicious, and my sister's magical hands could turn them into food fit for gods.

I made a mental note that maybe Aly and I could go out there and get some content for her feed.

"All right, y'all, food's ready. Let's sit!" Gran called us in, and she set a giant bowl of pasta on the table with the salad. My mom came with a basket of bread and a bottle of wine. We all took our places and made more introductions to Henry. Gran was staring meaningfully at me, and I knew she thought Henry was cute. Plus, he had pulled her chair out for her. Gran and Mom sat next to each other, and of course Maggie was basically on Sam's lap. We dug in after a quick prayer, offered by Sam. It was a nice scene, everyone together around my grandmother's table, like Sunday night dinners of old.

"It's so good to be home!" my mom exclaimed.

"We're happy to have you back!" I was trying very hard to mean it.

"Jim told me you were on holiday in Italy?" Henry asked my mother.

"Holiday? That's what you Brits say, huh? Love it," she purred. "No, I was actually working! I was doing some training; I am a travel agent these days."

"Well, that's a fantastic job! I'm jealous; I haven't visited Italy in a long time. I have family in the south," Henry said.

"Oh?" My mother was practically licking her lips.

"Yes. In Naples." He helped himself to a hearty portion of pasta. "I have people in Naples, in Nantucket . . ."

"That's funny," I said, fingering the postcard in my pocket. "I was just thinking about Nantucket." Remembering the postcard picture and thinking it was Nantucket.

"Huh!" Gran exclaimed. It was a funny, loud noise that made everyone turn to look at her. She in turn looked at Henry. "You grew up in England, I'm assuming?"

"Yes, in a small town outside London. We moved to the city when I was a teenager. But—islands."

"You know, I've been dreaming about islands . . ." I said. "What is it about them?"

"We should talk about it."

"Have you been to Iceland?" I asked, picturing being alone with him, on a walk somewhere, talking about islands . . .

"All right, y'all, this isn't an interview," Maggie said. "Let the man eat. Mom, you'll have to tell me how authentic this sauce is now that you're an expert."

"Well, I was primarily in the north of Italy before I flew out of Roma, and as I am sure you are aware, red sauce, or *marinara* sauce, is more of a southern Italian thing. Right, Henry? However, I will be visiting the Amalfi Coast later on this summer, so I'll be sure to report back."

"The south is heavenly," Henry said. "Tell me where and when, and I can send along some recommendations if you'd like." He made a little happy grunt after he ate a bite of a meatball. "This is delicious, and exactly what you'd find in the kitchen of a nonna."

"Why, thank you! Those meatballs are all me, but the sauce is Maggie over there," Gran said in a voice sweet like honey. This guy was melting all the women.

Lily stuck her fork in the smallest bit of pasta, delicately twirled it on the prongs and into her spoon. I was guessing she was being protective of her white pants. She smelled the assembled bite, then set it down. "So, Henry, are you married?"

"Mom!" I whispered. "A little personal?"

"Don't be ridiculous, it's a simple question! Henry?" my mom said, looking at him through her eyelashes.

"No, I am separated, soon to be legally single."

"Oh, that's too bad. Do you have any children? What do you do for work?"

"Mom, is this family dinner or an interrogation?" Maggie poured out more wine and passed the green salad. "Chill."

"No, it's completely fine. No children. I am an investment banker by trade. I am currently looking into the hospitality market. Charleston is so hot right now; I'm looking for a more fun project." Henry waved his hand, as though this were all very tedious. He had cleaned his plate and was helping himself to another portion.

"Enter me and the Magic Lantern," Jimmy said.

"Oh, are you looking to buy a restaurant?" I asked.

"No, I want to open something new. An event space, perhaps. I met Jim a few months ago, when I was in New York on business. We met at a cast party. This bloke had me laughing till my sides hurt! He told me all about Charleston, especially Sullivan's, and as you know, I am partial to islands. I'll admit I was charmed by the experience at the Magic Lantern. The best fried chicken I've ever had in my life! Europeans are fascinated by American southern cooking. I had to come see it for myself." He smiled again at me, and I beamed involuntarily. Looking at him was like slipping into a warm bath. "And I love the old buildings—so much of the States is new-looking, and it's nice to be in a place with some history."

"I agree totally. I actually am really in love with the historical architecture in downtown Charleston. The wrought ironwork. Seems like all photographers love it, but I love it more."

"Do you, now?" Henry smiled at me.

"Yes, I do. I've always been entranced by the older homes, the cobblestone streets, and those gates that lead into—"

"Little secret gardens?" Henry finished my sentence for me.

"Yes, exactly!" I smiled.

"Was that your favorite book as a child? *The Secret Garden*?" he asked.

"Yes, actually it was," I gasped, and the table fell silent for a moment. It was a silly conversation, but for some reason it held weight. We looked at each other's faces.

"Mine too, actually. My grandmother Violet used to read it to me," he said, taking a bite of his dinner.

"You know, Violet has the cutest little place in Byrnes Downs," my mother said, putting an end to that moment of basking naked in his . . . waters? Jesus. I needed to get ahold of myself.

I cut my eyes over to Gran, who then looked at Maggie.

But Maggie caught my eye, noticing I wasn't answering right away, and made a face.

"I'm actually thinking about selling it," I said into my noodles.

"What?" Mom dropped her fork in her blate and cleared her throat in an effort to make me look at her. A pet peeve of my mother's was avoiding eye contact. She said it made you look weak.

"I was just thinking that it's a hot market and it might be a good time to sell . . ."

"I don't think that's a good idea. What does Chris think?" my mom asked. "What is he going to say when he shows up to no house? He will think that the two of you have no *future* together!" My mother shook her head, as though this were apocalyptically stupid behavior.

"Who is Chris?" Henry asked.

"Her ex. They still share a house together, but he lives in Japan . . ." Jim explained.

"Well, he's actually coming back . . ." I said in a portentous tone I really hadn't intended. "But I am unsure and undecided about our romantic status," I added.

"I see," Henry said into his own plate . . . or blate.

"I'd get the renters out first." Maggie's eyes rolled, and her eyebrows did a thing that made me feel not at all better about anything. The secrets I was keeping.

"Renters?" my mom said. "I thought things were on hold with Chris. You two have so much invested in each other."

"Yeah, just part-time, like on Airbnb. I decided to get a little extra income, you know: good to have an emergency fund when you own a house, things always come up, and then it actually turned out to be good money, and . . ."

"So, you're a secret entrepreneur, too, then? How nefarious of you." Henry wiggled his eyebrows at me.

Did he care that I had a boyfriend, or ex-boyfriend, or whatever, I was lying to about the house we co-owned, and the way I was maybe making money off it? Or was he so uninterested in me it didn't matter at all? Was he teasing me? I felt my cheeks redden.

"Of course! How smart of y'all, plus you can surprise your soon-to-be husband with a beautiful new cottage to return to." My mother was smiling at me with what I could only describe as delusional enthusiasm. "It makes perfect sense to me."

"Mom, we are not engaged!" God, I sounded nuts. I also felt nuts. Maybe I *was* nuts.

The heady conversation was interrupted by a loud bark.

"Jacques!" Henry admonished.

"The dog is Jacques?" Maggie asked.

"Yeah, after Jacques Pépin." Henry put his hands in the air, you-got-me style. "I confess. I am a super fan. Sorry, Chef Jacques probably smells the divine meatballs." Henry turned and called out toward the porch, "Jacques! Stop it!" Then another, much louder bark erupted from the porch, followed by some whining. To the table Henry said, "My apologies."

Then he made eye contact with me, made a face of sympathy. I would have appreciated the solidarity if I wasn't so mortified. *Why is my mother so hell-bent on Chris?* I asked myself. But more importantly, why was I all of a sudden back on the other side of the fence when hours before I was defending our relationship . . . whatever that was?

"Hey, Henry, come help me in the kitchen? Should we check on Jacques?" Jim suggested.

Henry and Jim left the room, clearing our blates.

Through the window I watched as Henry refilled Jacques's water bowl and gave him a treat from his pocket.

"Violet, have you discussed this plan with Chris?" Sam asked, breaking the awkward silence.

"Well, not yet."

"Violet, sell it," Maggie said, stoking my mother's fire.

"Stay out of this, Maggie."

"Okay, let's take a beat," Gran said, trying to break the tension. "Lily, you just got home. Let's let Violet explain herself."

"I don't need to explain myself to anyone! Chris has been in Japan for *a year*. It's a great opportunity to make a lot of money on a small house. Plus, we can take some amazing real estate pictures and sell for top dollar. I don't know what I want yet."

"Violet, don't do anything hasty!" Lily said. "*That's* all I am saying. You already own the house together; I mean, you're halfway there! Darling, you don't want to be single for much longer . . ."

"Uh, okay," Maggie said, bugging out her eyes and taking a savage sip of wine.

"Chris and I aren't getting married, Mom! We aren't even together!" I felt like a teenager defending herself rather than a grown-ass woman who owned half a house and had her own thriving small business.

A long howl came from the porch.

Jacques, who had been trying so hard to be a good boy, couldn't be good any longer.

He broke through the screen door, leash trailing behind him. We all watched, stunned motionless, as his large paws thundered inside, then launched his entire body toward the table, front legs outstretched, bracing for impact, knocking everything to the floor and sliding head-first down the entire length of the table. The pasta and all the meatballs were flung into the air, bursts of red sauce spreading like fireworks. That sauce sprayed everywhere, but mainly on my mother. On her face, her hair, and her outfit, especially her white slacks. Everyone else managed to get away, but my mom was now a spaghetti monster with a giant Lab trying to lick it off her.

"Oh my god. Jacques! Bad dog!" Henry entered the room, holding the dog's water, obviously mortified.

My mother looked like she might cry. I felt that childish protective tug, and for a moment I was frozen, wondering whose side to take. But then Gran caught the giggles, which set off Maggie, Jim, and Sam, and then I looked at Jacques, once a white dog, who was now a lovely pink shade from all the sauce. My mother shoved him off, and he started to roll around on the carpet. I couldn't help but burst into laughter right alongside my family.

"See, Violet? Aren't you glad we didn't use the linen napkins? Bounty saves the day again!" Gran said, handing my mom her napkin, and then getting her a few more.

"I am so very sorry! I am so embarrassed!" Henry was tripping over his words. "Do you have a hose?"

"This is horrifying!" my mother whimpered. "Not funny, and all of y'all are just *laughing* at me!"

"Oh, come on, Mom, don't get salty; it's not funny because it's you . . ." Maggie tried to be kind for a moment, but then she cracked up all over again. "Not *just* because it's you. Or because you're wearing all white. Maybe a Tide stick?" she said between hoots of laughter.

"Uh, it looks like a murder scene," Sam said. "A Tide stick would be—" And he broke off, chuckling.

Jim had meanwhile jumped into action. "Henry, let's get your chef cleaned up. You can't put that dog in your car like that. I know where the hose is."

Henry followed Jim away, shaking his head in shame, but also trying not to laugh . . .

I watched Mom as she got up and left the room, going upstairs to change, not saying a word. The room was silent. Gran and Maggie waited for me to say something.

Gran broke the silence. "You know you could just stay here forever!"

"That's sweet, and I would, but . . . I don't know, honestly. I am in a bit of a gray zone with Chris."

"What do you mean?"

"Well, I think he expects to pick up right where we left off . . . He doesn't know I'm not living there full-time. He doesn't know about the renters. That was obviously wrong of me."

"*Nefarious*, maybe, but not *wrong*," Sam said, reentering with shirtsleeves rolled up. "I did like that word. Sounded better in a British accent, though."

"Anyway, there's no one there now. And if Chris expects us to slip into the old routine, it would be so easy to fall right back into. But something in me doesn't want to do that." As soon as I said it, I knew it was true. I wasn't done with Chris, but I didn't want to just roll back into the way it had been. "I guess I need my own space, you know? I am overcrowding Gran's house, though. I probably do need to move forward, learn to live on my own."

"Like an apartment?" Sam asked.

I saw a quick transformation of Gran's expression. Had I hurt her? This had always been temporary. Or was the shift because she knew it would be easier with me gone? Maybe that look meant that she would be relieved to be alone but was afraid to tell me?

"Wait, what about my mom's place in Hampton Park?" Sam said to Maggie.

"Oh yeah! Sam! That could be perfect!" Maggie squealed.

"My mom owns this house in Hampton Park, downtown," Sam went on. "She's had it as a rental property for years. It's sweet. Needs work, but she is currently looking for the right family for it."

"Oh my god, Violet! Bunny is not a fan of mine but loves you! Call me crazy, but I bet she'd rent it to you for nothing! Just explain your situation to her! That house is beautiful, or could be after a few coats of paint . . ." Maggie was practically yelling, she was so excited. "Maybe you could enlist Aly to spruce it up, and then the next renters or owners or whatever would probably pay top dollar for it."

"Okay, I'll call her," I said. "But I do need to talk to Chris about it all. Maybe I'll float the idea of selling the house to Chris when we FaceTime tonight. If he's back, we can actually deal with that . . . I guess I've got some fish to fry."

"I have a recipe for that!" Maggie said, flipping her copper hair over her shoulder. She seemed to think everything was settled, but I wasn't sure that was how I felt. "You just gave me a great idea for a dinner special!"

CHAPTER ELEVEN

~~~~

Violet

There was this time of morning that always gave me peace. I liked to call it the "Violet hour."

Not because it was my alone time, although it was, but because the light was the prettiest blue violet. It was the hour before the sun would rise, turning the pitch-black velvet night into the fresh blue brightness of day. It happened right before the world woke up and gave me a slice of the morning to really think, or pray, or problem-solve. Sometimes I would just watch the light shift. I was never good at sleeping and seemed to always wake early. Once in a while, Gran would get up first, we'd meet in the kitchen for a cup of coffee, and she'd urge me to go take a walk on the beach. Those were my favorite and most sacred times to wander the shoreline and collect seashells or take pictures of the ocean. I was always hypnotized by how the weather affected the waves—how they could grow wild in a storm or turn calm in the sunshine. Pulling out and rolling back onto the shoreline. This was one of those mornings.

I was restless again. I looked at the phone and saw it was around five a.m., and I also saw three missed FaceTimes with Chris. I had slept so hard last night. I cursed and decided I'd apologize later. He'd sent me his flight info, though, and that made it real. He really was coming back; it wasn't just talk and speculation. I changed positions, fluffed my pillow, snuggled deep beneath my comforter, then stuck a leg out, then put it back in. I couldn't get comfortable. I decided to just give in and get up, put on an old gray pair of sweatpants that had holes in the legs, a beloved item left over from high school, and some flip-flops.

I walked down Goldbug Avenue, then Middle Street, then the two blocks to the public access to the beach at station 25. In the darkness, I felt like I was slipping through secrets. I approached the walkway. At each path to the shore, there was a little wooden boardwalk that led over marsh and dunes to protect the land. As I walked past the bushes and various greens, I heard the crickets announce my arrival. When I got closer, I saw the light breaking over the horizon. The beach was lit like a lantern. I exhaled tension I hadn't realized I was holding.

I kicked off my flip-flops and sat down next to them. I wasn't worried about someone taking them. Sullivan's Island was still a haven, and at this time of day I was practically alone, except for some fish and crabs. The air kissed my cheeks with a salty breeze, and I moved across the cool sand to the water. I knew I had some questions for the ocean to solve. I let my mind open. The water licked my ankles as I walked. I listened to the waves like I was listening for a voice. I wondered if my dad had ever done this. He was from here, so he could've. I'm sure he was here with us when we were little, but I wondered if he loved the beach like I did, or if he was indifferent to it, like my mom.

Had he found answers in the seaside places of this world?

Had he ever consulted these waters about us?

I wondered if Chris coming home really was all about the house.

He cared a lot about finances—neither of us had come from money—and the house was technically an asset. Some gut instinct, or paranoid fear, was telling me that he was alarmed by the mistakes I'd made, because I sometimes was an impulsive spender. I suspected that he knew something was up with the house and was just coming back to make sure his investment was protected.

Or maybe that was my insecurity?

The idea of getting my own place, putting some energy into that, excited me. Ever since it had come up at dinner last night, it had been churning inside of me. But maybe it was just another way of protecting myself, of not trusting Chris? The idea felt right, though. I wouldn't feel so "on hold" in a new space. I needed something that was mine. I liked the idea of painting walls and fluffing a nest.

I pondered being with Chris again, if that was on the table.

We couldn't go back to living together. We would need to start over, with the new versions of ourselves. Maybe we both needed a fresh start. A fresh canvas. I wondered what Bunny's house looked like. Maybe it would have a yard, so I could plant a garden like Gran's! I needed to fully heal before I could plant myself in *his* garden again. That made me chuckle.

I loved a good pun. I didn't have much of a green thumb, but I could try.

I had my camera around my neck and was instinctually taking picture after picture of my feet in the water. I felt still, despite the movement and change in my life, like the tide.

These dreams of far-off islands, lighthouses . . . What were they about? Like something calling me. That postcard my dad had sent, who knew when, with an image of an island in the Atlantic. I kept thinking of this *National Geographic* story I had read as a kid, about a matrilineal family of lighthouse keepers in Iceland, women who wore sealskin coats and were said by the locals to be descended from a Selkie woman. The Icelandic mermaids. Maybe I was like that—too much time on land, forgetting my true mermaid self, having lost my sea skin.

But I wasn't so lost. I knew some things. I had already made up my mind about the house. My quickened heart rate told me that I didn't want our old house anymore. I felt like stretching. I stopped walking and faced the water. I heard a few cries from a seagull probably looking for breakfast. The world was waking up.

I wiggled my toes and let the water wash over my feet, pulling away negativity and stress. I was a strong girl. I could be alone if I needed to. *I have everything in me,* I thought.

When I turned back toward home, the light was violet, and it lit up some shells in the morning rays.

Whatever is coming, I am ready, I can face it on my own, I thought. It was then that I realized that I already had been doing it alone.

~~~~

Back home, I padded across the old soft blue oriental rugs Gran so loved, through the dining room, and into the kitchen. I found Gran starting the coffee machine in her bright green fuzzy slippers and an Eileen West nightgown. She was staring out the window again, daydreaming. I was quiet, and she didn't notice me, so I was able to just watch her for a moment.

I lifted my camera and took her portrait.

Her silver hair was slept on, but in a loose bun pinned back with bobby pins, a style she had worn forever. A few white wisps had escaped the bun and were curling with the day's already brewing humidity. There was a time when hairstyles were more formal. When women would "set" their hair in curlers overnight. I wondered why that trend had died. I had always thought it was a little glamorous. Still not noticing me, Gran moved through the kitchen, grabbing a mug, sugar, the milk, the coffee grounds, and water for the tank, so gracefully she could have been sleepwalking. When she opened the old faded cabinet door to pull out her favorite mug, she did it blindly. Her focus was still on something outside, far away. It brought up my worrying that she might suffer a stroke. She was getting older, my sweet Gran, and anytime she got dreamy my mind thought the worst.

Everyone in the household had a favorite mug, handmade by Gran when she took a pottery class. All her mugs looked alike-ish, but each person had their own color. Like us, all different, though we all went together somehow. Mine was obviously purple; Maggie's was dark olive green, similar to the leaves of her name flower; Gran's was rose red; and my mother's mug was white with silver sparkles. It all made sense to us, and we drank almost exclusively out of our own special cups. Gran had tried to paint our corresponding flowers on them, but though she was creative, she was no artist. The bad art made us treasure them more.

I snapped another picture of her daydreaming. It was sneaky, but she looked beautiful. Standing over the sink, waiting on the coffee, with only the small sink light to illuminate her silhouette. I thought I knew this woman inside and out, but in that light she had an air of mystery.

Maybe we all held secrets, deep in our layers. I had been keeping this thing from Chris, after all. And I resisted the idea of telling him now, telling him about the money that I'd saved.

"Gran, you okay?" I asked her. "Something on your mind?"

"I just miss your grandfather sometimes." She gave me a sad little smile. "He loved this time of day, when the world was blooming awake."

"I miss him, too. I bet he'd like to go on these little walks with me." I shared her smile.

"Yes, I imagine he would." She gave me a squeeze and passed me my mug, now full of hot coffee that was infusing the morning with cheer.

"Do you ever think of finding a new friend?" I asked quietly.

"Oh god, Violet. No!" She huffed and pouted like I was being ridiculous.

"Why not? I mean, it might be nice to have someone to cook for other than Maggie and me. Or, like, go see a movie with or something."

"Are you a matchmaker now?" She gave a little laugh. "You have someone in mind?"

"No, I was just thinking that it might be nice is all." I swirled a little honey into my coffee. "Gran, I think I've been taking up too much space . . . I think it's a good idea for me to live on my own for a while. I think it'll be good for you. You seem worried—"

"Oh, Violet, that's not what I'm worried about."

"But you are worried about something, right?"

"Yes. There's something I need to tell you—"

"What's this?" my mother trilled, floating into the room wearing a sheer tasseled animal-print caftan. I realized that I'd smelled her a few seconds before she arrived. That was some powerful perfume she was wearing. "You girls keeping secrets from me?"

"No," Gran said. She shook her head emphatically.

Wait, *were* we keeping secrets?

"*Buon giorno!*" I said. "No, Mama, just a little morning coffee before I start my day. And speaking of a new day, what does yours hold in store?"

"Oh, I don't know. Lots of laundry as I get ready for the next adventure and write up my last one," she said. "I'll probably be in the office most of the day."

"Well, that's good. Do you know where you're going next?"

"Ricky, my boss, said he was considering sending me out west. Not sure where, but I'm hoping for Montana. Maybe Phoenix. There are a lot of very cute high-end hotels there and some great restaurants."

"Speaking of travel, guess who's just booked a flight?"

"Chris, I hope with a diamond. I'm *gently* suggesting you don't bring up the house until he's on American soil."

"Ha ha," I said, rolling my eyes. But it was a little blow to the heart, her saying that. I stood to leave. "Anyway, I should get to it. Lots of work to do before Chris comes back."

"Good girl. *Ciao, ciao!*" my mother called after me.

I could feel Gran's eyes on me as I left the room. What had she been about to say? I wondered. Or maybe it was my mother's gaze, looking critically at my behind, thinking I really should have been going to the gym more in anticipation of Chris's return . . .

CHAPTER TWELVE

~~~~~

Aly

Sweat dripped down my back. Our air-conditioning was broken again. It was already brutally hot, so hot I wished I could take off my skin, and there wasn't even a whisper of a breeze outside. I had work to do—a brand strategy Violet and I had begun that I wanted to nail down—but the heat was too relentless to allow me to think. I was in the kitchen in the big house, on a call with the repairman, who was over an hour late. The heat wave was knocking out everyone's units. I opened the fridge and stood in front of it. We had to get the AC under control. My dad was in his seventies!

"Oh, Aly, you look absolutely flushed!"

I turned to see that Joyce, my dad's new girlfriend, had entered the kitchen. She was smiling, but her tone told another story.

"But please close that door; your father wouldn't like that."

I loved when she spoke with authority about my father, a man she'd known only a few months. By *loved*, I mean *hated*.

I rolled my eyes and closed the fridge door. "Joyce, aren't you dying in this heat?"

"No, I'm actually a little chilled." Her arms wrapped around her slender shoulders.

"Oh." I resisted the urge to ask if it was because she was a lizard person. She was the type who put the heater on in April.

"Any luck with the repairman?" she asked.

"On hold right now." I switched the phone to speaker and went to my dad's stash of cherry tomatoes, but they weren't there. "Do you know where the tomatoes are?"

"Oh yes, I moved them to the fridge. They last longer that way."

"We like them room temperature and eat them so fast they don't even have time to age," I said lightly.

"Well, I like them cold." She stood in front of the fridge, her back to me.

I couldn't wait to tell Violet of this blasphemy. My mouth opened and closed.

Wait, were we actually fighting about cherry tomatoes?

The repair company finally picked up, and I was relieved to be having a conversation with literally any other human.

"Sorry about the wait, Ms. Knox. We should have a technician out there by three."

"Okay, thank you." I hung up and looked at the clock. It was just noon. "I'm going for a swim," I told Joyce. I rolled my eyes again and left her alone in the kitchen.

As I made my way through the house, bright colors flashed in the corner of one eye. I turned around to face the bookcase and spied two new plastic frames with sea creatures all over them. They reminded me of Lisa Frank, but coastal. So tacky. I picked one up and saw that it was a picture of them kissing in front of a fountain. By *them*, I mean my dad . . . and Joyce. The other neon green one was her with her hand possessively over his chest, clutching his sweater in her claws. Good lord. How long had they even been dating? This woman was marking her territory in a big way. Wasn't she too old for this? I guessed desperation didn't age. I put the frames in a drawer.

I quickly changed into my red bathing suit and braided my hair. I was on the beach in minutes. The sand gave way under my heels as I ran toward the water like I had when I was a little girl. I always did that. I was never *not* excited about jumping in the ocean. I let a wave crash into me and dove through the next. The cool water instantly lowered my body temperature. I came up for air and opened my eyes, spitting out some salt water. I flipped onto my back and let the waves hold me for a moment.

As the tide gently rocked me back and forth, I thought about my dad. Was he happy? Truly? I knew he had to miss my mom, and I knew he didn't want to be lonely. I didn't want that for him either, but I was finding Joyce really hard. She was so unlike my mom, cold and harsh, whereas my mom had been described as "human sunshine." My mom was super successful, as was Joyce, but Mom was generous with her warmth and power. Joyce was always inserting her opinion where it didn't belong and constantly putting everyone on the spot by doing petty, transparent, pathetic things like asking people about their credentials. I guessed my dad saw something in her that I didn't.

Or maybe he was settling? He had made a few comments about being tired of the dating game. Apparently, this had been going on awhile, the dating; he'd been sneaking around and not telling me about it long before he told me that day in the kitchen. Joyce, it turned out, was one of his first dates once he started to date again.

I had suspected that this day would come, him having another significant relationship. He was a handsome man, after all, and kind, so why wouldn't a woman want to be his companion? I just wished he had chosen someone more . . . fun. The void of my mother's death was an absence of joy. She'd had a riot of a life, and now I felt like I was in the letdown stage that followed any really good party.

Maybe Joyce sensed that somehow . . . that she'd come on the scene too late? Maybe she was just nervous around me? The water had cooled my hot head, and I realized I should probably give her more of a chance. She was spending more and more time with us and clearly was wild about my dad, so at least she had good taste.

Swimming helped me figure out questions I didn't know I had. I swam until I felt my muscles get sore. When I was finished, I toweled off my hair and decided to grab a Diet Coke from Dad's outside fridge. He always had them stocked. I checked my phone for emails. My Google calendar reminded me that I had made a reservation for mah-jongg with Holy Mahj at the Charleston Place that night. After some ladies had given me and Violet a tip at the nail salon, I discovered mah-jongg had taken over in Charleston. There seemed to be posts every day on my Instagram about girls playing together at mah-jongg parties. I thought the trend might give my Insta some new content, and I loved the Charleston Place Hotel downtown. It was so pretty and had the best events. I'd have to select the perfect outfit. As I came into the house, I paused to google-map the distance, see how long it would take me to get there.

Just then Joyce appeared. She made a face and sighed heavily.

"What's wrong, Joyce?"

"Nothing, it's just you're dripping all over our floors."

"Our?"

"Yes, *our*."

She definitely meant *your*, but I'd let it slide. "O-kay."

"You know, Aly, your father and I are getting more serious, and unfortunately I find it very upsetting sharing with another woman . . ." She smiled like this was a joke, but what she said next had a serious bite. "I'm *very* territorial."

I took a short inhale. I agreed with her self-assessment but couldn't recall ever having used that word to describe a woman. A dog, maybe, but not a woman.

"Joyce, I really value your honesty, but this is the family home."

She nodded like a patient teacher trying another tactic to explain a simple concept to a slow student. "I'm sure you'd have trouble with any woman coming in here."

Whoa, this did not feel like it was going anywhere good. "That's not true! I look at it as a bonus relationship with a woman from an older generation!" Did that sound like a dig? I didn't mean it that way—did I? "And, you know, I really like living close to my dad. He's been encouraging me with work, and I'm going to redo the apartment to promote my brand."

"Oh, Aly. You need your own *space* to work in. Would you want *me* working in your home?"

"What do you do?"

"I'm a Harvard-educated lawyer, Aly."

"Uh, well, if you need to use my house to hold court and prosecute a criminal, then I'll let you."

"Aly." God, it was awful when she said my name.

"Joyce. What you do and what I do are very different. You and I are different."

She smirked and said, "Well, I guess we all need to decide if this is your house, your father's house, or the home I am making with your father."

"Not to be rude, but I don't think that's your decision, Joyce. I think that's up to me and my dad. You don't live here; you're in *my* house."

Just then my dad came around the corner.

"Minnow, this is *my* house."

"I mean it's the family home, Daddy."

"It's *my* home," he repeated.

I felt like I was in a belfry and the bell had been rung.

I looked over at Joyce, who had a smirk on her face, and she exited the room like a cat, swishing her butt as though it were a tail. On her way out, she straightened the framed pictures—the ones I had most definitely put in a drawer but that were now right back where she wanted them. My dad watched with a face that did not in any obvious way communicate disgust. I felt sick.

"What's happening here, Dad?" I asked him, feeling the room start to move.

"Listen, Aly, as a favor to me, I'm asking you, please, I think it would be a good idea for you to think about when you might get your own space. That could be good for both of us. Help your dad out." He cleared his throat. I could tell this was making him uncomfortable. But somehow, I also knew these weren't his words.

So, Joyce had my dad by the balls.

"I live over the garage! This is a huge house! She doesn't even live here!"

"I know, you're right, it is totally big enough . . . but I want to keep the peace. Plus, you don't want to live with your old man. I'm okay now. I promise. You are going to step in for your mom's brand. It's going to take off. This could be very good timing." He smiled, and I felt tears prick at my eyes and my heartbeat in my ears.

I glanced over at the shelf where my mother's cookbooks lived. *Had* lived. They were gone now.

All of a sudden, my safe place, my mother's dream, was being snatched away from me because of this . . . *viper*. How was he attracted to *her*? How could he move on from my wonderful, talented, funny, kind mom to this? It was blasphemous. It was sacrilegious. It was disgusting.

"Well, this chat was lovely, but I guess I've done enough damage to your floors, so I'm going to change into some clothes. I have work to do."

When I got to my apartment, my heart was galloping. Who did this woman think she was? I was sure my dad didn't align with this; he was the one who'd suggested I move in! God, next thing I knew she would be taking measurements and repainting the house!

I needed a good shower. I stepped into my bathroom and tossed one of those shower steamers that smelled like lavender on the floor of the shower. I needed to relax and think clearly. I turned the water to a temperature that could only be described as that of the flames of hell itself. Once I got in there and stood under the water, I felt myself almost start to cry. I loathed confrontation, and I was embarrassed. Especially in my own kitchen. The same space in which I had cooked countless meals alongside my mother. The kitchen with the counter-tops that she taught me how to roll out pastry on, that we used for making Christmas cookies. I squirted some shampoo into my palm, applied it to my head, and started to scrub. Then I got really mad.

I thought, *How dare she speak to me like that?* Telling me what to do. Trying to manipulate me into moving out. Over my dead body . . . over my mother's!

No, I wasn't going to fall into her trap. I wasn't going to let her take over. Not my father, not my family, and not this house. She could pee on every single wall, but it would never be hers. Ever. I needed to talk to my dad, and quickly. Joyce had messed with the wrong girl. As soon as my dad saw the real her, I was sure she'd be history.

Thank goodness I had a competitive activity lined up in my social calendar.

I needed to do something with my foaming rage.

CHAPTER THIRTEEN

~~~~~~

Violet

The day finally arrived. I had been waiting for so long to see Chris, and I guessed I had thought the sky would be brighter, or the birds would be singing arias or something, but instead it was just a normal day. Maybe I didn't believe it was actually happening, or maybe I wouldn't feel anything until I saw him. I thought that if I could just get my eyes on him, if I could smell him again, then I'd know. But what if I didn't feel anything? What if he wasn't attracted to me anymore? What if I or both of us had changed too much to come back around?

Then I really would be all alone.

I was a blender of emotions.

Chris had sent me his flight information, and we'd had more than a few hours on the phone going back and forth about what this all meant. But in the end, we just agreed that the only way to look at it all was "We'll see when we see each other." I still hadn't told him about renting out our place, but I did make it clear that I wasn't living there anymore. That I was at Gran's, helping her out, but was figuring out a new situation, and we could revisit cohabitation in the future. Chris could stay in the house, but I wouldn't be moving in with him. I had said it loud and clear, probably two times more than necessary.

And I insisted I'd still be paying half the mortgage. It was only fair. Plus, then there would be no financial argument he could make about me moving back in . . .

And plus, there was that money I had tucked away from the house rentals and wasn't planning on telling him about.

I blew out my hair, straightened it, put on a full face of makeup, and chose a black shift dress that I knew was flattering. I put on my red stacked-heel sandals and my grandmother's gold bracelet, which she had given me for my birthday last year. It was a simple look, but classic. I needed to feel confident when I saw him. I added a swipe of red lip gloss and spritzed on some perfume for good measure.

On the way to the airport, I played some of my favorite girl anthems.

I needed to feel less nervous, and every mile closer to Charleston International Airport gave my stomach another rotation, but no amount of Beyoncé or Kelly Clarkson was helping. I turned off the radio and called Jim through the speaker in my car.

"Today's the day!" I told him when he picked up on the second ring.

"OMG, is he in the car? I'm going to throw up!" he squealed.

"No, I'm on the way to pick him up," I said.

"Are you wearing those red shoes? The strappy ones that look like they belong in *Vogue* but you bought at T.J.Maxx?"

"Of course I am, and lip gloss to match," I said.

"Good girl. Shave your legs?"

"Jimmy!"

"Please, I know you did. Can't have a proper reunion without clean stems."

"James, I am shocked and clutching my pearls. I will not do the deed with him the first time we've breathed the same air in months!" I gasped, then giggled. "Plus, I don't think I remember how, anyway."

He laughed. "Pretty sure it's like riding a bike."

"Let's hope."

"So, you *did* shave."

"Duh."

"There's my girl. Perfume?"

"Chanel No. 5."

"Kill him." I could hear him smile through the phone.

Now I did relax a little. Joking with Jimmy, I felt strong. It was good having him back in town. We'd fallen right back into our old closeness.

And he was right: I did like it, the whole ritual of glowing up to fetch my man.

Chris and I would be okay. Or we wouldn't. Only one way to find out. "Eh, whatever," I said into the phone.

"Breezy. I like it."

"Well, the one that cares the least controls the most."

"Is that what you're telling yourself?"

"James, it's my motto."

"Oh my god, it *is* . . . ! Stop trying not to care! Violet, you have to allow yourself to be *vulnerable*."

"I'd rather go with breezy."

"Y'all almost had a kid together," Jimmy said gently. "We are past breezy."

"I'm nervous, Jimmy. What if I'm just hanging on to the old best memories of him? What if all the best old memories are just fantasies?"

"Well, that's normal. We all romanticize the past. Just be careful. Everyone deserves a second chance, but also remember that he didn't step up when you needed him the most. Go slow."

"Thanks. Okay, I'm here. I'm going to park. Love you, Jimmy."

"Love you, too. Good luck!"

I found a spot right by the elevator, thank God. I was sure Chris would have a ton of luggage. I took a few deep breaths and strode into the airport. We had said we'd meet at baggage claim, and when I arrived at the big silver carousel, I checked his incoming flight on the monitor. His flight from Atlanta was on time. I would see him any minute. My heart started to race as I looked around at the people exiting the gates and greeting their waiting loved ones. Big hugs between family members, kids running into their parents' or grandparents' arms. I always loved airports, because everyone was about to go on or was returning from an adventure. But as the minutes passed, there was no sight of him. His flight had landed about thirty minutes ago. Odd.

I started to sweat. What if he had never gotten on the plane? What if he had changed his mind?

All that bravado with Jimmy, it left me now. My neck got hot. I pulled my hair up into a ponytail. I walked around the carousel. Maybe he was waiting on the other side? I thought I saw him and then realized it was a much older business type, not really Chris-like at all.

More and more bags came out, and then they started to slow, and more people left.

Then I felt a tap on my shoulder. I spun around, and there he was.

My Christopher Charles, towering over me, in a wrinkled suit and with a sly smile.

He was beautiful. He took my breath away. I tilted my head up toward his and allowed my whole face to break out in a smile.

"Hey, gorgeous," he said, and pulled me in for a hug.

"Chris!" I whispered. I took a short inhale, let his massive arms swallow me, and breathed in his familiar scent. This was my guy, and he was home, and everything was going to be all right.

I pulled away, and he cupped my face in his giant warm hands.

"God, you're more beautiful than I remember. It's so good to see you, Violet."

"I can't believe you're finally here," I said, tears threatening. I looked into his eyes and realized they were about to spill over with tears.

"I was going to wait. I was going to take a few days to settle in, but

Violet . . . I love you still. Seeing you—I just *know*. I don't ever want to live without you again. I was a fool. Please forgive me."

"I was a fool to let you go, Chris. I love you, too." Happy tears spilled down our cheeks, and he pulled me in for a world-stopping kiss. As his lips pressed into mine, I felt my heart soften. It was as though in an instant all the damage had begun to heal. All the loss, all the heartbreak, all the fights and harsh words. Forgiven. I had waited so long for this and hadn't known I desperately needed to hear it.

"Let's start over. From the very beginning."

"Okay." He paused a beat. Grinned. "Hey, I'm Chris. Can I have your number?"

I laughed and pulled his neck down for another kiss.

We stayed there in each other's embrace for a few minutes, not caring that we were drawing attention. Someone whistled at us, and we pulled away.

"Let me get a good look at you." Chris took my hand and twirled me around. "My girl. Perfect as always."

"Well, I'm glad you like what you see," I said nervously. "It's been a while."

"You are my ideal. Let's get out of here."

We took all three of his giant roll-on bags to my car. I insisted on driving because he was beyond jet-lagged. I turned on the radio, and he held my free hand, gave it a squeeze, and promptly fell asleep. I liked that—how easy it was, like we were already a couple, confident and relaxed together.

My phone buzzed in my cup-holder. At a stoplight I picked it up to see a text from Aly inviting me over to her house for a party this Monday. I immediately accepted. Her home was on the water right on the beach. It would be beautiful. It was going to be nice for Aly to meet Chris finally; she would get to put a face to a name.

We pulled up to what used to be our shared home in West Ashley. The giant magnolia tree in the front yard was a beauty. Maybe we could plant another one to mark a new beginning . . . or was I getting way ahead of myself? *Take it slow*, Jimmy had said.

I gently shook Chris awake. "Hey, you. We're home."

He opened his eyes and saw me. "What a face to wake up to. This is home? We're home?"

I gave him a smile. "Yes, well, *you're* home. I'm staying at Gran's, remember?"

"Violet, stay with me. Just tonight. I want to be next to you," he said in his sleepy voice.

"Chris, we have to go slow. I want to give this a shot. I'm not ready for that yet."

"We don't have to do anything; I just want to hold you."

I felt my skin prickle. I wanted that, too. More than anything. But I had to stick to my plans. There was so much love and history between us. We had shared an unspeakable loss; it was the kind of thing that would test even the strongest relationship. At the very core of us, though, we were good. And that goodness had to be protected, nurtured back to full strength. If we wanted any chance of salvaging this, I had to be strong.

"I'd like that to happen, too, but I know us. If we start just snuggling, it won't end with our clothes on."

He gave me a devilish smile. Ugh, why was the wrong choice so very tempting?

"Okay, Vi," he said, putting that wolfish grin away. "You call the shots. You're right. We are worth this. Do you want to come in at all?"

"Yes, I do, but I actually have an early day tomorrow," I said as I got out of the car. "I left you something in your fridge for dinner."

"Tell me it's lasagna."

"Of course it is. I remember what you like."

"God, you're so good to me. I remember what you like, too, baby." He gave me a significant look, and I felt a shiver.

It had been a long time since I had been touched. "Chris . . ."

"Okay, just one more kiss, then?"

"Okay."

We stood outside the door of the home we'd once shared together, and the weight of the change of our situation felt heavy, but hopeful. He took a step closer, and a rush of desire flooded through me as I looked into his eyes and saw them take me in. Every single inch. I shivered again, despite it being super humid. He took my hand and pulled me closer to him. I let out a sigh. He ran his finger against the inside of my wrist and traced the inside of my arm, ending by cupping my face and gazing into my eyes.

I closed my eyes. "Hi," I said, making myself say the words. "My name's Violet, what's yours?"

After a beat he said, "Chris. Chris Charles. And I'd love to take you on a date sometime."

I stepped back from him. "Nice to meet you, Chris Charles. I'd like that, too."

When I opened my eyes, he was smiling at me, and I could tell he wasn't going to push me anymore. He offered his pinkie, and I looped mine with his. "Fresh start?"

I nodded. "Fresh start."

"Okay, I'll pick you up for a date soon. Stay tuned for the details."

"I'm looking forward to that," I said, and did a slow, confident walk back to my car. I was feeling buoyant, excited by this game we were playing. The game of starting over. And I wanted him to have a nice eyeful of what he'd been missing.

~~~~~

The week went along swimmingly. I was excited about my date with Chris—a real date, like you'd have with someone who was courting you. But at the same time it was Chris: we were familiar with each other, I already knew I liked him. The idea of moving into Bunny's was grounding. We'd scoped it out, and Bunny had agreed to give us a friendly rate for a six-month rental. I spent the morning working on some editing for a cool wedding that had been downtown at Lowndes Grove. I was feeling my independent streak. But I guessed I was feeling other contradictory things, too. As I clicked through the pictures of the bride, surrounded by her loved ones, my mind slipped into fantasy planning . . .

Once I was happy with my work, I made a few calls and took a break to help Gran knock out a few projects around the house. A loose cabinet door that needed tightening; a few lightbulbs that had burned out. Things I'd been meaning to do for months that seemed to have a deadline now that I was readying myself to move out any day. Then, feeling frisky, we polished her silver.

"Are we having a party, Gran?"

"No, life *is* a party. That's why I want to start using the good stuff. If I wait around for the perfect occasion, my mother's silver will never be used."

"This seems like a big switch from the woman who wanted me to use paper napkins the other day."

"Oh, hush, that's just being smart. Look what happened to your momma!"

"Gran, you seem like you have laid down some burden."

She sighed. "I haven't. I have been avoiding it like you wouldn't believe. I just promised that I would by the end of today," she said. Then she took me by the hand and brought me to the wall by the stairs with all the portraits and pictures of our family. "Okay," she said, and took a deep breath.

"Gran?" I whispered. It was still humid as hell, I could feel the pressure on my skull, but the temperature seemed to have dropped. I was hot and chilled and sick-feeling.

Gran pressed her lips together. Her eyebrows were knotted. She wrung her hands, and then she said, "I am going to ask you to just . . . keep an open mind here. There are reasons, and I'll tell you everything, but here's the lord's truth. I've been keeping a secret from you and your sister. A big one. And from your mother, too."

"Gran, you're scaring me," I said, feeling my heartbeat pick up.

"I bet. I'm sorry, but it's time I came clean. It's beyond time."

"Came clean? Gran? You have always been straight with us."

"Look. Violet. That time in the hospital. I almost died. It made me look at my life and my past choices clearly. Or at least more clearly. I always have made decisions about you, Maggie, and Lily based on the best, safest information I had at the time. I'm not perfect. Sometimes I made the wrong decision. But I wanted to keep you three safe. I love you all so much."

"Gran! I know, we all know you do," I tried to reassure her.

She let out a long sigh, and I could see she was trembling a little. Her hand shook slightly as it reached for the picture of my great-grandmother Daisy. The one that was always a little crooked. The one that had been a little *too* straight the other night, when I had found that postcard tucked between the frame and the wall. Now she slid the frame all the way to the side, and I saw a little dug-out hole. In it were two thick stacks of postcards and letters. They were tied together with string. She took them both out and handed them to me. I stared at them and then at her.

"Gran? What are these?"

Her eyes were searching and deep. "Please, don't hate me forever, Violet. I am so sorry."

I flipped over the stacks and saw that they were all from a man named Scott.

Scott.

Scott . . . Jones?

My father. How could he have written so many in the short time our lives had overlapped? Impossible, and yet . . . The one on top still had its stamp, its postmark. My vision was a little blurry, but I could read well enough to see that this postcard was only six months old.

"He—Scott—is . . . ?"

Gran nodded.

I took a few steps backward and tried to center myself. My mind was spinning, and I struggled to not let the room go with it. I went around the corner and into the kitchen, sitting down hard on one of the kitchen's barstools. My mind was struggling to make sense of it, and I really had no idea what the rest of my body was doing.

My father was alive.

CHAPTER FOURTEEN

~~~~~

Rose

At the time, I had to. There's no other way to spin this story. It was necessary. I knew that eventually the truth would surface, but I figured the girls would be older by then. I was the mother and head of this little female tribe of mine. So, the hard decisions fell on my shoulders. I separated my head and heart and made a call to serve the greater good of this family. This was back in the nineties. I knew I could put my feelings and emotions aside and hurt them a little to save them a whole lot of hurt over time. After his motorcycle accident, and a stint in rehab, I knew he was too unsteady. I ordered Scott to stay out of our lives.

He agreed, so long as he could write to the girls. I took that deal, but I never promised I would give the cards to them. At least not immediately.

Now you might think, wasn't that implied?

But you might also think: they were too young to understand, and the point was that I was protecting their childhoods, so wasn't it my responsibility to go on protecting that a little bit longer?

So, I hid the cards and made the decision to tell them Scott was dead.

Because that seemed to me the only way they would never go looking for him.

I know now that it was wrong. Children shouldn't be denied a relationship with a parent. And it wasn't my decision to make. But I made it, the way women in my family have always had to make hard decisions. Most women in most families, if you ask me.

And now I had to face the consequences of my actions. I truly thought at the time I was protecting them from a lifetime of heartbreak. As a mother, all I wanted to do was keep the fox away from my chickens, at least as much as possible.

Back then, Scott was a broken man. He and my daughter, Lily, had gotten into a seriously toxic relationship way too young. Stupidity and carelessness resulted in Maggie and derailed my daughter from her lifelong dreams. I was angry at both of them for being so stupid, but once Maggie came into this world, and Scott proposed, I thought that, despite their youth, they were doing the right thing by getting married. Age is the best teacher, though, since marriage isn't always the right thing when a baby comes into the world. I know that now, because it was the worst thing for those two.

So many mistakes followed that first mistake. So many vices. So many times things spiraled out of control. So they broke up, he took off, and the girls moved in with my husband and me. I thought the problem was solved. It wasn't. Lily was heartbroken. She was convinced she'd let the love of her life go. She was so angry with the kids all the time, mainly Maggie.

A short time later, my daughter got in her car and disappeared for over a week. She didn't tell us where she was, what was going on, or when she was coming home, if ever. A phone call came in the middle of the night from Arizona. It was Scott. Lily and he had been on a bender, and she had overdosed. Then she was in an accident. She was alive; he thought I should know.

Eddie flew out the next morning to bring her home.

I was wild with fear for my girls' futures, and I made a deal with

Scott that night. I said I would give him some money and I told Lily he was gone. I lied. God help me. I told her he was dead.

I couldn't—I *wouldn't*—have him back. Destroying my grandchildren's lives.

When she returned to Sullivan's Island to the girls, I told Maggie and Violet the same lie. She was sad but took the news better than I had expected. Lily, not so much. But her life did improve. She still battled demons, but she came to work in the restaurant, and having structure was good for her. The girls' lives were happy. They were safe.

There were moments that I wanted to tell them the truth. Scott kept up his end of the bargain, communicating through postcards. He was diligent and sent them often. I read them, and I couldn't bring myself to destroy them, so I put them in a stack in a hole behind my mother's picture on the wall. Sometimes I would look at the photograph, thinking that she looked like she stood with me; other times it was like she was guarding something she disapproved of. But what was done was done. I honestly thought Scott would forget them.

But he did not.

Scott had never filed for divorce. Sometimes that pulled at me. I mean, he never had been that responsible about paperwork or legalities, but he was popular with women, and I guess I had always assumed that would be what blew up my lie. That day never came, though.

And then it did.

He had met someone about a year ago and written me an email. I was scared. I didn't respond. He wrote another. When I ignored that one, he just showed up on Sullivan's Island. He was getting married and finally needed the divorce, and he wasn't going to be ignored.

CHAPTER FIFTEEN

∿∿∿

Violet

I tried to go about my day, get back to work, pack up my clothes, but I couldn't seem to do anything. My mind was crazy. Where was my father? How could I contact him? I needed to read those postcards, but I was too distracted to do it yet. I put them in a drawer in my bedroom. I needed to get out.

It was 4:30. That was something to hang on to. And I had a text from Jimmy.

It seemed like it had been sent from another planet.

A planet where dead fathers stayed dead.

Hey there, princess. Meet me for a drink? Been dying to
try the Post House. The chef there is a cutie!

His message made me smile, despite everything. Of course he wanted to go to a restaurant purely because he had a crush on the chef!

I was about to tell him it was a bad time.

But the idea of talking about this situation with someone not directly involved, like Chris and Maggie were, was appealing.

Yes. I have some major news. Could use some feedback.
Meet you at the bar in forty-five? Can I invite Aly?
I might need reinforcements. And it's time y'all met.

Yes of course! Perfect! xo.

I called Aly on the way over. I didn't tell her anything; I just made it sound like a casual meetup, which was maybe unfair, but I honestly couldn't figure out how to tell her what had just landed on me, at least not over the phone. She was thrilled, though, to finally be meeting Jimmy. It was going to be nice to get them together, but I also needed input from both of them on my father.

I rode over to Old Village in Mount Pleasant on my old bike, taking it slow and being cautious. I definitely had less than all my wits about me. Biking through that part of town did calm me a bit, though. It was such a charming pocket of Charleston, and right on the water. I pedaled up over the Ben Sawyer Bridge and looked out, watching boats and people enjoying themselves. I spied a fat gray pelican sitting on a wooden post. His feathers against the sparkling cobalt blue water were stunning. He caught sight of something delicious and dove in after it, sending up a spray of water behind him.

And now my thoughts were dark again.

My father.

I wondered what my father would know about that. Was nature the kind of thing we'd have talked about, if he'd been around? I'd always felt that on the water, I was close to everyone who had come before me.

I continued down Pitt Street, passing the old pharmacy with its soda fountain bar. The Post House Inn shone like a bright white stone. It was one of those "in" spots in Charleston. It had changed hands a few years ago, and the renovations reminded me of the set of a Wes Anderson film. I found parking for my bike right next to a golf cart.

I pushed the door open and was greeted by a sweet young girl.

"Hey there! I'm Naomi, welcome to the Post House! Do you have a reservation?"

"No, I'm just meeting a friend at the bar."

"Okay! We've got room! You came at the right time! Try our spicy margarita."

She led me around the corner to the bright front-room dining space in front of the bar. It had an old-world vibe with new-world finishes, the 1930s combined with now. The giant wooden bar wrapped around the left side of the room, and in the center of the wall hung a beautiful colorful painting that could only be by Mickey Williams, a local artist and, in my opinion, a genius. No one captured Charleston like he did. I scanned the room and found my Jimmy, elegantly nestled into one of the velvet chairs at a small round table by the window, sipping a glass of water.

"My love!" Jimmy said. Our eyes met, and he rose to give me a hug hello.

"Jimmy darling! It's been too long!" I said, matching his drawl. This was our thing. We always greeted each other like old Hollywood movie stars. Had been doing that since the third grade, when Jimmy fell in love with Katharine Hepburn (though he soon realized he was actually more in love with Humphrey Bogart, or Cary Grant, and really just liked Katharine's jaw, voice, and costumes).

"Violet, my flower, can I get you a drink? A wine spritzer?"

I was sort of glad we had the melodramatic tone set already, because there was really no other way to say what I had to say. "Jimmy, I'm going to need something a little harder than a spritz," I whispered. "I just found out something shocking. My father is alive."

His mouth opened and closed a few times, and his eyebrows knit together. Then he said, "Gin it is. Hold that thought." He gestured to our server, pressed his fingers to his temples, did an actorly voice warm-up sort of thing. "What on earth?"

I started to tell the story, but then our server arrived. She was blond with the brightest smile, warm and friendly. I instantly liked her despite her interrupting my tale.

"Good evening, and welcome to the Post House. I'm Kelly, and I'll be taking care of y'all this evening. Can I get you something to drink?"

"We need, and I can't stress *need* enough, three martinis. Gin, please, shaken, light on the vermouth—dirty, but still a lady—three olives."

"I love how you order that," Kelly said, marking her pad.

"Well, darling, if I say, 'extra dirty,' it comes out like swamp water, and if I say 'dirty,' it's never enough. 'Lady' captures it perfectly."

"You capture everything perfectly, Jimmy!" I said, laying my head on his shoulder for a little extra ballast.

Just then Aly walked in. She was wearing a blue-and-white-striped button-down dress casually belted with a leather strap the exact color of her sandals. Her gold hoops glistened in the soft lighting of the bar. She looked at home here, but then again, that girl could look like she belonged anywhere. She had on lipstick, and I wondered if she was aiming to impress Jimmy.

"Hey, girl!" she said brightly at me, and then turned to greet Jim. "Hi! It's so great to meet you! Gosh, I feel like I'm with a celebrity!"

"You are," Jim said, giving her a cold stare.

"Oh, I . . ." Aly's smile dropped away.

"Just kidding, gorgeous. I wanted to tease you a little." He pursed his lips. "I guess I'm slightly jealous over your new friendship with my Violetta."

"Hey, I don't want to step on toes," she said, looking relieved. "The more the merrier!"

Kelly was still standing there, patiently waiting on our order, so I asked, "Hey, do y'all want to split a few things? I'm starving and need at least a bite of the famous burger."

"Fine," Jimmy said, "but I want my own fries, and a side of mayo, please."

"Same!" Aly clapped her hands. "French fries are my love language."

"Now I know why you like her."

Once Kelly left, I looked over at my friends. One had always been there for me, and the other was new but felt like she would always be there for me, too. Seeing their faces made me feel slightly more confident that I would sort out my life despite this wild monkey wrench having been thrown into it. They would help me. I was obviously stressed-out, and anxious . . . and, well, feeling all the things . . . but seeing Jimmy, and seeing him and Aly joking and getting to know each other, slowed my racing pulse. Jimmy was a beautiful man. He was so elegant and reminded me of an old movie star, like the ones he idolized. There was no better heart on the planet, and no one more loyal.

"Okay, first things first: your nails look great!" Jimmy said.

"Why, thank you," Aly said, dangling her fingers with their fresh coat of lemon. "Speaking of which, I should wash my hands . . ."

After Aly excused herself, Jimmy asked me if Aly knew the secret, not knowing if we should pick up our conversation. I told him she didn't, so he waited until she came back and then I gave them both the headlines. It sounded crazy. I almost couldn't believe it myself. I was glad I had said it out loud to people I loved, though. For a moment, we sat in silence, taking in the magnitude of it, and then Kelly returned with—God bless her—three beautiful cut-crystal coupes containing ice-cold martinis.

"Have y'all dined with us before?" she asked, laying down our menus.

"No, this is my first time," Jim said. "I am back for the summer. Rumor has it the chef is a genius! Saw his handsome picture in the James Beard newsletter last month."

"Yes! He was nominated for Best New Chef for the Southeast," Kelly gushed. "Fingers crossed he'll win."

"So, Kelly, tell us, is he single?" Jimmy wiggled his eyebrows.

"No, Chef Carmine is happily married and has two beautiful children," Kelly said, sorely disappointed.

"Rats! Well, please tell him he has a big fan in the dining room," Jim said through a pout.

"Will do. Tonight, he's got some amazing specials to delight y'all!"

"Oh, I need a little delight. Let's have it!" I said, my mouth watering as I remembered the last time I was there, when Chef Carmine made a delicious roasted pepper dish over whipped house-made ricotta. If my life was going to be completely turned on its head, the best course of action I could think of was eating well.

"Tonight, Chef Carmine has two specials. He has an heirloom tomato salad, sourced from Ambrose Farm on Johns Island, over house-pulled mozzarella with a salsa verde and a twenty-year-old balsamic vinegar," Kelly read off her notes. "He also has a braised pork shank over creamy polenta, made with goat cheese and fresh herbs. That is served with a Madeira wine reduction and some rainbow carrots braised in orange juice and honey."

"Wow. Well, what's your favorite thing?" Aly asked Kelly.

"Honestly, those specials. I always try and snag the last order. And, not to be basic, but we do have the best burger in Charleston. Little Jack's is pretty good, but I love ours the most!"

Jim went ahead and spoke for us. "Okay, so let's stick with our order of the burger, and let's have one of each special. The tomato salad and the pork shank. I do love some polenta, which to me is just fancy grits."

I relaxed into the hunter green velvet club chair. I felt like I was in a bubble. Being with Jimmy was like that for me. I always felt protected and taken care of. I hoped Aly was okay with someone else ordering for her.

"Sorry, Aly, is that okay? Jim and I always just order . . ."

"God, yes. Please. I'm so tired of making all these little decisions. It's nice to have a handsome man do something for me!" Aly's flattery made Jimmy beam. That boy was a sucker for a compliment.

When Kelly was gone, Jimmy picked up his drink, and we clinked our glasses. "To new chapters, new friends, and daddy issues."

"Thank God you are here, Jim," I said, sipping on the perfect martini.

"So, back to the father situation . . ." Jim hinted.

I filled them in on everything Gran had told me. Our food came, and we devoured it between my monologue and the good questions Jimmy peppered me with. Aly made a few key points, too. The two of them on the opposite side of the table looked like executives trying to hatch out a business plan.

"So, what now?" he asked, mouth open, eyes wide.

"I . . . I want to find him, I think. I want to know him; he obviously wants to know me, too. Right? I mean, why keep sending those postcards if he wanted nothing to do with us? But also, how am I ever going to . . ."

"Forgive Gran? How's Maggie taking this? Furiously?"

"She doesn't know yet. Mom either. I mean, Maggie will be furious, and so will my mom once she finds out . . . She almost married another man! All this time she's still been *married*."

"Wait, oh my god. I would be furious!" Aly said.

"I mean, was Gran ever going to tell her? Her whole marriage could have been annulled and never valid! I'm shocked. Or maybe she was just putting it off . . . Who knows how many times she *almost* told us?" I said.

"Well, I've known Grandma Rose a long time," Jimmy said, signaling Kelly for more martinis as she passed by. "The one truth I know in my bones about that woman is that she loves her family. If she made a decision like this, I cannot imagine that it was easy or that she didn't really think it through. Good ole Rose protects her flock."

"That's true," I admitted, and Aly nodded in agreement.

"That being said, I can imagine how it could have seemed like a good idea that then spiraled out of control. Perhaps she made this call and then thought that she would deal with it later? Or that life would take care of him? I mean, for sure the statistics weren't in his favor, with an addiction like his. I don't know. I feel like she probably put it off, waiting for the right moment to tell your momma."

"Is it bad that I'm not angry at her?" I asked.

"Well." Jimmy pulled a face. "You're not angry *yet*."

"I don't think I'll ever be. Maggie will be for sure, and that's fair. But as the family peacekeeper, I kind of get it."

"What do you mean, Violet?" Aly prodded.

"Well, if I was a mother, and my child was in a bad way with a partner that she would never leave, and I knew in my bones that them staying together would only eventually or ultimately hurt her, I would do everything I could think of to remove him, children or not."

"That's very wise of you. But don't you wish you knew your dad?" Aly asked.

"Yeah, of course, but maybe, in a small way . . . it's better that I didn't? I'd like to know him now, I think I could handle it, whoever he is . . . but I wouldn't want a childhood full of disappointment from *both* of my parents. Mom was enough. And even if he writes beautiful words, he might still be a bad guy. Do I want to know him?"

"Maybe it was all your grandmother could handle, too," Aly added. "I mean, if she took on you and your sister, and then had to also take care of your mother . . . She's her daughter, but your father she didn't owe a thing to."

"That's true . . . but the postcards. That is the part that I hate."

"Why do you hate it?" Jim asked.

"They just seem so passive-aggressive," I said. "Sort of weak sauce, you know?"

"I mean, the man wasn't going to burst into your life again when he had been told to stay away," Jim added.

"I don't know . . . Aren't we worth causing a scene over?"

"Vi, you have no idea how the initial conversation went. I am sure your gran put up a massive wall," Aly said.

"Maggie, she always wanted a dad," I said. "I was so young when he left that I don't really remember him. This is all I've ever known. Maggie had him for a little while. So, it's always been different for her."

"So, where does he live? Are you going to reach out?" Jimmy asked.

"I don't know. I'm sure it's all in the postcards," I said.

"It's very romantic, sending postcards. Old-fashioned, I mean. He could have found you another way, like Facebook, or Instagram, or by picking up the phone," Aly added.

"I guess, but . . ." I shrugged. It was all feeling so speculative and sad. "I also feel like he didn't want to intrude?"

"It would kill me not to know my children," Aly said. "I mean, I have a good family, and we're all so close. Secrets don't last very long in our house, so I see why you are a little spooked."

Jim gave me a long look. "What if you don't like what you find?" he said.

"But what if I do?"

"Okay. What about the others?"

"You mean Gran, my mom, and Maggie?" I said. "I don't know. Some part of me wants to just think about my own needs first for once. Also . . . I mean, this felt like big news this morning, and now it seems like nothing, but I want to move out."

"You do?" Aly asked.

I spent the next few minutes explaining to them about Bunny's rental downtown, until Kelly returned asking if we wanted a third round.

"No, honey, we need to move to wine if we are going to stay upright," Jim said. "I think just a nice Chardonnay. Maybe the Simi?"

Once we were alone again, Jimmy leaned in, elbows on the table. "So, I have a confession."

"Now you spill the tea. Let's have it."

"I got fired from my show." He glanced away, made a vicious little hand gesture. "Well, not *fired* fired . . . but they killed off my character. Got the script last week. I film my last show Wednesday . . ."

"Oh, Jimmy!" I said. "I'm so sorry!"

"So, what's next? Auditions?" Aly asked.

Kelly came and went, leaving the crispest, most perfect golden Chardonnay in our wineglasses. Jimmy seemed to settle. "Actually," he said, "I think I might take a break?"

"Oh?" I exchanged a glance with Aly, who already seemed to understand the momentousness of this.

"I want to do more theater. I think I need to get better, and the real actors are onstage every single night. I need to return to my roots."

"I have a wild idea . . ." Aly said.

"Move in with Violet and work at Charleston Stage or the Dock Street Theatre?" he blurted.

"Yeah! Oh my god, we'd have so much fun!" I said. "I mean . . . Wait, so you're not here for just the summer, then?"

"Right. At least a year. I need a New York City pause. Find out about the house, and we can go from there."

"Done and done." We clinked our wineglasses. It seemed like this was one of those get-it-all-out nights, so I went ahead and said it. "Also, Chris is home . . ."

"How's that going?" Jimmy asked, and I wasn't sure, but it seemed like he was trying a little hard to seem neutral and curious. He was acting, and overdoing it.

Aly gently said, "I feel like this will be different."

"I think this time it's for real, but we agreed that for it to be a real shot, we have to take it slow," I said cautiously. Aly nodded. "It's kind of fun, starting over with someone you know really well, you know?"

"Violet, y'all have a lot of history, but since you parted, time has passed. Maybe he's grown up a little. I'd want to see if the fire was still there, too. I don't blame you one ounce. However, if he starts his usual bullshit, please throw him out. Everyone deserves a second chance . . . but not a *third*," Jim said.

"Thank you for supporting me," I said. "Maggie is going to kill me."

"Yes, she is, but it's your life, Violet. You get to make the decisions." Jimmy gave me a wink. "Trust yourself, babe."

He said it like it was the easiest thing in the world to do. Maybe it was. "You're right!" I said.

What did they say in Mom's meetings? "Fake it till you make it"? Maybe that would work for me, too . . .

CHAPTER SIXTEEN

~~~~~~

Violet

I took Gran's truck over to my house in Byrnes Downs. I paused in the driveway, wondering if it was too late to turn around, if I should just go home to Gran's. Then I wondered if showing up tipsy on my own doorstep, which was not now my doorstep, was a bad look. But Chris answered before I even had a chance to ring the bell.

"I know we said we'd—"

"Hey," Chris interrupted, and then covered my mouth with his.

"Oh," I whispered when there was a pause in the kissing. All of me felt good and warm.

"I was hoping you'd come," he said.

"I'm a little . . ."

"Buzzed? I can taste it on you."

"You don't mind?"

"No. Where am I allowed to kiss you?" he whispered.

"What do you mean?" I asked, confused.

"How about here?" he said as he brought his lips to my wrist. "Or here?" He moved to the inside of my elbow. He grabbed me by the waist and pulled me in, pressing me hard against him. Pretending not to notice me flinch as I felt the strong length of him through his slacks.

"Gracious, Chris!" I gasped. I was a little shocked at his forwardness, and my own boldness, but my heart was racing.

"You're flushed, princess." He grazed his perfect mouth along the nape of my neck, said, "What about here?" and then took a slight nibble at my earlobe.

"Jesus," I moaned.

"I love to make you feel good. Please, Violet, you drive me crazy. I've missed you."

I was almost panting as he pressed into me again.

"We can't," I said. "I want to, but . . ." Before I finished my sentence, he covered my mouth with his.

"Then why are you here?" he asked.

I opened my mouth to protest—it was the vino, or the daddy ish, but who cared, really? He was right. I had come here for this. I felt myself arch into him and welcomed every moment afterward. He led me through the front door, and I playfully pushed him against a wall in what was once our living room.

"When did you paint this wall, by the way?" Chris said between kisses.

"I made some changes, Chris. Had to. Do you want a tour?"

"Not of the house, not now. All I want is to taste you everywhere."

"Jesus."

"Come here. The bedroom is still plenty good."

"I changed a few things there, too. I guess you didn't notice."

"I've changed, too; we both have. You've gotten even more beautiful." He led me into the bedroom. "If you want me to stop, I'll stop, Violet. I don't want to push, but if you don't stop me right now, I'm going to devour you."

"Christopher."

He moved closer and slid off the strap of my dress. My heart was throwing itself against my rib cage. I felt my body betray my mind, and against all better judgment I said, "Take me."

Was it the martinis talking? They'd definitely made my voice husky.

He slid off my dress, and I stood there in my bra and panties. Black lace. And my red sandals. He made a noise that was a lot like a growl. I felt a wave of confidence as I watched him take in my lingerie and body. He came closer to me and started kissing my neck, cupping my breasts.

"Are you sure?" He nuzzled me, and I took his face in my hands and kissed him. "I like this idea of our date, of starting over. But I want you so bad."

"So sure."

He picked me up by my butt and threw me on the bed. I let out a giggle at his playfulness.

In a moment I watched him as he, with one hand, unbuckled his belt and snapped the leather off the loops of his pants in a single fluid movement. My breath caught, and a delicious fear tightened my stomach. I had never seen him like this. So . . . primal. He had picked up some tricks in Japan. I pushed that line of questioning out of my mind.

If someone else had broken in this saddle, well, I was going to enjoy riding it.

In the next moment he flipped me over on my stomach. And in a flash, he pulled my panties off and told me to spread my legs. He gently kissed up them starting at my ankles and going along the insides until he took a devastating pause.

"Get up on all fours."

I did.

"Good girl."

The next few hours could best be described as "concerning to feminism."

If anyone had witnessed my actions, I was sure I would have to turn in my eyelet seersucker, pearls, and Gloria Steinem books. But, oh, what a way to burn. I would go to confession in the morning. I hadn't had an encounter like that since . . . well, ever. He had changed during our time apart, and it scared me a little, but I was appreciative.

Of his skills, and of our thick walls.

~~~

When I returned to Gran's, it was still dark, but of course she had left the porch light on for me.

As I climbed the front steps, I saw that she was sitting on the porch—having woken early, or never gone to sleep, I wasn't sure which—staring off in the direction of the water.

Maybe I was still feeling the effects—or vibrating with what Chris and I had done, I don't know—but holding anything back right then felt really pointless. I asked, "Gran, what is my father like?"

She turned around to face me, looking deep into my eyes as if to determine if I'd really just asked that question. Then she gave a little nod to herself and answered me.

"Well, the young man I knew all those years ago wasn't the same man he is now. He struggled with life for a very long time, and as I understand it, he has a firm grasp on the wheel now."

"Oh."

"Violet, if you want to know him, know him . . . but I didn't like him very much when I last saw him. Still, I suppose he deserves the chance to explain himself."

"I would like to hear it."

She took a long sip out of her mug and sighed.

"He was handsome. Very much so. But in a wholesome way, which made his behavior all the more unexpected. He was funny, and always had your mom laughing."

"You know what I remember? It's so weird: I've been trying to pull something significant from the vault, and all I get is the smell of cinnamon."

"Ah, yes, that would be because he loved it. Especially when he was nervous. He loved you both—still does, I'm sure . . . but he couldn't be the kind of father you both needed, and the type of man your mother needed."

"I don't want to argue, but shouldn't that have been Mom's decision?" I asked.

"I know it was wrong."

I opened my mouth, trying to figure out how to say what I wanted to say. Probably she was right—it was wrong—but I wondered if maybe it wasn't also in a lot of important ways right. He was *alive*—that didn't seem bad to me. I didn't really know him, I was curious about him, and her choice probably had shielded me from a lot of unpleasant experiences of the person he used to be.

Before I could get any of that into words, I reconsidered. I was afraid of what Maggie would think of all this, but Maggie should be here; she had a right to know about Scott, too. She had the right to be caught up at the same speed as I was getting caught up . . .

"Gran, I think I should go to bed."

"That's a good idea. We can talk about all of it when the sun is up and you've had some black coffee . . ." I must have looked a little ashamed, because Gran patted my hand and added, "Don't worry, you look like you had fun, and you know what? You certainly deserve some fun."

~~~~

When I woke up, the sun was strong, and the heat was serious. How far into the day had I slept? Much, much longer than I had in a long time. It was well into the late afternoon!

My phone was buzzing. That was what had woken me. I was dimly aware that it had been buzzing for a long time. It was Maggie.

The call ended. A text came through. 9-1-1! EMERGENCY!

I dialed, and she picked up on the first ring.

"Violet!"

"What? What's the matter? Are you okay? Are you hurt?"

"No—yes—oh my god. But you have to be careful. I had to warn you to look out. For him. Before he—before he—"

Even though I knew the answer, I interrupted, asking, "Maggie, what is this about?"

"Dad's alive!"

I closed my eyes. Gran must have told her. Which was only fair. But I realized at that moment that I'd wanted just one more day of it being my secret to hold and no one else's. Mine to figure out how to feel about.

Maggie was breathless and shouting, "He came into the restaurant!"

"What?" Now I really was confused.

"He's alive. But don't worry. I told him to get the hell out of Sullivan's Island. I scared him good. He's never coming back."

CHAPTER SEVENTEEN

~~~~~

Maggie

That day started out ordinary. The season was turning in the South, and in the spirit of early summer I figured that lemon-and-rosemary roasted chicken was always welcome. I'd tried it recently, and it had been a big hit, one of the classics that made everyone feel good. Also, recently I had tried the famous roasted chicken at Vern's. My first thought was *This is the best thing I've ever eaten,* so naturally I needed to rival it. As soon as I got to the restaurant, I got to work with my cooks, and we broke down what seemed to be a hundred chickens, saving the bones and wing tips for chicken stock. We tried not to have any waste, which was one of the ways we were keeping our costs down, and it was working.

I reminded Ben, my sous chef, of the drill. Classic roasted chicken. Quick marinade for about twenty minutes. Lemon juice, olive oil, salt and pepper. Maybe a dash of red pepper flakes. "Let's keep the skin on those legs and thighs," I told him.

"Okay, then what?"

"Season the actual meat, salt and pepper. Medium-heat pan, a little olive oil, and a tab of butter. Brown them skin-side down for six to eight minutes. Get it nice and crispy. Then grab a hotel pan and put them in there, skin-side up this time, add potatoes and capers, then put it into a four-fifty oven, drizzle the whole thing with the leftover marinade. Roast them for about forty minutes. Warm them in a butter sauce just before pickup. Squeeze some lemon juice over the plate."

"Can I make a suggestion?" Ben asked. "What if we fry the capers? Might be a good additional texture. Also, they're pretty!"

"Great idea! Let's do that. Half in the marinade for salt, and then fried over the finished plate. Love it!" I returned his smile. Ben had come to me entirely green, and I was slowly teaching him everything I knew. He was a quick learner, and I was proud to see his progress.

"Thanks, Chef. On it." And off he went to fetch the capers.

Soon the kitchen was rocking and rolling. The air was filled not only with the aroma of the chicken special but also with some sweet tunes from the Rolling Stones and Hall and Oates. Occasionally some of the cooks would sing along as they sliced and diced their way through the prep work. My kitchen was not just *my* happy place. Since I had taken over, little by little I was elevating it. One of the things I was the proudest of was the baking station that I had added last summer. We now made our own bread, and while lemon chicken with rosemary smelled good, you couldn't beat fresh bread.

When the chicken was done roasting, I demonstrated the pickup. I lightly sauced the plate with the lemon butter demi sauce and piled the baby potatoes in the center, creating a nest; then, skin-side up, I placed the golden chicken breast in the center and topped it with some fresh, bright green rosemary. I showed Ben and the other cooks how I wanted it presented on a plate, and we all tasted it. It was wonderful. I walked Ben through the plating and brought it out to the dining room so the front of the house could give the chicken a try before service. It was important to me that the servers knew what they were selling.

I pushed open the swinging doors and took a few steps. It was early evening. The dining room was starting to fill up with early diners, and it was buzzing with conversation. I sailed past a few regulars, said a few quick hellos. But then, as I got closer to the bar, I saw a familiar-looking man.

His face stopped me in my tracks. It was that vague recognition, like seeing a character actor who's played a family member with a handful of lines in the kinds of movies you watch on airplanes. I took a small step forward. Blinked a few times. I stared for a moment and shook my head. This had happened before, and I knew it was stupid. I would think it was him, and of course it wouldn't be, because it couldn't be. He was gone. Dead. The man shifted his weight and turned to me. Then there was no doubt in my mind. It *was* him.

"Hey there, Maggie May." He smiled at me, and my plate crashed to the floor.

I stopped breathing for what seemed like forever. I brought my hand to my mouth. I felt like I would faint. How could this be happening? I must be hallucinating. A ghost was talking to me. This wasn't real. *It wasn't real!*

He took a step forward, and I smelled his cinnamon gum.

I took in his height, his dark hair. The same shade as Violet's. He still had a short beard, but now it was peppered with gray. The creases around his eyes were deeper, but I remembered the shape of them. They always reminded me of fans framing his green eyes. *My* green eyes. It was him. I had seen him often enough in dreams, but that made sense. Of course you dreamed about dead people, especially parents. But this wasn't a dream, and he wasn't dead.

My heart was pounding in my ears. I swayed a little in place.

"Dad?" I said in a very tiny voice. "What are you doing here?"

He reached out to me. I stepped away.

He was still smiling—why was he smiling? "I just could not wait to see you," he said.

Hot anger flooded my veins. The heat spread across my chest, and I felt tears pricking at my eyes.

He wasn't dead. It hit me like an anvil. He was just a *deadbeat*.

He had played dead to skip out on us, and now he showed up? In *my* house?

How dare he show up in my restaurant in the middle of service?

This was something my mother would do, trap me in public and make a scene, and I'd had about enough of her this week already. My fists clenched. I took short breaths as my heart rate quickened. I saw red, literally, and then everything went blank for a moment as I stared at him in horror and fury.

"Oh, my girl," he said, apparently unaware of the molten rage that was overflowing and spreading his way. "How I've missed you."

"Get out," I said through clenched teeth.

He blinked at me, and the smile fell slightly, his expression becoming confused.

"Maggie, I want to explain myself. I was hoping we could ease into it, but you deserve to know, if you don't already. Your grandmother and I had an agreement. I promised I wouldn't intrude, but that I'd always write, and . . . and . . . I always did."

"Liar!"

"I know it probably did feel inadequate, those postcards. So many postcards! All the time! God, for years, it was like all I thought about was postcards. But I would have written more if—"

"*Postcards?*" Was this man insane? "What are you talking about? I never saw anything from you! Nothing! Not a word! And why now? What took you so long?" I tried to remember the people around me, the *customers*, and get my emotions under wraps, but I was keenly aware that wasn't at all possible.

What I needed to do was escape.

"Magnolia, sugar . . ." he said, his face all fake, confused and pained.

"Don't talk to me." My body was rigid with anger, hurt, over a lifetime of wishing for this, only to get it now, horribly, because of a deadbeat's lie. "Don't come an inch closer."

But he did. He took a step and reached out his arms. What was he thinking? That this was going to be a reunion? Not on my life. So I made an offensive move: I stepped over the broken plate and shoved him hard. He lost his footing, and on his way to landing on his butt, he grabbed two empty barstools. The crash reverberated across the Magic Lantern. The whole dining room went silent.

And so, what? I was seething. I could have thrown a barstool all the way across the street right then, I was so angry. Years of abandonment and sadness pumped through me. My heart felt freshly torn in two all over again.

"Please, Maggie, can we go somewhere where we can talk? I can—"

"Absolutely not! Get out of my restaurant!" When he didn't immediately do as I said, I stalked toward him, nearly screaming, "And I mean, sorry for *what?* For lying, for abandoning us, for leaving us with *Mom?* For letting me be the girl with the dead father all these years? What is the *matter* with you, thinking you can just show up like this? Where *were* you?"

Frankie tried to reach me. She was at my elbow, gently saying, "Maggie, come on, let's get you out of here," but I pushed her away.

"You aren't welcome here. I don't want anything to do with you! Get out before I call the police."

"Maggie, please. I'm sorry. I'm so sorry, I would have come—"

"Do not talk to me. Get. Out." I took another aggressive step forward, and he nodded, seeming to finally get it, and climbed to his feet. "If you come near me or my sister, I swear on all that is holy, I will end you," I shouted at him as he retreated from the scene. "You hear me, Scott? You come near me, you are going to get a black eye. You come near Violet, and I will *end you.*"

Once I was sure he was gone, I pressed the heels of my palms hard into my eye sockets. I sensed Frankie nearby and nodded that I was fine. Shame welled up in me over the scene I had made.

"Everything's fine, y'all. Sorry about that! Just a little family drama supper theater, ha ha. Go back to your meal! Frankie, give everyone a round on the house." I smiled big, heard a few good-natured chuckles, and hurried back into the kitchen.

I started to shake and needed to get deep into work to block out the past traumatizing ten minutes. I started slamming pots around, barking at everyone; the music was off, and it was silent except for the professional noise of the kitchen. Frankie came in while I was reading the orders as they buzzed through the ticket machine.

"Maggie?" she asked. "Do you wanna take a break?"

"Not now. Two burgers, fire table twelve."

"Maggie, come on, let's take a minute." She nodded over to Ben. "Can't Ben expedite the orders?"

"I got it. Need to work."

I turned around and grabbed a pot that was on the stove, forgetting my side towel. Instantly I pulled my hand away, and I dropped the pot, splashing hot liquid all over my legs. Thankfully I was wearing long pants, or it would have been so much worse. The shock had worn off. My hand was screaming in pain. I had grabbed a cast-iron skillet at over four hundred degrees. I barked out a colorful expression.

"Fine, after I get the burn cream," I said, and walked off the line.

"I got it, Chef, no worries," Ben called after me. "Fire table four. That's three chickens all day on deck."

A loud "Yes, Chef" was spoken in unison, signaling that the cooks on the line had heard him.

The chicken special was running out fast. At least that was going as planned.

I went into the bathroom. I took the burn cream from the first aid kit and ran my hand under ice-cold water. I looked into the mirror and took a deep breath. My face was pale. Which made sense, because I had just seen a living ghost. I had dreamed so many times that I would run into him, that it had all been a mistake, but I never once thought I would be so angry. And maybe that shouldn't have been a surprise. With me, anger was always the first reaction. My hot temper wasn't strength, exactly, as I sometimes thought, but I always felt that anger kept me safe.

I came back around the corner, saw Frankie, and nodded to the walk-in refrigerator. She followed me there. Everyone in the food and beverage industry knew that the walk-in was where you went to get emotional, cry or scream or laugh hysterically, in some peace. Things got volatile in a kitchen from time to time, and it was a good place for privacy.

"So stupid," I grumbled. "I *never* burn myself."

She sat down on a short stack of milk crates.

"I know I was a little unhinged."

She smiled at me. "I didn't say anything."

"I can hear your thoughts. And you're right. I should have taken a break before I jumped back on the line."

"I get it."

"So, what the hell is happening right now? My dad's alive? Does anyone else know?" I stared at the ceiling.

"I don't know . . ." Frankie said, and I shot her a look. I shouldn't have been so close with an employee, but, honestly, Frankie was family.

"He lied about his *existence* for this entire time! This must be my mother's fault."

"How could it have been?"

"Someone must've hidden this. Helped him, I mean. And why come out as alive now? I wonder what his next move will be. I can't deal. Who knows, maybe Scott will go to the house. To Gran's."

"Scott—you mean your dad?" She was just clarifying, I knew, but the word "dad" made me furious all over again.

"No, I mean *Scott*. My dad died for me a long time ago."

"Okay, Maggie, I get it, but—"

"I need to call my sister." I pushed open the door and left Frankie alone in the refrigerator. "I have to protect Violet from Scott."

CHAPTER EIGHTEEN

~~~~~

Violet

After listening to Maggie fulminate, I put my phone down. My head hurt from last night, and my heart was confused by all that had transpired in the past twenty-four hours.

Maggie was really on one about Scott. I looked over to the drawer where I'd left the postcards, which Gran had given me and which I had been planning to read after I discussed things with Aly and Jimmy. I hadn't even really been able to tell her about them, she'd been on that much of a tear. I opened the drawer and quickly realized they weren't where I'd left them . . . or had I left them? I remembered reading them last night downstairs.

"Oh no," I said out loud to my bedroom. I had forgotten them on the kitchen counter.

That was when I heard my mom screaming.

"What is this? What the *hell* is this?"

I hurried in the direction of her voice, which seemed to fill the whole house. I rushed around the corner to find Gran standing in the kitchen.

"Mom?" I called out. Then I saw Gran, who had blanched. "Gran, you okay?"

Her eyes were downcast.

My mother burst into the kitchen with the force of a thousand horses, red-faced, with rivers of black mascara running down her face. She was angry and wild. I hadn't seen that in . . . well, maybe ever. Not at this voltage.

My mother fell to the floor, and it was then that I saw the handfuls of postcards in her fists. "Oh my god," she wailed.

"Lily, I am so sorry. I am so sorry." Gran went over and knelt next to her. My mother sobbed and got up. She threw the cards at my grandmother, who ducked; the cards fell over her like confetti.

"Your father is alive, Violet." My mother had a manic expression on her face. She spoke as though she were telling on her own mother, like a five-year-old tattling on an older sibling for the vilest sin. "Scott is alive, and Gran knew that and was *keeping* him from us!"

My throat got tight, and my ears started to pound. I had wanted her to find out in a totally different way, but here we were. Mom was hysterical. Feral. Grabbing all the postcards one by one and screaming at Gran, who just knelt there and let her. Years of heartbreak and deception were whipping through our house. I didn't know what to do.

"What else is there? Are you hiding anything else?" I heard my mom say.

"Well, it's all there in the cards and letters. But he did email me recently," Gran said. "I've been planning to tell you. All of you. I guess that's why he showed up . . ."

"Showed . . . up?" Lily was shaking. "Why?"

"Well, because he . . . he needs a divorce, honey."

"I'm sorry, what?" my mother shrieked. "I am being *divorced* by a *dead man?*"

"Well, he's alive," Gran said. "He does want a divorce, but he's not a dead man."

"You knew? You knew all along? This was your doing from the very start. How *could* you?"

"I'm so sorry, I'm so . . ." Gran said. But my mom screeched with venom. The sounds of her upstairs door slamming and the old lock clicking into place felt like slaps.

Gran looked at me and then silently went upstairs, too. I heard her door quietly close.

The deafening silence of our childhood home was eerie. I decided to take a hot bath to wash it all off. My swirling, desperate emotions, one of the central facts of my life being overturned suddenly, whatever had happened with Chris last night. Maybe a soak would help me sort my troubles out. I climbed the stairs, past the wall of portraits, and looked at Daisy's picture.

The one that was always crooked.

I knew where my father had been hidden all these years. So close, it turned out. I had been looking for him my whole life, and his words, and his thoughts of me, had been right there all along.

I felt like a balloon that had been let go of. I was aimless, searching for some truth to anchor me. In a dim sort of way, I understood that this was traumatic. I understood why my mom was carrying on like she was on fire . . . which, emotionally, she was.

But my temperature was only slightly elevated.

I knew I *should* be angry, but I just . . . wasn't.

Was my anger shoved so deep I couldn't access it?

I turned on the tap and put some bath salts into the tub. I lit my favorite candle and turned off the overhead light, allowing just the candle and the night-light to illuminate the room. I got into the tub, let the warm water fill up around me, and squeezed out some lavender-scented bubble bath.

I tried to remember what he was like, my father. I wondered if the things I knew were my own memories, or a collage of collected stories and memories belonging to my sister that she'd told me and I'd strained to make my own. He had left when I was so young. All I could remember were large hands and the smell of his cinnamon gum.

I knew we had the same hair color and that he rode a motorcycle. I thought I could hear the engine rumbling if I listened hard enough.

I remembered the day he had left, or what I could patch together of it. I was so young, but it was my last, and strongest, memory of him. I remembered him not looking at us.

There was a reason I never thought about him, but sometimes, in my dreams (nightmares?), I could still hear his laughter, low like thunder and gritty like sand.

I looked at my phone. The water was turning tepid. I pulled myself out of the bath and grabbed a bath sheet, a large extra-fluffy towel, and wrapped myself up like a burrito.

I had questioned how my mother would handle this, and now I worried about her sobriety. And beneath all that—my obsessive strategizing and putting it all together, my ruminating about everyone else—there was the little seedling of a question. Scott was alive—could I find him? Gran had said he was in town, but I hadn't gotten any more information out of her, and judging by Maggie's reaction and her big story of how she'd gone about heroically kicking him out of the Lantern, I didn't foresee him returning.

Then my brain decided to chime in. It was like my hand already knew what to do—already I'd clicked into the apps.

Social media.

I had never searched for him before, because why would a dead man be on Instagram or Google or Facebook? Why would I go looking for someone who wasn't there? As far as I knew, he'd departed the planet before most people had left a digital footprint. In moments I was staring at my father's life. Pictures of time in Montana, showing that he liked to hunt and fly-fish. He had recently moved to Nantucket.

Nantucket. An island up north.

Seemed he was really into food. I kept scrolling—he was a chef!

Maybe Maggie would like that? I could tell her that.

Oh, lord, Maggie! I wanted to reach out to him, but it wasn't going to be easy to convince her that we should. I would message him, but only after I spoke to Maggie; we should do this together.

Maybe then we could connect.

I heard a low rumble of thunder. A storm was blowing in from the ocean. Man, sometimes Mother Nature knew just when to throw a fit.

~~~~~

Later that night, after my bath, I walked down the hall, pausing at my mother's door. Through the wall I could hear that she was crying, but I knew that knocking or doing anything wasn't going to get me anywhere. I didn't feel like being rejected for showing compassion. Heat rose up my throat and inflamed my cheeks at the thought. This wasn't just happening to her. But I was worried about her. I knocked.

"Go. Away!" she screamed.

"Mom, it's me," I said.

"Not now, Violet." Her voice softened.

"Mom, this is happening to me, too," I said in a small voice.

I waited a few seconds and heard her bed creak, and then I heard her walk over to the door, but she kept it closed. It sounded like she slid down on the other side and leaned her back against it. I heard her take a deep breath, sniff, and sigh.

"Violet, I'm sorry. You're right."

I sat down in the hallway. I had never heard my mother give up a fight so easily.

"I'm sorry, too, Mom. This is a . . . it's a weird one, it's really weird."

She opened the door a crack. "Can I be honest?"

"Sure," I replied. "I think some honesty would be good around here."

Just barely making eye contact, my mother said, "I knew."

"What do you mean, you knew?" I felt as if I had stopped breathing.

"I just felt it. I mean, I didn't *know* know, but I knew in my heart that he wasn't gone. Scott and I were and always have been very connected. I just *knew.*"

"Oh." I was, if I'm being honest, a little disappointed. I guess I was hoping to hear that she had seen him or something, that she had real information. "So, what do we do now? Find him? Do you even *want* to see him?"

"I have to! I'm still married! That's so . . ." She sighed deeply, and it was like I was breathing out, too. "It's been such a long time. If I had known he was writing, that he was trying to reach out, I would have . . . I don't know, I would've done something different. Oh my god, Violet . . ." She opened the door wide then and stared at me.

"What?"

Mom had a look on her face that I had never seen before. Her eyes were extra wide and she seemed to be frantically searching through her inner filing cabinet.

"I almost got remarried! To Buster!"

Mom remained motionless in her doorway, the weight of it all pressing down on us.

"Mom?" I said, and she went back into her room and closed the door.

No one in this house was going to explain any of it to me. I had to ask him. Scott.

My phone buzzed.

I'm out early. What's up? Maggie texted.

I have to talk to you, I texted back.

Can it wait? Maggie texted.

No, I texted back.

Fine, she texted back, and I swallowed hard.

I had a moment of jealousy. I knew all she wanted to do, what she had *planned* to do, was go over to Sam's house so they could have a cozy night together, while here I was at ground zero of a family fight. I envied her for her breezy lifestyle, beholden to no one. Then it occurred to me: I had chosen to live in my childhood home. This was the price.

Every woman in this house was emotional. I decided to move forward. Pancakes were the answer.

I went into the kitchen and opened the baking cabinet, pushed back the pancake mix, and found the stash I hid when my mom was home. Three bottles of wine I always had for emergencies. Emergencies could be anything from a fight with Mom to, like . . . this.

I poured the dark purple Merlot into my violet mug. Mom didn't need to see me with a wineglass. I decided to pour a larger-than-usual amount. I was saving time this way, I rationalized. I wouldn't have to refill so often. I drank the first half down and stared into the front yard.

I had stood out there early that morning, before the sun had come up. Now the sun was down again. A lot could change in mere hours. I had a father who was alive.

I heard Maggie's loud footsteps before I saw her. She always ran up the porch stairs. I heard the key above the door scratch along the doorframe as she found the keyhole with her hand and let herself in.

"Anyone home? Anyone armed?" Maggie called out.

"Girl, stop, you have no idea. Also, glad to see you among the living," I said as I dashed over to the door to hush her. I had been afraid to see her, afraid of her opinions, but now I was glad she was here. My big sister. The other half of my heart.

Maggie arched an eyebrow and jutted her chin in the direction of my mug.

"Okay? You got enough for two in there? By the look on your face and the vibe of this room, I might need some hard stuff." Maggie shook her head in wry disbelief.

"I only have wine," I said, following her into the kitchen.

"Nah, little sister, you just need to know where to look." She opened the cabinet next to the baking one, where the secret stash was, and pulled out some whiskey.

"Uh . . ." I mumbled.

"There's always *another* secret stash. This is just Mom's favorite hiding spot," she explained, tilting the bottle up to the light.

"Do you want to talk about Dad?" I asked.

"I don't know how I feel about all of this . . . but I'm guessing Mom found out and flipped out. What's going on?" she said, and took a sip, then shivered. She liked to pretend she could drink the hard stuff and that she was a badass, but every time, she'd wince. I took her mug, poured it back into the bottle. Maggie gave me a little pout. I stuck my tongue out at her and rinsed her mug, then poured some of my bottle into it.

"Oh, you have a secret stash, too?" she said.

"Yeah, behind the pancake mix. Carbs. Mom would never look there."

"Looks like sneaky runs in the family," she said. "We're all a bunch of squirrels. So, let's have it."

"Maggie, I don't even know how to begin . . . Mom saw those postcards."

"What? What are you talking about?" Maggie said, almost choking on her sip of wine.

Maggie took a second to let what I had told her process. I could feel the wheels of her mind whirring.

"So, he was telling the *truth*?" she said. "He really did send us lots of postcards?"

"Yes, there are hundreds of them. They were hidden in the wall over on the staircase behind Great-Grandma Daisy's picture." I guessed I'd decided it was best to get the facts out quickly.

"How did you find them?" she asked me.

"Well, I found one the other day, but then Gran told me. Yesterday. She gave them to me, but before I had a chance to look at them, Lily found them."

"That picture was always askew. Maybe our great-grandmother wanted us to find them."

"Maggie, can you imagine what she's thinking right now?"

"How about what *we're* thinking? Where's Gran? Did she know Mom was hiding this?"

"No, Maggie, you don't understand . . . *Gran* hid the postcards. She's known the whole time, and now you know . . ."

"*Gran* hid this?" Maggie said, dumbfounded.

"Yeah, and I can't get my head around it. She said she wanted to tell you. Us. But I have so many other questions first . . ."

"Violet, I'm going to need to see those postcards . . ."

It was almost like I could see it physically happening. A heavy wave of sadness crashed into my sister. Large tears that reminded me of hot summer afternoon raindrops poured out of her eyes and down her cheeks. They were thick with years of questions, abandonment, and longing, fast as a spring river. Her eyelashes, when soaked, looked black instead of their usual golden copper color. She wailed, and a sound came out of her that I had never heard. She stopped looking at me and sat down on a stool, folded her arms on the kitchen bar, and buried her face in them, sobbing.

I was stunned, watching her, at how rapidly her shoulders heaved with her sobbing.

I didn't know how to comfort her. There was just this strange inner inertia. I felt so still.

My mother was furious, my sister was devastated, but I was . . . something else entirely.

What?

In my head and heart was the pulse of a thousand questions.

Why was our father hidden from us, after she kicked him out?

If he really loved us, why didn't he try harder to see us? Gran could be scary, I guess. But we hadn't been minors for a long time.

"Maggie, come on, I know this is hard, but we should be celebrating, right?" I gave her back a rub. "I mean, now we can find him!"

"Find him? Screw him! How dare he be alive and just send us stupid postcards . . . Seeing him the other night . . . now her betrayal on top of it . . ."

"Maggie, we don't know what those cards even say . . . I bet he really did miss us."

"You miss us? Come get us!" Maggie blew her nose. "He could have saved me from years of torment from Mom, and we could have . . . had a dad."

"We don't know what happened, and obviously there is a story here."

"This was a *big* lie, Violet. What makes you think Gran'll tell us the truth now?"

"I don't know, but I don't think—"

"Violet, it's okay to be mad at someone if they intentionally hurt you. This changes everything; don't you see that? About Gran, I mean. Not about *him*. He's still dead, as far as I'm concerned. I don't want to know him. He didn't really care enough to know us . . . Put him back in the wall, or in the ground. I'm fine without him. *Been* fine." She wiped her tears and gulped. "I gotta go."

With that, Maggie left and slammed the door behind her.

I stood in the kitchen, searching for words that wouldn't come.

My eyes caught sight of something sticking out from under a stool by the kitchen bar. It was a postcard that had escaped my mother. She had taken all the others to her room, but this one must have gotten away. I pulled it out and saw a picture of a cowboy with a lasso.

It read, "Greetings from Montana!"

My heart stopped, remembering all the biscuit orders the Magic Lantern had had over the past several years from a Montana man . . . Could there be a connection? Maggie had started a side hustle selling biscuits in an effort to help our family's restaurant, and we had always found it funny that some random man in Montana, of all places, loved her biscuits. He would order a hundred almost every month. I liked to imagine he was a police officer or something and would bake them for his team. I didn't know why I had always thought he was in some sort of protective service . . .

I refilled my mug almost to the top and took the card out to the back porch. I sipped slowly as I turned it over.

"To my Bouquet Girls—I have been dreaming about you again. I am moving to Nantucket. There is a restaurant there right on the water. It's so beautiful, and I will be the head chef there! I know it's still far away, but at least we'll be on the same coast again. Missing you girls, with everything in me. Love, Dad."

It was dated last year.

Nantucket. The restaurant he had tagged . . .

I didn't feel anything but my overwhelming desire to meet my father.

I almost didn't care who I discovered—broke, mean, duplicitous, whatever—as long as it was him, and I finally got some answers.

My pulse was racing. Mom could be sad all she wanted, and Maggie could be angry, and I guessed that was justified, for them anyway. But I was pulled in a different direction.

I was going to know my dad—it felt like a good secret, my own little secret, buoying me up. I was not going to stay stuck. I was going to move forward.

First step, move in with Jimmy until I decided if Chris was real this time. He had been spending time looking for a new job and we had not connected often. Second step was to plan a trip to Nantucket.

CHAPTER NINETEEN

~~~~~

Aly

I opened my email to find a message from Rosemary, my mother's business manager.

> Aly—
>
> So great to hear from you! As previously discussed with your father, you could potentially be a fit for Callie Knox. Taking into consideration a shift in audience participation and demographic change, having a young, fresh voice on her brand would be ideal. I am sure having her very own daughter would bring in old followers and encourage a new generation. I think, in a lot of ways, a transition to your style would be seamless, and I am open to hearing your ideas and thoughts about this new direction. That being said, we have to consider a rebrand over the company as well. We have a long-established relationship with various larger companies, such as Crate and Barn, who might be hesitant to tack on an unknown. Or someone with her/his own smaller audience. Let's keep talking. I am excited about this opportunity to work with you.
>
> All my best, Rosemary

She had taken a while to respond, so I was glad to finally hear from her. But the response wasn't as full-throated as I'd hoped.

In fact, I was a little confused. Rosemary had known me forever, and my dad had made it sound like the business was sort of already figured out, and now it seemed like I was being tested for this role that I had thought was already mine.

But I saw her point. The Crate and Barn deal was a huge part of the company's income, and without it our brand would be hard to sustain. And then I reread Rosemary's message and realized it wasn't as negative as I'd thought. I could totally make a segue into leading Mom's brand; Rosemary had said that pretty clearly. And I had brashly told her I could increase my following exponentially, with no real plan for how to do that.

Well, *now* I had a plan. I was going to redo the apartment! But Joyce had stymied that.

But whatever—if Rosemary wanted to keep things totally professional, I was going to have to show her, my dad, and the rest of Mom's staff that I could do it. I decided to keep cool—I had to keep it positive, think about serving my mom's audience the way she had, and keep on homing in on my vision.

I managed to get a workflow going that lasted about three straight hours. I finished up a draft of a blog entry I was going to post later on about mah-jongg and started to work on an outline of my dream for my mother's brand. It couldn't be called Callie anymore, much as I wanted it to be. It would have to be Aly.

How could I carry on with its still having her core identity, though?

She had always believed in telling the truth but making it beautiful.

Was that the key? Maybe I could go with the tagline "Seeing beauty in the everyday, with Aly Knox." I liked it, but it was too long.

What was my mother's brand really, truly about? I thought about her linen line, the one we did together, the tablecloths and napkins and those really pretty seersucker place mats. I remembered her choosing the fabric; it had taken her forever to decide on a shade of navy. It had to match the water; she kept insisting on that. The magic was in the details with her; that was something we agreed on. Everything she created was practical, beautiful, and high-quality. Then I started to think about what we had in common, and what made us different. She was more formal than I was, but we were both totally transfixed by and obsessed with a coastal lifestyle. She was more into contemporary, while my taste in interiors skewed traditional.

How could we mix the two?

Then it hit me. I wanted to call the refreshed brand, the new outpost of Callie Knox, "My Mother's Daughter."

It felt right. I wanted the new brand to be about honoring yesterday's women, who had shaped the women of today. Passing down tradition but making it your own. I would start to design things that honored the past but still could be useful. So where would I begin? What was one item everyone seemed to have that could be improved upon?

Water bottles! Every single person these days was concerned with hydration levels, something my mother never was . . . I didn't think I had ever seen her drink water, nor did I remember her being concerned about it when I was younger. I didn't go to school with a water bottle, but now every child had one on them at all times.

I would use coastal looks to design a water bottle. I thought about Charleston, and right away images popped into my mind. Little ink shrimp, pearl necklaces, oysters, the pineapple fountain, a shrimp boat, a sand dollar . . . and then the Charleston sweetgrass baskets. How cool would it be if I could somehow tie together the textures of the sweetgrass baskets and . . . ? Then I was on to remembering this Instagram account I had recently come across.

Violet had mentioned Nantucket, and that led us down a social media rabbit hole when we were brainstorming. We found this girl in Nantucket who wove baskets in the Nantucket style. She made earrings, bracelets, and drink cozies! I wondered if I could do this in the style of Charleston. I sent her a DM and sat back. This could be awesome. I checked the clock and saw it was time to get my act together if I was going to make it to mah-jongg. I headed to my closet for something to wear.

Shuffling through my dresses, I landed on a new dress by Hill House. I was starting to be a walking advertisement for them; their feminine smocked dresses were perfect for summer. This one was white with purple flowers. I slicked my hair into a high ponytail. I finished up my look with a long silky bow barrette. A quick swipe of eyeliner and a little rosy lipstick and I was set. At the last minute I added three of my mother's antique bangles. I was ready for some girlfriend time, and I was excited to be learning mah-jongg. I grabbed the keys by the door and flew downtown.

~~~~~

The Charleston Place Hotel was one of the most elegant places in Charleston. Every time I walked into its grand lobby, I got chills. It had always been beautiful, but after some new renovations, it was elevated to give its guests the feeling of being Lowcountry royalty, which made sense, because that was exactly who was at the Thoroughbred Club, the dark-wood-paneled bar in the lobby.

Maybe one day I could be like them—I could make a name for myself in the community. Since I was early, I decided to go into the bar and have a drink, see what that felt like. I had time for a quick glass of wine before my mah-jongg lesson.

I entered the bar and found a seat right away. A handsome bartender welcomed me and handed me a menu. I heard the jazz musicians start to play. *Nice touch, Charleston Place*, I thought to myself. I scanned the menu and decided to just order a glass of Merlot. After a few minutes it arrived, alongside a small plate of truffle fries.

"Oh, these smell wonderfully dangerous, but I didn't order them!" I told the bartender.

"They are a gift from the gentleman at the end over there."

"Oh, okay. Well, tell him thank you?" I leaned forward to get a look past my chic bar mates and locked eyes with the finest jawline and the sexiest smile I'd seen since I had fallen in love with Brad Pitt in *Interview with the Vampire* when I was a little girl watching things I wasn't yet old enough for. Wait, had my mouth dropped open? I shut it quickly and gave the Brad Pitt type a little wave. God, he was gorgeous. I exhaled a little breath and took a fry.

"Oh, my lord, these taste as good as they smell." My eyes rolled back; I'll admit, it had been a while since I had allowed myself a carb. These were too good for me not to have another, then another. I let out another moan.

"Oh, I do love to make a woman moan," a deep voice said behind me.

I turned around in my seat to see the man from the end of the bar. He was dressed in what had to be a custom blazer. I would have bet this guy had a house account at Ben Silver, the gentlemen's store on King Street. The blazer was a dark navy with a slight pattern on it, and underneath it was a crisp white button-down, unbuttoned just slightly. The jacket was tailored exactly to his body, not hiding the fact that this guy was no stranger to a gym.

"Well, that's a little forward . . . but I have to hand it to you. Fries beat flowers any day," I replied.

"Glad it worked. I saw you float in here and I had to meet you." He stuck his tanned hand out. He was also no stranger to the sunshine. "Everyone calls me Charley."

"Hey, Charley. I'm Aly. Aly Knox. It's nice to meet you."

"So, what brings you to Charleston?"

"I actually live here; I'm not a guest at the hotel. I'm here tonight to play mah-jongg for the first time with some girlfriends."

"Not a boyfriend?" He pumped his eyebrows, making a joke of his forward question, though I could tell he really did want to know.

"Not tonight," I teased him.

"What about tomorrow night?"

"Not tomorrow night, either."

"Then I'd like to take you to dinner if you'd let me."

"Do *you* live here, Charley?" I asked. "Or are you just passing through and spoken for in some other city?"

"What do you think?" he asked, and I detected a southern accent. Then he said, "Yes."

"Yes to which question?"

"I am a local, born and bred, and a little insulted you couldn't tell." He made a gesture of mock horror.

"Forgive me, Charley. I love Charleston like a native, but I'm from elsewhere, originally . . ." I took a long sip of my Merlot, which really was a perfect pairing for the fries. "So, are you married?"

"What? No. I wouldn't ask you to dinner if I were married."

"It's just that I'm not going to dinner with any more Peter Pans."

"Peter Pans? Right. Got it. Allow me to reassure you I am a grown-up. My mother would have my hide if I were married and attempting to take women to dinner. But you're right, this is Charleston, the hottest bachelor and bachelorette troublemaking destination of our time. Are *you* married?" He lifted a brow, and I couldn't help it: I smiled. "Whew, the lights just blew out in Georgia with that smile."

I felt my cheeks burn. I had never had anyone be so direct with me before. He was smooth. A little too smooth? I felt a strong need to change the subject. "What do you do, Charley?"

"Can I tell you a secret?"

"Okay."

"I really am a grown-up, and when we go to dinner, I am the sort of Charleston gentleman who picks up the tab. Don't think I'm some lost-boy dreamer. But what do I really want to be? A writer."

"Why are you embarrassed? That's wonderful."

"You think so?"

"Yeah. Actually, I'm trying to build a creative career right now. I mean, it's not like high literature or anything, but—" I broke off, embarrassed but smiling somehow just to be in this Charley person's company.

He grabbed his chest like my smile hurt him. I giggled. He might be a little too smooth, but he was playful, and somehow that made it all seem cute, not manipulative.

"What do you do, Ms. Knox?" he asked me.

"I am an aspiring decorator for home interiors, and I have a blog, too."

"Oh, so you *are* a writer."

"Well, I don't know . . . It's just a blog."

"Do people pay to read it?"

"Well, some do. I offer subscriptions, but some of my content is free."

"In that case, you're a real writer." He sounded like he meant it. I straightened up a little.

I had this feeling like I could spend a long time in the warmth of his company. Maybe for that reason I stood up to go. "I have to get moving to my mah-jongg class. Here's my card. Call me."

"I will. Enjoy, Ms. Knox." He gave me a wink. The bartender came over with the bill on a tray, and of course Charley wouldn't let me pay.

"But you're a writer!" I said. "Writers struggle, in my experience . . ."

"Well, I'm a writer who mostly writes legal briefs. My day job is as a lawyer."

"Okay. In that case, thank you. Nice to meet you, and thank you for the drink and fries."

"Till next time," he said, "when we can share something delicious on purpose."

I felt *that* in my Lowcountry. "See you later, Charley."

"Good night, Ms. Knox."

I left the bar feeling like I had just walked off a movie set. I might have blamed the giant floral arrangements for giving me a contact high with their amazing scent, but I knew it was the banter and the way Charley had looked at me. It made me feel good; what can I say?

I looked over my shoulder and saw him watching me walk away.

Holy Mahj was the company that was holding the mah-jongg class in the Palmetto Cafe, per the hotel's website, and it was located on the hotel's first floor. I click-clacked across the marble floor and was welcomed by a beautiful blonde named Ann and a tiny, pretty brunette named Caroline. They were sharply dressed and had both accessorized with fun jewelry. Both gave me big smiles. We had become fast friends in the world of mah-jongg.

"Wow, what a great venue!" I said. "I'm definitely going to post about this."

"Please do," Ann said. "Tag us, okay? Last time you posted about us, we got a ton of traction!"

I took a look around and saw all the card tables set up with colorful printed tablecloths. Each table had a small lamp in its center, a pile of tiles, and four racks called pushers. Before I even learned the rules, the aesthetics of this game had me sold. The women all dressed to the nines when they played, too, in various sundresses and dangly earrings. It felt very sophisticated.

And that was what Rosemary had said I needed, after all. Sophisticated followers!

I was hoping this game might become a bridge between my mother's established audience and my growing audience. It was a ladies' game.

I scanned to find my friends.

I saw Maggie right away. With her copper red hair, she was hard to miss. I was surprised she'd come. It was Monday, and she did usually take Mondays off, but she was almost never without her boyfriend, Sam. Plus, she wasn't the type to put on a frilly dress. She was more of a let's-get-tacos-and-throw-back-shots-of-tequila kind of gal.

"Hey, Maggie!" I said, and she spun around to give me a kiss on my cheek.

"Hey, girl!" she exclaimed, putting on a warm smile. "Good to see you!"

She was dressed in a white linen shift and had a chunky turquoise necklace on. It was a minimal look, but effortlessly chic. It was good to see her out of her chef's whites.

"You look great! I love your dress!"

"It's actually Gran's! Vintage from the seventies!"

Just then Violet walked in, arm in arm with a gorgeous woman who had what looked like a million tiny braids and was wearing an African-print pencil skirt and a black blouse with see-through puffed sleeves. She looked fierce and chic, especially with the stack of gold bangles on her wrist.. You could tell she was in the fashion business in some way. I assumed this was Malory.

I knew the drama with Violet's relationship with her father was still touchy. It had been a few weeks, but she seemed to be making some positive changes—moving out of her grandmother's, cleaning up, trying new things, having fun. Her makeup was perfect, and she was smiling. I had an inkling it had something to do with this Christopher guy coming home.

"Violet, you look fantastic!" I gave her a huge hug.

"Got her coat shined, if you ask me," Maggie said.

"Maggie, stop it. Chris and I are taking it slow, okay? We were going to have our big first date tonight, but, honestly, with everything, I needed to be with my girls," Violet said. "Aly, this is Malory! *She's* the reason why I look good!"

"Hey there! I'm Malory. It's so nice to meet you. I've heard such great things!"

"Great to meet you! Can you make me as beautiful as Violet? I have some serious hair envy!"

"Of course! But you are already beautiful! I happen to have just had a cancellation tomorrow if you'd like a cut and color. I'm thinking of a beautiful brighter blond?"

"God yes!" I said.

"Oh, I want to be blond!" Maggie said.

"Have you lost your mind? Girl, people pay money for your shade. I think the beauty gods would chop my hands off if I dared to dye that scarlet mane," Malory said.

"Fine." Maggie looked around for our server. "I'm ordering fries."

"Oh, I just had some great ones at the bar! Met a cute guy, too."

"Oh yeah?" Violet elbowed my ribs.

"Yes, seemed fancy, too. One of those old Charleston aristocracy types. A lawyer."

"What kind of law?" Violet asked. "I hope he's not in a field similar to Chris's, because that's so much work . . ."

"Let's just hope he's not like Chris in any way," Maggie said, not under her breath at all.

"Maggie, Chris and I are starting afresh, so I need you on board with me."

"Okay, ladies, listen up!" Caroline called, before Violet could answer. This was probably a blessing—it seemed like Violet and her sister were about to get heated with each other. "Who's ready to learn?"

The night progressed nicely. As the hours went on, Caroline explained every single thing, and my friends started to pick up the rules. The shuffling of the beautiful tiles, the calling, the Charleston passing, and the traditions, like cheers when you got a "bird bam." It was all very girlie and wonderful. Violet and I took tons of pictures, and I planned the blog post I would do about it. Now my biggest problem was how quickly I could order some of those tiles for myself! I learned they were expensive, but, luckily, we were offered a discount. Now, to choose which ones to buy.

By the time we walked out to our cars, I was feeling much better. "Can I have a group hug?" I asked. "This was the perfect night; I needed to be out of the house with girls and do something beautiful!"

"Uh-oh." Violet shot me a sympathetic face. "Your dad's friend causing you trouble?"

"Joyce. Yeah. She has pressured my dad to ask me to move out."

"What?" Violet's expression conveyed how much she got it—how much this thing with Joyce displacing me was salt in my deepest wound. "Not from your mother's house!"

"Oh no, he made it very clear that it was *his* house." A lump was forming in my throat.

Maggie shook her head. "Oh, please. Who does she think she is?"

I shrugged bitterly. "My father's future wife."

"Over Callie's dead body," Violet said.

"Literally," I seconded.

"So, what are you going to do?" Maggie asked me.

Malory crossed her arms over her chest. "Revenge, obviously."

"Revenge?" I repeated, and held back a giggle.

"Absolutely. If she's making you move out, it's only right that you make her just as miserable." She cocked one of her beautifully shaped brows. "I got a few ideas."

"Y'all, that's funny, but, seriously, I'm sad about it. I don't want to move out of my home!"

"He didn't mean it, Aly, I'm sure . . . Why would he do that?"

"Because he's a selfish man who wants to get laid . . ." Malory made a face like *Tell me I am wrong.* "And I hate to say this, but he's taking advantage of the fact that you'll forgive him. Sounds like this Joyce throws one hell of a fit."

"I have a crazy idea," Violet said.

"What's that?" I said.

"Why don't you move in with me and Jimmy?" Violet said, and then squealed.

I frowned. I didn't want to cede any territory, and I'd gotten really excited about fixing up the apartment.

"Aly, you haven't even unpacked. We have an extra bedroom!" she said.

"It could be a real good story to post about . . ." I mused.

"Aly, Bunny said I can do whatever I want with the house!" Violet was bouncing with excitement.

"I'll think about it . . . I mean, it is tempting. I'm so angry and hurt by my dad, I don't really want to even go home tonight."

"Girl, this is a godsend. I say do it," Malory said.

I nodded, but I wasn't sure. "Let's sleep on it."

We said our goodbyes and got in our cars. On the way home, I listened to some good tunes, rolled the windows down, and let the ocean air mess my hair up as I drove over the causeway onto Sullivan's Island. Maybe Violet was right. My gut told me that I needed to get out of there. Maybe some space from my dad would be good. I was too hurt and angry not to get into a knock-down, drag-out fight, and I had to think strategically here.

If I caused a scene, Dad would think *I* was the problem.

I needed to give that woman enough time to reveal her true colors.

The house that Violet and Jimmy were making could only be temporary anyway—Violet was just biding time before she and Chris moved back in together, or at least that was what it sounded like to me. Making sure she had her own space so it didn't go *too* fast. And Jimmy would surely want to return to New York and the theater world before too long.

My dad would eventually see the real Joyce, especially if he was alone with Joyce all day and all night. Meanwhile, I'd move out, and he could see what it was like living with her full-time. Silent warfare, cucumber cool, that was the best way to take on a woman like Joyce . . . and maybe Violet was right about this being another great brand-building activity.

CHAPTER TWENTY

~~~~~

Violet

July

Aly, Jimmy, and I were painting the walls of Bunny's house in Hampton Park, which we were already calling home. It was so hot outside, I could barely see straight. We had cranked the air-conditioning, but the southern humidity was fighting to keep it even at seventy-five. Chris and I had been spending a little time together, but he was still trying hard to find a job and so we weren't seeing each other as much as we would have liked.

The house Bunny had rented us was a diamond in the rough. I hadn't realized that Hampton Park was such a happening neighborhood. When I was younger, living downtown, this area wasn't a great spot to be. Now it was full of young families who were buying up all these old houses. It seemed like the whole street was getting a makeover. Our home was over a hundred years old, and it needed a lot of work. Bunny was planning on selling it eventually but had agreed to rent it to us for a low price if we would do some of the cosmetic renovations ourselves, and because Aly needed a project, it had worked out for us.

Aly was also in the process of taking over her mom's brand, something that had been in the works for a while. She was going back and forth with her mother's old business manager and wanted to use our house for her portfolio. She wanted to build on her dream of being an influencer to have a full-on brand within a brand. It was great to see her in her element.

We had all purchased some cheap overalls from the Goodwill, and it was a good thing, because we were totally covered in colors. Sherman-Williams cabbage rose, dusty rose, true rose. Well, Jimmy and I were; Aly was basically a professional. I had thought it would be more laid-back, but once I saw her pull out the painter's tape and several brushes, I knew this wasn't going to be like college, when we ordered a pizza and a case of beer and got the job done, if a little sloppily. Aly was serious.

It made sense, since this was all going on her social accounts. She was steadily growing an audience by posting more, doing more lives and stories, doing more projects.

We were working off this girl's vision board. But I would be lying if I said Jimmy and I weren't smiling indulgently behind her back as she went on about "vibes" and "cohesive moods" when referring to paint colors. The calendar gods gave us a week to get it done, because that particular week I didn't have any weddings to cover. At first, we ate it up, but after three full days painting when it was over a hundred degrees, it was nigh impossible to keep a straight face when, for instance, I said I wanted a tan color for the living room and Aly quickly corrected me, saying the shade I was imagining should be properly referred to as "dune."

She obviously had talent, and the house was shaping up to be beautiful. But I was more than relieved when she told us to take a little break around noon.

After splashing water on my face and drinking a little sweet tea, I went upstairs to find Aly at her computer.

"Hey, girl, what are you doing?" I asked.

"Oh, just a little touching up of some photos."

"For your Instagram?" I asked.

"No, for me, I guess. Malory suggested I digitally alter Joyce's photos every so often and add like ten pounds each time. It was funny, but kind of evil. I'm not a fan of Joyce's, but . . . so I'm doing this instead."

"I can't see any difference between the photos, Aly," I said, looking at the original picture next to the newly altered one. "They look identical."

"Look more closely with your professional eye."

"Do you have a loupe? I mean . . ."

"Look at the birds in the sky . . ."

"Oh my god, Aly, they spell out 'Callie.'"

"Yup. It's for me. I need to not feel like my mom is totally wiped out. I just don't . . . Why does he allow her to put up all these pictures . . . ?"

"I was going to ask if your dad still thinks she's perfect."

"It's still early days. I've tried to talk to him, but nothing gets through. I don't understand it." She sighed. "What's your plan for tonight?"

"Oh, I've got a date with Chris. What about you?"

"Aww, man, I was hoping you would be home so we could start on the garden outside and maybe take a little trip to Hyams for some plants. The back and front need some love."

"Sorry, can we do that another day?" I said. "We're going to Park and Grove for dinner. It's this whole courting thing—it's cute! He took me to a 'first-date' restaurant, and a 'second-date' restaurant. Third date's more serious—so you know it needs to be a higher-caliber place. The chef from Post House left and is there now."

Aly nodded, but I could tell she was distracted. That was fine. I liked the game Chris and I were playing—taking it slow, courting. It didn't matter to me if no one else understood. "Let's go back to painting. I want to talk to you about color saturation."

"Like for a photograph?" I asked.

"No, it's a stylistic choice for the living spaces. I am going to paint the walls and ceilings in the living and dining rooms all the same colors. Farrow and Boll colors. Or at least I'll go to the paint store and have them matched. Trim, ceilings, walls, all of it. It gives off Jane Austen vibes. This house is so cool already. This is just the icing."

Another blessing of this endeavor was that Jimmy had discovered his love for handiwork. Before this, he would never have been able to tell you the difference between a flathead screwdriver and a Phillips. "Henry explained it to me," he said. "You know, Henry the yummy Brit?" And I felt a little sad that I couldn't have a crush on Jimmy's friend Henry anymore. I had to focus on the potential of Chris. Not that I was going to mention this to anyone. I had my pride to think about. But he still liked all my pictures on Instagram and watched all my stories. Yes, I was keeping track. Anyway, he'd certainly helped Jimmy become handier, or at least *look* the part. Now here the man was walking around with measuring tape, safety goggles, and a hammer in the carpenter loop of his overalls. He seemed really happy with his new hobby. I think Jim needed a distraction and something to throw himself into; frankly, all of us did.

I liked the way things were going with Chris. We were living separately. I was holding the line on that, though he kept asking when we could stop the charade and live together like before. Sometimes I wondered if I was being ridiculous. We did own a house—and I was contributing to the mortgage on it—and I knew who he was. But I figured if we did get back together, it would be for forever, and it was okay to give us some time to figure things out. It was nice to go on dates where he picked me up and dropped me off, nice to feel like I was starting over with him.

"All right, I think I'm going to paint my room pink," I said.

"Like a Barbie pink?" Aly's face was wide with alarm. "Please tell me no. It's important that the colors all vibe. The hues have to flow."

I showed her the swatch, trying to keep my expression neutral and not, like, break out in giggles. "I was going to go with this soft peony color."

"Let's test it out on the wall."

As we assessed the swatch, I asked Aly, "What's going on with you and your new guy?"

"Oh, him." She shrugged. I sort of admired how much Aly seemed to be able to take or leave relationships. But I didn't really get it. "We've been texting and talking on the phone a lot but haven't gotten together yet."

"Why's that?"

"Honestly, it's both of our schedules. I'm so busy. I've always been this way—with my family we're really close, so it's hard to make room for a new person, you know? For him, I don't know. Must be lawyer life. Is that how it is with Chris?"

"Yeah . . . though, I don't know, we're sort of doing this 'starting over' thing, so I like that we're seeing each other more like a courting couple, less like people who've been together years."

"Get that mystery back?"

"Yeah!" I grinned. It was kind of true. This new side of Chris had come out. It was exciting.

"I think I get it," Aly said. "With this new guy, I am enjoying having some distance. Just talking on the phone like kids, you know? He gives good talk, if you know what I mean."

"Oh, I like the sound of that! Spill it, girl!"

Just then Jim appeared. "Dare I think I hear gossip about to be aired out—gossip about the mystery lawyer man?"

"Yes. Charley. He's a spicy one. I just need to figure out when I can see him."

"What about tonight?" I suggested. "You aren't doing anything."

"Yes, girl. The yard can wait!" Jimmy said.

Aly frowned. "Can it, though? We have so much to do. And I'm really trying to grow my own audience. I'm so afraid of losing this important collab deal that meant so much to my mother. Anyway, what do your southern mothers tell you? Better to leave a man wanting more, right? Let's get back at it, then, y'all. I'm going to switch out the light fixture in the dining room. Violet, can you do some before shots, so I can do a before-and-after post?"

"Sure thing," I said. "Let me get this paint off my hands and grab my camera."

The rest of the afternoon went on like that until I had to get ready for my dinner date. I chose a red linen dress with a full skirt that made me want to twirl like I had done when I was a little girl. I paired it with some faux-diamond hoops and my gold slide-on sandals. Park and Grove was a great restaurant; I was excited to try their new menu. Since I was running late as usual, Chris and I decided to meet at the restaurant.

It was that time of day when the sun had finally tucked itself behind its cloud cover for the night, relieving us from its endless heat. The city was still humid, but relief was in the air. Park and Grove had a large covered outside dining option, and if it had been slightly cooler, I would have wanted to be there. However, the day's heat still lingered and threatened to melt my tinted moisturizer off. They had some live music inside; it was one of the things they did every Tuesday, along with offering half-price bottles of wine and happy hour charcuterie all night.

It was a charming neighborhood gem, and I was excited to be there on the arm of a handsome man who was familiar but also new again.

Chris was at the table in the corner next to the windows, wearing a starched blue linen shirt and pale tan slacks. He had his head buried in his Kindle and was sipping a white wine that looked like the perfect antidote to the hot day of painting I had just emerged from.

"Hey there! Sorry I'm late," I said, and sat down across from him.

"No worries, I was just finishing the new Baldacci. It's gripping." He set aside his Kindle to give me a warm smile. "Hi, gorgeous. How was your day?"

"Spent the whole day doing what Martha Stewart—I mean Aly— told me to. I could use one of those. What are you drinking?"

"Simi, Chardonnay. My favorite. Here, let me get you one." He signaled our server, and she was back in a moment with my glass.

The golden-hay-colored wine was a cool kiss. It was delicious, like honey, and as it slid down my throat, I felt my shoulders relax. Wine sometimes healed wounds that I didn't know existed.

"So, how goes the job hunt?" I asked him.

"How it always goes. Long. Lots of paperwork. I have an interview at a firm downtown next week, maybe." He made a gesture as though to say he wouldn't dream of boring me with this stuff and changed the subject. "What do you think about pickleball?"

"Pickleball? Well, like mah-jongg, it's all the rage these days. Why, are you thinking about trying it?"

"I thought we could do it together." He shot me a wink. "You know, if you can break away from work."

"I told you things were different now, Chris. My wedding photography biz has really taken off. But it should slow down now, until October, when . . ."

"Vi, I know October is the busiest month for you. Remember when we thought about . . . ?"

Of course I did. My stomach hurt, remembering. But here we were, with glasses of a beautiful wine, in a nice room that smelled of lavender and roasted potatoes. "You know what? We don't have to talk about that."

"You're right, Violet. You always are. Let's reset. I'll use the bathroom, and when I come back, we can start afresh. Excuse me."

Chris got up, and I watched him walk away. And I noticed the other women pause over their dinners to look at him. He was mine—I felt proud of that, glad those women would watch him walk back to me. I looked over the menu and preselected the peach and burrata salad. It felt like a summer dish, and South Carolina was in fact the best place for peaches. Georgia had the reputation, but we actually had the better peaches. Those who knew, knew. Then the pan-seared chicken breast. Then—

My menu strategizing was interrupted by a loud laugh.

I looked around the room at the mixed crowd, old and young, families, people on dates. My eyes settled on a beautiful woman in a purple dress. She was laughing so hard that her head was thrown back, and her hand was on the table like she was reaching out to hold, or had maybe just been holding, the hand of her companion. I realized they were speaking another language. I thought to myself how nice it would be to laugh like that. I wondered who she was laughing with, and then it hit me.

"Oh god," I said out loud, recognizing Henry. I felt a pang of jealousy. That woman was beautiful. Stunning, actually. Dark eyes, dark hair . . . sophisticated. I felt plain in my stupid red linen dress. Ugh. *Of course* Henry would be attracted to someone like this Eva Longoria look-alike. I suddenly was very aware that my legs hadn't seen the sun in a while, that I needed to get my butt on a beach. As the woman crossed her legs, I spied a sparkly anklet. She just oozed sex appeal. "Eva Longoria" shook her hair back off her face and gave another throaty laugh. How had my glass become empty? I motioned for our server to bring me another one.

Finally, Chris came back. I might have been drinking a little too quickly on an empty stomach, because I could feel the muscles in my legs start to relax.

"Sorry about that. There was a wait, and I had a call I had to take."

"Everything okay?"

"Yes, of course." Thankfully, our server brought over a bread basket. I ordered the burrata and peach salad and the pan-seared chicken, as planned. Chris ordered mussels and the bourbon-brined pork chop. Then he took out his phone, which annoyed me. I wanted Henry to look over and see how perfect and happy Chris and I were, joined in intimate conversation, just laughing our heads off. But then I realized that Chris being sucked into his phone would give me time to spy.

What was my mind doing? Was this the wine, or had my mom's line of thinking infiltrated my head? Henry and I had only flirted, so why should I care if this was his girlfriend or whatever? Oh god, not another Charleston slimeball. Why would he lead me on like that? Or worse, what if he was just being friendly, and I had made up our connection and spent all this time delusionally reading into the fact that he liked my Insta posts?

"So, what do the next few days look like for you?" I asked Chris.

"I am working like a monster. Work dinner tomorrow."

"Oh, okay." This wasn't really a gripping conversation. We clearly were not having as much fun as Henry and "Eva." "I'm going to use the ladies'. I'll be right back." As I stood, I realized that I hadn't eaten much while working on the house, and the wine had gone to my head and weakened my knees. But I would be fine. I'd muster up all my sex appeal and confidence and walk right past Henry, not even looking at him.

I steadied myself, stuck out my chin and chest, and breezed past their table. But this didn't work out as I had envisioned. In fact, when I walked past, he was so absorbed in what "Eva" was saying that he didn't even look up. *Ugh. Okay,* I thought, *I'll get him on the way back.* In the ladies', I reapplied my lip gloss, fluffed my hair, and pushed my shoulders back. I would exude confidence and elegance. I would be but a breeze of subtle mystery and sex. I would be a living goddess as I glided to my table, where my handsome prince sat. Henry *who?*

I took a deep breath, pushed through the door, and strode back toward the dining room, and that's about where it all fell apart. The first step out was fine, but on the second one, I took a little too big a sidestep dodging a server who came out of nowhere carrying a very large tray of dirty plates and glasses. He tried to swerve but ended up right in front of me, and the heel of my sandal met something slippery and my feet began to move in opposite directions, and my legs parted into the splits, a position that I hadn't visited for at least a decade.

I went down, and I mean *down*, hard and fast. Not just me, either. I took the server, who grabbed my wrist, with me and sent the plates flying in various directions. All my attempts to right myself just increased my momentum. As I slid right past Henry's table, I took his tablecloth and whatever was on the table with me. The worst part of this truly revolting turn of events was that I yelled "Oh, shit" louder than I've ever cussed in my life. As soon as my speed decreased, the bottle of red wine tilted and spilled all down my back. My hips hurt, and I was too embarrassed to look up, so I just sat there in a split, covered in food and bathed in wine.

At least there was wine.

I didn't know what else to do, so I threw my arms up like a gymnast and said "Ta-da!"

"Violet?" Henry said. Oh no. I could hear him getting out of his chair to help me up.

"Babe?" Chris yelled across the dining room in my direction. "Are you okay? Oh my god!" In a moment he had reached me. Before I knew what was going on, I had one hand in each man's palm.

"Uh, yes, mostly embarrassed. Hello, Henry, nice to see you." I flicked droplets of red wine from my hair, splattering Chris's crisp blue shirt.

"No need, this makes us even. You and my dog." Henry dropped my hand.

Wow. The guy was comparing me to his dog. I really *was* delusional.

"Do you know each other?" Chris asked. He was trying to seem like he didn't care about his ruined shirt, but I could see that he did.

"Yes, he's friends with Jim. Henry, this is Chris. Chris, Henry."

"Oh, you're the famous Chris! I see you returned from Japan safely." Henry passed me a napkin.

"I'm sorry, have we met before?" Chris asked.

"No, Violet was just saying so many nice things about you at dinner—a dinner where my dog jumped on the table and spoiled the meal. That's what I was referring to."

"I'm Samantha, his date," said the Eva Longoria clone.

"Hey, I'm Violet." I felt my cheeks redden, but thankfully I was such a mess it probably didn't show. "And I'm leaving now to go home, change, and drink myself to sleep. See you around, Henry. Let's go, Chris." I left as the servers arrived to clean.

"Wait, please let me pay for your wine, Henry," Chris said. I was shocked; he never offered to pay for anything.

"No need, really. Like I said, this makes us even," Henry said in a tone of finality, and sat down with Samantha.

I left my car and walked back home while Chris handled the bill. I texted him, saying he should meet me back at my place—I wanted to get out of these shameful, ruined clothes as soon as possible. When I arrived home, thankfully Jim and Aly weren't there. I took off my dress, and threw myself into the shower. After I washed all the shame off, I talked myself into several conversations I should have orchestrated back at the restaurant. Did I really say "Ta-da"? God, I was such a freak. I grabbed a short black sundress I had worn the other day and just threw it on.

I'd needed to come home and pretty myself up. But being alone with my thoughts, with my unbearably awkward self, was horrible.

Maybe Chris and I could watch a movie, make this whole episode disappear.

While I waited for him, I opened a bottle of wine. I was so embarrassed about making that scene. I was embarrassed that I cared that Henry had a girlfriend, embarrassed that I'd been secretly crushing on Henry when he was unavailable and uninterested.

Was I being ridiculous? A small, vicious, bossy voice in my head definitely thought so. That voice was very adamant that I should stop being absurd, that I had no right to be annoyed or hurt. Henry could date whomever he wanted. And why, honestly, would he want to date a ding-dong like me?

I was pretty well cleaned up, but still a real mess mentally, by the time Chris knocked at the door and suggested we go for a walk.

I tried hard to put away whatever I had just been feeling and was relieved to find that the weather was ready to accommodate me, help me shake off the uncomfortable feelings and play this game Chris and I were playing. We were a new couple again, just getting to know each other. A fresh start.

Outside, it was unusually cool and breezy. Giant clouds were rolling in, illuminated with early starlight. The light was almost a dark purple. Everything felt electric. It was the summer storm season, and we were in for a show. Chris took me by the hand to lead me out of the house, and we drove in his car toward the Battery.

We strolled along the seawall, hand in hand, watching the turbulent emerald sea.

I felt a shiver as the wind hit the back of my exposed neck. I wrapped my pashmina around my shoulders and squeezed Chris's hand. He squeezed mine back. I looked up at him, and we smiled at each other. Walking in silence, matching his pace, I felt small next to his towering height. I felt protected with his large hand holding mine. I had his attention, and I liked it. The wind could lift me up and away, it seemed, but still, he would anchor me. Chris was so strong, so sure of everything, and so sturdy. I liked the old familiar feeling of not having to make any decisions. I inhaled the salt in the air and smelled a faint whiff of jasmine. I had forgotten how nicely we fit together.

I dropped his hand and went to the railing. A sliver of a silver moon flashed, exposed by the fast-moving clouds, along with a sprinkling of stars. Chris came up behind me and put his arms around me, pulling me to him.

"I've missed you, Vi," he whispered into my neck.

He pushed my hair aside and kissed the soft spot where my neck met my shoulder. I shivered again, not from cold.

I wanted him, I wanted us; we weren't over. Maybe we had just begun.

I looked deep into his eyes. "I missed you, too, Chris."

I knew that he had some making up to do, that we needed to talk through our issues and maybe even get some counseling if we were ever going to reestablish ourselves as a couple . . . but right then, at that moment, I just wanted to give in to the tug of what felt like fate between us. Wrong or not, I could make that decision later. Right now, I wanted to feel like just a woman, uncomplicated.

I spun myself around, got up on my tiptoes, and reached for him around his neck, pulling his lips to mine, our mouths opening to each other. He kissed me slowly at first, and as the wind picked up, so did the heat between us. His tongue parted my lips, and I took a deep breath in between fast kisses. His hands slid down past my back and grabbed my hips. He pressed himself firmly against me, and I could feel the familiar tug. The air was colder then; I felt my skin get bumpy, and he rubbed my arms. With my back against the railing, he slid his hand up underneath my dress and tugged at my panties.

I was a little shocked—he was usually such a gentleman—but something about his urgency excited me. The last time we'd made love—the first time in a while, since he had been in Japan; the night I found out about my dad—I had noticed he was more direct. I looked around, and thankfully we were alone. There was no one anywhere. I heard the low roar of thunder and a few waves crashing against the rocks. A giant pull, and a huge spray of water splashed up against the wall, misting us with salt. It felt like the whole universe wanted us to undo each other.

We needed a fresh start, and this felt sexy and naughty. I was reminded of the heavy make-out sessions we'd had so many years ago in the back of his truck in my grandmother's driveway when he dropped me off after movie-and-fast-food dates. I felt his fingers push aside my pink hanky-panky lace boy shorts and slide inside me.

"Chris!" I gasped.

"Come on, baby, let me show you something new," he murmured at the same time as I saw a flash of lightning.

"Okay . . ." I whispered. I couldn't help it. The way his fingers were moving prompted me to whisper, "Yes."

"Yes, sir?" he asked as he pressed his length against my leg. I felt a rush of fire through my veins.

"Yes, sir. I'm yours." I bit my lower lip. He growled low in my ear, and I tried not to think about who else had seen this side of him.

This wasn't my familiar Chris. My polite gentleman. It was a powerful sexual being, and all I could do was give in, roll with him like the tide behind me—a little rough, but very wet. The sky opened then and sent fat raindrops plopping against the cement Battery. My dress was stuck to my body like a second skin, and Chris pushed the hair off my face to look at me.

For a moment I had this flash of insecurity. Some old, old self-critical habit. He could see all my curves.

But then he said, "God, you're beautiful, Violet," biting his own lip, and I forgot to worry about my soft tummy.

A giant crack of lightning blazed in the sky, and I let out a yelp.

"I love it when you scream," he said. "Please let me make you."

This was new.

"Think you still can, Chris?" I teased, trying to keep it light, though everything was feeling vertiginous and urgent.

"*Sir.* Call me 'sir,' baby." He was licking his lips and staring at my chest, which was entirely visible through my soaking wet linen dress.

My stomach flipped. I'd never felt more wanted in my life. His hunger was big; I could see it and touch it through his now skintight, drenched khaki trousers. I let my eyes linger, and through my soaked eyelashes I looked up at him and said "Yes, sir" in a husky voice.

"That's a good girl. Come on." He took my hand and led me into the park across the street.

We hurried, jumping over puddles, to the gazebo in the center of the park. I did a quick scan and couldn't believe how alone we were and how dark it was. Underneath the roof we stood looking at each other, heavily breathing. I had never felt this wild and unleashed. I couldn't stop my mouth from finding his mouth again and again. He stepped forward, and I took a sharp breath in, almost bracing myself for impact.

With one arm he scooped me up against him and with the other he palmed my breast, finding my hardened nipple between his fingers and giving it a hard squeeze. I gasped. I had never been touched like that; I had never danced on the line of pain and pleasure. My heart was racing, but my body begged for him to go on.

He pushed me up against one of the columns and kissed me on my mouth, neck, shoulders. He pulled down one of my dress straps and slid the bodice low enough to expose one of my breasts, which he gently licked, then bit. A small moan escaped me.

"More, baby?" he asked.

"Yes, please, sir." I moaned again, and arched my back, pressing my pelvis up against him. I wasn't in control anymore, and I couldn't tell if it was him, if it was me, or if I was bewitched.

He took my hair and bunched it in his hand, pulling my head to the side, exposing my neck, which he gently bit and kissed. Took me around my waist and sat me up on the railing that wrapped around the gazebo, my back still against a column to steady me. He parted my legs and worked his way between them. He slid the skirt of my dress up, and I felt my sandals slide off. I wrapped around him and felt my thighs tighten up as I rocked against him.

"Oh god, Violet. I want you right now."

"How much?"

"Forever."

It was what I had wanted to hear for so long. I inhaled his scent then, and he smelled so, so good. "Take me, then. I'm yours."

He pulled back, licking his lips. "Take off your panties."

"What? Chris, we're in public!" My heart was beating in my throat. "I don't care."

"You can't go to jail; you're a lawyer."

"Then we better not get caught, baby." He unbuckled his leather belt and slid it through his belt loops, cracking it like the lightning that was firing around us.

"Oh my god, Christopher!" I let out a giggle, but I was getting nervous. This was sexy, for sure, but it was going too far. I didn't know what to do. His eyes were so dark.

"I said take off your panties."

I felt a flash of fear then, but he looked so intent and so wild. He wouldn't really want to go all the way in public, would he? Surely this was a game of chicken.

"Yes, sir." I maintained eye contact and slid off my undies, kicking them to the side.

He picked me up in a breath and sat me back on the railing. Parting my legs, he slid his fingers inside me again, pulling them out for a moment to suck them.

"I call the shots. I am in charge. Let me worship you, baby," he said, a little too sternly.

"Chris . . ."

"Open your legs wider," he demanded. So I did.

He slid his hands under me and picked me up, carrying me to the other side of the gazebo. Up against the pillar, he wrapped my legs around him and removed his stiffness from his pants.

"I love you, Violet. You are my queen."

"I love you, too, Chris. You are my king."

Then he shoved himself inside of me, and I almost saw stars.

"Remember me, little girl? Remember how much you need me," he said in a hoarse whisper. He pumped into me, and it felt fantastic. "You make me wild, baby."

"Chris, oh my god, we need to . . ."

"Never. We are never stopping." Between deep breaths he slid his free hand around my throat and squeezed.

I tried to breathe and felt my eyes go wide.

He'd never done anything like that before. I tried to protest, but his hand was getting tighter, and the words wouldn't come.

"See? I knew you'd like that, baby. Me in control," he said. "I'm almost there . . ." and everything went dark.

CHAPTER TWENTY-ONE

~~~

Aly

I woke up to a beautiful day and this fine sense that things were going well for once. The Hampton Park house was coming together, and my content was gaining traction. Everyone loved a makeover story, and they loved to watch Jim. Jim was having a blast and totally leaning into being the handyman around. His celebrity following brought people to my page, too. His soap fans loved my style. We were now thinking about doing a YouTube series together.

After a long session working on the house and filming each other for our various socials, we'd gone out and celebrated. I was having fun, and I was proud of myself. I was trying not to get too excited or ahead of myself, but I was thinking this all had a lot of potential; it was going great.

Maybe I was really good at this? Maybe I really was meant to take over Callie Knox?

If Crate and Barn didn't want to buy into our plans for the Christmas line, someone else would for sure pick it up.

I went downstairs to find Violet up way earlier than usual.

"Hey, girl!" I said brightly.

"Hey, good morning. I'm going to just take this coffee upstairs." Violet lifted the mug in my direction, avoiding eye contact.

"Long night," she added as she disappeared up the stairs.

That was weird.

I had wanted to tell her the latest about Charley, but that did not seem to be in the cards.

Last night, after much prodding from Jim, I had finally made the executive decision to call Charley and ask him to dinner. Enough was enough. Sure, this bold move of putting myself out there had been fueled by sass, but, in the light of day, I was grateful for the push. I had resented my dad's implication that I should be out dating, but the truth was, it had been far too long and it was time to get back in the game.

I went back into the kitchen to find my phone and check my socials. I had gained almost a hundred followers overnight! Everyone seemed to love the video Jim and I had done about picking swatches for the hallway, and also the video of us sanding the floors. That one was pure joy, with Jimmy riding the sander. I smiled, watching it again.

And there was a text from Charley, saying he'd planned a dinner for tomorrow night. Thanks for calling, gorgeous.

I was still smiling at this message when my phone buzzed with a message from my dad.

I've got some news, Min.
When are you free for dinner?

I'm free tonight . . .

5pm cocktails on the porch?

See you then! Xoxo

Jimmy entered the kitchen, looking a little rough.

"Hey, what's up with Violet?" I asked him.

"What do you mean?"

"I don't know. I just saw her for a sec, and she seemed, like . . . spooked."

"Spooked?"

"I don't know how else to describe it. She was a little jumpy."

"She had dinner with Chris last night. Maybe that didn't go so well. I'll check in with her. I think I need to go back to bed; I have a Zoom audition later this afternoon, and then a call with a director downtown. The Dock Street Theatre is looking for a male to join their troupe."

"Well, that sounds fun! Break a leg!"

"Thanks, chica," Jim said, and left me alone in the kitchen.

I knew I had some work to get done, so I decided to go to a local coffee shop with my laptop. It was so hot outside, and the only remedy was iced coffee. I was going to do a blog post about some of my summer favorites. I would make sure to include things that I was loving so I could get double usage out of some content pictures. I was repeating using my Hart Jewelry Charleston charm necklace, so I decided to write a little about the designer on my blog. She was so sweet in real life, too, and I loved the opportunity to shine a light on local talent.

Last week I had submitted everything to Rosemary, and I was waiting on her email back. I wanted to make her and my father proud. I wanted to take over the brand and make it mine, but on my own merit. I needed to earn it. They had loved "My Mother's Daughter" as a new brand name, and seemed enthusiastic about the logo I submitted. I sent over another video of our living room transformation and was excited for her feedback. I wanted the whole team to be impressed.

I decided to call Violet and check in on her, but she ignored my call and it went right to voicemail. This wasn't normal. I checked her location. We had shared our locations when we moved in together, for safety reasons. The app on my phone said she was at the house. Maybe I should go talk to her directly at home. But then I saw the time, and realized I was going to have to hustle if I wanted to get home and changed to drive out to Sullivan's. The day had totally escaped me.

When I walked into the house it was dead quiet, which was kind of freaky, so I went upstairs to Violet's room and knocked on the door.

"Vi?"

"Hey. I'm just lying down."

"Can you talk for a sec?" I asked.

"Um . . . yeah, hold on."

I heard some things moving around and a drawer closing. Then she opened the door. The room was a mess, which was very un-Violet. She wore a robe, and her face was pink.

"Everything okay?" she asked.

"Yeah, of course . . . I'm just checking on you."

She still wouldn't make eye contact. "Okay."

"Violet, what's going on?" I said.

"Nothing. I had a bad night. I'll be fine."

"Is this about your dad? I think we should talk about it. I'm having dinner with my dad, but I have some time."

"No, seriously, I'm fine."

"No you're not. Meet me in my room in ten."

I went to my room and started pulling out different outfit options for my dad date.

I had been really busy the past two weeks, I hadn't really seen him, and I obviously had some questions. In a few moments, Violet appeared with two ice waters, the glasses already fogged by condensation.

"This might call for adult beverages later," she said, putting the glasses on the nightstand and then plopping down on my bed.

"Uh-oh. Do you want to save it till after dinner, then?" I tried to make her smile, make her laugh. "I'll grab matches and we can do a séance? Make a voodoo doll? Who do we hate?"

"Funny." Violet sighed and dragged her finger down the screen of her phone. "Me. I kind of hate myself."

"Okay, tell me . . ."

Suddenly she gasped and jumped to her feet. "Oh my god!"

"What? What's going on?" I was actually finding it a little hard to process Violet right now. It was like she was becoming a different person every few minutes. Not the controlled, accomplished girl I was used to. Maybe Chris and her thoughts about her dad were stressing her.

"Jesus. Yes!" she happily shrieked.

"If you don't tell me what's happening, I might faint, Violet."

"My dad! My dad just sent me a message on Instagram! Oh my god."

Jimmy appeared in the doorway, holding a martini with two plump olives. "Violetta, I couldn't help but overhear . . ."

"Isn't it great? I'm so happy! I was afraid Maggie had scared him off! I had sent him a few messages, but he left me unread . . ."

"Wow, this is big." Jimmy took a long sip from his glass.

"Oh my god, oh my god, he says I should come up to visit him in Nantucket!"

"Whoa, how are you feeling about that?" I asked, because the energy in the room was a little crazed and I wasn't even sure how *I* felt.

But Jimmy just looked plain excited. "Do you think I need to come with you?"

"What? Jimmy, I don't . . ."

"Might be a lot, going there alone." Jimmy gave Violet a significant look. "That's all I'm saying."

"Thanks, Jimmy," Violet said, throwing her arms around him. "Would you? Oh my god, I'd be so scared, honestly. I know Maggie is going to be dead set against this, and I could use some company, I think."

"I bet that's why he took a minute to respond. That steel Magnolia probably scared him good."

"So, when does he want you to come?" I asked, putting on my gold hoops. I was glad to see Violet perk up, but I was a little on Maggie's side of things. Change should be approached slowly.

"He says as soon as I can, and that he'll send me a ticket, and Maggie, too, if she wants to come. He knows that might be tough, and he doesn't want us to feel pressured, but the door is open." Violet was clearly thrilled. "But, shit, what am I going to tell Maggie? Will she want to come?"

"Oh, lord, Vi, wait a sec on that, maybe?" I said, turning from the mirror.

"Yeah." Jimmy's eyes went from me to Violet. "She isn't on the same page as you."

"I have to tell her, though, so she can consider it. Right?"

We all nodded, and Violet left the room to call Maggie in private.

"Can you believe that?" I said.

"I'm happy for Violet, but Maggie is going to be upset." Jimmy shook his head and sucked his teeth. "She'll see this as pushy."

"Does she know that Violet's been trying to contact him?"

"I don't think so . . ."

I gave him a wan smile. "And I thought I had complications in *my* family."

Jimmy sprawled back against my bed. "What's the latest with the potential stepmother?"

"It's actually been pretty quiet on the western front, but I think Dad's still got a roaming eye, so there's hope . . ."

"*Quel scandale!*" Jimmy sat up a little at that and wiggled his eyebrows.

"These senior citizens are wilder than us!"

"So, when do you see your summer lover?" Jimmy asked, pursing his lips.

"Tomorrow, finally."

"Finally!"

Just then we heard Violet speaking forcefully into the phone. "It's not disloyal, Maggie! I want to know Dad!"

"Oh, boy," I said.

"You finish getting ready," Jimmy said, dutifully getting to his feet. "I'll take care of Violet."

~~~~

The drive out to Sullivan's Island always reminded me of the times my mother and I would drive from the airport over the bridges when we'd just arrived for the summer. She would roll down the windows, let the salt air in, and tell us all to inhale. I loved how Charleston had grown up alongside my memories. The dark navy blue harbor stretched out on either side of me, dotted with sailboats and streaked with giant container ships. I missed my mom. I had to strain my memory to remember her laugh. I turned on the radio and found a song she would have loved.

My car rolled down Coleman Boulevard, passing the antique malls, the Kickin' Chicken, and the Village Bookseller. I was making good time; my dad would approve. He always liked me to be a little early. His brief time in the Army had given him the mindset that "on time" was actually late.

At my dad's house, I went up the front steps, turned my key in the lock, and let myself in.

There was Joyce, sprawled out on my father's couch, reading. She sat up, looking startled. "Aly! I didn't know you were coming over! Goodness, you didn't even ring the doorbell!"

"I used the key, Joyce. I have my own."

"You have your own key to this house? *And* you just come over unannounced?" Her mouth was hanging open as though this were shocking. I was starting to feel that I *had* done something wrong.

"Um, no. My dad and I are having dinner."

Just then my dad appeared around the corner. "Oh, Minnow! Hello! Ah, shoot, I forgot about our dinner!" He was looking at Joyce when he said this; she got up and sailed past us both, not making eye contact, and went into the bedroom.

"Uh-oh," I said.

"Uh, yeah. Whoops. Let me go see what's happening there." He disappeared into his bedroom. I sat down on the couch and scrolled through my phone. Great. A few minutes went by, and I decided to check my email. I had one from Charley.

"Can't wait for our date tomorrow. See you at Melfi's downtown. Seven p.m."

My stomach did a little flip. Was I nervous to see him? I couldn't wait to go to Melfi's. I hadn't been, and everyone was raving about their spicy Caesar salad. For a while I scrolled, looking at similar influencers, at the feeds of artists and creators I admired. Then I checked my watch and realized my dad and Joyce had been gone for over thirty minutes. Luckily, we were going to High Thyme on the island, and they were usually pretty accommodating to us. But it was very unlike my dad to let anything get in the way of a meal. I walked down the hall to his bedroom, then knocked and slowly opened the door to check on them.

"Hey, y'all, everything okay? I can come back. We can reschedule."

My dad quickly got up from where he was sitting and blocked the door.

"Give us another minute, Minnow. Dinner is still on," he said, and closed the door.

A long silence followed, and then a closing of what I assumed was the bathroom door. I shook my head and decided I had heard enough. I went back into the living room and started to notice that things were looking a little different. There was a new rug in the hall, the dining room had been painted a bright orange, and there were three more of those framed pictures of the two of them.

My mother's house was being invaded by her total opposite. When I was younger, my dad and I had butted heads, but with the loss of my mother, we had grown closer. My mom had always encouraged our relationship. She would arrange our father-daughter dates. She knew I needed a dad, but I didn't know it until I lost her. Now all the work that we had done to get on solid ground was in jeopardy. I wasn't going to let Joyce convince Dad that *I* was the problem!

Then Joyce came out, a brilliant smile on her face. "Sorry about that, Aly," she said. "Your father and I had a little scheduling mix-up."

"O-*kay*," I replied. She had said the word "sorry," but there was nothing apologetic about her manner. "Should I go? Is he not even going to say bye to me?"

"Oh no, don't be silly; he's just getting cleaned up for your dinner."

"Oh." What was this? My shoulders were rigid with distrust. "Will it be the three of us?"

She ignored this.

"Here," she said. "I got you something."

The way she was smiling at me was terrible. I accepted the wrapped present. The paper was a pretty jewel-tone floral pattern; I was actually surprised she'd chosen something so subtle, until I remembered that my mother had used that paper a few Christmases ago. Joyce must have been poking around my mother's crafts room. I should have taken those things for my own projects. My fingers were a little trembly as I undid the ribbon and saw two items: a pastel-colored paperback of *The Motherless Daughter Club*, and under that was a frame. A nice frame, the kind I would choose.

"That was so thoughtful of you, Aly, to contribute to our house makeover. *Thank you* for making me feel included! But I'm really going for a specific look, so I don't know if that one fits. Maybe it would work in your little Hampton Park project."

Wow. This was another level, a silent escalation. My fingers were still and calm now. I stood up, my smile as bright and insincere as she was. She took a step back. I took a step toward her. She watched me, and then I threw my arms around her.

"Thank you," I said.

"Oh . . ." She shrank a little from my embrace; obviously she had anticipated more fight from me. "You're welcome."

"It's been hard for me to accept Dad moving on," I went on. "I can admit that. But thank you for caring *so much* for him."

"Oh, I . . ."

"In fact, can I tell you something?"

"Sure."

"It'll be his first birthday without Mom, and I know he'll be afraid to talk to you about it, but it's our tradition to have all the siblings together for that, and Mom always made the richest chocolate cake she could imagine. It was a whole thing, every year, a richer, denser, more delicious chocolate cake."

"Oh?"

"I can see Dad is trying to please you, but I bet he'd be so happy if we could make that happen for him this year . . ."

Joyce nodded at me. I smiled back. "That's great," Joyce said. "Thank you for that thoughtful suggestion."

"What suggestion?" my dad said, appearing from the bedroom.

"Oh, Joyce and I were just talking about your birthday! She's so excited and wants your brother and sister to come out for it!"

I could tell Joyce had not been planning on taking my sugges-tion, but it was too late now. Plus, I had already invited them. My dad grinned. "That's great!" he said. "Wow, it's so good to see you two getting along . . ."

"We're going to have so much fun. Right, Joyce?"

"Definitely," she replied.

"Are you sure you don't want to come, Joyce?" I asked.

"No, you two enjoy," she said.

I gave her a smile and laid the book and the framed picture on the couch. "Let's go," I said, linking arms with my dad. "Want to take the golf cart?"

We left Joyce and drove down Middle Street to High Thyme. I loved the ride. I loved to see what the neighbors were up to, who was having a party, who was coming off the beach and piling into their

Broncos and Jeeps. I inhaled jasmine. It was hypnotic air laced with salt. I missed living over here . . .

"Dad?" I said.

"Yeah, Minnow?"

"I don't want to have to fight for you."

"Too many hens in the henhouse, I think."

"It isn't her coop, Dad."

"No, it isn't. But, Aly, it might become . . . We might try living together."

I took a long inhale. I was glad I'd invited my siblings—that I had backup coming.

"Why?" I asked.

"She wants to get married. I don't. This is a compromise."

We found parking in front of the restaurant, a little wink from my mom, or so I liked to imagine. When she was around, she could find parking anywhere, so whenever I got a spot, I always silently thanked her for lending her power to me.

We were greeted at the door by Emily, the owner. "Hey, y'all, it's been a minute! How are you, George?" She patted my dad on the back and gave him a kiss on the cheek.

"Oh, better after that kiss. How about another one? We can be European."

"Oh, gosh, George! Dinner for two?"

"Yup, here with my daughter!"

"Hey, Aly! Nice to see you!" she said over her shoulder as she led us to a table by the window.

I looked at the menu and decided that, as usual, I'd order the Caesar salad with grilled chicken. Maybe I'd get the street tacos? Moments later, our server arrived.

"Hey, y'all, how are you?"

"Lisa! My favorite! How are your boys, Grady and Brody?" my dad asked.

"Oh, keeping me on my toes, I'll tell you what!"

"That's what little boys do. Got anything special tonight?"

"Yes, we actually have seared wreckfish over fresh succotash. We also have shrimp and grits tonight. Local shrimp over some stone-ground yellow grits. Both are delicious."

"Well, I love wreckfish. I'll have that. Aly?"

"I'm going to get my usual salad with grilled chicken, please."

"Sounds good. Anything to drink?" Lisa asked.

"I was so excited about the fish special I forgot to order wine. What's the matter with me? We'll have a bottle of the Cloudy Bay," my dad said.

Lisa left, and I sat in silence as my dad scrolled through his phone, texting Joyce, or so I assumed from the heavy sighing. Lisa returned with two glasses of the wine and put the rest of the bottle on ice for us.

"Are you sure you want this, Dad?" I asked in a small voice.

"The wine? Of course!" he said, grinning.

"No, Dad. I mean Joyce."

"I'm not getting rid of her, Aly."

"Do you love her?" I asked.

"I might. I really don't like dating, Aly, and I want a companion."

"Have you been dating a lot of other women? I just, respectfully, don't want you to settle, Dad. I want you to be happy . . . and she's just so different from Mom."

"But who could ever be like Mom?" He was having a hard time looking directly at me.

"Okay. Just don't let her push you into marriage if that's not something you want," I said.

"I won't, because I don't. Why get married again?"

"I don't know. She comes across like she's aggressive and usually gets what she wants."

My dad wiggled his eyebrows.

"Oh, gross, Dad! Please!" I gave him a look of mock disgust. My father had always had a dirty sense of humor, but sometimes I loved it because it broke the tension. "I just wish you'd found someone who was a little more . . . fun."

"She's fun to me," he said.

"Okay, but what about the rest of us?" I said. "Doesn't that matter?"

"Of course it does, Aly. Nothing will ever come between you and me. As for your brother and sister, we'll find out. That's such a nice idea of yours. So glad they can come help me ring in seventy-five!"

"That's awesome! I can't wait to see them. It'll be good to get everyone together."

"They can meet Joyce."

Exactly, I thought.

Our food arrived, and it looked fantastic. My salad was fresh, with generous, giant shavings of Parmesan cheese and cool, perfectly seasoned slices of grilled chicken. The dressing was, thankfully, light on the anchovies but still full of freshly cracked black pepper. Every bite was refreshing. My dad's plump, golden fish sat atop a bright little pile of fresh vegetables. Yellow corn, green okra, and red tomatoes, coupled with dots of fresh goat cheese. It smelled divine.

Dad took a bite and closed his eyes in appreciation. He loved seafood like no one else. I recalled how, when I was younger, we had caught fresh fish together one summer. He showed me how to clean a fish. His hair was roughed up by the salty ocean air. There was something about my dad and the sea. It relaxed him. His life in finance kept him clean-cut and buttoned-up, but by the ocean, on the water, he could be free. I smiled, remembering his face that night at dinner when we cooked the fish we had caught. He nodded then in approval, like he was doing now.

"Do you miss the Midwest ever?" I asked him.

"Nope. Turns out your mother was right about this place. It really is the center of the universe. At least for me."

"Mom usually was right." My throat got tight and I lost the battle, as I did only when it concerned my father. "Dad, I don't want to lose you, too."

"Minnow! You don't need to be sad. I'm here." He grabbed my hand across the table. "I'm sorry, Aly. I promise I'm not going anywhere. No one will come between us. Ever. I'm here forever. You're my little girl. I promise."

I knew in my gut I could do nothing about this except try not to be awful. He had never considered himself a pack animal. I needed him—I always had—but in his mind, he was a lone wolf. I didn't want to lose him, and I knew then and there that if I was difficult, I would only give Joyce ammo to push me totally out of his life, and she would win.

CHAPTER TWENTY-TWO

~~~~~

Violet

It was early evening. I was sitting next to Aly with a giant bowl of boiled peanuts between us, sipping an ice-cold Diet Coke with slices of lemon and watching a giant summer storm roar through the sky. She had her head on my shoulder, and we were silent. She sensed something was wrong. I hadn't heard back from my dad since we had DMed on Instagram about coming to see him, and I hadn't told her about Chris yet, because I wasn't ready to talk about it. Aly and I had known each other only about a year, but it had been an intense year for both of us; our friendship had blossomed quickly, and it already felt like a lifetime. Jim came out to join us, the slamming of the screen door startling me out of my thoughts.

"Hey, ladies," Jim said.

"Tonight was a doozy," Aly said.

"Spill it." Jim sat down in the rocking chair, pulling it toward us. "Joyce?"

Aly grimaced. "I thought for a second that I was feeling closer to my dad. I had become more valuable. We felt close in a new way, like he really admired *me*, and for the first time I felt cherished by him . . . and now I know that I never was, and never will be. And it isn't his fault; it isn't anyone's fault. It's who we are. So, I get myself overly involved and help others, so they will see my value. If anything good has come of this vile situation, it's *that*—that understanding. It's the beautiful, painful honesty that happens when I listen. She's a codriver, but she isn't in charge. He is. Even if it hurts, I see him now. It's how he's always been."

"Oh, honey. That's not . . ." Was this what it felt like to have a father? I wasn't sure if it was Joyce or me who needed to hear what I said next. "He loves you, Aly."

"This isn't about loving or not loving; it's how you choose to express your love. I know that he holds me as close as his own trauma, or whatever is wrong with him, will let him." Aly shrugged bitterly. "But if it's between me and a good time, he's always going to choose what makes him the happiest. It's just who he is."

"That isn't true," I whispered. What if my dad never wrote me back? The fear was really biting at me. What if no one would ever love me but Chris? What if that was my last, best shot at getting married, even though now he scared me? "It can't be."

"It is, actually, and I'm okay with it. He's so generous in so many ways, but emotionally he's very guarded. Honestly, it's for the best. I'm not a little girl. But I don't know . . . I just had this idea that he was my new North Star after my mom passed."

"Be your own damn North Star, Aly," I said, my voice sudden and urgent.

"What?" Aly blinked at me. I held her gaze. It didn't feel like it was me who'd said it, really, but some wise woman from above.

"She's right," Jimmy said. "Look, we all know there will never be another Callie Knox, but you are Aly Knox! You're just as funny, warm, and talented as she was. The world will see it soon. You need to just trust yourself. You aren't lost without her; you don't need to replace her; every wondrous thing she guided you to and from is in you. She did her job. You are the new North Star."

I pulled her into a hug, kissed the top of her head. She giggled. "I got you, sister," I said. "We all do. You can do this on your own. But if you need us, you have an army."

"Thanks, guys. I got you, too."

"Oh, we know. This house has never looked better. Your mom would approve for sure."

"You think?"

"The hot pink lacquered spindle bed? She raised you to be this beautiful, talented woman—now go be that woman!" Jimmy exclaimed.

"Yeah, well. Enough about my daddy issues. What's happening with yours, Violet?"

"Not much. I sent him a message after he contacted me saying he wanted us to visit, but I haven't heard anything back. No call, no direct message or text, no email." It actually pained my throat to say all that. I tried to sound brassy with a tossed-off "Nada."

"Damn, am I tired of chasing these men! Dads, boyfriends, romantic or otherwise. It's exhausting!" Aly huffed.

"I hear that." Jimmy sucked his teeth.

"Well, not you, precious. Obviously," I said, pinching Jimmy.

"Obviously." He gave me a hard look. "All right, let's have it."

"Have what?" I said, pretending, not very effectively, not to know what he was talking about.

"Violetta, honey child, you've been moping around this house all day, barely saying a word. I haven't seen Chris; you haven't worn lipstick . . . I'm worried. What happened?"

"She'll tell us when she's ready," Aly said.

"No, nope. I haven't seen that little Chatty Cathy do a silent strike since she lost the ticket lottery to Britney Spears in seventh grade. Spill it, sister friend."

I looked out at our yard. The rain was soaking the ground. I folded my arms. "Chris has changed," I said.

"Uh, isn't that good news?" Jimmy said.

I paused to gulp my Diet Coke. "I mean, I think he's grown to like a romantic style that I'm not really into."

"What are you talking about?" Aly said.

"He, uh . . ."

"Oh my god, Violet!" Aly gasped. "Did he hurt you?"

"No, it didn't hurt. I mean, but it was during . . ." I closed my eyes. My cheeks were burning. In a whisper, I managed to say, "*Sex*."

"Honey, that's all the kids are doing these days, so rough." Jimmy shrugged and swirled his wine. "But it should be consensual. Did you discuss this with him beforehand?"

"Obviously not. My god," I said, and refilled my glass.

"Well, I see why you're upset. What do you want to do?" Jim asked me.

"Can I be totally raw honest?" I was feeling the need for some truth-telling.

"Yes, duh." They said it so fast, and at the same time, that it made me laugh.

"The first time we were intimate after he got home, it was different, but kind of sexy. Like, I thought it was just super passionate and he was acting like he was starving for me. It was hot, and I felt wanted, and I wanted to be sexy for him. We were starting over, from a new place, and I felt the rekindling of a spark I thought had died a long time ago. But then," I went on, relieved, "I started to feel slightly out of control, and I'm not going to lie and say that I wasn't into it—I was. It was a shifting of power, and having a big, strong man toss me around and be a little rough with me was . . . it felt like he would devour me."

"Oh, like in a romance novel!" Aly said.

"Yes, kind of like that. Like I was with a new pro in the bedroom, and he had to have me. But it got . . . a little *too* rough," I said. "I didn't want to seem boring to him, so I kept meeting him where he was, but then . . ."

"He took it too far?" Jim said.

"Yep . . . he choked me out."

"Jesus, at home?"

"We were . . . outside."

"Where?" Jim asked.

"The Battery. In the gazebo."

"Good lord in heaven, Violet! This is *not* where I thought this conversation was going."

"He was super sweet afterward and apologetic. But I don't think . . . I think I'm too weirded out now. Like, where's the line, you know? It scared me. I haven't called him or returned any of his calls. I know he knows he crossed a line."

"Feels like we are flirting with abuse, Vi," Aly said with a firm shake of the head. "I'm gonna be real with ya: I don't like it."

"Me, either," Jim said. "He knew who you were."

"Well, yeah, but he left *that* girl for Japan. I didn't want to be that girl anymore."

"So, you let someone squeeze the ever-living life out of your throat? No, thank you, babe." Aly lifted the bottle to refill our glasses, but it was empty. "I'm going to get another one, and maybe a gun to go kill that fucker."

"No, Aly," I said. "No to murder, but yes to more wine."

"No worries, we don't have a gun," Jim said. He gave me a face. "Are you okay?"

"I think so. But I know I don't want that."

"Well, there's something to be said for clarity."

"Then why do I feel so confused?" I asked.

"Because you love the guy." Jim threw up his hands. "Stupid as he is."

"I do." I squeezed my eyes shut and shook my head. "I'm not like some big prude or something; I just know it isn't my cup of sweet tea. You know? I like the sweet stuff. I'm a Disney Princess, I guess."

"Well, my love, there is nothing wrong with that! Vanilla is a classic for a reason. I think, though, you should have a conversation."

"I'll talk to him."

"Give him an opportunity to talk about why or what . . ."

"This is awkward. I love you, Jimmy, but I can't."

"You just had sex in public! We are way past shy."

"But it feels overwhelming to do that deep relationship work right now. I'm not doing a great job at focusing, and fall is just around the corner, and that's busy wedding season. I'm being offered more jobs than I can realistically do, but I'm afraid to say no to the money. I might actually hire an assistant and really get back into the swing of work."

Aly returned with more wine and a smile.

"Why the smile, hon?" Jim said.

"Charley!" she said. "Just got a cute text. He's good with words."

My phone buzzed. I opened it to see that I had finally gotten a response from my dad.

"Y'all, my dad answered!"

"Did the moon just get full or something? What's in this wine? It's like liquid closure!" Jimmy held up the bottle as if it was some sort of magical elixir. "Hey, wine, let me know about my audition with Charleston Stage?"

"What does it say, Vi?" Aly asked.

"He's getting married," I said. "That's why he wants me to come up soon—so I can meet her before . . ."

"Whoa, how do you feel about that?" Jim said.

"Happy for him? Flattered he cares enough to have me meet her? That feels inclusive to me," I said. "I'm dying to get to know him. I'd love to see Nantucket. But Maggie's not on board with it."

"You gotta do your own thing," Jimmy said. "Whatever you think is right. And my offer still stands to come with you."

"Thank you, Jimmy. Where would I be without you?"

Later, upstairs in my room with another glass of wine, I typed out a message to my dad saying next week should work. But I couldn't bring myself to send it.

I wanted to talk to my mom and Maggie, but I didn't want to open up old wounds. My mom hadn't spoken to Gran since that night, and

Maggie had fully moved in with Sam. Gran was alone in that house. It wasn't that I wasn't speaking to her, but we weren't talking like we used to. Maggie wasn't speaking to her, and I was the only one who was, but she kept me at a distance out of shame, I assumed. Either that or she didn't want to battle with me, and the feeling was mutual.

I did a full skin-care routine, put on my coziest pajamas, cranked my window air-conditioning unit to a chilly sixty-eight degrees. When I got into bed, I saw I had a text from Maggie.

> I got an email from Dad offering to fly us both up to Nantucket. I'm not interested in doing that but I respect that you have to make your own choices.

Whoa. I wasn't sure what to say. Thanks, I texted. I'm going to go talk to Gran this morning, Maggie. She's hurting. This needs to end.

> Go for it.

> Maggie . . .

> I have nothing to say right now. I need to figure out how I feel about this before I hear more excuses.

My heart was beating fast. It was true, I had to talk to Gran, but I wished Maggie would, too. I needed her to set things right so I could move on with my life.

In the morning, I drove over to Sullivan's. When I got to the Ben Sawyer Bridge, I realized I had forgotten beach traffic and boat traffic. The bridge was up, so I sat there and baked in my car for fifteen min-utes while we waited for a sailboat to pass underneath.

As I sat waiting—frustrated, wishing my car could sprout wings and sail over all the backed-up vehicles—I realized that it was true what Maggie had said. Whether or not she actually did respect them, I needed to make my own choices. I was the only one who wasn't angry at Gran, and it was time to have some questions answered, and my sister's stubbornness and my mother's pain were things I couldn't let hold me back. Enough dust had settled. I didn't want my family to live in this emotional limbo forever. I didn't want to be stuck there, either.

As the bridge lowered and the cars ahead of me began to inch forward, I thought how I was tired of waiting around to see how other people felt before I made a move. The radio was saying another storm was on the way, but ahead of me the sky was pure blue.

CHAPTER TWENTY-THREE

~~~~

Aly

I was in the cellphone area of the Charleston International Airport, waiting on Jessica, my big sister, who was flying in from LA, where she worked in the movie business. I was so excited to welcome her back to the Lowcountry. My plan was to let her encounter the beastly Joyce on her own. I hadn't told my sister much about her; I had decided to let her and my brother see for themselves. My brother, Mike; his wife, Cate; and their kids were arriving later that evening. Our plan was to go to the Magic Lantern on the island. Violet had gotten Maggie to do a special menu for us, and we would be eating in their new private dining area, which was the old side porch that they'd screened in.

Jessica was the oldest sibling, very career-driven, and Mike was in the middle. I was the baby. We had all been very close growing up, but our lives, commitments, and geographical locations had created some unavoidable distance. I had summoned my siblings in part to show Joyce a united front—the Knoxes were not to be messed with—but I was truly glad to be getting together with them. My phone buzzed with a text from Jessica, so I pulled the car around and there she was, barking into her phone. She was dressed all in black and had a tiny silver roll-on bag behind her. When she saw me, she threw her phone into what looked to be a very expensive bag and got into the car.

"Aly, oh my god, you are so tan and . . . blond! Ahh, I've missed you, girl, come here!" She leaned over, pulling me into a huge hug. She smelled like airplane and French perfume.

"I missed you," I said, relishing the hug. "Welcome back to the Lowcountry!"

"I always forget about the humidity. You could swim through it! My poor hair!" She took off her black blazer and threw it in the back seat. She pulled out a black leather case, unzipped it, took out a hair tie, and wrapped her hair into a tight, low bun. "Man, I forgot my hair wax."

"Hair wax?" I said, piloting us out of the airport parking lot.

"Oh my god, it's a must! How will you ever tame your flyaways without it? But what do you care? You are living the mermaid lifestyle now, always in that dang ocean . . ." She kept talking, telling me all about the LA life. The yoga studios, the fresh juice bars, the film industry. I was soaking up my sister. I felt like a carefree teenager when we were together, transported to our childhood summers.

"All right," she said, as though her speed talking had worn her out. "Tell me about Joyce."

"I'm going to let you form your own opinion on that one." I turned on the radio, but she immediately turned it off.

"No, ma'am, spill it."

"Jess, I'm serious. I want to see what you think. It'll validate if what I see is really there or not."

"You don't want me to be influenced, Miss Influencer?"

"Exactly." Yet I couldn't resist adding, "Mikey's gonna hate her."

"Oh, and I'm not?" Jess said. "You guys are way more forgiving than I am."

"Yeah, but you are a big-time career lady, and so is Joyce. So maybe you'll understand her better than I do."

"Now I'm curious. What's for dinner? We're eating at the Lantern, right? I'm starving for some real food. There's only so much avocado someone can take!"

"Oh, and you can eat something that requires a knife, not a damn quinoa bowl."

She smiled and rolled her eyes at me. We drove over the bridge, and I watched my sister take in the view. "It's so peaceful watching the boats. I could look at this all day."

We made it to the house, and I let Jess lead the way. She carried her suitcase up the front steps and tried to open the door, which she found was locked. She turned around and gave me a face. I tried to keep my own expression neutral, without much success. Joyce would never leave the house unlocked. Ever. She wasn't from around here. She didn't realize we kept things casual.

Jess bent down, flipping over the front mat to look for the key, but it wasn't there.

"Aly, throw me your key."

I climbed the stairs, trying to keep my voice even. "I don't have one. Mine doesn't work anymore."

She gave me a hard look. "Got it. So should we ring the bell?" She pressed the bell.

The door swung open, and there was our dad.

"Jessica! Aly! Why did you ring the doorbell? Just use the key . . ."

"There's no key anymore, Dad. Remember?"

"Oh, right, well, you have your key, Minnow."

"The locks were changed."

"Oh, that's right . . . I'll have one made for you. Welcome!" He held his arms open, and we both hugged him. Joyce slinked around the corner and put her hand on his shoulder as though to shut him up about that.

When she saw Jess, she put on a big fake smile. "Oh, hello there. Welcome!"

"You must be Joyce, the lady keeping my father young! So nice to meet you. I'm Jessica." She went to hug her, but Joyce jutted out her face for a double-cheek kiss.

"Lovely to meet you, Jessica. Your father tells me all about what you're up to in Hollywood. Says you just landed a film deal. Very impressive."

"Oh, yeah, thank you," Jessica said, and shot me a face.

"Well, we have you all set upstairs in the guest room," Joyce said.

"The guest room," Jessica repeated. "You mean my and Aly's old bedroom?"

"We redecorated. It's a *guest* room now." Joyce giggled and side-hugged my dad, who looked at his feet. "And sometimes my gym."

"Great. Okay, let me drop off my luggage and we can get ready for dinner. Should we take the golf cart?" Jessica said.

"Yeah! Like old times!" I said. "Is Mikey renting a car?"

"We can all fit in the cart, no problem!" Dad said.

"I just got my hair done! This humidity will ruin it!" Joyce said a little too loudly. "Your father and I will drive."

"I guess we're driving," my dad said.

We stood there for a moment and let the first of what would be many wet blankets settle over us. I followed my sister upstairs. We got to our old room, shut the door behind us, and took in the changes.

The room was painted pale blue and now had two white wicker twin beds. Both had duvet covers with seascapes on them. The bed on the left had shell pillows, and the one on the right had a shark. Gone were our family pictures. They had been replaced with wooden signs with beach-themed phrases written on them in white paint. I couldn't tell if they were from Home Wears or if Joyce had painted them herself. Over the bed there was a mermaid clock, that in the center, read, *You're on island time now.*

Jessica mimed throwing up. "You have got to be kidding me."

"I wish I was surprised to see this," I said.

She went over to the dresser and paused as she took in the shell pulls on the drawers. She picked up a teal frame with a 3D sandcastle on it. It was a photo of our dad and Joyce kissing at what looked like a beach restaurant. In front of them was a seafood tower. My stomach knotted.

Jess turned on a shell-shaped lamp, put her suitcase on the bed, and picked up a book. With a pastel cover. The one Joyce had tried to gift me. "Um, what the fuck is this?"

"Oh, that's a self-help book on how to get over the loss of your mother," I said. "She highly recommends it."

"I need a drink," Jess said. "Or, better yet, a gummy."

"Gross, Jess!"

"What? Oh god, Aly, loosen up. You're on island time," she said, quoting the sign, and popped a gummy into her mouth. "Everyone in LA does it. Plus, it's just CBD. It's fine."

"Enjoy."

"Joyce is aggressive. You know what she's doing, right? She's trying to erase Mom." Jess pulled a red tank dress over her head. My sister was a shark, so calling Joyce "aggressive" was big.

"Well, she can't do that," I said. "Right?"

"I don't know. If he marries her, that's exactly what she's going to do. That bitch is taking over. Have you talked to him?"

"I tried. He doesn't see it, and whatever he sees isn't enough to make him let her go."

"Ugh. Why does everyone feel like they need a person? I'd rather be alone than with the wrong person."

"Same. But men are different. They need a wife, especially after losing one. I mean, Mom did so much for him, I'm sure he feels lost without her. I guess he's . . . I mean, Joyce does fuss over him quite a bit. Maybe he finds that endearing?"

Jess groaned. "Whatever. Let's get outta here." She slipped on a pair of Chloé sneakers.

"God, Jess, those are, like, a zillion bucks! Looks like LA is treating you well this quarter."

"I'll send you a pair for Christmas. Do you think I should grab socks? I forgot to pack a pair; I usually wear these without socks, but it's so hot I don't want my feet to get sweaty."

"Well, everything I had here is gone, but I can go steal some from Dad's room."

Once I climbed down the stairs, I realized the house was quiet. I called out and looked at my watch. Dad and Joyce either were out on the porch or had left early. The bedroom door was open, so I let myself in. Dad, if memory serves, kept his socks in his bedside table.

I opened the drawer, my eyes not believing what they were seeing, and then slammed it shut quickly and let out a little shriek of shock.

"Aly? You okay?" Jess yelled.

"No! I mean yes, but . . . wow!"

Jess entered the room. "What happened?"

"I don't want to tell you what I just accidentally discovered in Dad's sock drawer."

"Please don't."

Then the door opened, and Dad and Joyce stood there.

Shit.

"Hey, guys, we were looking for some socks. Jess forgot to pack them and didn't want to get blisters."

"No problem!" Dad pulled out a pair from the chest of drawers across the room.

Jess was avoiding eye contact with me.

"You girls are so free over here," Joyce said. "You know, none of my adult children would ever enter my bedroom without permission."

"Well, we are more open in this family, Joyce," I said.

"I can see that." She leaned into my dad, who just cleared his throat.

"Last chance for a golf cart ride!" I said to Joyce and Dad. Dad looked over at Joyce, and she pulled his arm back.

"Nah, Minnow, have to protect the hair."

Jess and I piled into the golf cart and waited for Joyce and Dad to drive off.

The whole drive to the Lantern, Jess peppered me with questions, and I told her about the last dinner I'd had with our dad. She just shook her head.

"Let's ignore her. That's the best thing to do. Let's not give her space to ruin our weekend. This is about celebrating Dad, not playing her dominance games."

~~~~

At the Magic Lantern, I pulled the giant, heavy wooden door open, and the warm golden light and delicious smells spilled out to greet us. I felt hungry for the first time in a while. We followed the hostess to the private area where Mike, Cate, and their two children were sitting. Della was coloring, and George Jr., whom we called JR, was deeply concentrating on his Nintendo Switch. It had been a long time. With Mike being busy with his kids and his company taking off, we rarely got together. But, looking into his big brown eyes as he took me in, there was my big brother. I knew I had missed him. I did a little hop at the sight of him.

"Mikey!" I squealed. He rose and picked me up in a huge hug, and I felt ten years old.

"Missed you, kid," he said, and all was right with the world.

"Aly, you look so beautiful! It's so good to see you! Della, JR, go say hey to Grandpa!" Cate said as she pulled something out of her daughter's hand. Her shiny brown hair and freckles felt as welcoming as a summer breeze. She was so sweet, and she was the only woman my mother would ever have approved of for her only son.

"Jess! Whoa, clearly you've been letting yourself go!" Mike joked as he hugged my sister. "You're harder than I am!" We all laughed as he pretended to be crushed under her arms. She playfully punched his arm, and he gave her a noogie. We were all in our thirties, but when we got back together, we were kids again.

My dad's laughter boomed. Joyce's eyes were as big as dinner plates.

Mike engulfed her in a bear hug. "You must be Joyce! My father's new flame! You live with my old man? We're family now!"

When he let go, she immediately smoothed out her dress.

"Sorry, Joyce. I'm a hugger!"

"I see, I see." Joyce attempted a smile and gave my father a look.

We all sat down at the long table, which was tastefully decorated with small gold and blue flowers, my dad's favorites, and a nod to Michigan University, his alma mater. I had printed out some pictures from his lifetime, all in black and white, and Violet had helped me make them into cutouts that were all over the table in small silver frames. It was the perfect setting for a family celebration. I saw Joyce pick up some of the pictures and put them down, raising and lowering her brows.

"Aly, I love these pictures!" Cate said. "I'm glad I got some of them to you on time. But especially this one of Dad and Mom. She'd be so proud of all of us coming together!"

"Yes, she would!" Dad said.

"But you know she would have that cake with, like, seven hundred candles on it," Jess chimed in.

"And she would bring out the fire extinguisher!" I laughed.

"And the cake would always be a fatal density of chocolate. God, she was fun," my dad said.

Joyce stood up. "I have to use the ladies' room. Where is it?"

"Right past the bar in the main dining room," Cate told her. "Do you want me to show you? I could use a trip myself. Della, do you want to come?"

Della nodded, and the three of them stood and left.

A moment later Frankie arrived. "Hey, y'all, and happy birthday, Mr. Knox. We are so thrilled you have chosen to celebrate your big

day with us! Chef Maggie has a special menu she's prepared for you."
She handed out long rectangular menus, and immediately I spotted
chicken potpie, Dad's favorite.

"Oh, my gosh! Chicken potpie!" My dad licked his lips and patted
his tummy.

Frankie shot us a wink. "Yeah, y'all are in for a treat! She's been
cooking up a storm for days!"

"May I see a wine list, Frankie?" my dad asked.

"Sure can, but the wine has been preselected for the evening."
Frankie gave me a nod, and I nodded back. My siblings and I had had
several talks and group calls about this evening, and Cate had gotten
some special wine labels made on Etsy that had different pictures of
our dad on them. We'd had the staff at the Lantern slip them over
some of his favorite wines, which we had ordered for the evening. I
was excited to see his face when he saw himself on the bottles.

We all chatted a little and looked over the menu, which had my
mouth watering. JR was explaining Minecraft to me on his game thing,
and Mike, Jess, and Dad were having a fake argument about who was
the fastest sandcastle maker, which led to him challenging us all to a
contest the next morning. Joyce returned to the table and sat next to
my father, grabbed his arm, and whispered something that caused him
to frown.

"Where are Cate and Della?" Mike asked.

Joyce glanced at Mike but didn't reply. "Darling, did you order the
wine yet?"

"Here's the wine!" Frankie said as she set the bottle in front of my
dad so he could appreciate the label.

"Oh my god, it's me on my wedding day," he said, beaming.

"Is it? I thought it was a holiday or just a normal day fishing!" Jess
said.

"No, that morning . . ." He paused and cleared his throat. "Your mom got me that boat as a wedding present. That morning, we took it out on the lake to watch the sunrise."

Dad gave Joyce a look.

But she smiled what seemed like a totally natural and nice smile and said, "I bet it was beautiful."

"I'm a lucky man to have a lot of beauty in my life," my dad replied, and kissed her forehead.

Was she being sincere, or was she just getting wilier?

I knew she had lost her husband, too, and I wondered if that was what they had in common. Broken hearts. Maybe Joyce really cared for my dad, even if she wasn't great with everyone else? That moment of humanity was confusing.

Just then Cate came back to the table with red eyes, Della skipping ahead of her. She sat down next to Mike, who was oblivious. I caught Jess's eye, and Jess then caught Cate's. Cate gave her a brusque "I'm fine" nod. But it was clear she wasn't.

Chef Maggie appeared then with a few servers, and they placed the first course in front of us, a pale yellow liquid in a shot glass. Maggie was so cool in her chef whites and leopard-print chef clogs. "Hey there, George, and welcome, y'all! Happy birthday! I am so thrilled to present the first tasty bites of this evening. We have a chilled corn bisque with fresh crabmeat and a cilantro oil. Take it in one or two sips to amuse y'all's bouches," she said with a giggle.

We did as she instructed, and there were many nods of approval going around the table.

"Oh my god," Jess said. "That is unbelievable! Is that a little spice I detect?"

"Yes! I added only a slight hint of Fresno peppers." Maggie was beaming at the facial expressions her soup was causing. Everyone was in a state of euphoria.

"Can I have another?" Della asked.

"Me too?" JR asked.

"It's okay with me if it's okay with y'all's parents, but we have a lot more food coming out, so you might want to save room," Maggie said, and smiled at the kids.

"What's next?" JR said, putting his game down for the first time.

"Next up, we've got our first official course. It's a small tomato tart with goat cheese served alongside a chilled arugula salad dressed with a lemon vinaigrette and shaved Parm. Give me a moment to clear this round, and we'll be back shortly . . ."

When they were gone, Mike said, "So, Joyce, tell me about you!" his warm voice booming. He finished his glass of wine and began refreshing everyone else's, making a show of it and focusing on Joyce.

"Wow, first time anyone's asked me a personal question!" Maybe Joyce was trying to make a joke, but it didn't quite come out sounding like one. "*Kidding!* I'm sure you all are so excited to be together, it's just hard to get a word in!"

"Joyce." My dad put his hand on hers.

"I am a lawyer born and raised in California. But now I practice down here."

"What brought you to Charleston?" Jess asked.

"I had a friend move here and wanted to be close by," she replied, waving off an offer of a wine refill. "One and done, thank you."

The tarts arrived and were inhaled. They were paired with a delicious Chardonnay, and the label that was around this bottle showed Dad holding one of us as a baby.

"Well," Dad said, "that was one of the happiest days of my life."

"Who was that?" I asked.

"That's Jess. Man, you were such a little pumpkin. Came out with red hair!"

"Wish I still had it!" she said.

"Dad, what was the happiest day of your life? Which one takes the cake?" I asked.

"The day I married your mother." He smiled. "Here's to Callie! Without her I wouldn't have you all, and thank you. I know we have more ahead of us, but I appreciate you all coming here, traveling, bringing me my grandkids, and going through all this effort to make an old man happy. I love you all so very much." We clinked glasses.

Joyce added that she didn't hear what my dad had said and asked us what we were talking about, and I gently told her. But I gave her a warm smile, because it had to be awkward for her. I had all my siblings now, and she was one against the pack. I still wanted to chase her out, of course—but it would be easier for everyone if she maintained some dignity. She smiled back and simply said, "Oh."

The next course arrived, with more wine, and on and on it went. Sharing stories about Dad's life and memories that he cherished. We asked him some of his favorite lessons that he had learned in his seventy-five years on this earth, and he gave us a few, which Mike wrote down. I could smell a Christmas present brewing. My brother was so thoughtful like that, and Cate was so creative. I looked around and felt full. All my most loved ones at one table. My mom would be so proud to see us carrying on, loving one another, and embracing the changes in one another's lives.

Maybe Joyce wasn't so bad. She was trying so very hard, and we were a tight group despite our geographical distance. It would be hard for anyone in her shoes *not* to feel insecure, and, on second thought, good for her and for what was in that bedroom drawer at her age! To be sexy was ageless, after all.

I decided to make a toast before the cake came out, but Joyce beat me to it. She tapped her wineglass with a knife and snapped her fingers to get the attention of a server.

"We are ready for the surprise!" she told the server. "I wanted to contribute to this lovely evening," she told us, "so I took the liberty of having a cake made."

"Wait, but Dad gets his special cake every year." Jess glanced at me for backup. We were both picturing the rich chocolate, stuffed with as many candles as possible.

"Well, it's time to make some new traditions," Joyce replied.

"I'm all for some new fun!" Mike, ever the positive one, said.

Then the cake arrived, a very large sheet cake. Vanilla, which my dad hated, covered in sprinkles, which he also hated, with large icing flowers, which he would never . . .

I sank into my chair.

"Oh," my dad said, painting on a smile.

"I love you, darling!" Joyce said, wrapping her arms around him and planting a huge, long kiss on his mouth.

The rest of us had an opportunity to lean forward and get a look at the cake, which was decorated in the center with an enormous picture of them both.

CHAPTER TWENTY-FOUR

~~~~

Violet

On our way to the airport, Jim and I stopped in at the Magic Lantern to give Maggie once last chance to go to Nantucket.

It was afternoon, high sun despite the weather that was supposedly moving in from the west, and Maggie was outside, taking a break. Dinner service was still hours away.

"This is just so crazy," Maggie said flatly when I got out of the car and walked over to where she was sitting on a crate by the kitchen door.

"I know." I signaled to Jimmy that Maggie and I just needed a moment to ourselves. "But maybe crazy in a good way?"

"Our whole lives we thought Scott abandoned us and died, and now it's only one thing. And actually, abandoning us by dying—not much he could have done about that one. But abandoning us and still being alive . . . I mean, it's worse, Violet."

"Yeah, but . . . I don't know; isn't it sort of like a movie?"

"Yeah, a movie with a terrible writer. This isn't normal." Maggie crushed the can of seltzer she'd been drinking and tossed it on a heap of them. "I'm sorry, I don't mean to be ugly, I just . . ."

"I know," I said, seeing a little crack in her armor, hoping she might be capable of opening up. "But don't you want to see what he's like now, hear what he has to say?"

"I have questions." Maggie shook her head, as though it were all she could do to keep her fury contained. "I for sure have *questions*."

"I think this is our chance to get answers."

"Honestly, I think his absence is the thing that shaped me more than anything else."

"Me too, Maggie. I think that's why I'm always trying so hard to make a life with someone who doesn't want to make that same kind of life with me. It's crazy: when Chris was away, I'd spend days dreaming about our wedding. Now he's here. Now he wants to shack up and do the domestic thing, and you know what? Suddenly I'm not sure if I ever really wanted him. If I ever really knew him at all. And I don't know if that's because he's wrong or because I'm just so damn trained to dream about men who aren't there."

Maggie stood up with an abrupt, aggressive energy. "You know what? That's a *you* problem. That's not something chasing another absentee guy is gonna fix for you."

"Okay." I was afraid she was right. My heart was tight with that thought. But I was determined, too. I had to head for the horizon; I had to go find out for myself. "I'm going through with it, Maggie. And I'd love it if you came with me and asked your questions."

"Ask your own damn questions!" Maggie yelled. For a moment I was hurt that she had taken that tone with me. But in the next moment I knew it didn't have anything to do with me. She was angry and hurt, and it was very old, that wounded feeling that was firing in my general direction. It was a response to *her* experience, though, not mine. "Like, why didn't he fight? Why didn't he get on a plane and find us?"

"Those are your questions, Maggie," I said quietly.

"I know!" she shouted, and stalked off into the kitchen, letting the back door swing shut behind her.

I turned around and saw that Jimmy had been hanging on her every word. He didn't have to say anything; I knew he felt this one in his heart. He was close with both of us—he'd always taken it personally when we fought. I got in the car, and we drove silently toward the airport.

"You okay?" he asked after a while.

"Yeah, but . . . oof."

"She's fire. You know that. If she's going to come around, first she's gotta burn it all down."

"Yeah, but I wish she could be a little more supportive, too. My water sign tendencies, you know? I want to try and know him, or at least get a little more information out of him. I want to know how he could ever stay away."

"Well, keep your mind open, but remember sometimes it's better not to ask questions you might not really want the answers to."

"What do you mean?" My heart sank. Did no one think this was a good idea? "I want to know why he left!"

"I know you do, but you might find . . . he's a different person than he was. Maybe a fresh start would be more productive in the interest of building and rebuilding a relationship than rehashing the past and opening up old wounds. Like, just move forward."

I nodded and absorbed this. "I just think we're different, and that's okay. She feels abandoned by him, whereas I hardly knew him and barely remember a world where he was. It's totally different for me."

"Right. For you it's a lovely second chance at something you thought wasn't ever a possibility, but for Maggie, it's coming from a place of pain. I support you, honey. And who knows, maybe you'll have some fun, too! Meet someone cute . . ."

"Oh, Jimmy, come on. I have Chris; I don't care about romance."

"Oh, you don't care about romance? Yeah, right. You care," Jim said.

"Okay, maybe. But I wouldn't do anything; it's still on with Christopher."

"Please." Jim rolled his eyes at me hard before turning back to the road.

"Jim! What do you mean, please? I haven't decided fully if I'm done with him," I said.

"The other night on the porch you had more clarity. What happened to that?"

"I don't know . . ."

"You're waiting for the other shoe to drop, but it feels like it already did, right? If he's into that sort of thing, I don't think Ms. Lilly Pulitzer over here will be hitching her wagon to that particular cart."

"Rude. But maybe."

"I'd say keep your options open on this trip up north. You never know who you'll meet."

Then "After the Glitter Fades" came on the radio, and we turned it up and crooned along to Stevie Nicks telling the true rock 'n' roll woman's story. The airport was in sight, and the DJ was happily saying that the storm was missing us and heading up the coast—we'd get a few droplets, that was all—when Jimmy's phone rang.

He answered immediately. As he listened to what the caller had to say, a glow suffused his face. "Yes . . . Wow . . . Tomorrow, got it . . . Thank you!" When he hung up, he was smiling huge. But that big grin faded when he looked at me. "Violet, I'm sorry, but—"

"You got a callback, didn't you?"

"They think I'm perfect, and I'll be doing a read-through with the other lead, the one they already cast. But that means—"

"Don't even say it! You *have* to, Jimmy. This is a big new thing for you, and this is a big new thing for me. It's okay. I gotta go on my own steam, you know?"

We had pulled up to the drop-off curb. "You know what I was going to tell your dad when I met him?"

"What?"

"I was going to look very serious and protective and say, 'I'm Jim Williams, sir. I have been both of your daughters' best friend all our lives. I belong to both of them, and if you hurt either one, you'll have to answer to me.'"

I threw my arms around Jimmy. "You know what? It's just as good hearing you say that to me like this. I love you."

"I love you, too. Now go catch your flight!"

I blew him a kiss and dragged my carry-on toward check-in.

"Don't forget, tomato juice is classic, but it bloats!"

∿∿∿

By the time I reached Boston, the world had changed.

The sky looked low and dark. I had fallen asleep on the plane and woken up feeling small and frightened. It was a long day of travel Scott had scheduled for me. Suddenly it was feeling a little scary to say "my father"; suddenly it was feeling very much like I was setting myself up for more pain. The Weather Channel wasn't helping any. The storm that had been promised in the South had cut a different course: it would soon bear down on New England. On the arrival and departure monitors, I could see that many of the later flights to Nantucket were canceled.

Not mine, though. Apparently the storm wasn't close enough yet, and the next few flights would be allowed to take off.

I nervously scrolled for weather news on my phone. But instead I got an update from the constantly churning weather system that was my family.

Maggie had sent several of those questions she'd wanted to ask Scott my way.

Did you ever think of us while you were out there?

Were you relieved when Rose asked you to go away?

There were more, but I stopped reading them. I had some of those questions, too, but I wanted to meet Scott with an open mind. I didn't want to color our first interaction with a lot of projection, especially not projection that wasn't even my own.

Then there was a text from my mom, accusing me of betraying her by choosing the dead man who was divorcing her.

And then there was Chris.

> Where have you been? Why haven't you been returning my calls?

> This house needs a woman's touch, Violet.

> The silent treatment is really immature. We have plans to make . . .

> Is this about what happened at the Battery?

Meanwhile, they were announcing that ours would be the last flight out to Nantucket. After that, the skies would be too dangerous.

Not wanting to think about that, or my family, I opened Instagram and saw that Aly had just gone live. That made me feel a little better. A little calmer. I smiled.

She was sitting cross-legged in her room at our house, looking pretty and a little manic.

"So, like, do any of you have any extra-special recipes for poisoning your potential future stepmother?" she was saying. "Asking for a friend!"

I saw that a torrent of comments was coming in—mostly expressions of solidarity and jokes about how to do away with Joyce (*she sounds like a real b!*; *rat poison ratatouille!*). But there were a few who didn't seem to think Aly was being very funny. *Maybe she's right, maybe you are too close with your dad* . . . someone had written. *Grow up, girl.*

> Hey, Aly, I texted. I know Joyce sucks but are you sure you want to air this publicly?

I couldn't tell if Aly had seen my text, but she seemed to answer me in the next moment.

> I just want to be real with y'all. That's what my mother always said—if you want to have an audience, you've got to give them all of you, the good and bad. You show them how to make their lives beautiful, but you don't pretend life isn't ugly sometimes, too. And, y'all? I am my mother's daughter. And my mother, she would not have tolerated a vanity sheet cake on her table. Love you! Good night, Knox fam!

I decided that my phone was causing me too much agitation, and so I put it away.

Soon the gate attendant made an announcement asking anyone on the flight to Nantucket to go to the desk.

"Well, that's never a good thing," said the older gentleman sitting next to me, looking up from his *Wall Street Journal*.

"I'll go see what it's about," I said. At the desk, I told the attendant that I was on the flight to Nantucket and braced myself to be told that it wouldn't be taking off after all, and I'd have to wait even longer to meet my dad. I felt a strange tide of emotion at the thought—part relief, part disappointment, part some debilitating childhood loneliness and sorrow.

"Name and your weight, please." The attendant didn't even look up at me; he was chewing his gum so hard I could hear his jaw spring.

"Excuse me, weight?" I asked, suddenly feeling anxious in a whole new way and also very much like a cow.

"Small plane; it's standard." The attendant glanced at me, then continued typing furiously into his computer.

I looked around to see if anyone was close enough to hear me. I was a southern girl, for crying out loud! This was an invasion of privacy.

"Violet Adams, and I'm, well, I've put on a little *extra baggage*." He still didn't look up, and I guessed my joke had gone over his head. This was annoying. I felt anger rising in me, and then I just went ahead and said it, my real weight, not even in a quiet voice, and whoever was listening would have to deal with it. This was me, right here, right now. The attendant—apparently unimpressed one way or the other—recorded this information without looking up.

A few moments later the passengers on my flight were once again summoned to the gate, and now we were led down onto the runway, where we saw a very small plane. Tiny. Too small.

Had I made a terrible mistake? In my indignation over being asked my weight, I had failed to check the Weather Channel again, failed to make one last-ditch decision about whether this was safe or suicidal. Now I was down on the tarmac. The atmosphere was seemingly volatile, dry and electric: you could tell that something big was coming.

Just in case, I sent the same text to Chris, Maggie, and my mom: There's something I have to take care of for myself. We'll talk when I get back. Love you.

Then I put my phone away and looked up at the puddle jumper that was apparently going to deliver me to another island.

"That's the plane?" I said.

"Looks like it," the man who had been reading the *Journal* replied.

"Was it made by Playskool?" I said, trying for funny but not feeling very funny at all.

God bless him, the man smiled at my joke and said, "I know, right? I've seen helicopters larger than this."

Then I remembered that I had taken Jimmy's warning about tomato juice more like an invitation and had had a few rounds on my first flight. Had I added a couple of pounds of water weight? Had I lied to the attendant? Was I the reason we were all going to go down howling into a rough and seething Atlantic? Maybe I looked a little panicked, because the man said, "We will be totally fine. They make this flight like ten times a day. I've done it dozens of times."

Then the flight attendants came and collected our personal items; apparently there was no room in the cabin. Once we boarded, I saw that there was absolutely no room for anything extra. The seat belts were not much more than rope, and it was so hot. My heart was pounding.

"Sorry, are we going to have air-conditioning?"

"Nope, but you can open the windows," my friend—he was now my friend; I was desperate for any friend at this point—told me.

I glanced around at the other passengers, some of whom appeared nervous, some of whom were totally blasé. None of them seemed to find this news remarkable. "Excuse me, what?"

"They just tilt open up there at the top. It's the way all planes used to be. They don't fly as high as other planes, so it's totally safe. Right above the clouds—it's cooler."

I went to buckle my seat belt and tilted my window open, because I was starting to sweat from anxiety. I noticed that the armrests still had ashtrays. This plane had been around the block. As we rattled along the runway, noisily picked up speed, and tilted toward the heavens, I tried not to think about plummeting to my death.

What would Maggie say? *I was right and you were wrong?* What would Chris do? Bring another bride home to my house, someone thinner and wilder in bed?

"It's so loud," I managed, once we were in the air.

"That's little planes for you," the man said. "It would sound the same in a big plane—worse, maybe—but they have all that insulation so you can't hear what's going on outside."

I took a breath, and tried to let his calm demeanor rub off on me.

I looked outside and even though my stomach was in knots, I couldn't help but notice how beautiful it was, dodging in and out of giant white, puffy clouds like a bird. I felt like we were flying, which, of course, technically we were. But I'd been on plenty of flights before, and none of them had truly felt like, well, *flight*. With the added breeze from the much cooler air, I considered what kind of bird I would be. The pilot was saying that we'd be above the clouds soon, and then he could level the plane out and give us a smoother ride. I felt it—in more ways than one, I was aloft.

"There's the Cape to your left," the pilot was saying. Below me, I saw the land narrowing as it reached into the deep-green sea. My stomach still felt high up in my torso, closer to my heart, but I kept my eyes open as we sailed through the atmosphere, moved a little by the wind. I felt precarious, I felt my body moving through space, and I knew that the future was uncertain. I could not know whether I was doing the right thing until I got there, and I could not control the future—not in any way, shape, or form, and certainly not from my safe old life.

The pilot announced that we were approaching Nantucket, and then I saw it—the old lighthouse that had been featured on my dad's postcard, and I knew that whatever else might happen, I was going to make it back to land just fine.

CHAPTER TWENTY-FIVE

~~~~~

Aly

The morning after the welcome/birthday dinner, I woke up feeling emotionally foggy and missing my mother. Then I checked my phone, and remembered.

My Insta was flooded with comments. Overnight, my following had increased by 10K.

Apparently there were a lot of women out there with a Joyce for a stepmother, or a sister-in-law, or a best friend's boyfriend. And, wow, did they have some inventive ways to shame the sheet cake. But also there were a lot of Joyces out there, too, women who had been excluded when they came into a new family, run out of town by their boyfriends' kids, women who really wanted me to know how unfun it was to date when you were over sixty-five.

I stumbled downstairs for a glass of water, feeling mortified.

What would my mother think of all this? I wondered. She had had grace. She didn't go in for shock value. But she really did say you had to show people the real you and share what you felt so that they could feel something, too.

But maybe I was looking at it from the wrong perspective. Was I just demonizing Joyce because she wasn't my mom? All of a sudden, I was mentally checking myself all the time. Was I projecting, was I being defensive, was I being open and allowing this person in? I had always prided myself on knowing exactly how I felt about a situation, but these were uncharted waters.

I had a fury burning inside me that just wouldn't die down. Every time it cooled a little, Joyce came along and stoked it.

I drove over to the house on Sullivan's as planned. I found the door unlocked and the house filled with the sounds of my family waking up. Della ran past me, being chased by her brother, who was screaming in glee.

"Hey, Aunt Aly!" they said in unison.

"Hey, guys!"

"Morning, Minnow!" my dad greeted me with his arms outstretched. "Give your dad a hug!"

I hugged him. Joyce was right behind him. My cheeks burned, seeing her in reality after I'd named her to my virtual rabble. Probably she didn't Insta, but you never did know. "Hey, Joyce," I said.

"Hello, hello," she said flatly.

Dad gave her a shoulder pat, then said to me, "Hey, Aly, thanks again for last night. It was really wonderful."

Just then the kids tore through the house again, shrieking with delight.

I called out to them to be careful and slow down, but my dad told me to let them be. "Reminds me of when you were all little, running through this house," he said, smiling.

"Oh, well, then good!" I glanced at Joyce, who was frowning and looking off into the distance. "Where are the rest of us?" I asked, meaning Mike and Jess. "I smell coffee!"

"Mike brought his own, you know," Joyce said, making a face at my dad.

"Mikey has always been very serious about his coffee," I replied, aiming as best I could for a neutral tone and hoping he'd brought the local brand back from Michigan.

I walked into the kitchen and found Jess and Mike, who was brewing the coffee.

"Hey, Jess, how did you sleep?" I asked my sister.

"Great after that gummy," she said.

"What gummy? Melatonin?" I almost jumped at the sound of Joyce's voice. I hadn't realized she was lurking behind me.

"Ha! No. A CBD gummy. Can't travel with the real stuff, but this helps me sleep."

"Wait, *you smoke marijuana?*" Joyce asked my sister. The room got quiet.

"Well, yeah. Sometimes." Jess shot me an "Is she for real?" look. "It's legal in California."

"Does your *father* know this?" Joyce's eyebrows were laboring heroically against her Botox as they tried to rise.

"She's a grown-up. She does what she wants," Mike said, amiably enough, while looking straight at Joyce, who mouthed "Wow," turned on her heel, and left us in the kitchen.

"What the hell was that?" Jess asked me.

"That," I said, "was pure Joyce."

"Was she born in 1932? Why is she so afraid of a little pot?"

"Girls, give her a break," Mike said. "This is a lot of family time. Our family is a lot. Now, who wants coffee?" Mike went to find the mugs but stopped when he opened the cabinet. "Where are our mugs?"

"What do you mean?" I said.

"Our mugs, Al. Like, the ones we always used?" he said. "These are all white."

I went around the counter to the cabinet he had opened, and saw that instead of the family mugs, there were sixteen bright white mugs with silver rims lined up like pawns on a chessboard. My mom and dad had collected mugs over the years from vacations or as gifts. Mike's kids had painted a bunch. I had my favorite mug I always used here, one from the College of Charleston, but it was nowhere to be seen now.

"I bet Joyce threw them out," Jess said.

"No, Dad wouldn't let her do that," I said. "He loved those crazy mugs."

"Jesus," Mike said under his breath. "Dad's in it."

"Whatever, he's a grown-up, like me. Right, Mike?" Jess said.

Then my dad came into the kitchen.

"Hey, Dad, where are the mugs?" Mike asked him. "You know, like the one that looks like a pig and the one from Café Du Monde?"

"Oh, Joyce was organizing my kitchen for me. I'm sure they're somewhere. I'll ask her."

Mike gestured forcefully, showing my dad the cabinet like it was an exhibit in a criminal trial. "Okay, because we only found these uptight white ones."

"I'll go ask her," Dad said again, and left the kitchen.

The kids came into the kitchen then, radiating sunshine.

Mike brought both kids around the counter to face the stove and pulled a stepladder out so Della could see what was happening. He put aprons on them and let Della mix the batter for a minute, complimenting her on her skills. He then made a big show of flipping the pancakes. JR was begging him to let him flip one.

"Please, Dad? Come on, let me. I'm seven! I can totally do it!"

"Uh, I don't know, kiddo. This is Papa's house, and I'm not sure he'd like that."

Just then my dad entered the kitchen with Joyce.

"What wouldn't I like?" Dad asked Mike.

"He wants to flip pancakes, and I'm a little nervous about potential kitchen hazards."

"Here, JR, why don't you help me get the fruit salad ready?" Jess asked.

"Don't be silly," my dad said with a grandfatherly air. "In this house, the answer is always yes! Go right ahead, JR. The cleaning crew are coming tomorrow!"

"Papa said it was fine! I'm doing it!" JR's eyes got wide.

"Me too!" Della said.

"Are you sure, George?" Joyce said.

"Yes, I'm sure. Go right ahead!" Dad smiled patiently at Joyce, but his voice was firm, which I appreciated.

"Fine, but if you make a mess, you're cleaning it up!" Mike told them.

JR grabbed the frying pan and flipped his giant pancake up into the air. Both kids tilted their heads to watch it almost hit the ceiling. Instead it tumbled down, landing perfectly back in the pan.

"Wow! Good job, buddy!" I said, and we all cheered him on. Della then tried, too, but couldn't really get her pancake to lift.

Cate entered the room, gave everyone a kiss on the cheek, and then went about finding dishes to set the table.

"Where are the plates?" she asked. "They used to be here . . ."

"Oh, I moved them. They are now over here," Joyce said, showing Cate where things were. Everything, down to the forks, was in a new location.

"Oh, okay, thanks." Cate seemed strange; she wasn't making eye contact. "I'm sorry. I'm just used to the old layout, I guess."

"Well, it makes much more sense this way," Joyce responded. "I'm going to go cut flowers for the table. George, are you joining me?"

We all looked at my dad, who made zero eye contact with us as he followed her out.

"I'm sorry, the woman rearranged the kitchen. This isn't even her home!" Cate said.

"Get a load of this!" Jess said, and pulled out a pad of paper that was by the house phone.

"What does that say on top? 'George and Joyce' stationery? Oh my god, this isn't her house! Unbelievable. Mom would hate her," Jess said.

"She's just so . . . aggressive," Cate said. "But maybe she's just nervous?"

"All right, you hens," Mike said.

"Hens?" Jess repeated pointedly.

"Let's just relax, okay? It's a lot. She's an outsider. I bet she calms down after she gets to know us a little more."

"Listen, I've been playing nice for the whole summer," I said defensively.

"Have you, though? Have you gotten to know her? Do you know about her children? Have you asked her anything about herself? Don't be so dismissive," Mike said.

This sort of made my blood boil. But it also sounded a little bit correct. Maybe he was right. I didn't really know anything about Joyce. Maybe I had been telling myself that her relationship with my dad would run its course or something and getting to know her wouldn't be worth it. I had a bad habit of being dismissive of people I didn't like. Maybe there was still time to flip the script here?

"You know what, Mike? You're right. We should give her a real chance," I said.

"There's the little sister I know!" Mike said as he piled the pancakes on the platter.

"No way, I smell a rat. You should be a witch right back at her," Jess said, stealing a strawberry out of the fruit salad.

"Jess, come on. We live out of state. Aly has to deal with this woman much more than we do. I think it's a delicate game here. If she acts like a jerk, that only gives Joyce ammo," Mike said. "Why don't we make it a point at dinner to ask her about herself?"

"Okay, guys, let's get the food on the table," Cate said.

We took the pancakes, syrup, forks, knives, fruit salad, and sausage links out to the dining room. All the furniture had been replaced by clear Lucite chairs and a very modern, industrial-looking dining table. It made us all stop dead in our tracks. Our dining table had been a wedding present from our mother's parents to her and my father. It was solid wood and a beautiful antique. We had made many memories around that table, and now it was gone. Like the mugs.

I took a deep breath.

"Girls, let's just try, okay?" Mike said. "I mean, maybe Dad needs a fresh start. This could be a good sign that he's healing."

Jess gave a slow, sad shake of her head. "It doesn't even match the rest of the house."

We set the table and put the platters out, then called the kids over. My dad and Joyce came in, and Joyce placed the flowers in the center of the table. She had chosen to cut some of my mother's roses, my mother's *favorite* roses. She'd actually done a nice job arranging them, but that only made it worse. It was like Mom was here in the room with us, casting her magic.

My dad did not seem to have noticed. "Breakfast looks great, guys! Must be my favorite grandson's expert flipping abilities."

"I'm your *only* grandson, Papa!" JR said.

"Well, you're still my favorite."

"Oh my god, these are the best! Totally because of the flipping," Jess said, giving JR a little squeeze.

"So, Joyce, how old are your kids?" I asked her.

"I have three daughters," she said. "My eldest, Clara, is just like you. My middle child, Kristen, is your dad's favorite. They get along so well. And Kennedy is thirty-nine and living in Dallas."

"Oh, Dad, I didn't realize that you've met Joyce's children!" I said.

"Yes, we've had a few dinners together. Nice kids," he said, helping himself to another pancake.

"You should see how your father gets along with Kristen! They are like peas in a pod! It's really wonderful!" Joyce said.

"That's great!" I said, feeling it was anything but. First she replaced the mugs, then the daughters? *Hell* no. "Well, I'd love to meet her!"

"She's very accomplished," Joyce was saying. I could sense that she was really ramping up. My finger dragged across my phone and began another Insta Live. I had the phone propped up against a water glass to capture Joyce's gross, self-satisfied expression as she continued talking. "She's a doctor and has won so many awards. Went to Harvard. All my kids did. They didn't have a choice! But you know how it is, right, Cate?" Joyce said.

"Oh, I don't know where my kids will go to college." Cate gave her husband a look. "They aren't even in high school yet."

"Oh, I knew my kids would get into my alma mater. They all had Harvard onesies!" Joyce smiled at her own "joke."

"I want to go to Harvard!" JR said.

"Well, you'll have to work very hard and be the best at everything you do to go there. It isn't for everyone," Joyce said to JR in a voice that conveyed how unlikely she thought that would be.

"I like to work really hard, right, Mommy?" he said to Cate.

"Yes, baby. But you don't have to go to Harvard, and you have a long time to decide where you want to go and who you want to be," Cate said.

"That's right. Most important is to be a good person. Accomplishment can be measured in lots of ways, kiddo," Mike said.

"Not if you want to have a good job," Joyce said under her breath.

I put my phone on selfie mode, gave an eye roll to the growing audience for my live feed, then surreptitiously turned it back on Joyce as I asked, "Do you have grandchildren?"

"Yes, I do. I have four grandchildren and another on the way. All my kids are your ages and married." Joyce was methodically cutting up a single plain pancake.

"Well, that's wonderful!" I said with forced cheer.

"That's exciting to have another baby!" Cate added.

"Yes, and they all have Harvard T-shirts, too! I'm *such* a tiger mom," Joyce joked with obvious pride. That seemed like a good place to end the livestream, though I glimpsed how many comments were flooding in and had to repress the urge to go look at them right away.

Meanwhile, Jess slid a gummy across the table to Mike, who put it right in his mouth.

"Thanks, Jess," Mike said.

Cate stood up. "Who wants a mimosa?"

"Oh, that would be lovely!" Jess said.

Mike and I also voted yes, and I left the table to help Cate make the mimosas, slipping my phone into my back pocket.

"At least Dad keeps the champagne in the same place," I said, pulling out a bottle.

When I went back into the dining room to get a headc ount, I ran into Joyce in the hallway.

"You have to stop this, Aly!" Joyce said, clearly upset.

"Stop what? Are you okay? What's wrong?" I asked her, panicking a little that she knew I was bad-mouthing her to the world.

"You are allowing your niece and nephew to watch as their parents *take drugs* and *drink*!"

"What? They aren't *taking drugs*!" I was trying hard not to laugh, but I was also absolutely boiling with rage, and the contradictory emotions were pulling at my features in odd ways. "They are taking CBD gummies to relax, not to get high, for God's sake. Am I misunderstanding you?"

"No, you very well are not. This is *outrageous*. Might I remind you that in the state of South Carolina it is illegal to take THC."

"Joyce, it's CBD, you can buy it at the gas station," I said, now very much regretting that I didn't still have my livestream going. I felt for my phone.

"You know, I've served on many juries in my life and watched many people's families get taken apart. Parents lose their children all the time with this kind of thing. I've been a part of it. It's heartbreaking to watch, but the right thing must be done . . ."

"Joyce, please. No one is doing anything illegal. It's all going to be okay; I think you just don't understand what is happening . . ." I tried to finish, but she pushed past me and went into my dad's bedroom, slamming the door.

"Wow," I said to no one, and continued to the dining room table.

"How many mimosas?" I asked.

"Two, please." My dad must have heard the door slam, but he was still smiling affably. "One for me and one for Joyce." Joyce appeared in the dining room again.

"Oh, no, *I* don't drink during the day. Can I talk to you for a moment?" Joyce said to my father.

"Later. Let's finish breakfast first," Dad said, and I could tell she didn't like being brushed off one bit. Mike was laughing with JR over something, and Della crawled into my dad's lap.

"One for me and one for Mike!" Jess said. Joyce shot me a look, which I ignored. She was actually seeming pretty unhinged, which was giving me a weird and delicious feeling of satisfaction.

I left the dining room and went back into the kitchen.

Cate and I got the mimosas together and brought them to the table.

"You know who would really like this scene of all of us together?" Cate said with a warm smile. "Your mom. Right, Dad?"

"Oh yes! She loved family gatherings," he said. "And she sure loved a party!"

"God, did she ever!" Mike said. "But she really loved birthdays! Remember ours, guys? Remember that *Little Mermaid*–themed one you had, Jess, or that nail polish party? Everything had nail polish on it for years. Or my eighth birthday, where we all played laser tag? Even you, Dad!"

"I kicked your butt," Dad said, chuckling.

"Remember the cakes she would make?" Cate said.

"Yes! Remember that time she made me a Barbie cake? She stuck the doll in the middle and the doll's skirt was the cake?" I said, smiling at the memory.

"Callie knew how to have fun," Dad said.

"She did," Cate said. "To Callie!" She raised her glass, and we all cheered. "Man, I miss that woman."

"You were all so lucky to get along. Getting along with your mother-in-law, that isn't very common," Joyce said pointedly to Cate.

After breakfast, I stayed at the table a little to hang with the kids. I loved seeing my dad with them. They made him so happy. He was a natural grandfather, and now that he was semiretired, I thought he actually enjoyed being around children more. He laughed and smiled so big. I couldn't remember him having been so hands-on when we were younger, but now he was all play.

"Hey, Papa! Can we go in the ocean?" Della said.

"Yes!" my dad said. "Go get your suits and let's go for a swim! Aly, you're coming, right?"

"Sure. Who's going to find the most sand dollars?" I said to the kids.

"Me!" JR said.

"I'm going to find a starfish!" Della said.

"Let's find shells so we can paint them as Christmas ornaments!" JR said.

I found my trusty black one-piece in the laundry room with the beach toys (apparently a zone Joyce hadn't gotten her hands on yet) and headed to the beach. My dad was already in the water with the kids, splashing around and laughing throaty laughs. The kids shrieked in delight as they bobbed in the waves in their bright swimsuits with giant smiles. I ran to the shoreline. Sometimes it took a kid to shake you loose from the shackles of adulthood.

The many heavy loads I'd been carrying seemed to be lifted from me.

We were in the waves a good long while. Long enough for me to really let go of the whole shit show at breakfast. Afterward we all took a quick rinse in the outdoor shower, getting the sand and salt off. We toweled dry and headed inside, our bodies slightly blistered but our hearts happy. The kids got into their pajamas early and curled up on the couch with JR's iPad. I took a few pictures of them cuddled together like kittens. This whole day was so sweet. Seeing my dad so happy and just enjoying his life was a salve for my broken heart. *My mother would've loved this*, I thought again. So, I decided then and there that even though these kids weren't my children, I would enjoy them and drink up the joy for the both of us. I would love my family a little extra for her.

"You kids need an ice cream?" I asked, and they both nodded yes, so I headed into the kitchen, where I found Cate crying.

"Hey! What's going on? Are you okay?" I asked her.

"Yeah, God, sorry. Fine. Sorry," she said, wiping her tears.

"Sorry for what? Is it Mike? Do I need a tarp and a shovel?"

She did laugh at that, but then her face fell again. "I hate conflict," she said. "I had too many mimosas, maybe? I'm so tired. Those kids, man. They are amazing, but, whew, a vacation with kids isn't a vacation; it's a *relocation*. I'm so stressed-out."

"Cate, what did he do? We're sisters. I told you I'd keep you over him in a divorce!"

"It isn't Mike, but it might be soon. He's outside cooling off."

"What happened?" I asked her. I kind of knew, but I guess I was resisting going back into my Joyce fury after that blissed-out hit of ocean.

"It's Joyce. She cornered me and Mike." Cate sighed. "You know I'm trying, right? I'm an outsider, too, and I know it's hard to break into the Knox Club. You are all so close. But she's just . . . I don't get it. She told me I was making your dad uncomfortable by bringing up your mom," she said.

"Oh, no, Cate, that's not true. Dad loves talking about Mom, it doesn't make him upset! I think it keeps her memory alive!"

"I don't want to cause trouble, Aly. I just want to have a nice visit. We all miss your mom. Man, I feel stupid," she said. "You know she was the one who encouraged me to . . . well, do anything I wanted to do."

My dad came into the kitchen and saw us. "What's all this? What's happened?" He came over to Cate and hugged her, and she looked like she was struggling with the impulse to bear-hug him back.

"Dad, I . . . uh, I'm so sorry."

"What are you sorry for?" he asked her.

"For bringing up Mom. I shouldn't do it so much. I don't mean to upset you! I just miss her and know . . . I didn't mean to . . ."

"Cate, you can always talk about Callie. Where is this coming from?"

"Dad, Joyce told her that it upsets you to talk about Mom," I said.

"No! God, no. Never! I love remembering her. You are free to discuss any topic you want, Cate. You are like another daughter to me— you gave me grandchildren! You are family. Please don't cry; come here! How about a glass of wine? A nice Sauv Blanc?" He shuffled over to the fridge.

"Dad," I said.

"I'll talk to Joyce, okay? Here you go, kitty cat."

Dad slid a glass of wine toward Cate. She took it and drained it.

"Where's Mike?" he asked us.

"Outside. I'd let him be for a moment," Cate said.

I walked over to the window to see if I could spot my brother, and I saw he was talking to Joyce.

"Uh, he's out there with Joyce," I said.

"Oh, God," Cate said.

"I'll go." I raced outside, but by the time I got to him, Joyce had left, and Mike was smoking a cigarette. A habit I thought he'd kicked years ago.

"Hey there, big brother. You okay?" I asked quietly.

"No, I very much am not, Aly Cat," he said. "Where's Jess?"

"No idea. We just got in from a swim with the kids and found Cate in the kitchen really upset."

Mike made a face and tensed a fist. For a moment I thought he might punch the wall. "She threatened to call Department of Social Services on me and Cate for taking drugs," he said, taking a long drag off his cigarette.

"You have got to be kidding me!" I said.

"Nope. She said she knew we were engaging in illegal activities and she had played a part in removing children from, get this, *unfit parents*." He tossed his cigarette down and crushed it with his toe.

"This is insane. Who does she think she is, coming for your kids?" I was boiling.

I honestly felt like a superhero, my blood coursing through me with superhuman strength. It was a good thing Joyce wasn't there, because my hands really, really, really wanted to break something right then. Then I felt this heaviness in my stomach, a fear of other sacred things already being broken. I had told Mike to come for this birthday party, knowing it was going to be a shit show, selfishly wanting backup. "You both are the best parents I've ever seen! Those kids are fantastic, and that doesn't happen from bad parenting!" My cheeks were blazing. It was one thing to insult me to my face, but to go after my brother and *his* family? "I'll take care of this," I said. "I'll talk to Dad."

"Okay," Mike said absently, glancing at his phone. "I need to go talk to my wife. I am glad I live in Michigan." Then he stood and shuffled back inside.

I stayed outside and looked up into the sky, which had suddenly gotten dark. The clouds were gathering and threatening rain. The wind was picking up, and the air felt cool. I turned to go inside, but a sign caught my eye.

It was a permit for construction, right by my mother's garden.

Joyce was going to put a pool in, over my mother's garden. I was flooded with nausea. I looked up at the sky, wishing someone from above could explain why in the world we had been cursed with this woman. Was there a lesson here we weren't getting, or was she just a terrorist?

I couldn't ask my siblings. I couldn't ask my dad. Violet was off on her adventure, and Jimmy's audition was coming up. My phone was already in my hand, and I was circling the garden like I was a detective in a prestige cable drama and this was a crime scene.

"Hey, Callie Knox women," I said as I let the live function linger on my mother's red roses and herb patches. "This right here is the holiest of holies, my mother's garden. This is where she grew the roses she'd put on our table for the holidays. This is where she grew mint for tea and lavender for sachets and belladonna for—honestly, I always wondered, but maybe she knew this day was coming? My mother did have a kind of sixth sense for things . . . Maybe she knew that someday her soul mate would fall prey to a woman who would move in, insult his family, and pour concrete over her garden . . ."

I could see that the comments were coming in hot now, and I kept going.

"Some of you say I don't have sympathy for widows going out on the dating scene, but you know what? I *do*. In fact, are there any of you Callie Knox fans out there who are looking for a great guy? My mother was magic, and I know some of you are magic, too. Maybe you have the kind of magic that can save me and my family from this massive b—"

And then I did it. I gave my dad's name, address, and phone number to an Instagram Live audience that was now apparently upward of ten thousand people.

When I shut off the live feed, I was feeling about ten feet off the ground. I was feeling pretty mad, honestly. As I climbed the stairs to the front door and felt my phone buzz, I was relieved to see the text was from Charley.

Hello, Ms. Knox. Fancy a boat ride tomorrow? Sunset?

I smiled. This was what I needed. I needed to be away from the pressures of this moment, the horror show that my beloved family was becoming.

Sounds lovely. What can I bring?

Just you. And hopefully a bikini . . .

I blushed, but I also kind of liked the forwardness. This was exciting.

See you tomorrow, mister.

Can't wait.

I chewed on my bottom lip. This was a nice little pick-me-up in the midst of the current situation, but I still had to go back inside and deal with the fallout. On some level, I knew it was wrong of me to be putting these livestreams out for public consumption, but another part of me felt like I was stepping into my power. Like I was finally speaking in my own voice.

I went up the porch steps and pulled on the front door, but it was locked.

CHAPTER TWENTY-SIX

~~~~~

Violet

As soon as I exited the plane in Nantucket and felt the solid ground under my feet, I realized how rigidly controlled I'd been. Not just on the airplane but for the whole past year, maybe all my years. When I first arrived, the air was wild, and I could feel a few big drops beginning to fall. The wind was fierce. It felt like a new energy was whirling around me, whirling around everything. But then that passed.

The next day was lovely.

In the morning, I reread the email from Scott. The place I was staying in belonged to Annabelle, Jimmy's aunt; she had a small cottage that she had lent me for the visit. One of her husbands had bought it for her for their wedding. It was a place to hide, and she was currently in Europe, so the cottage was mine. It was called Rose House, which of course made me think of Gran, who, by the looks of the scenery, would adore Nantucket.

It was Nantucket gray, and all one floor. A deep white porch. A bright pink door that opened onto the coziest living room. White couches, handmade quilts, basket storage, and dozens of seascape paintings. Old weathered, lacquered wood-plank floors. I could imagine loving it here in any weather. The working brick hearth conjured up images of rainstorms, books, fuzzy socks, and hot tea.

When I arrived, I found a note on the coffee table:

> *Welcome to Nantucket! Shoot me a message and let me
> know you've arrived. I have a reservation for us for dinner
> at Galley Beach Restaurant tomorrow. In the meantime,
> get rested up and holler if you need anything. Can't wait.*
> *~Dad/Scott/Whatever you feel comfortable with*

I replied immediately, letting him know I'd arrived, then took a soak in the claw-foot tub, toweled off my hair with a fluffy navy blue towel, and fell into a deep sleep.

My father was working the next day, so I relaxed at the cute cottage. I searched the bookshelves for something to read and found an Elin Hilderbrand novel. I devoured it and loved all the Nantucket references. Honestly, I needed the rest. I had been burning the candle at both ends. As the time for our dinner approached, I dressed with care. I was happy to have packed something on the more formal side—a black crepe dress with flutter sleeves and a smocked bodice, which I wore with my slide-on gold sandals and bangles on my wrists. I slicked my hair back in a low ponytail, swiped some lip gloss on, and called an Uber.

The driver took me past dozens of chamring gray-shingled homes.

I tried not to think about the future or the past and just really look at exactly where I was.

All the window boxes were filled with plants featuring bright pinks, greens, and purples. Huge blossoms of blue hydrangeas seemed to line every fence. The charm was strong; the houses here gave some of the homes in downtown Charleston competition. And the cobblestone streets made me think of the side streets in Charleston. Nantucket and Charleston seemed like sisters to me. Both were port towns, so they had a similar feel. But there was something lovestruck and spooky about this island.

"First time in Nantucket?" the Uber driver asked.

I said it was and asked him what the best spots were. I was feeling so many things—nervous, elated, tired, wired, hungry, big, tiny—and was relieved when he just launched into tour guide mode.

"I would say that the best shops are on Main Street and on Centre Street. There is a great sandwich shop on Centre Street and also a scrimshaw shop. One of the only ones left. You can't miss Murray's Toggery Shop to pick up some red pants or a dress. You can go to one of the boutiques and see some of the famous lighthouse basket bags. They are expensive, but I think they sell cheaper fake ones at Murray's. Make sure to grab a drink at the Lemon Press, eat at the Company of the Cauldron—fun fact: the chef's brother is that famous chef Thomas Keller."

"Wait, what?" That was a name I knew from Maggie, and suddenly all my feelings were magnified ten times, because Maggie wasn't here with me to have her own experience of Scott.

"Thomas Keller. The guy who had that restaurant in California, I think?"

"The French Laundry?" I wanted to text Maggie immediately, but I resisted the impulse. I also wanted to stay in this moment, uncomfortable as it was.

"That's it! Yeah, he opened up his own little restaurant. It's a must-try. The beaches also are all great, and if you need a good book, head over to Mitchell's Book Corner. Ask for Tim—he knows books!"

"Obviously I'll be going shopping," I said.

At the restaurant, I was met by an impossibly beautiful hostess who led me to our table. The crowd could have been featured in *Vogue* magazine. Tall, tan women in various bright caftans all kicked off their sandals to let their perfectly pedicured feet slip into the cool sand beneath the tables. Men in linen pants and needlepoint belts took out their designer shades to protect their eyes from the bright mango sun, which was slipping behind the violet clouds. Giant beige canopies billowed in the ocean breeze like the sails of a pirate ship. The seating was right in front of the ocean, and I was temporarily hypnotized as we watched the waves rolling in and the sunlight dancing on the sparkling water and the foam as it crept up onto the shore. Everything was bathed in orange. It was breathtaking. I wondered where our father was, but after about a minute a man appeared—handsome, with Maggie's eyes and my hair—wearing chef whites.

I stood up. "Scott?" I said. I wanted to say "Dad," but the word was a lump in my throat.

"Welcome to Nantucket and to Galley Beach," Scott said.

"This is your restaurant?" I said in disbelief. He'd always been a wayward kind of man in my mind; it seemed incredible that he was the head chef of a place like this. But it was also hard for my mind to get around the fact that he was here, alive—that I had a father.

"Yeah, kid, but not as good as the one you and your sister gave a second life to. I've been following all that. I'm very proud of you both."

"That's all Maggie, really."

"I bet that's not true."

"So you got to eat at the restaurant? Before . . ."

"Maggie threw me out on my behind? Yes, yes, I did. I had a rough go of it last time, nothing I didn't deserve. But I'd had a more peaceful meal at the bar on an earlier occasion. You were there, by chance, and I was so happy to see you grown and looking well; it made my whole lifetime."

"You were there? At the Magic Lantern? When I was?"

"Yes. You were eating a delicious plate of fish and talking to the manager."

"Why didn't you say something?" Suddenly I felt cheated—of that night, when we might have talked, and every night since, when I might have spoken to my dad. I remembered it then—the smell of cinnamon, this man saying something along the lines of *the bad things make food delicious, but sometimes wholesome things are delicious, too . . .*

"I didn't know if it was my place. I didn't want to disturb your evening. Honestly, I was scared. I wish we'd had a peaceful conversation that night, just us. Hopefully, we can start with me serving you a meal as good as the one I had at the Lantern that night."

I felt this big sob working its way through my body. It seemed almost too enormous to let go of. I threw my arms around my dad's middle—he was definitely my dad all of a sudden—and tried to let the reality that he was real, and here, and alive, and good, wash over me again and again.

"We have a lot to catch up on," Dad said. "Let me get cleaned up and we can get started . . ."

As my father departed, a tan server with a foreign accent came up wearing a white button-down and a navy apron. He dropped off a bottle of champagne and a dozen oysters with lemons.

I happily filled my mouth with the brine from the oysters and the acidity from the lemons. I took a sip of the champagne and felt deliciously taken care of. It was all pretty perfect and glamorous. The sun continued to set, and a few seagulls called to one another. Then, suddenly, it seemed my father had been gone a long time. A little panic rose in my throat, constricting my airways. What if he was leaving?

What if this was me, alone at a table, forever trying to appear glamorously together?

But as soon as that fear arose, he was there, refilling my champagne glass as he lowered himself into the seat beside me and asking, "How were the oysters?"

"They were amazing, thank you," I replied with a rush of appreciation for this place.

"Wellfleets from the Cape."

"This is the most beautiful restaurant—it's unreal."

"Yeah, I am very lucky to be at the helm of the ship. This restaurant has been around forever, since the nineteen twenties. It actually started out as a clam shack, if you can believe it. It has gone through a ton of changes but always had the seating directly in the sand, looking out on the water. Plus, it has the greatest people-watching."

"Well, I much prefer this to a clam shack," I said. "Though I do appreciate clams and shacks, too."

"Me too. Also, it has a wine cellar with over five thousand bottles. Are you a wine lover?" my dad asked.

"Yes. Love it. I have very happily left my Pabst Blue Ribbon days behind me."

"Wine comes with the chef life for sure. But there is always a time and a place for a good beer . . . Maybe not a PBR, but . . ."

"Hey, now, a hot day on a boat? Nothing like a PBR," I said, and he laughed and raised a glass to me.

The server returned to clear the oysters and consulted with my dad over the menu. They got very serious, and I could see that my father was a little nervous: he wanted to make sure I was happy, that I was fed and watered and treated like a queen. The funny thing was that his nervousness made *me* a little nervous, too: Was this night going to continue to go well? Were we all going to be okay?

But then the dishes started to come, and the conversation flowed, and we were giddy with so many things to say to each other. I took a transcendent bite of lobster and thought, not for the first time, that this would be a good thing to share with Maggie. "Is it just, like, a ton of butter? It's usually butter when Maggie gives me something good."

"It is, but it's miso butter."

"The vegetables are so fresh, especially the sweet corn and peas with the lobster. But I loved the vegetable plate."

"I'll try not to take it too hard that your favorite dish is the least showy!"

"I mean, I love all of them, but . . ."

"It's okay; Hannah feels the same way about it. She loves her fish and chips, but she says she needs to mix in a vegetable plate here and there."

"Is Hannah the woman you are going to marry?" I asked him.

"Yes, that's the plan. She's the sommelier here. If you are up to it, I'd like you to meet her, and I'd like you all to come to the wedding at Christmas."

Dessert arrived, and a round of coffees.

"This is my favorite. I want to know what you think. It's a turmeric lemongrass panna cotta made with almond milk and macadamia nuts and finished with a drizzle of lavender syrup."

My spoon sliced through it, and when my mouth closed around the bite, my eyes closed in satisfaction. "It's delicious."

"I thought you'd appreciate it. I love our crème brûlée, but you can get that anywhere. This is special."

It was all so perfect. Could I trust in it? I reached out my hand, touched Scott's forearm.

"Everything okay?" he asked.

"Yeah, I think so." A few tears were running down my face, but I was smiling, too. "Just trying to reassure myself you're real."

"I'm real."

"So you say, but I'm going to need reminders from time to time."

Scott smiled. "I got you."

CHAPTER TWENTY-SEVEN

~~~~~

Aly

The weather was what I liked to describe as *thick*. You could swim through the air, it was so humid, but from a breezy porch or a boat ride or through a window, you could enjoy the South showing off. Summertime glimmered here, despite the heat. The season of long, lazy afternoons spent on the beach that turned into bright evenings. Barbeques everywhere, and the hypnotic night choruses of cicadas. Summertime was, in my opinion, the best season anywhere, and Charleston was made for it.

All season long I had been doing my best to post about that magic as much as possible, and it had grown my audience slightly. Nothing had grown it like my Joyce coverage, though. Engagement on my socials was high, and the comments were fast and furious.

Hadn't that been my goal?

Apparently not. Rosemary emailed me bright and early to say Crate and Barn was nervous that this turn in my content was going to alienate the core Callie Knox audience. I saw her point: I'd definitely had some folks announce they were unfollowing me, but the new followers more than made up for them. I didn't really know who these people were, though, whether they were the kind of people who bought lovingly designed tableware.

Thank God I had a distraction lined up. Charley and I had finally figured out a time to get together, and that time was late this afternoon. I was feeling unmoored and I needed something to take out my big energy on.

It was so hot, but so beautiful. Charley said he wanted to spend our time together on the water. The perfect Lowcountry date. He was taking me out on his boat, and I was bringing us a picnic from Harris Teeter, a southern grocery store that had recently joined forces with the famous New York City cheese store Murray's Cheese. So now we had access to some of the best cheeses in the world. I thought that would be an impressive addition to my cooler for this date. But after just walking from the hot parking lot to the store, I was sweaty when I reached the cold air-conditioning. As I stood at the cheese counter, I had second thoughts. On the one hand, I wanted our date to be romantic, with cheeses and charcuterie, but on the other hand, it was so hot that the cheese would get gross and the meat would sweat. Not exactly cute. Should I pack sandwiches?

I was Callie Knox's daughter: I was supposed to know beauty! The simple charm of a Charleston picnic was *my thing*. But I didn't know what Charley would want to eat. I was putting pressure on myself.

I headed over to the deli section and was unimpressed. Ugh. I decided to text Maggie. She would know exactly what to do.

> Maggie. Date emergency. I am going out with Charley finally, and he's taking me on the boat. I said I'd bring the food, but I am uninspired. What should I bring?

I grabbed a bottle of champagne and put it in my basket. She texted back.

> Where are you?

> Harris Teeter.

> Girl, I'm about to blow your mind. Go over to Hamby.

> The catering company?

Yes! They have a market, and they sell, get ready, boat
totes! They're prepackaged boat picnics! Ask them
for the chicken salad or the pimento cheese.
You're welcome.

> I knew you'd know what to do! Thanks!

I paid for the champagne and headed toward Hamby Catering.

Pretty soon, at the take-out counter, I was getting the full lowdown on the fabulous boat tote and doing a series of Insta stories on the whole amazing concept. My feed was still a little hot from my Joyce posts, but the engagement was really high, and I wanted to keep that going.

"Girl, we got you sixteen pinwheel bites on sun-dried tomato wraps. It's enough for four people. They have turkey, cheddar, roasted red pepper, and a yummy spinach pesto aioli. Also, there's a box of our famous chicken salad sandwiches, fresh fruit, a spinach dip with chips, a Mediterranean pasta salad, and lemon bars! It includes an insulated tote so you don't need to battle this heat!"

"Wow, that's a ton of food! Plus, I'll have leftovers, so that's cool."

"Where are y'all going?" she asked me.

"Not sure; it's a first date, so he's taking me out on the boat, and I'm in charge of the food."

"Well, you're covered. And if it's a first date, have these on the house—a bag of the best cheese straws in Charleston," she said. "Great with wine!"

At home I took a quick shower to wash off the heat, applied makeup, slathered myself in sunscreen, and gave myself a good squirt of my favorite perfume. I selected an easy-breezy white linen sundress and put on my black string bikini underneath, piled my hair up in a high bun, and finished the look with a black headband and my Jackie Kennedy sunglasses. Now that it was all happening, I was excited and felt the flutter of butterflies in my stomach. The conversation between us had been very flirtatious, and I was eager to see Charley again.

I wondered if he'd kiss me. I felt like he might, so I dug around my bag for mints . . . just in case.

At five—our planned meeting time—I walked down the boat ramp and heard some beautiful jazz music at low volume. Then I saw him standing next to the boat. He was wearing a bright blue linen shirt and red shorts. He was deeply tanned, and his hair was moving in the breeze. When he turned and saw me, he shot me a bright smile. I noticed that he had a linen napkin over one arm and his other arm behind his back, like a proper server. I giggled.

"Well, hello there, Charley!" I said. "What is the napkin for?"

"For this." And he brought out a very expensive bottle of champagne from behind his back and, in an over-the-top formal display, wrapped the bottle with the napkin and popped the cork, gently pouring the bottle's contents into two plastic champagne glasses. Presenting me with one and taking me by the hand, he escorted me onto his boat. It was little, but polished, clean, and cute.

"Welcome aboard the *Poppy*. It's an honor to have you, ma'am."

"Oh, the honor is mine. What kind of champagne is this? It's delicious." I felt the tiny bubbles slide down my throat.

"It's Dom Pérignon."

"Goodness, Charley, I'm a spoiled lady. I brought us a bottle, but it isn't like this."

"Only the best for the lady." With a flourish and a wolfish smile, he put the bottle in an ice bucket and ushered me into the seat. "Did you know that it was invented by monks? Dom Pérignon was the first to add sugar to champagne, and legend has it when he shared it with the other monks he said, 'Come quickly, for I am tasting the stars.'"

"Well, aren't you a font of charming information!" I said. "What else do you know, Charley?"

"Not much, but I do love trivia. So, mostly silly information, sadly. Well, I also know that Veuve Clicquot was run by a woman. That house has a lot of history," he said as he slid the boat into the water and started the engine. We glided past the almost neon green marsh grasses. The breeze was a welcome reprieve, touching our necks and kissing our cheeks with salt. My shoulders relaxed a little.

I went and stood next to him as he drove. As the boat propelled itself forward, I felt powerful. It cut through the water like a tight wire through clay. I caught a whiff of Charley's cologne and had a strong feeling that if he didn't kiss me, and soon, I might die. The wind wrapped his blue shirt tight around his body, and he gazed down at me through his dark lashes and smiled, biting his lower lip and shaking his head slightly.

"Goodness, Aly, you are about the most beautiful woman I've ever seen! I can't help it!" I was amused by his accent. These boys down here were all rascals, but damn it if they weren't fun. I giggled at him, and he put his large warm hand against my lower back. I felt a small jolt of electricity as he curled his hand and rubbed his knuckles up and down. I was in trouble with this man.

He slowed the boat and refilled our glasses. I drank mine more quickly than I had meant to, but it was so yummy, and I felt it cool my insides and relax my body. I leaned into him a little as the boat rocked, and he steadied me by wrapping his arm tighter around my waist. He smelled so good.

"Do you know how to drive a boat, Aly?" he asked me.

"No—my dad has a boat, but he always drives; I never learned."

"Come here." He took our glasses and placed them in the cupholders. Then he slid me in front of him, placed one of my hands on the lever, and showed me how to increase the speed while holding my other hand on the wheel. He pressed against me from behind, and I arched my back. He gave my neck a light kiss. It was well over ninety degrees, but a shiver rocked the length of my body.

"So, Aly, you want to go to my island?"

"You have an island? Wow."

"Ha, well, I don't own it, but as a kid I would come out here with my dad for picnics like we're about to have. So, it feels like it's mine."

"I'd love to see it." I leaned my head on his chest. "Should I move?"

"Please don't. Stay right there." He casually took over the wheel with one hand and put his other hand on my hip, keeping us pressed together, as close as we could be.

It was feeling a little *too* good—for both of us, I guess, because in the next moment, he said, "Okay, I need you to move now or I won't be a gentleman."

I swayed my hips a little as I sat down and watched him gently drive the boat onto the shore of a tiny little island. There was something so attractive about a capable man, I thought as he docked the boat. I watched the muscles in his forearms tighten.

"Good lord, Miss Aly, I don't know if I like the front or the back of you better," he said with a whistle.

"Well, I'm all yours tonight. Hope you're hungry."

"For you? I'm starving."

"No, silly, for the food," I replied with feigned horror. "Behave yourself and I'll share my lemon bars."

"I can't make any promises. But I'll do my best." He docked his boat up against the sand bar island. Like a true gentleman, he got out first and held my hand as I playfully jumped out onto the sand. Then he spread out a huge blanket. We sat down, and I took out the boat tote, and he refilled our champagne.

"Here's to new adventures!" he said, and we clinked our glasses. "Here's to finally getting together."

"Thank you for letting me on your island, Gilligan. It's really special," I joked.

"I don't think there's any buried treasure out here, but you could score some sweet shark teeth."

"I've always wanted to find them, and I never have."

He smiled at me. "I can help. I'm an expert."

"Gotta love an expert."

"What's in that box?"

"Oh, I got us a bunch of goodies from Hamby's; those are the chicken salad sandwiches."

"Oh, man, you *are* perfect. How could you know they are my favorite?"

"It was a friend's suggestion! I've never had them."

"Give me that box. Please." I passed it to him; he cracked it open and handed me one of the sandwiches.

The chicken salad was unbelievably light. It was on the perfect soft white bread with the crusts cut off, and the whipped buttery texture of the salad was amazing. The exact right amount of mayonnaise. It was heaven. I moaned.

"Well, now I'm going to take credit for making you moan again."

"Listen here, sir, that was from food."

"Oh, I bet I could make you make that sound in other ways, too . . ."

I arched my eyebrow and slipped off my sundress, exposing my bikini.

"Miss Aly, are you trying to kill me? You are lethal, girl."

I threw my head back and laughed. It was wonderful to feel adored. I grabbed my suntan lotion and opened it.

"Allow me," Charley said, and I arched my brow again. "I promise you'll like it . . . I'm very good with my hands." He was cheesy-flirting with me, and I loved it.

"Are you? Let's see." I handed him the bottle.

"Oh, yes. In fact, I've been told before that I could be a profes-sional." He popped the bottle open. I sat up and twisted my hair, exposing my neck. He squirted some lotion into his hands and made a show of rubbing them together.

"I want it to warm up a bit so it doesn't shock you."

"Mm-hmm."

He placed both his palms on my shoulders and squeezed, and immediately I knew he wasn't joking. Those hands *were* capable. Of what? I couldn't wait to find out. The combination of the hot sun and his warm hands as they moved down my back gave me the feeling of a hot stone massage. I smiled to myself. This felt good. He moved his thumbs in circles, and as he found a little tension I shifted slightly.

"Want me to fix you?"

"Oh, that's a tall order, but if you'd like to get that knot, be my guest."

"Yes, ma'am. Just let me know if the pressure is too much," he said, and went to work.

His thumbs got under the small knot in my shoulder and pushed it forward. There was a little jolt of pain, but it subsided once he got it to move, sending a warm rush up the side of my neck.

"Too much pressure?" he asked me.

"Just right," I said, and felt my whole body relax.

He added a little more lotion to his hands and moved on to my other shoulder, lightly kissing my exposed skin.

"Too much?"

"No." I turned around to face him.

"Can I keep going?"

"Please."

He leaned down and kissed my mouth gently, parting my lips and slipping his tongue inside. I cupped his face with my hands and felt him push himself against me. I pressed into him.

"You are delicious." He ran his fingers up my arms, then pulled back and stared at me, eyes shining.

He put some more sunscreen on his hands, and I realized our breathing had intensified. When he applied the lotion to my lower belly and thighs, I bit my lip.

"Tell me if it's too much."

"Okay," I replied a little hoarsely.

He leaned forward and palmed my stomach, lightly working in circles again. I shivered. He moved up between my breasts, and I inhaled sharply.

He pulled slightly on the string of my bikini top.

"It's very hot, and there's no one around to see us," he said.

"That's true."

Slowly I pulled the string and undid my top, letting it fall down.

A breath escaped his mouth, and he dropped to his knees.

"See? I can make you moan, too."

"I never doubted that." He looked up at me, said, "You are a goddess," and kissed my legs. Then he brought me to the ground, kissing my stomach, my breasts, all of me, and playfully biting my nipple gently.

I gasped at the little jolt of pain and pleasure at the same time.

"More?"

"More."

He kissed and licked until I pulled him on top of me. I had to have him. I didn't care that it was daylight and we were outside. I was grinding up against him, begging for him to take me right there and then. My body was on fire, and we were both sweating from the heat. This was igniting at a fast pace, and if I wasn't careful, I would bite him back. The next time he kissed my neck, I decided to let myself go. I needed this.

"More," I said between heavy breaths.

"More?" he growled.

"Yes."

"I like that word, Aly. Flip over."

I lay on my towel, grateful for the soft sand under me.

He straddled my lower back and got on top of me, running his thumbs along my spine all the way up to my neck. He was working in that suntan lotion. There was no UV ray that could hurt me. I might walk away with sand in my hair but not any sunburn. He worked in sections on my back, and I agreed that he could be a professional. Then his hands went to the sides of my bikini bottom and flicked the strings.

"Too public?" he asked.

"Yeah, I'm more of a private show girl," I joked.

"Let's move behind that dune."

I grabbed my towel, and he went to grab the champagne. Right behind the dunes the land was covered with thick bushes and trees. I could hear birds and bugs, and I even spotted a small brown rabbit hiding under one of the bushes. I spread out the towel and sat down. A few fiddler crabs scurried away.

"Now, where were we?" Charley said in a suave voice that made me laugh.

"You are so cheesy," I teased.

"Is it working?" He wiggled his eyebrows.

"Maybe."

I lay back on my elbows and looked at him. He was a beautiful man. He took his shirt off, and I was blessed with the sight of his golden-toned stomach. He reminded me of the *David* statue in Florence. If someone had told me that Michelangelo had hand-carved Charley, I would have believed them. His muscles rippled across his strong chest and shoulders as he lay down next to me, his body giving off heat.

"Jesus, you're sexy." His fingers lightly moved across my skin. "The things I want to do to you . . ."

"Yeah? Like what?"

"Well, I'd pull on this string first." He pointed to my bikini bottom. "With my teeth."

"That sounds good; then what?" I said, feeling my heart beat a little faster.

"Then I'd . . ." And then he undid one side of my suit.

"Too much," I said, and he put his hand up.

"You're the boss," he said.

"I'm a lady . . . or, usually I am, and . . . this is our first date. As much as I want to do this . . . I have a hard no-sex-on-the-first-date rule."

"Sounds good. But I can kiss you?" he said as he retied my suit.

"Yes, kissing allowed."

"Thank goodness." He leaned in, and I felt him against my stomach, hard and strong. My heart was racing, and it was all I could do not to give in to him. He was kissing my lips, neck, and breasts again, his hands on my back pulling me as close as possible. I could smell the salt water on him, and his own scent filled the air. I let him kiss me deeply, and my head started to get almost dizzy with lust. It felt like I was a teenager again. I couldn't remember the last time I had been this hot for someone. I wanted him. Badly.

"Can I kiss you here?" he asked, pointing to my stomach.

"Yes," I said, and he lightly kissed the top of my belly.

"Can I kiss you here?" He pointed to right below my belly button.

"Yes." He ran his tongue along the top of my bikini.

I squirmed a little. "Kisses . . . are . . . okay," I said in between short breaths. I was on fire.

"Oh, good. I bet you taste as good as you look." He got on top of me, pressing his entire body against mine. I pushed my pelvis against him as he kissed me, and I was mentally transported into another space and time. He tried to pull away, but I wouldn't let him. I grabbed his bathing suit bottoms and pulled him to me harder. I reached my hand down, because I needed to know what future equipment I would be working with, and barely got my hand around him.

"Whoa," I whispered.

"Not yet . . . right?" he whispered to me.

"Not on the first date."

"But kisses are allowed?" he said as he pushed himself into my hand and I rubbed him through his suit. He kissed me again, then moved to my neck, my shoulders, my breasts, then very slowly, kiss by kiss, to the top of my suit again. He pulled the strings off me and gently removed the swimsuit bottom, exposing me.

"Can I kiss you here?" he asked.

"Yes. God, yes. Please kiss me there," I moaned. It was technically still kissing, right?

"Oh, *baby*. I love to hear you moan," he said, and gently and slowly licked me. A full shudder ran through my body, building up pressure inside of me till I couldn't see straight. Small, fast licks; long, slow licks; and slightly sucking me . . .

I wasn't a stranger to this kind of behavior, but I'd never known it like this. Not so unbelievably targeted and confident. I would have let him do anything to me at that moment, but I stayed firm in my rule, and I was imagining him sliding his enormous self into me when, finally, the wave of pleasure overcame me and every muscle in my body tightened and then completely relaxed. He wiped his mouth on the blanket and casually refilled our champagne. He handed me my glass, and I was so tingly, I could barely hold it.

"I love making you feel good," he said, and clinked my glass with his.

"Thank you. I feel selfish." I pulled my bottom back on.

"Every goddess needs a good worship once in a while. And I'll make you repay me later."

I pulled my knees up to my chin. "Make me?" I said.

"If I'm lucky." He laughed.

"I don't like having open debts," I said, and looked right into his eyes.

"Well, Ms. Knox," he replied with a wicked grin, "I always collect."

I emptied my glass and returned his wicked smile. Was this a brazen afternoon? Yes. Would I regret it? Possibly, but I felt empowered and sexy and wild on this little, secluded island.

A warm breeze picked up, and I wrapped my arms around him and kissed him again. We must have made out for a long time, because when I finally came up for air, the sun was setting, bathing us in gold. We returned to the boat, and I pulled on my top and sundress. I relaxed at the front of the boat, allowing the setting sun to bathe me in its mango-colored light. I watched Charley, and he caught me looking at him. Was he the real deal, or was this just a summer fling? I didn't know if it mattered. It felt . . . *good*.

And given the craziness of the past twenty-four hours, it was a welcome reprieve.

But I couldn't help but second-guess myself. It had been a long time since I'd entertained the idea of letting a guy into my life. The loss of my mother and the building up of my online presence had been massive distractions. Come to think of it, it had been a while since I had gone on a date, but this was so easy. Charley was a smooth operator. He was well-seasoned and knew what he was doing, what to say to get what he wanted. That made me nervous. I still couldn't believe he'd undone me like that. I looked at the sun shining through his hair; uh-oh, I liked this guy.

He dropped me off at my car just as darkness was setting in and gave me a kiss good night.

I was floating on air.

Against my better judgment, I looked at my phone, and saw a text from my dad: Aly, what have you done? Whatever, I would deal with that later.

When I got to my porch, Jess was pacing there and talking on the phone. I blew her a kiss hello and let her inside.

"Sorry!" she mouthed. With an eye roll, she added, "Hollywood!"

"I'm gonna get a quick shower—there's some wine in the fridge," I whispered. "Help yourself; it's a screw top."

When I came downstairs again, my sister was on my couch, looking like she had always belonged there and texting like a madwoman.

"Hey! Everything okay?" I asked her.

"*Slight* emergency, but thank you for letting me come in! This is such a cool space! You totally have Mom's gift!"

"Aww, thanks, Sister! What's going on, though?"

"The male lead in the new film just dropped out. So, we are scrambling to find a replacement. Hollywood. It's going to be a five-alarm fire until we get someone else."

"Oh, man, who was it?"

"Do you know of William Potter?"

"The guy from that awful holiday movie last year?"

"Yup, that's the one. He's having some sort of emotional breakdown."

"Who's up for the role now?"

"That's above my pay grade. I work on budgeting." She handed me a glass of wine and gestured that we could close the subject. "So how was the date?"

"Jessica, if I told you the truth, you'd kill me. But I think I *like* the guy . . ."

"Oh, no, you caught feelings?"

"Yeah, I think so. Ugh."

"Embarrassing." She shot me a smile. "Boys are stupid."

"Have you just thrown in the towel on men?" I asked.

"For now. I mean, every time I think I want to get out there again, I have to seriously ask myself if I even want someone in my life. I'm pushing forty years old. I don't want children. I like where I'm at in my career, my social circle; I like my apartment. If I had someone move in with me, I'd have to compromise on the style of the apartment I've spent the last decade developing and collecting for."

"I know how you love your vintage hunting."

"It's just, anyone who came in at this stage of the game would have to be additive. I'm an established woman. They would have to enhance my life, and that's a tall order, I think, for guys. It's hard to be a partner of a girl like me. I don't need some kind of void filled, you know?"

"I guess I can see that."

"I enjoy being alone, maybe because I don't really *feel* alone. I have you guys if I need family. And I have a really vibrant social circle in Los Angeles. I'm happy. I'm not craving change."

"I hear you. I wasn't really, either; this just fell into my lap, so to speak." I blushed at that phrase, but Jess didn't seem to notice. "And who knows where it'll go?"

"You've always been more romantic than I, Aly Cat."

"Stop, no, I am not," I said. "You've had relationships before! It isn't like you're a stranger to romance. Don't you sometimes miss having a partner?"

"Not when I see the shit show Dad's signed up for! I mean . . . *whoa*. And it got even worse today, if you can believe it."

"Oh, yeah?"

"Yeah. Something happened, I don't know what, but doors are slamming. Dad and Joyce are going at it."

"Maybe he's breaking up with her?"

She pursed her lips. "Not sure I can hope like that. But I'm glad I'm here right now and not under the same roof as Joyce."

"Do you want to spend the night here? Violet's away; you can have her bed . . ."

"Sure! Although I'll miss the pancakes in the morning with the kids."

"I thought you didn't see the value in kids," I teased.

"These mornings are precious to me because they are rare. But the thought of having to make breakfast for kids every single day . . ."

"Cate is a saint."

"All mothers are. Man, I miss ours," Jess said.

"We all do, Jess."

"Does Dad? He's moving on pretty fast."

"I think he's so used to having a partner. He thinks he needs that. Maybe he's afraid of being alone, like all of us, and this is his way of dealing with it."

"Look, watching how sad Dad was . . . Even if I found the right person, I don't think I'd want to be that vulnerable. If I allowed myself to truly love someone, then I'd be allowing myself to be destroyed, ultimately, by losing them. Devastating. I mean, I guess every love story is a tragedy if you wait long enough."

Jess's words hit me like a truck.

"Whoa, it must be real bad over there," I said. I was glad I still had some fizz from my afternoon escapades, which buoyed me even as I took in what Jess had said, how committed my dad was to this difficult woman, how scary love could be. "And you are definitely staying over. Pass the wine."

CHAPTER TWENTY-EIGHT

≈≈≈

Violet

The morning air in Nantucket was crisp, even in late July. I was thankful that I had packed a sweater. I pulled it on and grabbed a pair of shorts. I left the cottage and went across the street to an enormous graveyard. The gravestones were beautiful—carved, weathered; any with dates indicated they were over two hundred years old. Nantucket was so similar to Charleston, and I felt as if I were walking with her buttoned-up Yankee cousin.

I started to imagine the lives of these people in a world so far away from my own. Many had died or had been lost at sea. The whaling industry here was famous. I couldn't believe that people had used to light their homes with oil from whales. It seemed prehistoric, but really, in the grand scheme of things, it wasn't that long ago. These people had fought with their families, fallen in and out of love, dealt with heartbreak and unexpected change. Over such a short period, we as a people had changed so much, and yet the joys and sorrows seemed pretty much the same.

I walked down the grassy aisles and inhaled the scents of flowers. The light was turning yellow with the advance of the morning when I tripped over a small grave. It was unmarked and beside a larger one; I realized it was a mother and her child. My heart tightened. I hadn't thought about my own loss in a long time. I had been avoiding my grief. The loss was too big, a lot of days—a missed life, a whole future that I had planned in detail, mentally bought a whole wardrobe for. A song I knew the music to but had never gotten to perform; I had forgotten most of the words. I pushed the memory of her face out of my mind—the little baby I had wanted and lost before she had taken a breath.

My throat tightened. For a while, I had begun and ended every day with tears, but now the grief just grabbed me when it wanted me. Grief was a debt that demanded to be paid. You could give in or push it down, but it would come back either way and charge you double.

So, I sat next to that tiny grave of another life that never was and had a good cry.

Once I opened the floodgates, my tears were rivers, and I realized I wasn't crying just about her; it was about my father, and Maggie, and my mom, and Gran, and Chris. All of it, it just came and came, and I allowed it to wash over me. I had been burying myself in work and the excitement of knowing my dad. I hadn't been over *this*; I'd just pushed it off. I sat there in my sadness and let my chest heave with the release of stress and broken dreams. I called out and I let myself call for her. I looked to the sky and asked God why He would do this to me or this child, long gone. Why give us promises of children and then take them away when we most yearned for them? Why let my body go that far, only to snatch her from me?

I let myself cry for a good five minutes and then sat back on my heels.

I took these tears as a good sign, and I let out a deep breath. I knew then, with perfect clarity, that I had rushed into welcoming Chris back into my life. I had allowed all the other things I wanted to color my understanding of him. We had work to do if we wanted to be together, and I didn't know if I really wanted to put in the work. Actually, I knew I didn't. He had obviously changed, and so had I.

That house in Byrnes Downs—it was just an asset. I had made some money off it, and I wasn't ever going to tell Chris. It was never going to be a home again.

"Violet?" a voice called out. I whipped around at the sound of a British accent and saw a handsome, familiar face.

"Henry? Oh! Oh, my goodness, I . . . I . . ." I mumbled, trying to collect myself, wiping my face on the arm of my sweater.

"Violet, are you all right? I'm so sorry to disturb you, I just . . . Can I help?" he said.

"Oh, my gosh. I thought I was alone, it's so early . . ."

"Yes, I always go out this early for a walk when the light is purple"—he gave me a shy smile—"or violet . . ."

"I . . . me too. It's the Violet hour!" I immediately hated myself for saying anything.

God, he really brought it out in me. The goofiness.

"It is, indeed. Are you sure you're all right? I heard a woman wailing . . ."

"I wasn't *wailing* . . ."

"No, of course not . . . A ghost, maybe?"

"I'm sorry, Henry, but . . . what are you doing here?"

He knelt beside me, offering a handkerchief.

"Do people use those anymore?" I started crying again, but this time it was a little more of a laugh-cry. Everything was feeling really crazy right now. "This seems very old-fashioned."

"Why, yes, they do, and it's hand-embroidered, too, and this is a graveyard on a misty morning, and maybe, just maybe, we are in a novel by Jane Austen."

"Oh my god, that would make so much sense!" As I wiped my eyes with his linen handkerchief, it started to mist rain. "Austen at the beach."

"Are you all right?" he asked, and put his hand on my cheek. It felt warm and intimate but not totally out of place. I leaned into his palm.

Suddenly the mad coincidence of his presence here, the strange turns of my life—it all just seemed like *life*. I pulled away.

"Well, I just found this child's grave, and . . ."

"Ah, yes. Those always get me, too."

"She was less than a year old."

The sadness inside me was feeling unwieldy.

"What are you doing here?" Did that sound accusatory? I didn't mean it to be. But we'd had this moment of intimacy, and it had scared me, and now I was rigid, saying all the wrong things. Hastily, I added, "I'm staying at the cottage across the street."

"I was taking my morning run and decided to cut through."

"Are you here for the week with your girlfriend or . . ." What was coming out of my mouth right now?

"Girlfriend? I haven't had one of those in a while," he said, maintaining eye contact.

"Oh, but . . . the woman at the restaurant?"

"My cousin, who was leading you on. Who you dazzled with your . . . flexibility."

I blushed. "That was mortifying."

"Violet, you don't need to be embarrassed. You seemed in fact a little . . . 'vulnerable' isn't the right word, because I think that's a good thing. But something like that. Out of sorts? I was so happy to see you, but a little worried, too, I suppose."

"Oh, no, I'm okay. I'm fine, really. It looked painful, but it wasn't really. I promise. Totally, totally doing great. When do you go back to Charleston?"

"In a few days. But, listen, I hope this doesn't sound forward, but I like you. A lot. That day at the coffee shop I had this instant good feeling for you. When you've made a mistake in love, like I have, sometimes it's just more obvious—the people you have time for. I have time for you, Violet. I like your vulnerability—what you call 'mortifying.' I don't know, I guess I feel like I see the real you."

"Oh." I wondered if they could hear my heart beating in the houses across the street. It felt that loud.

"I have a family house here, but the real reason I'm here is that Jimmy told me you were coming. He knows I took a liking to you, and I had told him that if you were single again, I'd like to know; I'd like to be able to take my shot. He was upset he couldn't come with you, and he asked if I'd come up—just in case. I said I'd been meaning to visit Nantucket; it was no big deal. And, either way, I wanted to know if you were okay. Violet, the reason I'm here is you."

All I could think to say, idiotically, was "Your family has a house here?"

"Yes, since I was a child. Islands, remember?"

"Right. I—" What could I say that would adequately convey the beating of my heart? "I remember now. I'm really glad to see you, Henry."

"I know you must be going through a lot here. Jimmy told me about Scott; I hope that's okay. He was feeling a little guilty he wasn't at your side, and, well, I think he was hoping I'd keep an eye on you. No pressure. But, if you find yourself free or would like some company for your next graveyard visit, text me," he said, and gave me his number.

"I will." We had a hug goodbye. Then I quickly crossed the street and returned to the cottage.

As soon as I walked in the door, I texted Jimmy. Oh my god guess who I ran into.

He texted back. I have *no* idea.

You know I'm still trying to sort things out with Chris, I texted, even though I knew I wasn't anymore.

You aren't married, girl.

I love you, Jimmy. But you know where he found me? In a graveyard. I tripped over a child's grave, and it triggered me. I don't know. I'm fine now. But it was a moment. It was like I needed to just, like . . .

I sent the text, not knowing how to finish that sentence, but then Jimmy responded immediately.

Release?

Yes, exactly. I don't know. I'm still not over it.

Baby, no shit, who would be. You went through a real trauma. It's a lot. But might I say, I am so proud of you?

Proud of me? Lord. I don't know that I'm doing anything worth being proud of.

Violet, you are handling this with grace! Your career is thriving, you moved out of Gran's, you are starting your own life on your own terms! It's inspiring! The way you're there, showing up to meet your dad. It's very brave.

I'm not the brave sister, Jim.

Honey, yes you are. You think Maggie could face this if you didn't first? No way, Jose. She'd hide behind her anger forever. You are handling this for the family. Queen shit.

Thank you, Jim. I love you.

After I put my phone down, I felt a tremble go through me. I was still nervous, and a lot of emotion was coursing through me all the time. Scott seemed like a good man. A little rough around the edges from his life choices, but he really did seem to care. I wanted to believe in him. I felt the creep of Maggie's suspicions, and also the weight of responsibility—because it was true: I was facing it for both of us.

And it sort of sat funny with me that we'd only heard from him because of his new marriage, because he needed the divorce, and once we were of age and didn't really need anything from him. He hadn't mentioned our mom, who was, it had to be said, a pain in the ass—but who hadn't really been treated very well in all this.

On the way to breakfast, I passed the whaling museum. I made a mental note to visit. I hardly knew a thing about that industry and would have loved to learn more. Shops had Nantucket Reds in their windows, and beautiful basket purses. This trip had beauty, whatever else might come.

At the Lemon Press, the breakfast spot the Uber driver had recommended to me, I looked around for Scott. The bright little bistro was buzzing with well-dressed vacationers, who all looked happy sipping colorful smoothies. Abundant yellow flowers lined the brick walls and arched over the doorways, and long wooden tables with Parisian café chairs made the room cozy and inviting. The pastry case was filled with fresh breads, croissants, cookies, and Danish garnished with fresh berries. Another case held takeaway salads and fresh juice. An elegant ribbon of coffee aroma cut through the air. My stomach growled in anticipation—a hard conversation, a delicious meal.

I spotted Scott—Dad, whatever—reading a newspaper with a pair of reading glasses on and his legs crossed. He looked like he belonged here. He was relaxed and not at all nervous like I was. My energy was staticky. When I sat down at the table across from my father, I half expected to shock him. It got quiet then, and he put his paper down, half rising and giving me a kiss on my cheek.

"Did you sleep well?"

"Yes. Thank you again for dinner; it really was amazing."

"My pleasure. I can't tell you what it's like for me to see you so grown-up. You're both so beautiful and smart, you and Maggie. Thank you for taking time out of your busy life to come and see me. I know this is difficult, and I just want you to know that I am willing to answer any questions you might have about the past. Even the hard ones."

Menus were placed in front of us. "Do you come here a lot?" I asked, feeling uneasy suddenly. Last night had been so easy and nice, but probably we would have to confront some difficult topics. I realized I really wanted this to work . . . and that probably meant saying some hard things.

"I'm friends with the owner. She is very passionate about this place. It's fun and cheerful."

"Scott—Dad—I want to give us another chance, you and me. I'm not like Maggie—she runs hot, and I know she didn't show her best self when you came to the restaurant. But part of me feels that way, too, you know? It's been this big hurt all my life, you being gone—but I never thought it was a *choice* you made, staying away from us."

"I wouldn't have if I had known all the facts," he said. "You two weren't the only ones kept in the dark."

"Yeah, but . . . Gran's been the most stable person in my life, and it was her decision, so I have to believe that on some level it was deserved." It pained me in an almost physical way, saying this out loud, saying it to Scott's face. "Right?"

A friendly server approached our table. I think we were both relieved about the interruption, which also allowed us to order coffee, orange blossom waffles, and the Persian breakfast with date chutney and feta.

"We will be better off fed," he said.

"Better than dead," I joked. As soon as it came out of my mouth, I regretted it. "Sorry, too soon. Maggie actually always says that. I've been feeling that it's weird she's not here."

"Maggie worked at Bar JP, huh? In New York City? What was Jean Paul like?" Scott asked. "I was so impressed by that."

"Yeah, she said he was a genius but rarely there. Everyone in that kitchen was an animal."

"It's wild that we are both cooks," he said. "And you . . . you're an amazing photographer! I saw your website, how in demand you are. It's wonderful."

"Thanks, I guess. I like my work, but sometimes I'm worried I don't have anything creative and big like Maggie does. I'd love to go somewhere wild and remote, you know? Take real pictures for once . . ."

"Then we have something in common, too! An adventurer, like me. Why not go?"

"I guess adventuring seems pretty scary to me," I said carefully. "It feels awfully close to abandoning people, or like it would lead me to risk being abandoned. And that's a raw nerve for me."

My father rubbed his neck. "I know," he said. "I know."

"But as Maggie and apparently you say, better fed than dead!"

For a moment, I thought I'd said something that had led us to a place we couldn't come back from. But then he burst into laughter, and his laughter was like a thunderclap that broke all the tension. Earlier I had mourned, and now there was this break, this wash of warmth and joy. The absolute absurdity of our situation was now at the surface of this deep well of complicated emotions. There was something about being on an island, so close to the water, that made my heart sing louder. Happy or sad, I felt things more intensely by the beach.

"This is just so crazy!" I said between belly laughs.

"Isn't it?" he said.

"I mean, look, I have *questions*."

"I hope I can give you the answers."

"I am having a hard time even believing this is happening. Not to be dramatic, but your absence has shaped me—all of us. Maggie actually said that to me, but it's true."

"I'm sure."

"How could you do that to us? How could you stay away if you were really around?"

"I know, it hurts me so much to think you didn't know I was always thinking about you. I guess I thought the postcards were conveying that to you and that you knew you could reach me when you needed to."

"Why didn't you fight? Why didn't you get on a plane and find us?"

Scott looked out the window for a moment. I could see that some-one was calling me, but I flipped my phone over to avoid being distracted. The coffee arrived, and then our breakfast. Beautiful plates, smelling like heaven. The owner had sent over cocktails, seeing that a fellow chef was dining, and they came with crushed rose petals. The presentation was lovely, but it also reminded me of a broken heart.

"Here's the thing, Violet. The honest truth. Rose was right to do what she did. I was . . . I am ashamed of what I was, okay? She could never trust me. She was right not to. I was given very strict instructions that I could never come back into any of your lives, and I knew you were better off that way. At first, anyway. Then, as I began to clean up, I did start to hope. That maybe we could find a way. I guess I knew she wouldn't be sharing the postcards right away, but I didn't think it would be forever, that she would keep me a secret. I have a lot of guilt about it. There were more than a few times that I thought about showing up, saying . . . but I also didn't want to show up unwanted. I did believe you knew I was out there but thought you had lost interest in me or never forgave me or whatever. But the bottom line is, I wasn't worthy of you girls, or Lily, and I am going to have to live with that forever—that when you needed a dad most, I wasn't capable of being one. I am now, and I'd like to be a dad to you in whatever way you can accept me."

Scott's hand was on the table, balled into a tight fist. I reached across and grabbed it. I could feel the table vibrating—which made sense to me; it was all so much, I was trembling. With very wet eyelashes, I said, "It's okay. I understand. I think I needed to hear that, but I get it, I really do. It's a second chance if you want to take it."

"I never stopped wanting you," he said. I moved over next to him and hugged him.

"You still smell like cinnamon."

My head was in his chest, and he was holding me so tight that my sobs got a little smothered in his shirt. We were broken, we had made mistakes, but we wanted each other, and we wanted forward movement. I believed that Maggie would, too, in time. She wanted family; I knew she did. Broken or not, we would make it work.

After what seemed like forever, and once the rush of the public display of yet another emotional moment had washed over us, we got back to our food. The meal's mood changed into rapid-fire questions. Scott asked me about my life and my photography business. We were starving for information about each other, and it felt . . . joyous. The table was vibrating again, and I realized it was my phone. I turned it over and saw I had a number of missed calls, but whatever. I tossed the phone on the banquette, and we devoured our food and ordered another round of coffees.

I could feel unknown parts of my heart healing. Dad-daughter relationships were special; they made you believe in safety, not only for your physical self but for your heart and mind. I hadn't realized it until that moment, but I had never believed someone would have my back unconditionally.

Finally taking accountability . . . It made me think of Chris, who would never do anything like this. Admit defeat? He could never.

"I'd love for you to meet Hannah. Would you come over? We'd really like to have you for dinner."

"I'd like that, too."

"Let's do it tonight . . . Listen, I *do* want all your attention while you're here, but that phone of yours is blowing up."

I looked, and I saw that I had several missed calls from Sam.

My heart dropped.

Was something terribly wrong with Maggie? Or . . . was she mad? Like, never-ever-forgive-me mad?

"I'll get the check," Dad said. "You see what the emergency is."

Sam picked up on the first ring. "What's wrong?" I asked as I maneuvered through the restaurant to the sidewalk.

"Violet, I need to talk to you," he said. And I could tell that it wasn't the kind of emergency I had been afraid of. It was a different kind of emergency. The kind that makes breath short and hearts lift.

"Oh, crap, Sam, not now," I said, trying to make a joke of this thing I realized I'd been afraid of for months. Suddenly I was feeling sick to my stomach. "It's too late for us!"

"I—" Sam broke off, and I could tell that he was in an intense place and couldn't process my teasing him.

"Kidding. What's up, Sam?"

"Look, I'm sorry I called you so many times; I must seem crazy. But I have to say this because it's been on my heart . . ."

"Oh god, Sam, what?"

"I just wanted to touch base with you. I know we've been through some things, and . . ."

"Sam, oh my god. Stop. We didn't work out. It's okay, seriously, you are like a brother to me . . ."

"I'm happy to hear you say that because I wanted to . . ."

"Oh my god. Sam!" I said, feeling the world stop. He was going to ask my permission to marry my sister. Over the phone, after the morning I'd had, on this sweet little street lined with flowers and beautiful people. This day already felt like a very dramatic week, and here he was, asking me. Not my father, not my mother, not Gran . . . me.

"I love your sister."

"I know."

"She is my person."

"I know."

"I am only at my best because of her; I don't make sense without her. I want to . . ."

He wanted to marry her. My sister was going to be married. I was younger, it was silly to feel this way, but I had just gotten used to thinking I'd be the one to get married first. "Sam, I get it. You want to marry her."

"You know?"

"Of course I know," I said. And I did. "Y'all are salt and pepper shakers! We were never like that, Sam."

"Violet, thank you for saying that. I wanted your permission!" He was laughing, he was so relieved, and I wished I could have such a natural response. I didn't want him; I just felt like the world was moving so fast and the things I had wanted for myself were spinning away from me. "I needed your blessing before I proposed."

"Sam, of course you have my blessing." I closed my eyes. It was good we were on the phone. I could put all my genuine happiness into my voice and let the pain work its way through my face, the pain and the fear that I was being left behind. "Do you have a ring?"

"I have my eye on one, but I wasn't going to pick out a ring without Jimmy's eyes and your blessing."

A photo message came through then, and a tiny dark red velvet vintage box opened to display a beautiful bright diamond smiling back at me. A cushion cut with a small ruby on either side. A little acceptance settled in my head when I saw that ring. I couldn't explain it any other way, but this stone had sass, just like my sister.

I put the phone back to my ear. "It's perfect, Sam."

"I'm so glad you approve."

"I've always approved."

"Well, she has to agree first."

"She will. She isn't as dumb as she looks."

My father came out to the street then, offering me his arm. I told Sam I had to go but that I would be excited to hear more when I came back home.

"I'll send a cab for you later," Scott said. "Say, six o'clock? I can't wait for you to meet Hannah, and I want to hear about this potential mate of yours, too . . ."

We began to walk down the street, and I nodded, smiling as though that was a fine topic. But I couldn't help it: the whole idea of Chris was an ache in me, the ache of a dull dead end. And I couldn't admit I didn't have a domestic life about to open up for me, just like my sister . . .

CHAPTER TWENTY-NINE

Maggie

I pulled into Gran's driveway and spotted her in her garden, watering her tomatoes. It was early; she always liked to get out there before the day got too hot. She was wearing her giant straw hat, and when she noticed me, she gave me a warm smile. I almost forgot about the drama for a moment, that burning in my chest cavity. Seeing her *was* home. I had missed her, and no matter what she said, and whatever her reasons were to have kept a secret from us, I already forgave her. She loved me unconditionally.

"Hey, kiddo."

"Hey, Gran." I gave her a big hug. When I went to pull away, she held me for a moment.

"I've missed you, Maggie," she said.

"I missed you, too, Gran. Let's go inside and talk about it."

"Just made a fresh pot of coffee."

She led me inside after kicking off her soil-covered garden clogs at the door. The house was super clean, and there was a giant magnolia floating in the middle of her best crystal bowl. It was like she had been conjuring this, us finally facing off. The kitchen tempted me with the smell of hot coffee, and I could feel the welcome our home was giving me. Gran pulled out our flower mugs and filled them, making my coffee exactly how I liked it.

"So, Gran."

"It's so good to see you, Magnolia."

I gave her a small smile.

"I know I let it go on for too long. I should have said . . . I don't know what. It's hard to go back to that place. I'm not perfect."

"Yeah, none of us are."

She let out a little laugh. "Well, I am sorry to inform you, but I can be pretty stupid. It's a big day when you realize that none of us actually knows what we're doing. We just make the best choice at the time with the most information we have, and we try to protect the ones we love."

"That's why you did it?"

Gran sighed. "Listen, back then things were really dark. I mean like *pitch*. Your momma was so in love with Scott, and he wasn't . . . he just couldn't be the man you all deserved. Although he did get better. But who knows, perhaps the separation was the reason he did. I'm sure you know that I've been in contact with him almost this whole time. I was upset when he showed up because we were meant to come clean to you all together, but I understand why he was just taking things into his own hands . . . and, man, was that some bad timing."

"Does Mom know he was here?"

"Not that I'm aware of. She isn't talking to me at the moment."

"Well."

"She is so angry with me, and she can't understand my motives. It was a wild series of mistakes."

"Violet's in Nantucket right now. Did you know that? With him."

"She did inform me of that. And you, you didn't want to go?"

"Well, I might want to hear his side of the story."

"Hopefully it will be a trip full of answers for Violet, and she can share some," Gran said. "And you can take that trip when you're ready. He didn't know y'all thought he was gone; he thought y'all just thought he had abandoned—"

"He *did* abandon us."

"Yes and no. I honestly feel he did the best he could." Gran sat up straight, met my eye. "I just want you to know I understand what I've done and I will weather whatever you and Lily and Violet think I deserve."

"Gran, I truly believe that you love us . . . I'm still going to name my first child after you."

CHAPTER THIRTY

≈≈≈

Violet

As I walked into the cottage, I received a text from Maggie.

> Girl, I am sorry. Honestly I was trying to make my anger yours. You are brave to face the big bad. If it means anything to you, I finally talked to Gran. We've made peace.

I smiled. It did mean something to me. But then I put my phone down.

I had come all this way by myself. I wanted to soak it in, feel my feelings, the nice ones and the uncomfortable ones, too, and see who I would be once all that had moved through me . . .

The morning air was full of the smell of sea grass and ocean. I took the cab my dad sent but had the driver stop early so I could walk the rest of the way to his house downtown. He was renting the bottom floor of a historic property. Impressive window boxes were overflowing with flowers. Every house seemed to have a whale or another nautical hint on it. Maybe it was the Charlestonian in me, but I adored older homes. In older homes, you could find glittering chandeliers, oil portraits with ornate gold frames, soft and colorful rugs, and character. All the new houses that were going up all over Charleston lately were soulless. Give me some fringe, needlepoint, and chintz—that style made me feel like home. Why did everything have to be tan and white? Where were everyone's books?

I felt my phone buzz in my purse, and I dug around to retrieve it. It was a text from Henry.

> Violet, I am sure you are busy tonight, but perhaps you'd fancy a late-night snack? I can meet you downtown somewhere. I'd love to see you.

I felt my heart start to race. I wondered about Chris—I was on a roller coaster with that. But who said two friends couldn't have a drink if they met on vacation?

Just then a delicious cool breeze kissed my neck and gently lifted the hem of my dress. I texted him back.

> Having dinner with my dad and his girlfriend. Should be free around nine. Where should we meet?

> How about Dune? I have a few ideas I'd like to run by you. I would love your insight.

Oh. Maybe I had, in my heightened emotional state, mistakenly thought he was saying he was here because he was looking out for me. Maybe this was just a business thing, and he was being polite? Now I was confused.

But I was at least a little flattered that he was seeking me out for my opinion.

Anyway, I knew I'd have to face Chris, and even just the fact that I knew my dad was going to ask about him made me not want to complicate the situation with projection.

I knocked on my dad's door. In a few minutes the door swung open, and I was greeted by a very petite woman in her late forties who had two long braids down her back. She was wearing short overalls and a bright orange tank top with bare feet.

"Hey! Nice to meet you. I'm Hannah," the woman said. "Come in! Your dad's making a feast in there!"

The house was sectioned off into three apartments, Hannah explained; it had been built around the late seventeen hundreds or the early eighteen hundreds and had survived two fires and been battered by who knew how many storms. I looked at the windows and realized the glass was warped with age. Old glass always made me remember that it had been made by someone's breath and was alive and moving with time. The wooden floors were original to the house and creaked as we walked across them. She led me down a hallway, past a giant staircase, and through the front door of the apartment.

As soon as the door opened, we were embraced by the most delicious smell of fresh seafood and spices. The apartment was small, but all the windows were open, making the main room feel larger than it really was. The walls were painted white and were covered in artwork of all kinds. Collections of tiny black-and-white photos, oil seascapes, portraits, and vintage framed posters. The old cracked and worn leather couch was covered in soft pillows and had a throw blanket over each of its arms. Soft jazz music was playing, and about a dozen candles were lit, bathing us in warm light. We walked around the corner into the kitchen and I saw my dad by the stove.

"I love this music!" I said. "Miles Davis?"

"The king, yes, ma'am! When I cook, I listen to him or opera."

"Maggie likes to cook with music, too. Fleetwood Mac, mostly, but this works. Can I help you with anything?"

"Help me cook?"

"Yeah, if you'd like me to. I mean, I'm no Maggie, but . . ."

I could see that the idea of cooking with Maggie was something he'd thought about before. Was cooking with me disappointing?

"Yeah, kid. Come here." He beckoned and handed me an apron.

"What are we making?"

"Lobsters, of course!"

As I chopped parsley and squeezed lemon juice, I thought about Maggie and our dad cooking together and decided I would try to make that happen. After Hannah set the table on their back porch, she entered the kitchen and poured us all a glass of wine.

We toasted. And then my dad brought me in for a hug. "I know you haven't had Maggie's experience, but you have some pretty good knife skills." His apron smelled like lemons and rosemary. Fleetwood Mac's "Don't Stop" came through the speakers, and we did a little spin before returning to our chopping. This was my first time in this house, but it felt like I had been here a thousand times. My dad smiled down at me, and I suddenly unearthed the memory of his smile from the deepest corners of my mind. This felt really good. We sipped the crisp white wine and toasted again to future kitchen dance parties.

Big ole happy tears slid down my cheeks. This was too much sweetness. It was like a hot honey bath slowly dripping down and warming me from the outside in. We were healing wounds that I'd thought had scarred over.

"Okay, Violet, you waterworks, get yourself together," I said, wiping away this latest round of tears.

But my dad was crying, too. "Why get yourself together when you can get real?" He laughed at himself.

When it was time, the three of us grabbed various pots of food and serving dishes and in moments were at the table outside under a dozen fairy lights and paper lanterns. Mismatched silverware and plates, but somehow it all went together.

"So, *Dad* . . ." I said, and we all let out a little nervous laughter. "Tell me about all that awesome art in your living room."

"Well, most of it is actually Hannah's, except one or two pieces." He cracked open a lobster tail and dipped the meat into the sauce. "Good night, this sauce is good, if I *do* say so myself! Pass that bread, I need to dunk." He ate like Maggie did, all the way in.

"It's really good," I told him.

"Thanks, it's just a lemon butter sauce with a little rosemary. Simple. A little yuzu."

The dinner went on for a long time, and when I checked my phone, it was eight thirty, so I decided to text Henry.

> Hey, the night is going a little longer than expected. Want to reschedule and grab coffee in the morning?

I waited a moment and saw him text back right away.

> Sure. Would nine work? I can meet you at your place, or should I meet you in the graveyard?

> Ha! I am staying across the street. The little cabin number thirty-one, Rose House.

> I'll bring the coffees.

I felt my tummy flutter a little.

"Was that your fellow?" my dad asked.

"Not exactly . . ."

"Oh, I'm sorry. You just had that *look* . . . Forgive me, I was mistaken."

"I own a house with a man!" I blurted. "And then we were apart, and now we are together again. I used to want that. Well, not entirely—it's not officially over."

"Wow." Scott and Hannah exchanged a glance, and then he nodded at me to continue. "And now?"

"Now? I guess it still seems like he is what I *should* want."

"Hmm," my dad said. Then he led us back to the living room and all the paintings.

I looked around for a moment and something caught my eye. It was three photographs, and they looked very familiar. I took a step closer and recognized them. They were three of my photographs from a high school project.

"Wait, are these . . . ?"

"Works by Violet Adams. Why, yes, indeed."

"How did you get them?"

"Silent school auction! I had Rose snag them for me." He put his arm around Hannah and gestured to another wall—framed reviews of Maggie's food. There was a printed-out article from *Eater* from when she had taken over the Magic Lantern. There were also a few pictures of us growing up over the years that I assumed Gran had sent to him.

He had been keeping track of our lives and silently cheering us on.

There was a picture of our mom with us, too. Although the pictures of me and Maggie filled me with emotion, the one of my mom threw me a little. "How does it feel to have Lily on your wall?"

"I truly believe that there are a lot of types of romantic love, and for a period in all of those relationships they feel good. But people change and sometimes grow out of each other. Part of loving someone is knowing if and when you should walk away. I'll always have love for your mother, for instance. But I don't want to be married to her. Which is something I need to address."

I thought immediately of Chris. Sometimes I knew to walk away, sometimes going back to him seemed inevitable. Why did I do that? I needed to heal myself and not slap a Chris-size bandage on that wound from losing our daughter. Had my season of Chris truly ended? Was I hanging on for no good reason other than familiarity? Except he wasn't familiar anymore.

I wanted a real love. I wanted to be partners with someone. I wanted to wake up and have coffee together, build a life with someone who valued and dreamed similarly to the way I dreamed, the dreams that haunted my heart. I wanted to be wanted and needed.

"You know what's funny about romantic love?"

My father smiled; he seemed to genuinely want to know what I would say next. "What?"

"I own a house with a man I've dated for years. But today I ran into this man, named Henry, in a graveyard. He's a Brit, he's from another country entirely, and I've only met him a handful of times, yet he puts me at ease. I feel I know him."

"Couldn't be Henry Tucker?" Hannah said to Dad.

My father shook his head. "No way."

"Yeah, actually it is. I mean, that's the Henry I'm talking about. His last name is Tucker."

"Whoa, young lady, if you have his attention . . ." Hannah said.

"Hold, please." My dad took out his phone and pulled up a picture. "This him?"

I looked at his phone, and staring at me from under the headline was Henry.

"Wait, what? He's famous?"

"He is a major deal," my dad said.

"Hence the Nantucket house?" I said.

"More like compound, but yes. His mother's family has owned their estate forever."

"It's so crazy how we keep running into each other! First on Sullivan's, now here."

"Don't you think that's a sign?" Hannah asked. "I mean, sorry, none of my business . . . but I know you mentioned another partner you're not sure about."

"Well . . ."

"I'm gonna go clean plates," Dad said.

"Can I help?" I asked.

"Nope, got it," Dad said, and left us.

"Violet, can I refresh your drink?" Hannah seemed to sense I was being put on the spot and was feeling uncomfortable.

"That would be great!" I said.

"You don't have to talk about anything you don't want to," Hannah said.

"Thank you. Maggie is just sometimes . . ."

"An older sister. I have two. Know all about this kind of thing. It's hard. They think they are entitled to know everything about your personal life and have a right to voice their opinion whenever and with authority."

"Ha! Yes. It's out of love, I know . . ."

"Sisters are tough. I am one of five girls. Right in the middle. I get it. But at the same time, I don't know what I would do without them. Women either build you up or tear you down . . . sometimes both on the same day."

"Don't I know it." I took the offered glass of wine. "Thank you."

"Sure thing, kiddo." She gave me a wink.

"Hannah, do you have any kids? Or . . ."

"All I want is a roof over my head and a place to make my art."

"So, painting?"

"All of it. Painting, drawing, sculpture, a little photography. Right now, ceramics are my thing, but I dabble in all forms of expression."

"I think all creatives do, a little. It's really about finding the vessel for your message at the moment," I said, not knowing where that had come from. "But you didn't answer me about the kids."

"I lost a child."

"Me too," I blurted, and realized that this was the first time I'd spoken about it, and it was to basically a perfect stranger. Maybe that was why.

"Oh, sweetheart." She looked at me with her honey brown eyes, and I felt a rush of sisterhood between us.

"Before she was born. By the time I held her, she was gone."

"I don't know what's worse, the two years I had and always wanting more, or never getting to know my child. Both are nightmares. I'm sorry you're in my club." She pulled me into a hug.

"Thank you, Hannah. Me too."

I looked at her and realized this was the first time I had heard about such a loss happening to someone else. I had carried this almost entirely by myself. Maggie, Gran, and my mom were supportive, but they hadn't gone through it. I decided then I liked Hannah. She was her

own woman, which was cool. I liked her creative spirit and her willing-
ness to be open with me. She would be a great addition to the family.

"So, how long have you known my dad?" I asked her.

"You know, I don't even know. Five or six years? Time is wacky."
She giggled. "He's great, your dad. He's a good man, I mean."

"I think he is, too. Or at least it seems like it."

"He's had a tough life, but he's pulled himself together. It takes
a lot of strength to turn your life around, and he's very talented. He's
why I went up two sizes."

"You are tiny; what are you talking about?" I said. She was like a
pixie.

"He made me love food again—and, honestly, myself, too. Another
fun club I'm a part of with a zillion other women."

"Oh, I mean . . . I don't know a woman who doesn't suffer from
some sort of body dysmorphia. I think it's a spectrum that the world
has put us on, obsessing over how we look. I fall prey to that sometimes.
My mother really struggles with it. The only one in our family, now
that I think about it, who doesn't obsess is Maggie, but she's got the
genetics. Sometimes I think if I take too deep a breath near a cookie,
I'll absorb it."

"That's funny. But you have to let that go, girl. Don't warp your
mind like my generation did."

I threw my arms around her. "I'm so glad we're going to be family."

"We feel like family, right?"

"Yeah, that, and you and Dad getting married!"

"What?" Her face wore a funny expression.

"Oh, shoot, did I ruin the surprise?" I covered my face with my
hands.

"Oh, no . . . no, we aren't!" Hannah laughed. "Why do men always
think women want to get married? I am perfectly happy just the way
things are. I have a sweetheart—why would I want something as cum-
bersome and boring as a husband?"

My mouth formed around an *oh*, but I couldn't quite get it out. I felt a little bad for my dad but mostly free for myself. Why *did* men always assume that women wanted to get married, that they would bow to any man who tried to put a ring on it? I could tell from the tenor of Chris's recent texts that he sort of thought it was outrageous I wasn't jumping right back onto the fast track to marriage with him . . . "Well, I hope I didn't ruin anything. But that's actually really refreshing to hear!"

"Come on, let's go find your dad. I think he's probably finished cleaning up by now." Hannah kept her arm around me and led me back to the kitchen.

"Dad, thank you. This was better than good."

"Love you, kid," my father said, and gave me a kiss on my forehead.

When I got back to the cottage, I fell into an easy sleep. My heart had had its questions answered, and I felt a peace settle over me. I knew that once I got back home, emotional wood would need to be chopped, but for now there was nothing to do but rest.

CHAPTER THIRTY-ONE

Violet

The morning came after a long, dream-filled night. I dreamed about the dark and deep waters of Nantucket, waves rolling on top of a vast, hidden universe. Oceans held so many undiscovered secrets—wild plant and animal life that had never been seen by people. Thousands of whales swam through my dreams underneath floating ships. I swam alongside a huge gray beast, and although his size made me nervous, we swam together and shared the sea. I emerged on top of the water to swim underneath hundreds of silver stars.

There was something so romantic about Nantucket, and sisterly to Charleston. Both were dreamy port cities covered in wildflowers and historic homes. Both held some dark histories, yet had evolved. Each place had its own vibe, but I knew I could have made a home in Nantucket, too. I was ready to return to Charleston to make hard decisions.

I was packing up the last few things in my bathroom when I heard the knock. Henry, right on time. I opened the cabin door, and the morning sun's rays almost blinded me, they were so bright. They lit him up in an ethereal glow.

"Good morning, Violet." He smiled and handed me a coffee. "I thought we could go for a little walk."

"I'd like that."

"Perfect, then. Shall we?" he said, gesturing to the sunny morning. "There's a lovely garden just around the corner I want to show you."

I gave him a smile. Man, he was handsome with a little extra color on his face. "So, how long are you up here in Nantucket?"

"I'll stay a few days and visit with my mum and some other family. I come here every summer. I like Charleston, but the weather here is much more civilized."

"Oh, I agree. But wait till December. You'll see then, Charleston wins."

"Yes, I like that about the South. Come winter, I'll do about anything not to be knee-deep in bad weather."

"I've heard that London has some dreary weather."

"It does. But good accents."

"The best. No matter what you say, you sound smart."

"No way. I find southern American accents charming. "

"Well, that is kind, but if you ever watch a movie with a southerner, there is a vibe."

"You're doing a good job right now."

When I turned to his smile, I noticed a perfect dimple. "Are we flirting?"

His smile widened. "I am."

Lord, I was already putty in his hands. "I don't know why, but I sort of convinced myself you had some practical, businesslike reason for meeting."

"No, dear. I am here because of you. We Europeans aren't so professional. We aren't always work, work, work like you lot."

"Guilty as charged," I said. They felt far away, my work obligations. But I knew they would overwhelm me as soon as I got back to Charleston.

"Well, we can do a little of both, if that would make you feel more comfortable."

"I guess so. What's on your mind?"

"Storytelling."

"Storytelling?" I said.

"Yes. In my world, or at least part of my world, the restaurant business is all about storytelling, and I am fascinated by your family's restaurant. I guess I'm a lover of history, and the American South really holds on to its traditions and heritage."

"That's the damn truth. Sometimes a little too tight, but yes, we do."

"So, I was wondering if you could tell me a little bit about the story behind the Magic Lantern."

I nodded. It felt good to talk about this, actually, tell him who we were. My great-grandmother Daisy. The era when the place had been a fried chicken house that sold blue plate specials for twenty-five cents. How it was the first restaurant in South Carolina to have a soda fountain. How Rose had come along and given it the bones it stood on now, adding a bakery and expanding and elevating the menu, making it an institution on the island and famous in South Carolina. How Lily had come and run it almost into the ground, and then Maggie had returned to Charleston and pulled it back up.

How we were technically in partnership with my mother's ex-boyfriend's daughters, but how, luckily, they had backed off and just collected checks now.

"That is a great story," Henry said, after listening intently for some time. "So where does the restaurant stand now?"

"It's not for sale, Henry."

"No, sorry, that's not why I . . . I was just genuinely curious. But it is useful to hear your story. I have found a plantation in the Ace Basin of South Carolina, Tall Pines, and its owners are looking to rent it out to people for weddings. It's for sale and I am considering it."

"Oh my god, I know that plantation; it's beautiful! I'd say go for it."

"Well, there's more to it. I don't really know what I'm doing. I need some guidance on where to start. I like the idea of it having a set caterer, cake maker, florist, and photographer. It makes it so much simpler on the money side of things. Charleston has become the number one wedding destination in America. I think that you and your family have a very keen eye when it comes to preservation of the local heritage. I think that it can translate well into events. I spoke with Jim, and he said you have experience running the business side of things. I like the idea of having a place that was the start of so many stories."

"That's why I like taking pictures. I wish I could really go out into the world, tell really unexpected stories, you know?"

"Like what?"

"Like . . . there's this place in Iceland. I saw a few pictures of it in a *National Geographic* when I was a kid. This lighthouse that was operated by a matrilineal family. The women wore these nineteenth-century dresses into the 1970s, and great full-length seal coats. They had these special sea caves they hung out in when they were fishing, or collecting seaweed, or whatever. The local people claimed they were Selkies . . ."

"Wow, you should go see if there are any of them left!"

"I know. But, I mean, it would be so expensive. No one is going to pay me for that trip. I'm not like you, you know. I didn't grow up with money. It feels really scary to go out and do something like that with no guarantee it will amount to anything."

"Maybe I could sponsor your trip, then—sort of like a patron?"

I clenched at the suggestion. I hated owing anyone anything. "Oh, no, I couldn't accept that."

"But you have to go," Henry said.

And then I saw it all happening, how it would go. I *did* have the money. I had been squirreling it away, planning to buy a wedding dress, or pay for a huge wedding, or need it for some domestic emergency. But it had never been for that. "You know what, Henry?"

"What?"

"It's not about the money. I'm just scared."

"You'll do it, then?"

"Yes."

"You have the money for it? I was serious earlier."

"Yeah, it's funny, but I've been saving up; I just didn't know for what."

"I'm going to check in and make sure you've bought plane tickets."

"Thank you." I smiled. "You know what? I'm so excited! Don't get me wrong. It's not that I don't love photographing weddings. I love to witness and be a part of someone's story."

"Of course. You are a professional and an artist. All art is a form of storytelling one way or another. An event is a story, too."

"I guess I never saw a wedding as a story," I said. "Just as more of a celebration of something you already had."

"Well, it's the beginning and end of a story for sure. People end their single lives and enter into a new life of partnership."

I nodded, taking that in.

"Can I call on you, then? For . . . advice?"

"Yes," I said. I would have said yes no matter what he had asked me, but I didn't mind that it was all of me just then—professional, personal, all of it.

We stepped through a wooden gate and into a hilly field where, when I looked around, I saw small, velvet-looking violets absolutely everywhere.

"I stumbled across this the other day while walking my naughty dog, and it reminded me of you. I had to show you. I took it as a sign."

"Henry, this is very lovely. It's beautiful. Thank you for showing me."

"I needed to see you smile after the other day."

"Henry, why are you being so kind?"

"Look, I am on a journey myself . . . The divorce will be final tomorrow."

"I'm sorry." But I knew that was false. I was not sorry, not one damn bit sorry.

"Thanks."

"I mean, not that sorry. I'm glad to be standing right here, with you."

"Me too. I don't scare you?"

I let out my own sigh. "Listen, Henry, I like this feeling. Being with you. Right here. But I should really tell you my situation. I am about to end it with my ex. I just have not said the words."

"Ah." He nodded, glanced away from me. "Jimmy gave me a précis on you, to be honest. When I told him I was interested."

I looked at my feet. "Yeah."

"Well, people can grow apart," he said.

"I thought I wanted a traditional life, that I wanted to be married with children, and that dream . . . didn't happen. I got more into my career, and for the foreseeable future that's what I want to do. I want to build something that's just mine."

"That's the right outlook. We don't always understand why things happen, but I do believe things happen so other things can happen. I think it is all part of a wonderful, beautiful story . . . even if it doesn't always feel that way. I've found that I am always drawn to those who have experienced true loss or tragedy. It just gives a person a real perspective."

"What's that?"

"Empathy, and an appreciation for joy."

"That's lovely, Henry. I agree with you. My happy moments now are deeper."

"Turning bad into good." He took a long drink of his coffee. "Well done."

I blushed at this appraisal, suddenly embarrassed.

"I have a confession," he said.

"What?"

"I want to spend more time with you. But I don't want to cause problems. I don't want to interfere with whatever's going on with your life . . . but, if you would like, I would like to take you to dinner." He smiled, and a little flush was on his cheeks.

"I'd like that." I reached out—it just felt like the right thing to do—and he held my hand.

He laughed. "Good. Life is short. How about I'll call you when I return to Charleston, and we'll set something up?"

"Yes. Okay. That sounds good." I gave his hand a little squeeze.

"You know what's crazy? Violets are sweet little flowers, but every woman named Violet that I've ever met has been tough as nails."

~~~~~

As my plane descended over Charleston, I leaned into the window, watching the green marsh grass and seeing the serpentine blue water carve itself into the landscape that was imprinted on my heart. It was good to be back in the Lowcountry. Nantucket was beautiful, but this was home. As we departed the plane and walked across the tarmac, the humidity hit me. I put my hair up because I could already feel it sticking to my neck.

As I watched Charleston through the windows of the Uber, my mind began to tick. I had no time to waste. I wanted to get on with my life, cut out all the old, flat stories. I needed to face Chris soon.

No one was home at Bunny's. I gave myself a quick birdbath and drove down 526 with the music blasting from the classic rock station. Then I took the exit onto 17 south and swung into the drive-through of Bessinger's Barbeque. This had to be done, but that didn't mean it was going to be easy. I got a giant sweet tea for each of us, barbeque sandwiches, and extra onion rings. I hadn't totally figured out what I was going to say, but I was going to be as nice as possible. I was going to ask him to buy me out of the house and I'd just gently move on. It was for the best. I drove into what was once our driveway. I took a deep breath, centering myself, telling myself not to crack, to see this through and deliver this decision.

As soon as I opened the door, I heard the yelling.

It was Chris. "Come on, we never said we were exclusive!"

Oh, shit.

Then I heard a very familiar voice.

"Charley, what am I even doing here? I can't believe you lied to me!"

Charley?

Oh, no.

I was frozen. I couldn't move. I needed to get out of there.

I knew that voice sounded familiar . . . Aly was so upset.

But *I* should be upset!

Strangely enough, though, I wasn't. I was just disgusted and kind of shocked.

Aly came out of the bedroom in a rage, and Chris followed her, holding a towel. Not wearing a stitch of clothing.

The expression on Aly's face changed abruptly, from rage to shock. "Violet! Oh my god! I swear I didn't know till I saw this was your house!"

"Um . . . I got barbeque?" I said awkwardly, holding up the bags and the teas.

Chris stared at me. I shook my head at him. Maybe there wasn't going to be any need to carefully and laboriously talk him through why we were going to break up.

"Violet! I'm so sorry!" Aly said.

I looked at Chris, but he just stared at me. It was all so clear, yet too convoluted to put into words. "Want to jump in here, Chris?" I said.

"Chris?" Aly spun around to face him. "I thought your name was Charley?"

"Well, that's actually my middle name . . ."

"Shut up!" She shoved him in his chest, and he stumbled. "Shut up, shut up, shut up!"

"Uh, let me go put some pants on." He went into the bedroom and closed the door.

"Oh my god! Violet! I didn't know!" she said, and burst into tears. "He looks so different than the guy in the picture you showed me!"

"It was an old picture . . ."

"I swear I didn't know!" she sobbed.

"Girl, I know you didn't know. I didn't, either. But this does make what I came here to do a lot easier. Here, let me get you a tissue," I said, and went into the bathroom. I heard a crash in the bedroom and went to check on Chris.

I was mad as hell, but that hadn't sounded good.

I opened the door and saw that the window was open; he had crawled through. I heard his truck start up. The lameness of him running away was actually as shocking as what he had been pulling here, cheating with my best friend. I went back into the living room and gave Aly the tissue. She was really crying.

"Welp. Charley-slash-Chris ran off through the window."

"Are you kidding me?" She ran to the door and opened it to see Chris's truck peel out, tires shrieking.

"Charley! I mean Chris, or whoever the hell you are, I hope you got your pants on fast enough, because with that kind of driving you'll have a tougher audience with the state troopers soon enough!" she screamed out the door.

I laughed out loud. "Aly!"

"Please, don't be mad at me, I really didn't know! I met him at the bar at Charleston Place. I had no idea he was your Chris. He told me his name was Charley."

"How could you have known?" I said, still laughing.

"I should have! That picture in your room was . . . Wait, are you okay?" She sniffed.

"He was ten years younger and wearing a baseball hat and sunglasses in that picture. Please. Also, I was here to break up with him. Yes, I'm fine. This is just stupid ridiculous," I said in between heaves of laughter.

"What? Okay, I mean, shouldn't you be crying, not laughing like a maniac?"

"Girl, I'm done with that guy."

"God, what a slimeball." She took a huge sniff. "What's in the bag?"

"Bessinger's Barbeque. Want some?"

"Yeah. If he's going to ruin my night, might as well eat his dinner." She grabbed an onion ring.

"So, um, what happened?"

"He invited me over to see his house, and I got here about thirty minutes early. I obviously realized it was your house when he sent me the address, and I wanted to face him to give him a piece of my mind, but then I walked in on him having phone sex on a Zoom with some girl. I don't know all the details, but she looked young. I think probably it was something he paid for . . . I don't know."

"Super," I said.

"Yeah. Gross. I'm such an idiot."

"Chris is really smooth. He has a long history of getting exactly what he wants out of people and making them believe whatever he wants them to. He's a lawyer, for god's sake. The guy knows how to spin a narrative." I took a bite out of an onion ring.

"Why are you not raging out right now? You should be angrier, I feel . . ." Aly said.

"Yeah, maybe I should be, but I'm oddly kind of grateful that this happened. Makes dumping him easier. Plus, you did enough yelling for the both of us."

"I never yell, either. He unleashed some pent-up emotions." She covered her face with her hands. "Oh, I feel gross."

"So just because I want to be clear, this is the guy from the boat?" I asked.

"Yes. Ugh, I'm so sorry!"

"Don't be. It's okay," I said. "Truly."

"I need a bleach bath!"

"This is how I know sexuality isn't a choice. I'm embarrassed I'm attracted to men. Disgusting creatures."

"Let's get out of here."

"Forever," I said, and put my arm around her as we walked into Charleston's warm summer embrace.

CHAPTER THIRTY-TWO

~~~~~

Aly

For the second time in twelve hours, I turned on the shower. I was still full of the ick of knowing that I had carried on the way I did with Charley. Or Chris. Or whoever he was, really. Ugh. I had this urge to exfoliate with broken glass. He was still all over me; I was disgusted with myself. Violet had been more than understanding, which was a little concerning. She was cool as a cucumber, and not at all upset. It was almost like she'd been waiting for an excuse—like she was grateful to have been given the out. I, however, was scrubbing my skin raw in the shower.

"Aly! Honey! You're using up all the hot water in there," Jim called from outside the bathroom. "And I have to go meet with the director!"

"Sorry! Just conducting an exorcism in here!" I yelled back.

"All right, girl, get the sin off ya."

"Give me ten!" I lathered, washed, and repeated. Toweled my hair and briefly considered just shaving it. This was going to take time.

Soon I would head over to Sullivan's for a family dinner. It was my family's last day. Jess and I had been texting furiously; she'd been apprised of Charley/Chris and had informed me that Mikey and his squad had spent most of their time out of the house. At either the aquarium or the children's museum. On the family text chain, I had promised Mike and Jess that I'd come visit next year, once I was through Christmas and figured out what was going on with Callie Knox.

Downstairs, I paused to fuel up a little with a nice cold and crisp Diet Coke and found Vi in the kitchen making a tomato sandwich.

"Are those from Gran's garden?" I asked, eyeing the plump tomatoes.

"Nope, they are actually from Sam's farm on Johns Island." She was using a serrated knife and slicing one up in perfect circles. "Everyone knows the best tomatoes are from Johns. Even Gran only grows cherry tomatoes now. Want one?"

"I feel like this is how I know I'm not from here. Just tomatoes and mayo? Uh . . ."

"I can throw on some bacon for my favorite midwesterner if you'd like, and some lettuce."

"All right, fine. I'll try one of your sandwiches," I said. "Do you use Hellmann's or Duke's, Violet? I know that's a big debate in these parts."

"Well, I refuse to get political, so I use Maggie's homemade basil aioli."

"Oh, stop it." This conversation was making me feel a little better, I had to say. Violet had told me she didn't feel weird about what had happened, but it was hard to believe, so I was relieved we could talk like this. "You have to have a favorite."

"I like each of them for different things. Hellmann's for chicken salad, Duke's for deviled eggs." She shrugged. "I'm a mayo equal opportunist, you could say."

I watched her set out the slices of white bread and slather them with the pesto mayo. Laying the giant, juicy sliced tomatoes on top and sprinkling on a little bit of kosher salt and a few cranks of fresh black pepper. It did look good. She cut the sandwiches in half, placed each on a plate, and handed me one. I took a bite and felt my teeth press through the soft, pillowy bread. My tongue was hit with a lemon basil tang of the mayo and sweet tomato. It was heaven. Juice dripped out of my mouth, and I wiped it off with the back of my hand.

"All right, fine. This is amazing. You have converted me into a Lowcountry lady."

"Might need a few more of those if you want to call yourself a *lady* after that boat performance, miss."

"Please, don't remind me. I'm joining a convent next."

"Hey, Chris is a handsome guy! And from what I saw, he has some new moves . . ."

"All right, Vi, I mean, I'm grateful this is laughable for you, but really? You are so over it already?"

"Yeah, I've moved on. In the rearview mirror."

"Does this have to do with a certain English gentleman?"

She gave me a look. "Jim told you?"

"Of course!" I said. "But I kept assuring him that you were spoken for . . . and he kept insisting that Henry was into you."

"Ah, well. I'm just sorry you got pulled into his emotional bog." Violet finished her sandwich, took my plate, and stuck both plates into the dishwasher. "A lot of people live double lives. I don't know. In a weird way, I sort of feel sorry for him."

"Really?" I frowned. "I definitely do not."

"Look, I mean, Chris had a life in Japan. He was important and moving up in his company. He wasn't anyone's son over there; he could be whoever he wanted. Big, powerful, dominating, all that . . . When he came home, he fell back into his old life, and it didn't fit anymore. He's an ass, but . . ." Violet shrugged. "He sent me this email about his porn addiction, and how he got into paying for phone sex, and how he'd been going to meetings for that, but he fell off."

"Whoa." I could tell Violet sort of *did* sympathize with him, but that seemed pretty far off for me. "Aren't you a little bit angry?"

"Honestly, I am just relieved to be seeing it clearly. He's really sad. His ego is so fragile he had to have three women to keep him validated! But it's not my problem anymore."

"Well, I'm still pissed."

"You should be. He really lied to you. I mean, he lied to me, too, or kept things from me, but . . . I knew who he was, even if I didn't *know* know. He was still giving you his most charming self. And it's hard to be single! We can't all be Maggie, with cute doctor-farmers head over heels for us and planning epic proposals . . ."

"Sam is going to propose to Maggie?"

Violet rolled her eyes, and it was weird, but it seemed like this almost bothered her more than the Chris thing. "Yeah, he called me in Nantucket to ask for my approval, and my help. He wants to have a big party and surprise her."

"Oh, let's use my dad's house!"

"Really? That's a nice offer."

"Well, I'd have to check with my dad, obviously, but, yeah, we could have a surprise engagement party for her there . . ." I was thinking I could decorate, and do a story about it on Insta, and really piss Joyce off. Dad would never say no if it was for Maggie, especially after that dinner we had at the Magic Lantern!

"On the porch? That's a great idea! I'll text Sam."

"Wonderful. I'll ask tonight. I have to head over to Sullivan's for the last-night dinner. Everyone leaves tomorrow, so pray for us it's not a bloodbath . . ."

"Godspeed." Violet gave me a salute. "I'm gonna go text my Brit."

"Hey, Violet? I'm glad this didn't, like, break us."

"Please. You did me a favor, Aly. If that didn't happen, I might have lost my nerve, he could have manipulated me into something further or longer, who knows . . . But you and me? Unbreakable."

"Love you, Vi. Well, I wish the fucker well."

At Sullivan's, Jess was at the door before I even got to knock.

"Before you come in here, I need to update you." She looked over her shoulder, wild-eyed, as though we might be under surveillance. "Cate isn't happy and is lying down. Mike had the kids all afternoon, and I gave him a gummy. It didn't hit him right at all. He's high as a kite. Joyce is cooking dinner and is very behind. Dad is hiding in his office. The kids are running wild."

"Wait, why is Cate lying down?"

"She's just done. Said she'd get up to eat with us, but she's had it with Joyce. She's in a high critical mode right now; it's almost like she is malfunctioning."

"Should someone talk to Dad?"

"Go for it. But he's so afraid of confrontation, he isn't going to do anything."

Inside, I was hit with a rancid smell. Wasn't sure whether it could be described as bad personal hygiene or fish. Whatever it was, I thought, my stomach in revolt, was dinner. Mike was asleep in Dad's recliner by the television. That was probably for the best. I went to my dad's office and knocked on the door.

"Dad?" I called.

"Yes, Minnow, in here."

I opened the door, and he was sitting at his desk, smoking a cigar. The giant gray clouds were swirling around him.

"Hey, Dad, what's going on?"

"You know, it's been a tough weekend."

"I heard."

"Why didn't you come over?"

"Dad, respectfully, none of us want to be around Joyce; she's a tough cookie to eat."

"I know she is, but she makes a great deal of effort to make me happy. I'm not getting rid of her, if that's what you're asking me."

"I'm not asking you to, but I mean, we don't all have to date her just because you are."

"I think this is a lot for her. Let's give her another chance, okay, Minnow? For your dad?"

"Dad, I love you and will do whatever you ask me, but I'm not looking for more time with Joyce."

"Let's just try."

"Okay. I'll try, but . . ." I took a breath and blurted it. "Do you really love this woman?"

"I might."

"You're settling, Dad."

"No one will ever be Callie."

"No shit." Suddenly the grief of losing her was pulling me down again.

"No shit is right." That was intense. He never cursed. "I still miss her so much."

"I know, Dad. I'll try to do what I can . . . for you."

"Maybe you could start helping her in the kitchen, whatever she's doing in there . . ." He took another pull from his cigar. "Whatever it is, is not great."

In the past few days, Joyce had been shopping. She had moved on to the kitchen. Every old pot was gone and replaced, and gone were the mismatched crocks that had held mismatched cooking utensils. There were two new blue-and-white plaid dish towels, and Joyce was standing over the stove in a matching apron.

"Hey, Joyce, can I help you with anything?" I asked her.

"I have everything under control, Aly." She lifted the lid, and a giant puff of smoke filled the room. I was worried about the smoke detector, so I grabbed one of the towels and swatted the smoke around and away from it.

"I have it, Aly." The smoke detector went off, filling the air with awful, high-pitched beeps.

"Okay, well, it smells like something is, um, burning . . ." As she turned around, I noticed that her hair was singed. "Joyce! Your bangs!" I swatted her with the towel on reflex, putting out the flame, which was reacting to what must have been hair spray.

The screech of the smoke detector was overwhelming.

My dad came in and shut off the deafening alarm. "Everything okay in here?"

Joyce suddenly burst into tears.

"Your daughter just smacked me!" She ran over to my father, collapsing in his arms.

"What? No I didn't! Well, I swatted you with the towel, but I didn't—"

"Aly! Why would you do that?" My dad was looking at me like I was a crazy person.

"She was on fire!" I replied, a little louder than I had meant to.

"I was not!" Joyce wailed, but as she pulled back it was obvious that the middle of her bangs was totally singed off.

"See?" I said.

"Your family hates me!" Joyce wailed. "All I want to do is make you happy!"

My dad shot me a look, but I wasn't about to take that bait. I went over to the stove and turned it down. Two pots were bubbling over. The kitchen was a mess. I turned off the burners. Joyce stomped out of the kitchen, and my dad followed her, leaving me in the kitchen.

I did a quick Insta story on the carnage—a sweep of the scene— set it to "Welcome to the Jungle," and captioned it "For All You Joyce Fans, a Portrait of Her Inner Life . . ."

Then, to atone, I opened the cabinet under the sink, found the Lysol and a roll of paper towels, cleaned off the countertops, and threw the pots in the sink under hot water with Dawn soap. "Hey, Jess?" I called out.

She came into the kitchen. Her hand rose involuntarily to cover her mouth. "Oh *shit!*"

"I think we need to save dinner," I said.

"God, do we even have time?"

"Call Maggie over at the Lantern. Order one of her family meals to go. I suggest the lasagna and garlic bread."

"Good call. Okay, on it!" Jess said, and went to get her phone, and I went to work scrubbing and cleaning. Once the kitchen was a little more in order and there was the delicious smell of the Magic Lantern filling the house, I actually sort of thought we might have a halfway decent evening. But my (probably delusional) Zen was short-lived.

Jess, who had been trying to set the table, exclaimed, "Everything is rearranged, I can't find anything that . . . Are these all new?" she asked, pulling out a tablecloth, blue and white and covered in dolphins and fish. "That woman!"

Jess was interrupted by Joyce, who flew into the kitchen and grabbed the tablecloth from Jess and the forks from my hand. "Do you go into everyone's house and just help yourselves?" She sneered at Jess and me. "Didn't your mother teach you anything?"

"Excuse me?" Jess said.

"Well, this has been a nice night—first your sister attacks me, and now you are just going in and out of my cabinets in my house, acting like it's yours! You are *rude* girls!"

"First of all, Joyce, I'm cleaning up your mess in here, and secondly, this isn't your house!" Jess said.

"It *is* my house, it *will* be my house, and none of your dirty tricks are going to get rid of me, got that?" Joyce stepped up to me, shaking the handful of forks in my face so they rattled and gleamed in the light. "And you, *Aly Cat*." She sneered. "*Min*now. I know it was you—you who sent those women over with their sympathy cards, offering to show your father a better time than I could. I know it was you, and I want you to know, if you try that again, I will *flay* you."

A wave of shame rocked me. I had forgotten about that, or anyway put it to the back of my mind, my Insta Live telling my audience how much I loathed Joyce, that my dad was single, that he needed a better woman, and maybe one of those Callie Knox fans was that woman. I blinked. Then all my anger rose right back up. "Joyce? You couldn't flay a Christmas pear."

I knew that whatever happened next, I wasn't going to have any control over. The words flowed from my mouth like fire.

"This—*this* house—isn't yours and never will be. You can put up ten thousand frames, change all the linens, pee on every wall if you want to, but it is now, and always will be, to this family and to everyone else, my *mother's* house! You can tell yourself whatever you want, but that's the truth and you know it."

Jess looked at me and gave me a face. I had crossed a line.

"You're a little brat, Aly. I'm onto you. You'll see. I always close the deal," Joyce seethed.

"Joyce, I am not your competition! Dad asked us to try and make this work," I said.

"Yeah, he's your dad, not your husband!" she sneered again. "You know what I think? I think your mother was a great woman, and she would be *ashamed* of you, with your little Instagram hobby."

I wasn't sure if I wanted to cry or throw up.

Joyce smiled at me—she could see she'd landed a hard blow—and stalked from the room with the tablecloth and silverware.

I felt hot anger tear through me, but I swallowed it down. I was shaking a little.

"Come on," Jess said quietly. "If you let her make you look like any shade of what she just threw at you, you're going to lose. If you are the problem, she'll win. It's dinnertime. Smile, okay?"

I shook my head, wiped the tears from my face. "How do I do that . . . ?"

"I say we should go out there and pretend this little spat never happened."

"Are you joking? I'm not a good actress."

"Time to learn, girl."

We took everything out to the porch, where Joyce was fussing over the place settings. Lasagna, still bubbling and brown around the edges, the garlic bread toasted, salad tossed in a bowl. I noticed that she had put the silverware all together and not where it belonged, but Jess had given me my orders; she was going to be the picture of an easy daughter, so I didn't say anything. I also didn't even mention that the water glasses were on the wrong side of the plates. This was restraint.

Jess followed me with Cate out on the porch, where the kids and Mike were already seated. Dad joined us a moment later with the wine.

"Joyce, the table looks beautiful!" I said.

"That's nice, Aly; isn't that nice, Joyce?" my dad said.

The woman looked at me, moving nary a facial muscle.

We all sat down, Joyce of course right next to my father.

The night was beautiful, despite the bad vibe. Sullivan's Island, to be fair, was always gorgeous, even in a hurricane. The breeze from the ocean, wrapping us in its salt-air embrace. The sound of the waves crashing against the stone jetties, perfect background music, along with the hungry calls of the gulls. The sun was low in the sky, turning the clouds mango, bright pink, and coral. Those were my mother's favorite shades to paint her mugs with. It made me think of her, and I smiled.

"What's that smile about, Minnow?" Dad asked.

"Well, I just was looking at that beautiful sky, and I remembered how you and Mom used to catch the sunsets. All of her homeware line was always in the colors of the sunset. I wonder if that's where she got her inspiration from."

"You know my husband died, too," Joyce said, and I couldn't tell if that was a jab or not. I was feeling a bit terrorized. What could I trust that came out of her mouth? "It's nice you have these good memories of your mother."

I tried to figure that one out. It didn't sound entirely like vicious sarcasm.

Jess shot me a look. *Don't engage.* I looked over at Mike, who was reaching for another glass of wine already. Cate was cutting up the lasagna and passing out portions.

"These smell fantastic!" Dad said.

"This is not what I planned for dinner. I worked all day on that salmon," Joyce said

"Yeah, and that's probably why it caught fire," Mike said.

Joyce shot him a look.

"Joyce," my dad said, "it's okay. It's no big deal. They got takeout from the Magic Lantern."

"But, George, this is all carbs! You don't eat like this! *I* don't eat like this. What am I supposed to eat?"

"Who can resist the Magic Lantern's garlic bread?" Dad passed her a slice. "Come on, our diets can make an exception."

She took it and placed it on her plate. Then tore it in half and left it untouched.

"This is delicious, Joyce," I said. "You should try it. Maggie makes all the pasta in-house. I learned that the other night at dinner."

"Wow. That's so impressive. It's very labor intensive to roll out sheets of lasagna noodles," Jess added.

"I know how to make fresh pasta, too, you know. Learned in Italy. Your father and I are going to Italy in October." Joyce pursed her lips and made a great show of putting no more than three leaves of lettuce on her plate and a single cherry tomato. "Oh, it's already tossed in the dressing," she said.

"It's just a vinaigrette," Jess said. She was trying to sound reassuring, but she was only half succeeding. "So nothing too calorically high."

"You have to watch the oil amounts, and I'm sure there's too much salt in this . . . Even salads in restaurants have salt."

"That's why it tastes so good," Mike said, sounding a little bit ugly.

"That's right!" my dad said. "Isn't this fun?" Even he was sounding a little manic now. "Maybe next time we can all spend even more time together!"

"Well, Dad." Mike's gaze was lethal. "That would depend on the guest list."

"Mike . . ." Dad said.

"I mean, I can't risk having the authorities called on me . . ." He was on his third glass of wine, I realized. At least. Cate put her hand on his arm.

"Can I pour you some wine, Joyce?" I asked, and she stared at me, took a beat, and said, "No, thank you; if I want any, I'll share your father's glass."

"All righty." It took everything in me not to roll my eyes at her. Since the bottle was already in my hand, I filled my glass high.

"So, what's on the schedule for next week?" Jess asked my dad.

"Your father and I are going to have some friends over," Joyce said.

"Oh, that's nice. Who's coming?" I asked.

"It's just for adults," Joyce snapped.

"Are you implying that Aly's not an adult?" Mike asked.

"No, of course not. It's a seated dinner, and I didn't want her thinking . . ."

"That I could come? I'm all set, Joyce; I was just being polite."

"Joyce, we have more room. There's always room for you, Minnow."

I couldn't help scoffing.

"Aly . . ."

"Dad, it's fine. I was just asking to be nice." I gave him a forced smile. "I have a busy week next week anyway. I have that Holy Mahj thing; it's going to be a big event for my brand."

"Well, let me know what days you *do* have open. We can get dinner or lunch . . ."

"George! What did we talk about?" Joyce said, wrapping her arm around him.

"We can talk about that later." My dad was struggling mightily to keep his temper in check. I could almost see his internal thermometer rising. "You need to drop this."

"Georgie, you *know* it's probably a good idea for Aly to find another guest to take her out to dinner . . ."

My dad smacked the table, and everything rattled. "Enough!"

The kids were staring at the adults, wide-eyed and silent.

My dad looked at each of us, our stricken expressions and stiff postures. I saw it register on his own face that this was bad and that it wasn't going to get better. He cleared his throat and set his jaw.

"Cate, do you think the kids might like a walk on the beach?" he asked.

"Yay! Can we be excused? I want to find shells for our Christmas tree!" Della said.

The kids got up in a flash, pushing their chairs out and making a mad dash for the beach. Cate followed them as quickly as she could.

"Guys?" Dad said. "We need to talk."

I looked over at Jess, who looked over at Mike, who shook his head and stared at the ceiling of the porch.

"Listen, I think we are not off to a great start here," Dad began.

"What do you mean?" I said with the best innocent face I could manage.

"Aly."

"Fine, yeah, not a great start," I admitted.

"I'd like us to get along."

"Don't look at me! I'm the victim here," Joyce said with a pout.

"Um, I don't know if I'd call you the 'victim,' Joyce; you've been scratching at them like a cat."

"Only because they have done everything in their power to make it uncomfortable for me!" Joyce said.

"What are you talking about?" Jess said.

"You know what I'm talking about," Joyce said, leveling her gaze at me. She grabbed a piece of garlic bread, tore it into smaller pieces. "My husband's dead, too! You don't hear *me* ranting and carrying on about him."

"Are you kidding me?" Mike stood up.

My dad was shaking his head in disbelief over what she had just said. Jess had a tear rolling down her cheek. She never cried. This was insane.

"Joyce, the kids can talk about their mother as much as they want."

She did a little fake laugh. "But when is it enough, you know? When—"

"And so can I. It's never enough. This is their family home, and Callie was their mother."

I looked over at Joyce, whose eyes were as big as dinner plates.

"It's not crazy what my dad's saying," I said as evenly as I could. "We loved our mother. She was wonderful."

Joyce made this awful dismissive noise that sounded like she was clearing her throat.

"I can't." Mike got up, left the table, and went down the stairs.

Jess followed him. "Me, either."

My dad stood up. He was following them with his eyes, looking angry and desperate.

Joyce made another noise, stood, and went to the stairs. I thought she was going to follow them, hurling insults or something else totally unhinged. She started waving her hands around as though trying to get their attention. The sun was setting right behind her, and from where I was sitting, I couldn't tell if she was facing us or the ocean. Her arms became frantic, and she made a wheezing sound.

"Oh my god, Dad! She's choking!" I rushed to my feet, hurtling toward her.

She saw me coming and stumbled away, pushing frantically, but I grabbed her around the waist to keep her from falling. I gave her back a blow, and I gave her an abdominal thrust. How was this supposed to go? My body was lit with panic. I hit her back again and again.

Then I felt something give. A chunk of garlic bread flew from her mouth and landed in the garden.

Joyce sucked in a breath.

"Oh my god," my dad said, reaching for Joyce. "Oh my god, are you all right?"

She turned, pushed him away. "Don't you touch me!"

My father looked stunned in a whole new way. "What?"

"I was dying," Joyce said. "I mean, I could have *died*, George. And you—you were looking at *them*." She gestured toward the door that my siblings had disappeared through. "I know what you really care about now." She slammed the door on her way into the house, and a few speechless seconds later she reemerged, carrying her purse. "Good *night*," she said viciously, to no one in particular.

My dad and I just stared at each other as she put her car in drive and peeled out, disappearing down the street.

"Dad, I—"

"That's enough for tonight." My dad turned and went wearily back inside.

I closed my eyes. It was hard to feel anything. There had been so much fury in my heart, but that was gone now. I walked down toward my mother's garden, hoping I would hear some wisdom from her, that I would hear anything good at all. As I approached, I remembered the signs of construction, my conviction that Joyce was planning to build a pool over the place where my mother had grown her roses. But by then I could see clearly that I was wrong.

The garden had been weeded. Someone had done the work we had been avoiding: they had deadheaded the roses, carefully removed the invasive stuff, given some love to the beautiful plants my mother had nurtured over the years.

I turned around, looking for someone to point this out to, someone I could say *I was wrong* to. But they had all gone off to their separate corners, and there was only the smell of dune grass and the sound of waves crashing.

CHAPTER THIRTY-THREE

~~~~~

Violet

I pulled into Gran's driveway to find cars I didn't recognize. A bright red Mercedes and a black Volvo station wagon. I hadn't called, so I felt a little weird going into the house if she had company. It was during the shock that my dad was alive, at the height of my Chris confusion, that I'd left here, and I hadn't done it in the best way. But I knew I could always come home, and that knowing propelled me out of the car, opened the door to the house that I had been raised in.

When the front screen door slammed behind me, I was greeted with roars of laughter.

The house was buzzing with joy. I smiled, because I realized it had been a long time since it had been quite this raucous with delight.

"Gran?" I called out.

"Violet?" I heard her voice. "Is that you?"

Gran came around the corner, and I smelled her familiar perfume before I saw her. She was wearing a red-and-gold caftan, bright red lipstick, and her long pearls. She was glowing, and when she saw me, she opened up her arms and I noted her freshly painted red nails as she welcomed me with a hug. I almost ran into her arms, burying my head against her neck like a little girl. She wrapped her arms around me, and we stood there for a long time, saying nothing. She had a long-standing rule that she would never be the first to break a hug with Maggie or me. This felt like home, in her arms, in this house. She kissed the top of my head.

"I am so very happy you came home," she whispered.

I pulled out of the hug to see three women in the next room.

"These are my friends from high school, if you can believe it! We are playing mah-jongg. Do you want to join us?"

"That's so cool! Did you know Aly has gotten super into that? I'm doing a sort of social media shoot for her at this tournament at Holy Mahj; we've been planning it—"

"Oh, that is too fabulous! Can I come?"

"Sure thing."

"Listen, we don't start for another thirty minutes; we're waiting on some more friends. Let's go out on the back porch. Want some tea?"

"Of course I do."

I looked at the women and took them in. They were all in caftans or kimonos or other flowy and bright things. They were done up. I smiled, remembering the class I had taken at the Charleston Place Hotel downtown earlier this summer.

I guessed everyone got dressed up to play.

"We can finish setup, Rose. Hey, Violet, remember me?" one of the women said, coming away from the others. "I'm Lucy! We met at the nail salon!"

"Of course! I'm so glad you're back together." I said my hellos to the other women. Then I went out to the back porch and sat in the swing, waiting on Gran. She came out with a tray and two glasses of sweet tea with yellow wedges of lemon over ice in cut-crystal glasses on top of linen napkins. She had pulled out her good stuff. She was sorry. I knew it because linen napkins meant ironing.

"Gran . . ."

"Violet, I want to know how it went." She handed me the tea. "I was worried, you going up there all alone. Proud of you, too. I love you girls with everything I have in me."

"I know you do, Gran. So very much." I grabbed her hand. "I didn't know you were having company, though, I'm sorry to intrude."

"This is your home. You don't need an invitation over here!" She scoffed at me, then took a pile of postcards from the pocket of her caftan. They were tied together with string. "Look, I have something for you."

"Mom gave them back to you?" I asked.

"Yes. She's off at an interview in New York, by the way. Her travel company has an office in the city, and she is interviewing to relocate there."

"Mom did always want to live in New York. She was jealous of Maggie."

"How do you feel about it?" Gran said.

"You mean about her living there? Great: it's another adventure for her. New York is tough, but at least she can go see the ballet whenever she wants."

"That's the right attitude. Look—"

I interrupted her with a firm shake of my head. "You did what you thought was right."

"Maybe, but I let it get away from me. Look, your mother was in no place to . . . She was in a dark place. She couldn't handle you and your sister, so I stepped in. I told her I would take you girls, but on the condition that she never saw your father again. Truth is, I would have anyway—but I knew they wouldn't bring out the best in each other."

"I guess I just wish I could have made that decision myself. If I wanted to know my dad or not. You took that opportunity away from me," I said as gently as possible.

"I realize that now, and I'm so sorry for that. It was wrong, and it wasn't my decision to make."

"But you hid the cards! You could have thrown them away."

"Yes, I think now it was because on some level I knew it was wrong to keep them from you, and that one day you'd find out or he'd show up." Gran shrugged and sipped her tea. "I don't know."

"It's okay."

"It's not."

"It is now. I like him. I like getting a second chance with him, the man he is now. I like that I don't have any bad memories of him—just a big hunger for making new memories."

"My girl. I love you so." She gave me another hug. "Thank you."

"Okay, I'm going to go read these. And let you have your night with your friends. It's nice to see you socializing, you little butterfly. Your nails look good."

"Big Apple Red by OPI. It's a classic."

"Okay, well, I gotta go help Sam."

"Oh, yeah?"

"Yeah, he's going to propose to Maggie tonight. I gotta pick her up and take her over there—I guess he took her car in for an oil change or something and made up a story they needed to do some work on it so that I could deliver her at *just* the right time . . ."

As we hugged goodbye, I saw that several more tables were being set up in the living room. Snacks were put out by the racks and tiles. I was happy for my gran. It felt like she was getting out of her slump. After the accident, she had gotten so isolated, so this was healthy for her. Plus, her friends looked like fun. It made me happy to see her get her groove back. Even if it was a small step, it was on the right path.

I got into my car and drove over to pick Maggie up from the restaurant.

"Thanks for the ride, Sister," she said, climbing into the front seat.

"I'm glad you talked to Gran, Maggie."

"Me too."

"She looks . . . happy."

"Yeah, like a burden has been lifted, right?" Maggie whistled and shook her head. "Listen, I want to hear all about Scott and everything. But could we take a beat? I've had a hell of a week."

"Of course." I thought about the postcards in my purse and was glad they were just mine for a while.

"And, girl, you are not going to believe what happened!"

"What?" I asked her, slightly alarmed.

"You know Aly's dad's girlfriend? The one she hates? I almost *killed* her."

"Hold on—*what?*"

"She almost choked to death on my garlic bread!"

"Jesus Christ! What in the world?"

"I know! Total freak thing! Anyway, it was apparently the thing that finally sent her running from the Knox household. Sounds like Aly might be rid of her for good."

"How's her dad?"

"Angry, I guess. She was difficult, but they worked, somehow, and he misses her. She's not returning his calls at all. I mean, I bet she comes back to him—sounds like a manipulative tactic to me—and he seems to like her. You never do know what floats a man's boat, do you?"

"Oh boy, I need to check in with Aly. We've been texting a lot, but it's all about work. This mah-jongg tournament that's coming up, and she thinks it's make-or-break in her quest to take over Callie Knox . . . I guess both of us can get like that sometimes. If there's work to talk about, then talk about work we will."

We pulled up to Sam's house, which was basically Maggie's, too, and saw that the lights were off. "That's odd," Maggie said.

I checked my phone to make sure we were on time.

"That the lights are off, I mean. Maybe he fell asleep? He did have a late shift at Children's Hospital last night. He probably turned on a show and passed out."

We opened the door and heard some light string music playing.

There were about a hundred pillar candles all over the living room in different sizes, and in the middle of the room was Sam.

He took a step forward. Maggie put her hand over her mouth to cover her gasp.

I stepped quietly away from them, into the shadows, and brought my camera up. I had the settings preadjusted for the dimness of the room—Sam had insisted on candlelight, even though I had told him it was going to make for a certain kind of picture, not the typical proposal picture. It would be special, though. I could see that now. Special in a Maggie way.

"Maggie, my steel Magnolia. The best woman I've ever known. You are talented, strong, smart, funny . . . incredibly sexy and my best friend. The past few years we've spent together have made me believe in magic, because when I'm with you, I feel like anything is possible. Doing what I do, I know at a very real level that life is short, and if you don't take risks, you can't get the big wins. When you hit the back of my truck years ago, the sky opened up and poured on us. I knew then that I wanted to spend the rest of my life making you happy. Will you allow me to do that?"

He dropped to his knee and reached for Maggie's hands.

"I love you, Maggie, more than I ever thought I could be capable of loving someone. The real love. I would take a bullet for you, write music about you. I am a lucky man. Marry me, Magnolia. Please?"

I captured Maggie's glowing face; I captured Sam's earnest, hopeful expression.

They were totally unaware of me, and here I was, at the margins, documenting the beginning of their life together as a family. I could see it all—even their future children running down halls, their cozy Christmases, their days on the beach.

Meanwhile, Maggie had dropped to her knees. "Yes. In every lifetime, in every way, in every moment, I will love you. Yes, I will be your wife."

Sam pulled out a little red box and opened it, and nestled inside on a small velvet pillow was that beautiful ring. Jimmy had advised him well—that ring looked even better in person.

"It's so beautiful."

"Like you, Maggie. The most beautiful girl in the world." He cupped her face, and they kissed, and then he slipped the ring on her finger. It looked like it had been made just for her. They were made for each other.

Enough pictures, I decided. I had done my job. I went onto the porch.

I smelled the earth and looked out at the magnolia trees.

My heart kind of felt both heavy and light and trembling and alive. I was happy for Maggie and sad for me and what I'd lost, sad that I'd be starting over again, without a house, without a set path. It was a little scary to be at the beginning like that. But exciting, too.

My phone buzzed in my pocket. Jimmy had messaged that he had gotten the part. I smiled for him—it was a huge win! I sent him congratulations, and then I added, Jimmy, I know what I'm going to use the money for.

He replied, Come home and tell me about it?

Wine chilled? I'll see you in twenty . . . , I texted back.

Already, I could picture it. Chris and I would sell the house. He'd have to go along with that now. And then I'd have a good cushion; I wouldn't have to take every wedding that came along. And in the meantime, I had that money I'd squirreled away. It was enough for me to buy the plane tickets, head out to Iceland, to the remote lighthouse that was operated by a matrilineal family who lived by the sea, who kept strange ways and were rumored to climb back into their seal skins and take to the depths when they needed renewal away from the land of men. I could go and take the photos I had always wanted to, photos that weren't for a job or a family member or for anyone but me.

And I knew that when I came back, I would return to a father who wanted to build a relationship, and a Brit who wasn't repelled by my fumbling vulnerability. Who made me feel that I didn't have to transform at all. That maybe all I had to do was keep on being true to myself, as true as I could be on any given day, in whatever seaside town I found myself.

CHAPTER THIRTY-FOUR

~~~~~

Aly

After weeks of promotion of the Charleston mah-jongg tournament, the big event was here, and I was ready and excited to see it come to life. I had teamed up with Holy Mahj to lead the game with a few local women who made their own tiles and other mah-jongg accessories, like mats and racks. The room was beautiful. Softly lit and sprinkled with game tables. Right by the opening, Ann and Caroline from Holy Mahj had poured dozens of glasses of sparkling rosé, and Hamby Catering had provided their famous chicken salad sandwiches on glistening silver trays. The room was perfectly southern and positively brewing with excitement as the ladies entered.

Violet was there to film and photograph the whole event so we would have good content for my social media accounts. We'd do some stories in the moment and take a good-quality reel for later. My engagement was up and my audience had grown. It wasn't quite at a hundred thousand, though it was getting close. Rosemary had said that Crate and Barn was getting cold feet, though. My Joyce posts had been controversial; there was a lot of engagement around them, and that had brought in the eyeballs, but the company was afraid the material was going to alienate the Callie Knox core audience too much. I was afraid of that, too. But I had no choice. This thing was in motion. I had to keep going.

Violet stood in the corner and gave me a thumbs-up while I snapped pictures of the ladies as they arrived, signed in, grabbed a drink and a sandwich, and found their seats at their assigned tables. I watched as the women shuffled in, all wearing lovely, feminine, colorful dresses and really great jewelry. Everyone got all dolled up and seemed to be just as excited as I was.

The night was to raise money for a cure for the disease that had taken my mother, so that made it feel more important, but heavy, too. I had really hoped that my father could be there, but he wasn't able to attend. He had a prior engagement, he said. It was—and I would have laughed at the absurdity if I hadn't felt so wounded by it—that it was his and Joyce's hundredth day as a couple, and they needed to celebrate.

After the fight when my siblings were in town, she had coldshouldered him for long enough that they had gotten back together on her terms. Which was nuts, but whatever. I held back my comment, which was that a hundred days was a quarterly earnings statement, give or take, not an occasion for an anniversary. He had asked me to play nice, and though Joyce had never thanked me for saving her life, what I had done had softened her to the point that I was once again allowed to have my own key to the Sullivan's Island house.

Not that I wanted to go over there that often.

I spied Kate Daniel-Stith in the corner; she was setting out a display of her mah-jongg tiles.

"Hey, girl!" I said as I made my way over.

"Hey, Aly! Nice to see you!" She gave me a warm smile, her dark brown eyes shining.

"Your tiles are so beautiful! I love the Charleston-themed ones!" I said, picking up a joker to take a closer look.

"Thank you! I worked so hard at getting the colors right," she said.

"Well, you did a fantastic job! Are you going to play tonight?" I asked.

"Yes, of course. Table four."

"Oh, yay! We are together! Do you know who else is sitting with us?" I asked.

"No. It's you, me, and two older ladies. I've never met them."

"Well, I hope they came ready to play. I've never seen you lose before," I joked.

"Can't," she replied with a wink. "That would be bad for business."

"See you at the table!" I said, and went to grab myself a drink. At the drink table I picked up a glass and took a sip of the extra-dry and crisp rosé, which helped me relax. I was jittery with excitement; this was a big deal for me and my brand. Lots of important people were there! Rosemary would be watching when we went live, and so would our partners at Crate and Barn. I was so close to my goal of a hundred thousand followers, but Rosemary said there were some differences of opinion at CB about how I'd come by them. They didn't all like the heat around my taking shots at Joyce, saying it was bad for the Callie Knox community. But that was behind me now, and I could keep building in a slowish, steady, and ladylike way. I took another sip and went to find my table.

When I arrived at table four, Kate was there shuffling the tiles with another woman. I recognized her immediately as Lucy, the older woman I had met earlier that summer at the nail salon. The one who had introduced me to this whole world! The sound of the clacking tiles as they were shuffled and dropped on the tables, mine and those around me, was some satisfying ASMR. I loved to hear it.

"Lucy? Hi, I'm Aly. I met you—"

"Yes! Hi, honey! At the nail salon! I remember! Nice to see you again!" she said.

"You, too! Wow, your ring is gorgeous!" I said as I was temporarily blinded by a giant diamond on her left hand. The thing was practically a gumball.

"Oh, why, thank you! I decided it was time to settle myself down. Met this nice man who swept me off my feet, and got off the dating sites."

"Well, you look happy to me!" I said.

"Oh, I am. He's truly a doll. His name is Mark, and he's a chef! Well, retired now, but he chefs for me!"

"That's wonderful!" I said. "When's the big day?"

"Oh, no big day, just a big ring. Who needs all that racket? I'm too old for it!" She giggled and got out her playing card and took a small plastic line finder out of a monogrammed leather envelope. I was impressed by how stylish she was.

"Aly!" Violet called my name and waved me to come over to her.

"What's up?" I asked as I approached.

"You are not going to believe who's here!" she squealed.

"Who?" I said.

"Russell Powell!"

"Oh my god! She only goes to really good parties. If this soiree is on her radar, we did something right!" I said. "Do you know who she's with?"

"Yes! Kelli Hoff, the hairstylist. You know, she does all the celebrities. She flew in this morning. I was eavesdropping; she just finished doing a Sabrina Carpenter music video."

"Whoa," I said, impressed.

"Are you about to throw the event of the season?" She smiled at me.

"Think I just might. I can't believe all these people are here! Wait, is that who I think it is?" I looked over in the direction of Russell and Kelli and spotted Cameran Eubanks Wimberly, everyone's favorite former cast member of *Southern Charm*.

"Yeah! That's Cam." She nodded.

"Oh, *Cam*? Y'all are friends now?" I said.

"Ha! Well, no, but, man, I feel like I could be; she's so nice and real. She was stoked to see Hamby did the catering! The girl has taste."

"Should I go say hello?" I said, a little nervous.

"Yes, duh, this is your event," she said, and pushed me toward their table. I took a sharp inhale, smoothed out my dress, and approached.

"Hey, ladies, welcome! I'm Aly . . ."

"Girl, hey! I've been dying to meet you!" Cam gave me a huge warm hug. "I totally love your Instagram! I was such a fan of your mother! Thank you for organizing this tonight. Let's raise some dough!"

"Wow, well, I'm a big fan of yours!" I said, grinning wildly.

"Hey, I don't really know what I'm doing here . . . I've only played once with Jason and Palmer and my mother-in-law . . ."

"Don't worry, we matched everyone up based on experience."

"Oh, thank God. I also have only played once!" Russell said. "I'm a big fan of yours, Aly. I'm so happy to finally meet you!"

"A fan of mine?" I said.

"Yeah, girl, you are the talk of the town. A true gem in Charleston!"

"Y'all are gonna make me blush," I said, donning a fake southern accent.

"It's the truth!" Kelli nodded in agreement, and I was suddenly worried about my split ends.

We chitchatted some more, and by the time I took off, I felt like the coolest girl there. As I crossed the room, Ann grabbed my arm.

"Hey, I saw you talking to the VIP table. I hope they play well. When I matched them up, I did it on skill. I didn't realize who they were till they arrived, and then—"

"No! All good. They are all beginners and are actually super sweet."

"Okay, phew! Do you want to say a little something before we begin?"

"Yeah, everyone seems to be settling down. I'll make a little welcome." I grabbed a fork to clink my glass, signaling for their attention.

"Hello!" I said, and cleared my throat. "I wanted to take a moment to welcome you all to this fantastic night, not only for the very important cause of finding a cure for MDS, but also for me. As some of you might know, my mother, the great Callie Knox, passed away from MDS, and she always loved a party and a good cause. So I thought that the best way to celebrate her life and legacy would be to come together tonight to raise money for a cure and to raise awareness and stress the importance of early-detection scans! When I met the lovely ladies from Holy Mahj, I told them what I was thinking about doing, and they jumped right on board! They have generously donated their skills and equipment to this night. Also, a big thank-you to Hamby Catering for donating all the food and wine! Best chicken salad in the world! So please, enjoy some wine, snag a sandwich, and let's play some mah-jongg!"

Everyone clapped. I let myself take it in, that thunderous sound of approval, and then returned to my seat. I was feeling warm and excited. Ann and Caroline gave me smiles of giddy anticipation, and Violet handed me another glass of bubbles. This was a win; it was going to be a great night.

I looked around at my tablemates and realized that one chair was still empty. This was a sold-out event; surely that person must be in the bathroom.

"Yoo-hoo! Here I am!" This from an unmistakable voice that slithered through the room, got right under my skin, and wiggled around. "So *sorry* that I'm late!"

Joyce.

What?

Why now, on this night? Here? She and Dad had their hundred-day anniversary date or whatever. Had she just made that up to keep my father away from something that was important to me?

"Hello, Aly. Thought it might be fun for us to do a little girl-time bonding," she purred.

"Hey, Joyce. Glad to see you," I said as genuinely as possible. I was, after all, in public.

"Do you two know each other?" Kate asked.

"I'm Joyce, her father's partner," Joyce said, and stuck out her hand for Kate to shake, but it looked almost as if she expected her to kiss her ring or something. "That's what we call each other now—'partner.' 'Girlfriend-boyfriend' sounds so juvenile, don't you think?"

"Oh, well, this is nice, then," Lucy said to Joyce, meaning to be nice, I thought, though it came out sounding like a question. Which it certainly was. Would it be nice? And why was she here? There were honestly a lot of questions.

"I have dice; highest roll wins," Kate said (for Joyce's benefit, I assumed), dropping the dice on the table. "Ah, six."

"Pass to the right?" Joyce said.

"Sure," I said, and Kate passed them to me. I rolled an eight. Joyce rolled a two, Lucy a seven.

"Okay, it's me, then." I pushed out my wall of tiles. I divided the stacks in the right order, discarding my first tile before picking up one.

"Friendly reminder that jokers can never be used in a pair, ever. But you can only call for a pair in the event you have mah-jongg," Kate reminded us.

"Right."

"Okay, so now that we are together, I thought it would be good to talk about the upcoming season as we move into the holidays . . ." Joyce began. "One dot."

"Joyce, it's only the end of summer." I gave a little laugh. "Red Dragon."

"Well, I need to *plan* things with my family. It's getting complicated juggling all our children."

"Usually we do Christmas Eve after church and then eat fish."

"Oh, no," Joyce said, "we'll have lamb."

"Flower." Lucy dropped her tile and took a long drink of her rosé. Was she feeling the awkwardness of Joyce and me being together? I certainly was.

"Wait, you're going to have Christmas with us? My whole family is coming down . . ."

"Bird Bam!" Kate said, and we all clinked our glasses and took sips of our wine. She made a face at me. Both Lucy and Kate could tell I was getting annoyed.

"Yes! I need your guest list. I am sending out invitations. See?"

Joyce pulled out her phone and clicked on a picture of an invitation to my own house for Christmas. At the top she had their initials intertwined like a wedding invitation. A giant "J" in script over a bold block "G." Gross.

"What? Why the formal invitation? It's just family," I said, a little confused, and Lucy shot me a look.

"Because it makes everything more organized this way. Plus, I'm going to invite some friends, too," Joyce said. "Very accomplished lawyers, our friends, our kind of people, you know."

"We usually only do family . . ."

"Well, things will have to change. Now that we are blending our traditions."

"Then I guess we are eating fish alongside your guest list," I snapped back.

Oh boy, I was taking her bait.

"Oh, Aly, you must be flexible."

"I'll talk to Dad," I said, feeling my neck get hot.

"Are there any traditions that are super important to you?" she asked.

"I mean, there's the Polar Bear Plunge on New Year's Day . . ." I said.

"Oh my god, I love that! On Sullivan's Island? Four Bam," Kate said, putting a tile down.

"Last year my family got all dressed up as 'shiny happy people' from the REM song."

"Fun!" Lucy added. "Four Bam."

"We covered ourselves in gold paint. Glitter was everywhere. I still find it in my car." Kate giggled.

"I love all the street vendors outside with the collards and black-eyed peas," I added. "Five Crack."

"Oh! Call," Joyce said. "I'm sorry to say, Aly, but New Year's is for couples. We are planning on going to the Bahamas."

"Uh, *Valentine's Day* is for couples. All of us make a big deal out of New Year's," I said.

"New Year's is for *couples*," Joyce repeated, and I wanted to slap her.

"Okay, maybe we can work something out."

"Tickets are already booked," she sang out.

"Okay," I said, and I felt myself start to spin a little. It was at moments like these that I wondered why my dad just let her mow us all over. How was I going to explain to my brother and sister and the kids that their dad and grandfather was choosing a beach getaway with his girlfriend over us?

I wondered why she had even come tonight. Was it to look good to my father? Was it to actually get to know me? Or was it just a chance to have this argument in public, in a place where she knew I couldn't really argue back? I felt my cheeks get red and I saw her notice. She looked at me with a smug smile.

"Well, in my house New Year's Day is always celebrated by family. We all come over to my house, and I cook a ham, my mom brings the collards and black-eyed peas, and we all make wishes for the upcoming year," Kate said, coming in hot to my defense. I looked at her, and she gave me a little nod.

"Same at my house. New Year's Eve might be for couples, but the morning is about being with the people you love most," Lucy added.

"Well, that's the same thing for us," Joyce added. "We both want to ring in the new year with the person we love most . . . Mah-jongg!" Joyce clapped in her win.

I'm not going to lie: Joyce winning at this game I had come to love provoked my spite. But I knew it was probably better this way. I'd learned to move aside when she was coming through. It was best for everyone. We played our next rounds, the clink of the tiles and the beauty of the room carrying me away from my worst feelings. I forgot about all my enmity toward Joyce. I was actually having fun. Then our final round was coming to a close, and all of a sudden Joyce had won it. She'd called the final mah-jongg, and all around me people were clapping.

"I knew I'd win!" Joyce said, clasping her hands in joy.

There was truly nothing I could do about the face I was making, even though I was most definitely in public, and there were phone cameras recording the whole thing. "You did?"

"Oh yes, I *had* to. Your father told me about the trouble you've been having with your brand since you bad-mouthed me on your little channel. *Now* see how things will turn around!" Then she put her arm around me and turned me toward Violet, posing us. Violet fiddled with her camera, adjusting the settings. Behind her was Rosemary, who had been handling the Instagram live feed, keeping up with the Insta stories, all of that. "This is really beautiful what you've done, you know," Joyce said, hanging on to me as though for dear life. "For your mother, I mean. She must have been so loved. The way you all hold on to her even now that she's gone. You know what my greatest fear is?"

I was trying to hold my smile, wishing Violet would get it together for this picture so I could get out of Joyce's claws. "What, Joyce? What is your greatest fear?"

In a whisper, she said, "Dying alone. I saw it happening, that night I almost died—my windpipe blocked, your father turning away from me, gazing after his children, ignoring me—and it was just me, in my final moments, choking to death! Abandoned!"

I resisted rolling my eyes.

"And it was *you* who prevented it and saved my life. I've never mentioned that to you—I was trying to figure out how to repay you, in a sense. Your mother must have been quite a woman. She really raised you right."

I blinked. Oh god, I was going to cry. Joyce was so twisted, and she'd just said the nicest thing she could have possibly said to me, and now I was totally at risk of bawling in public. A big smile came over my face, and I could feel tears—of relief? Of joy? It was one of those big emotional bursts that aren't exactly good or bad but make you feel lucky to be alive. "Thank you," I whispered.

"Ready?" Violet said.

Joyce pulled me closer. "Thank you for that," I said.

"Of course! We are family now." I was feeling so positive, I didn't even really mind her saying that, and what she said next hit me as funny rather than horrifying: "And family doesn't let family fail at things that they must succeed at. *That* would be embarrassing. In my family, we always win."

When Joyce stepped away, I was mobbed by people. Women who had come out to celebrate Callie Knox and who'd had a blast. The fundraising person, who reported how much we had raised. Violet, who had seen that my Instagram handle had ticked up past the hundred-thousand mark and wanted to tell me I'd done it: I had achieved my goal. And Rosemary, who pulled me gently aside and told me that the Crate and Barn rep had been following the game with Joyce and loved that she was there to raise money in my mother's name—that we were friends despite it all. And of course they knew how much my following had grown, too. They wanted to do the whole Christmas line my mother had planned before she passed, plus a special limited edition of Callie Knox My Mother's Daughter mah-jongg tiles, which would raise money for cancer research. They thought the whole thing was vintage Callie, Rosemary told me. Fun and classy and beautiful and real.

I couldn't stop smiling. Violet was by my side again. She had put away the camera for once and handed me a glass of rosé.

"You see?" she said, raising her glass for a clink. "The more real you are, the more your real beauty comes through. You truly are your mother's daughter."

I put my glass down and threw my arms around her and squeezed, because when she said it, I really believed it. I felt it way down in my heart.

EPILOGUE

~~~~~

Violet

October

So, this was real life, it wasn't a movie, Henry wound up staying in Nantucket through September, I had a number of weddings I'd already committed to, and I knew my big trip to the sea-blown Nordic wilds needed real planning. I had my tickets purchased—Henry had checked in with me until I committed—but I decided I needed time to make contacts and a schedule. Plus, there was Maggie's engagement party to see through. For those reasons, on a Monday night, I found myself running around, getting things ready at Gran's.

Everyone was there, going crazy trying to make everything perfect.

Henry was coming—the first time we would be meeting since that walk in Nantucket—and I was warm with anticipation of the fact that soon I'd see his face.

Gran was at the helm of the food. She was the boss this evening, directing everyone. Each table had a theme and a color to represent it. Purple for eggplants, green for kale, and red for tomatoes. Aly was there, too, obviously, and she was helping with the decorations and the overall vibe of the room. She had officially been asked to take over her mother's brand and accepted the role, and she had been approached by an agent who wanted her to put together a lifestyle book. But she wasn't the only one about to break into the big time. Maggie had gotten an offer to do a cookbook based on the history of the restaurant, and Jimmy was officially part of the ensemble cast at the Dock Street Theatre. He was going to be Scrooge in their *Christmas Carol*.

Life was good.

Aly had asked if her dad could come to the party, and Joyce was with him. I could tell it wasn't easy, but it didn't seem as awful as before. They seemed to have accepted each other, foibles and all.

As busy as everyone was trying to make it an unforgettable night, I noticed that we all looked our best. Gran was in a red caftan with a matching turban; my mom was there, too, in a silvery minidress and a black leather moto jacket. She and Gran were still prickly, but she had taken that job in New York City and had started the paperwork with our dad for divorce. She dating a new guy who no one knew much about yet, but she seemed happy.

"Do I look okay? I'm unsure about this dress," Aly said.

"You look beautiful!" I told her. And she did. She had cut her hair chin length, and she looked like a little French flapper.

"Thanks, girl, you do, too." She gave me a wink and went outside.

"She's right, you really do," came a low, not-so-foreign accent. I swung around to face Henry, who looked every inch delicious. He towered over me. I had forgotten just how sharp his jawline was. I melted a little.

"Oh. Hey, Henry," I said, looking up at him through my eyelashes. My cheeks were burning. "You're early!" I said.

"I couldn't wait. And Jim texted me. He needs help hanging lights."

"Oh, the lights are out on the front porch. Join you in a sec?" Jim said.

"Yes, one second." Henry smiled at me. "I just had to get a look at you. Will there be dancing later? I want to dance with you."

I smiled back. "There will be dancing."

He gave me a light kiss on my cheek and then whispered in my ear, "Later," and I almost fainted.

"Good lord, Violet, if you don't kiss his face off, I will," Jimmy said, coming up behind me. "You are *blotchy*."

"Shut up," I laughed. "I can't help it!"

We got everything together after lots of teasing. The house was shining. Gran had hired a small bluegrass band to play, and we were blessed with cool weather, so we opened up the sliding doors to the porch on both sides of the house and let the ocean air and music waft through the rooms. Around six thirty, Maggie arrived in a bright red dress, arm in arm with Sam. They were the best couple in every way.

The evening was perfect, and the drinks were flowing. The mood was light and happy. Everyone was talking about how good the food was. Aly's dad had shown up and was in a corner with Gran, who was cackling. I hadn't heard her laugh like that in a while. I moved toward the bar, which was next to where Aly had set up a microphone. My mom made her way through the group, and I blocked her from going to the front.

My mother miked was not a great idea, especially when it had to do with Maggie.

"Mom, you are not obligated to make a toast," I said.

"Violet, she is my eldest daughter. It is expected of me," she said. "Plus, I have a surprise for her."

"Yeah, that's what I'm afraid of," I said.

"No, Violet. Let me, please! I promise you'll approve."

I looked at my mom, and there was an expression of joy on her face I hadn't seen in a long while. Was that pride?

"Okay, Mom, but please don't upset Maggie," I said.

"I won't. Now, move, child," she said, stepping around me.

I made the sign of the cross as my mother took center stage.

She grabbed the microphone and adjusted it to her height, then took her wineglass and tapped it with a spoon, and someone lowered the music. Jim went around with Aly and Gran, passing out champagne glasses. My mother cleared her throat, and I braced myself.

"As you all know, I'm Lily, and I'm Magnolia's mother. Maggie and I haven't always seen eye to eye, but I have to say today that I have never been prouder of my girl. She is smart, she is driven, she is talented, and she is loved. Not just by me, and her sister, and her grandmother, who is probably a better mother than I."

There was some throat clearing and some apprehensive nodding throughout the room.

"Anyway. Now she is loved by the most perfect man. Sam. Whom we all love back, and we cannot wait to add you to our family. You are the only one who can tame that tiger, am I right?"

There was nervous laughter from various corners.

"Right, y'all know what I mean: Maggie is such a tiger! That hair! Where was I—oh, yeah, being proud of you. Well, I haven't always known what to say or do, but I *did* have the privilege of getting to watch you grow up—something that your father never had, but I think that's about to change. Our family is growing this year by adding two men: Sam and Scott."

Just then the crowd parted, and my dad appeared and joined my mother. I had known he was going to make a surprise appearance— he and Maggie had been in communication, and it seemed a welcome visit—but I was still happily surprised by the miracle of his presence.

"Maggie, I am just getting to know the woman you are, and while I cannot take any credit, except for maybe your cooking skills, I am also just so proud of you. You are one of the most incredible women I've ever met, and I am so lucky to be back in your life. I love you, my little girl. I always have and I always will. Welcome to the family, Sam! Let's party!" my dad said.

Maggie had the most serene look on her face. I couldn't tell if she was struggling underneath her expression or not. She gave Sam a quick kiss on his cheek and went up to join our parents. I was a foot away from them.

"Thank you . . . *Dad*," I heard her say. "Thank you, Mom, I love you." Maggie gave them a giant hug.

"I love you, too, girl," I heard my mom say, and I couldn't help it. I joined the hug and then so did Sam.

"God, how cheesy are we?" Sam said.

"Wait for me!" we heard Gran call from the crowd. And then everyone was just piling on. At that moment, I knew everything was going to be all right. I had my feet on the ground and a big circle of love to fall back on. I was safe to set out into the world and see what it had to offer, with nothing more than my camera and my own two feet.

ACKNOWLEDGMENTS

I could fill an entire novel with thank-yous over this beast of a book. Yes, beast. They say that the second book is always the hardest, and I would agree. The first book rattled around in my mind for years. I believe that everyone has one novel in them at least, and the second one is what makes you a true writer. I guess I earned my elbow patches and tweed jacket. But I digress.

First, I would like to thank my editor, Carrie Feron, for her Jedi wisdom and guidance. There would be no book without you. You make me believe in myself as a writer and challenge my perspective all the time. On and off the page. I love your brilliant mind, and I am so blessed and honored to be on a team with you.

Second, to my agent, Suzanne Gluck. You are my literary fairy godmother, making all my dreams come true! Thank you for being my advocate and truth teller. I am so grateful for you and the doors you have helped open for me.

To Anna Godbersen. Jesus, you are talented. Never before have I met someone who just "got it" so quickly. Your guidance and advice on this book were invaluable. Thank you so much, my fellow sister.

Thank you to my team of Gallerinas! Jen Bergstrom, Aimée Bell, Jen Long, Eliza Hansen, Sally Marvin, Mackenzie Hickey, Caroline Pallotta, and Ali Chesnick! Y'all made me feel right at home in my new house! I can't believe I get to keep company with *Britney Spears*!

To Ryan Nelson and Kate Conway (a.k.a. Gorgeous Kate). You girls rock my world! To Liz Dorsey, for keeping my wildlings.

Thank you to my publicity team, Heather Waters and Jessica Roth.

To Adri. You are a warrior for me and have talked me off twenty-five ledges. Thank you for reassuring me that I don't write garbage and that I can do this. Thank you for being a sister and a friend and a general in my army.

Thank you to Adam, Charlotte, Roberta, Brian, Polly, Maddie, Liam, Hanna, Kat, Gage, Kelly, Lisa, Hunter, and Jenny—the list goes on. I am so lucky to have y'all to hold me up, read pages, and give me advice and opinions. Y'all make me laugh, mostly at myself, and keep me grounded. Around dinner tables, rocking on rocking chairs, walking along beaches . . . you all are fantastic friends, and I am so lucky to have y'all on my team. God, I love you.

To my mom friends and fellow mah-jongg mamas. Thank you for getting me out of my damn head for a few hours each week and for walking through raising these kids together! Safety in numbers! XOXO!

Thank you to my family: Carmine, Teddy, Thea, Roberta, Brian, and my dad, for keeping me focused and driven. Thank you for allowing me to lock myself up in the office with the white noise machine blasting and for supplying me with endless Diet Cokes and hugs. Kids, I want you to always know that you should chase your dreams. Even if it's scary. Life is short, so grab it. Fight hard for them. Dream bigger than everyone says you should. Never give up. Ever.

To the booksellers. Especially Polly Buxton, who at almost first glance became my soul sister. But also the ones I have met on tour the past two years. You are my people. Thank God there are people like you fighting for the love of books! You have the very important role of placing stories into the hands of people—stories that will shape their minds and hearts forever. Thank you for putting my book on your shelves and supporting this girl's dream. I am honored to know you.

And finally, a giant thank-you to all the wonderful readers of mine and readers of my mother's. Especially Michelle, Dallas, Katie, Katie, and Megan. Again, it will never be lost on me that it is because of you that I get to live this fantastic life of storytelling. Thank you for encouraging me to keep going, for showing up at my events, for making me love this career so much more deeply than I knew I could, and for helping me realize this dream of mine. It is an absolute honor and such a privilege to be able to do what I do, and it's all because of you. Thank you for buying my book, for taking a chance on me. You all support me in so many ways that I had never thought possible. I hope this book makes you proud, and I hope that you devour it on the beach this summer—but remember your sunscreen!